The
Six-Gun
Tarot

The Six-Gun Tarot

R. S. BELCHER

TOR®

A TOM DOHERTY ASSOCIATES BOOK

NEW YORK

THE SIX-GUN TAROT

Copyright © 2013 by Rod Belcher

A Tor Book
Published by Tom Doherty Associates, LLC
175 Fifth Avenue
New York, NY 10010

www.tor-forge.com

Tor® is a registered trademark of Tom Doherty Associates, LLC.

Library of Congress Cataloging-in-Publication Data

Belcher, R. S.
     The six-gun tarot / R. S. Belcher.—1
        p. cm.
     "A Tom Doherty Associates book."
     ISBN 978-0-7653-2932-5 (hardcover)
     ISBN 978-1-4299-4698-8 (e-book)
     I. Title.
   PS3602.E429S59 2013
   813'.6—dc23
                          2012026479

First Edition: January 2013

Printed in the United States of America

0 9 8 7 6 5 4 3 2 1

To my mother, who did the job of two parents alone,
and did it better than any two people ever could.

To my sister, who always looked out for me and let me tag along.

And to my beautiful, wonderful children, who are the greatest
creation I will ever be a part of.

The
Six-Gun
Tarot

The Page of Wands

The Nevada sun bit into Jim Negrey like a rattlesnake. It was noon. He shuffled forward, fighting gravity and exhaustion, his will keeping him upright and moving. His mouth was full of the rusty taste of old fear; his stomach had given up complaining about the absence of food days ago. His hands wrapped around the leather reins, using them to lead Promise ever forward. They were a lifeline, helping him to keep standing, keep walking.

Promise was in bad shape. A hard tumble down one of the dunes in the 40-Mile Desert was forcing her to keep weight off her left hind leg. She was staggering along as best she could, just like Jim. He hadn't ridden her since the fall yesterday, but he knew that if he didn't try to get up on her and get moving, they were both as good as buzzard food soon. At their present pace, they still had a good three or four days of traveling through this wasteland before they would reach Virginia City and the mythical job with the railroad.

Right now, he didn't care that he had no money in his pockets. He didn't care that he only had a few tepid swallows of water left in his canteen or that if he managed to make it to Virginia City he might be recognized from a wanted poster and sent back to Albright for a proper hanging. Right now, all he was worried about was saving his horse, the brown mustang that had been his companion since he was a child.

Promise snorted dust out of her dark nostrils. She shook her head and slowed.

"Come on, girl," he croaked through a throat that felt like it was filled with broken shale. "Just a little ways longer. Come on."

The mare reluctantly heeded Jim's insistent tugging on the reins and lurched forward again. Jim rubbed her neck.

"Good girl, Promise. Good girl."

The horse's eyes were wide with crazy fear, but she listened to Jim's voice and trusted in it.

"I'll get us out of here, girl. I swear I will." But he knew that was a lie. He was as frightened as Promise. He was fifteen years old and he was going to die out here, thousands of miles from his home and family.

They continued on, heading west, always west. Jim knew far ahead of them lay the Carson River, but it might as well be on the moon. They were following the ruts of old wagon train paths, years old. If they had more water and some shelter, they might make it, but they didn't. The brackish salt ponds they passed spoke to the infernal nature of this place. For days now, they had stumbled over the bleached bones of horses, and worse. Other lost souls, consigned to the waste of the 40-Mile.

During the seemingly endless walk, Jim had found artifacts, partially eaten by the sand and clay—the cracked porcelain face of a little girl's doll. It made him think of Lottie. She'd be seven now. A broken pocket watch held a sun-faded photograph of a stern-looking man dressed in a Union uniform. It reminded him of Pa. Jim wondered if some unfortunate wandering this path in the future would find a token of his and Promise's passing, the only record of his exodus through this godforsaken land, the only proof that he had ever existed at all.

He fished the eye out of his trouser pocket and examined it in the unforgiving sunlight. It was a perfect orb of milky glass. Inlaid in the orb was a dark circle and, within it, a perfect ring of frosted jade. At the center of the jade ring was an oval of night. When the light struck the jade at just the right angle, tiny unreadable characters could be seen engraved in the stone. It was his father's eye, and it was the reason for the beginning and the end of his journey. He put it back in a handkerchief and stuffed it in his pocket, filled with an angry desire to deny it to the desert. He pressed onward and Promise reluctantly followed.

He had long ago lost track of concepts like time. Days were starting to bleed into one another as the buzzing in his head, like angry hornets, grew stronger and more insistent with each passing step. But he knew the sun was more before him now than behind him. He stopped again. When had he stopped to look at the eye? Minutes ago, years? The wagon trails, fossilized and twisting through the baked landscape, had brought him to a crossroads in the wasteland. Two rutted paths crossed near a pile of skulls. Most of the skulls belonged to cattle and coyotes, but the number that belonged to animals of the two-legged variety unnerved Jim. Atop the pile was a piece of slate, a child's broken and discarded chalkboard, faded by sand, salt and sun. On it, in red paint, written in a crude, looping scrawl were the words: *Golgotha: 18 mi. Redemption: 32 mi. Salvation: 50 mi.*

During Jim's few furtive days in Panacea, after crossing over from Utah, he had been surprised by the number of Mormons in Nevada and how much influence they had already accumulated in this young state. There were numerous small towns and outposts dotting the landscape with the most peculiar religious names, marking the Mormon emigration west. He had never heard of any of these towns, but if there were people there would be fresh water and shelter from the sun.

"See, Promise, only eighteen more miles to go and we're home free, girl." He pulled the reins, and they were off again. He didn't much care for staying in a place named Golgotha, but he was more than willing to visit a spell.

The trail continued, the distance measured by the increasing ache in Jim's dried-out muscles, the growing hum in his head that was obscuring thought. The sun was retreating behind distant, shadowy hills. The relief from the sun was a fleeting victory. Already a chill was settling over his red, swollen skin as the desert's temperature began to plunge. Promise shivered too and snorted in discomfort. There was only so much farther she could go without rest. He knew it would be better to travel at night and take advantage of the reprieve from the sun, but he was simply too tired and too cold to go on, and he feared wandering off the wagon trail in the darkness and becoming lost.

He was looking for a place to hole up for the night when Promise suddenly gave a violent whinny and reared up on her hind legs. Jim, still holding the reins, felt himself jerked violently off the ground. Promise's injured hind leg gave way and both boy and horse tumbled down a rocky shelf off to the left of the rutted path. There was confusion, and falling and then a sudden, brutal stop. Jim was prone with his back against Promise's flank.

After a few feeble attempts to rise, the horse whimpered and stopped trying.

Jim stood, beating the dust off his clothes. Other than a wicked burn on his wrist where the leather reins had torn away the skin, he was unharmed. The small gully they were in had walls of crumbling clay and was sparsely dotted with sickly sage plants. Jim knelt near Promise's head and stroked the shaking mare.

"It's okay, girl. We both need a rest. You just close your eyes, now. I've got you. You're safe with me."

A coyote howled in the distance, and his brethren picked up the cry. The sky was darkening from indigo to black. Jim fumbled in his saddlebags and removed Pa's pistol, the one he had used in the war. He checked the cylinder of the .44 Colt and snapped the breech closed, satisfied that it was ready to fire.

"Don't worry, girl; ain't nobody gitting you tonight. I promised you I'd get us out of here, and I'm going to keep my word. A man ain't no good for nothing if he don't keep his word."

Jim slid the coarse army blanket and bedroll off the saddle. He draped the blanket over Promise as best he could, and wrapped himself in the thin bedding. The wind picked up a few feet above their heads, whistling and shrieking. A river of swirling dust flowed over them, carried by the terrible sound. When he had been a boy, Jim had been afraid of the wind moaning, like a restless haint, around the rafters where his bed was nestled. Even though he knew he was a man now and men didn't cotton to such fears, this place made him feel small and alone.

After an hour, he checked Promise's leg. It was bad, but not so bad yet that it couldn't heal. He wished he had a warm stable and some oats and water to give her, a clean brush for her hide. He'd settle for the water, though. She was strong, her heart was strong, but it had been days since she had taken in water. Strength and heart only went so far in the desert. From her labored breathing, that wasn't going to be enough to reach Golgotha.

The frost settled into his bones sometime in the endless night. Even fear and the cold weren't enough to keep him anchored to this world. He slipped into the warm, narcotic arms of sleep.

His eyes snapped open. The coyote was less than three feet from his face. Its breath swirled, a mask of silver mist in the space between them. Its eyes were embers in a fireplace. There was intelligence behind the red eyes, worming itself into Jim's innards. In his mind, he heard chanting, drums. He saw himself as a rabbit—weak, scared, prey.

Jim remembered the gun. His frozen fingers fumbled numbly for it on the ground.

The coyote narrowed its gaze and showed yellowed teeth. Some were crooked, snagged, but the canines were sharp and straight.

You think you can kill me with slow, spiritless lead, little rabbit? Its eyes spoke to Jim. *I am the fire giver, the trickster spirit. I am faster than Old Man Rattler, quieter than the Moon Woman's light. See, go on, see! Shoot me with your dead, empty gun.*

Jim glanced down at the gun, slid his palm around the butt and brought it up quickly. The coyote was gone; only the fog of its breath remained. Jim heard the coyote yipping in the distance. It sounded like laughter at his expense.

His eyes drooped, and closed.

He awoke with a start. It was still dark, but dawn was a threat on the horizon. The gun was in his hand. He saw the coyote's tracks and wondered again if perhaps he had already died out here and was now wandering Hell's foyer, being taunted by demon dogs and cursed with eternal thirst as penance for the crimes he had committed back home.

Promise stirred, fitfully, made a few pitiful sounds and then was still. Jim rested his head on her side. Her heart still beat; her lungs struggled to draw air.

If he was in Hell, he deserved it, alone. He stroked her mane and waited for the Devil to rise up, bloated and scarlet in the east. He dozed again.

He remembered how strong his father's hands were, but how soft his voice was too. Pa seldom shouted 'less he had been drinking on account of the headaches.

It was a cold West Virginia spring. The frost still clung to the delicate, blooming blue sailors and the cemetery plants early in the morning, but, by noon, the sky was clear and bright and the blustery wind blowing through the mountains was more warm than chill.

Pa and Jim were mending some of Old Man Wimmer's fences alongside their own property. Pa had done odd jobs for folk all over Preston County since he had come back from the war. He had even helped build onto the Cheat River Saloon over in Albright, the closest town to the Negrey homestead.

Lottie had brought a lunch pail over to them: corn muffins, a little butter and some apples as well as a bucket of fresh water. Lottie was five then, and her hair was the same straw color as Jim's, only lighter, more golden in the sunlight. It fell almost to her waist, and Momma brushed it with her fine silver combs in the firelight at night before bedtime. The memory made Jim's heart ache. It was what he thought of whenever he thought of home.

"Is it good, Daddy?" Lottie asked Pa. He was leaning against the fence post, eagerly finishing off his apple.

"M'hm." He nodded. "Tell your ma, these doings are a powerful sight better than those sheet-iron crackers and skillygallee old General Pope used to feed us, darling."

Jim took a long, cool draw off the water ladle and looked at Pa, sitting there, laughing with Lottie. Jim thought he would never be able to be as tall or proud or heroic as Billy Negrey was to him. The day Pa had returned from the war, when President Lincoln said it was over and all the soldiers could go home, was the happiest day of Jim's young life. Even though Pa came back thin, and Momma fussed over him to eat more, and even though he had the eye patch and the headaches that came with it, that only made him seem more mysterious, more powerful, to Jim.

Lottie watched her father's face intently while he finished off the apple, nibbling all around the core

"Was it Gen'ral Pope that took away your eye?" she asked.

Pa laughed. "I reckon in a matter of speaking he did, my girl. Your old daddy didn't duck fast enough, and he took a bullet right in the eye. Don't complain, though. Other boys, they got it hundred times worse. "

"Pa, why does Mr. Campbell in town say you got a Chinaman's eye?" Jim asked with a sheepish smile.

"Now, James Matherson Negrey, you know good and well why." He looked from one eager face to the other and shook his head. "Don't you two ever get tired of hearing this story?"

They both shook their heads, and Billy laughed again.

"Okay, okay. When I was serving with General Pope, my unit—the First

Infantry out of West Virginia—we were in the middle of this big ol' fight, y'see—"

"Bull Run? Right, Pa?" Jim asked. He already knew the answer, and Billy knew he knew.

"Yessir," Billy said. "Second scrap we had on the same piece of land. Anyways, old General Pope, he made some pretty bad calculations and—"

"How bad, Pa?" Lottie asked.

"Darling, we were getting catawamptiously chawed up."

The children laughed, like they always did.

Billy continued. "So the call comes for us to fall back, and that was when I . . . when I got a Gardner right square in the eye. I was turning my head to see if old Luther Potts was falling back when it hit me. Turning my head probably saved my life."

Billy rubbed the bridge of his nose with his thumb and forefinger.

"You all right, Pa?" Jim asked.

"Fine, Jim. Fetch me some water, will you? So, Lottie, where was I?"

"You got shot in the eye."

"Right. So I don't recall much specific after that. I was in a lot of pain. I heard . . . well, I could hear some of what was going on all around me."

"Like what, Pa?" she asked.

"Never you mind. Anyways, someone grabbed me up, and dragged me for a spell, and finally I heard the sawbones telling someone to hold me still, and they did and I went to sleep for a long time. I dreamed about you and Jim and your mother. The stuff they give you to sleep makes you have funny dreams. I remember seeing someone all dressed up fancy in green silk, some kind of old man, but his hair was long like a woman's, and he was jawing at me, but I couldn't understand him."

"When did you wake up, Pa?" Jim asked. Even though he knew the story by heart, he always tried to flesh it out with any new details that he could glean from the retelling.

"Few days later in a hospital tent. My head hurt bad and it was kind of hard to think or hear." Billy paused and seemed to wince. Jim handed him the wooden ladle full of cool water. He gulped it down and blinked a few times with his good eye. "They told me we had fallen back and were on our way to Washington for garrison duty. General Pope was in a powerful lot of trouble too.

"They told me I had lost the eye, but was mighty lucky to be alive. I didn't feel too lucky right that minute, but compared to all the lads who didn't come home at all, I figure I did have an angel on my shoulder."

"So tell us about the Chinaman, Pa!" Lottie practically squealed.

Billy winced but went on, with a forced smile. "Well, when my unit got to Washington, a bunch of us fellas who were pretty banged up, we all went to stay at a hospital. One night in the hospital, this strange little Johnny, all dressed up in his black pajamas, and his little hat, he came sneaking into the ward and he crept up beside my bed."

"Were you scared, Pa?" Jim asked.

Billy shook his head. "Not really, Jim. That hospital was so strange. The medicine they gave us, called it morphine, it made you feel all flushed and crazy. I honestly didn't think the Chinaman was real. He spoke to me and his voice was like a song, but soft, like I was the only one in the world who could hear him. He said, 'You will do.' I don't to this day know what the blazes he was going on about, but he said something about the moon and me hiding or some-such. Then he touched me right here, on the forehead, and I fell asleep.

"Well, when I woke up I wasn't in the hospital anymore; I was in some den of Chinamen. They were all mumbling something or other over top of me, and they were pulling these great big knitting needles outta my skin, but I didn't feel any pain at all. The one who came into the hospital and fetched me, he said that they were healers and that they had come to give me a gift. He held up a mirror and I saw the eye for the first time. He told me it was an old keepsake from his kin back in China."

"Did you believe him, Pa?" Jim asked.

Billy rubbed his temples and blinked at the afternoon sunlight again. "Well, I was a mite suspicious of him and his buddies, Jim. He told me the eye was real valuable, and that I should probably hide it under a patch, 'less crooks might try to steal it. That seemed a bit odd to me. He and the other Johnnies, they all chattered like parrots in that singsong talking those folks do. I couldn't understand any of it, but they all seemed powerful interested in me and the eye. Then they thanked me and told me good luck. Another Chinaman blew smoke in my face from one of those long pipes of theirs, and I got sleepy and kind of dizzy and sick, like with the morphine. When I woke up, I was back in the hospital, and it was the next day. I told the doctors and my superior officer what happened, and they just seemed to chalk it up to the medicine they gave me. They had more trouble explaining the eye. The hospital was pretty crazy on account of all the hurt soldiers. They didn't have much time to puzzle over my story—I was alive and was going to keep on living. They had to move on the next poor fella. Couple of them offered to buy the eye right out of my head, but it didn't seem proper to give away such a fine gift. And it gave me a great story to tell my kids for the rest of my life."

Billy grunted, and pulled himself to his feet. "A while later, the war was over and I got to come home. I never saw the Chinaman again. The end."

"Let me see it, Pa!" Lottie said eagerly, practically humming with anticipation. "Please!"

Billy smiled and nodded. He lifted the plain black eye patch that covered his left socket. Lottie laughed and clapped. Jim crowded forward too to get a better glimpse of the seldom-seen artifact.

"It's like you got a green-colored eye," Lottie said softly. "It's so pretty, Pa."

"That green color in it, that's jade," Billy said. "Lots of jade in China."

"Tea too," Jim added.

Lottie stuck out her tongue at him. "You're just trying to be all highfalutin and smart seeming," she said.

"All right, you two, that's enough," Billy said, lowering the patch. "Let's get back to work, Jim. Lottie, you run on home to your momma, y'hear?"

Jim watched Lottie dance through the tall, dry grass, empty pail in her small hand, the sun glistening off her golden curls. She was singing a made-up song about China and jade. She pronounced "jade" "jay."

Jim glanced to his father, and he could tell that one of the headaches was coming on him hard. But he was smiling through it, watching Lottie too. He turned to regard his thirteen-year-old son with a look that made the sun shine inside the boy's chest.

"Let's get back to it, Son."

He awoke, and it was the desert again. The green and the mountain breeze were gone. The sun was coiled in the east, ready to rise up into the air and strike. It was still cool, but not cold anymore. He remembered the coyote and spun around, gun in hand. Everything was still and unchanged in the gathering light.

Promise's breathing was labored and soft. The sound of it scared Jim, bad. He tried to get her to rise, but the horse shuddered and refused to stir.

"Come on, girl, we got to get moving, 'fore that sun gets any higher."

Promise tried to rise, coaxed by the sound of his voice. She failed. He looked at her on the ground, her dark eyes filled with pain, and fear, and then looked to the gun in his hand.

"I'm sorry I brought you out here, girl. I'm so sorry."

He raised Pa's pistol, cocked it and aimed it at the mare's skull.

"I'm sorry." His finger tightened on the trigger. His hands shook. They hadn't done that when he shot Charlie. Charlie had deserved it; Promise didn't.

He eased the hammer down and dropped the gun into the dust. He stood there for a long time. His shadow lengthened.

"We're both getting out of here, girl," he said, finally.

Jim rummaged through the saddlebags and removed his canteen. He took a final, all-too-brief sip of the last of the water, and then poured the rest onto Promise's mouth and over her swollen tongue. The horse eagerly struggled to take the water in. After a few moments, she rose to her feet, shakily.

Jim stroked her mane. "Good girl, good girl. We'll make it together, or not at all. Come on." They began to trudge, once again, toward Golgotha.

The Moon

The darkness filled with a terrible pressure behind his eyes. The pain was thick and settled over his skull like lead syrup. Jim opened his eyes and knives of sunlight stabbed into them. A groan escaped his cracked lips.

"It's all right," a voice said over the clatter of wagon wheels. "We got you, young fella. You're going to be right as rain."

Jim felt cool, spidery hands slide under his back and prop him up. He was under a wool horse blanket. It was scratchy against his red skin, but its shade was keeping the blazing sun off his head. A pale, cadaverous hand held a canteen before his mouth. There was a sour odor coming off the hand and for a moment he thought he was being ministered to by one of the dead pilgrims lost to the 40-Mile.

"Drink," the voice said, and he did, in greedy, silvery, cold gulps.

"Not too fast," a second voice said. "You'll get sick."

Jim's vision was blurry and his eyes felt sticky. He turned his head enough to see the man who was holding the canteen. His face was thin; his sparse gray hair was swept back from his high forehead. His features reminded Jim of a vulture. He looked concerned for the boy's condition, but he also seemed kind of fascinated by it too. Lottie had once looked at an ant she trapped under a Mason jar the same way.

"How is he?" the driver asked.

"Sick," the vulture-man said. "He's redder than a preacher in a whorehouse."

"Promise," Jim croaked. "My horse, is she okay?"

The cold hands turned Jim's head toward the back of the wagon. Promise was shuffling behind the moving wagon, her reins looped around the stakes that ran along the sides of the wagon. She looked tired, but she was moving and she snorted when she saw Jim.

The boy managed a weak smile. "See, girl, I told you we would—"

He fell into buzzing darkness again.

It was a hot July evening. The lightning bugs were drifting across the front acre like sparks from a bonfire. Jim was sitting out on the porch of the homestead, trying to find Sagittarius in the night sky. Lottie was already asleep in the loft, but Jim was allowed to stay up later to play fiddle with Pa on the front porch. Momma would sing as the lightning bugs danced.

But tonight there wasn't going to be any singing or playing. Jim could hear Ma and Pa fussing, inside the house, their voices gaining in speed and volume.

"Hush up now, William; the children will hear," Momma said.

"Hell with 'em!" Pa bellowed. "Maybe they'd like to hear what a man's gotta put up with just to have something to soothe his burning head."

"You're drunk," she hissed. "Please, William, if it's the headaches, we can go see Doc Winslow—"

"Doc Winslow can go straight to Hell, too!" Pa roared. "He ain't got nothing in his little bag that's gonna stop a Johnnyman's curse. This damn eye . . . like ants made outta ice crawling in my skull."

"Let me help you, darling, please."

There were loud crashing sounds—pots and chairs knocked about, Momma crying out in terror. Pa threw open the door and staggered out into the warm, sticky night. He froze when he saw Jim standing there wide-eyed and silent.

"Pa," Jim said. "Momma all right in there?"

Billy Negrey nodded slowly. Inside, Lottie was crying and Momma was calling out to her.

"Jim, you know I love your mother, don't you?"

"Yes, sir," Jim said.

"Sometimes this, this thing . . . in my head. I say things, I drink, 'cause it hurts so damn bad."

"I know, Pa. Ma knows too. She knows."

Billy staggered off the porch and toward the barn. He turned to regard his son. Billy's skin was dream-spun silver in the bright moonlight. The eye patch was hidden in shadow. Jim was taken by how old he looked—not the years but the awful toll this life had exacted on him. His God-given eye fixed on Jim's own.

"Take care of your mother and Lottie, Jim," he said. "I'm going into town."

A few minutes later he rode out of the barn on his horse and disappeared down the dirt road toward Albright. After a time, Lottie stopped crying. A little while after that, Jim heard the porch door close behind him and felt Momma's small, strong hands rest on his shoulders.

"It's all right, Jim," she said softly. "Your poor father just needs to find himself some peace, that's all."

She wrapped her arms around him and began to sing "Barb'ra Allen," her favorite song, low and sweet. It was old, like the mountains it came from, another place, another time. It was sad, but there was a beauty in the sadness that Jim didn't fully understand but that soothed him nevertheless; it was Momma's song. He picked up the fiddle and played it the way Pa had taught him.

The stars blazed and the lightning bugs drifted. The moon painted the world in smoky silver and endless ink. He felt her love, for him, for Pa, and all was right in the world then. It was all going to be just fine.

He never saw his father alive again.

Jim opened his eyes to a vast canopy of black velvet, sprinkled with silvery sand. He was on his back looking up. It was cold—a deep desert night. He struggled to sit up and blinked. He was under the warm horse blanket beside a crackling cook fire. About twenty yards to his left was the wagon he had been in earlier. To his right he could see Promise tethered to an emaciated excuse for a tree beside a pair of short paint horses. The mare seemed stronger, more alive than he had seen her since they had entered the arid hell of the 40-Mile Desert.

"She's a good horse," a man's voice said from across the fire. "Strong heart, strong spirit."

The man leaned closer toward the flames and Jim could make out his features in the frantic, shuddering firelight.

He was Indian, the first real one Jim had ever seen. His hair fell down to his shoulders in black, oily strands. His nose was crooked and seemed too thin and too pointy. His eyes reflected the firelight like spit on slate. His face was a grizzled topography of pockmarks and scars that made it hard to figure his age. His eyebrows grew together, colliding over the crook of his nose. He smirked when he saw the reaction his appearance created in the boy. The gesture revealed a mouthful of yellowed, snagged teeth and two very sharp, very straight incisors. The image triggered a memory in Jim that darted in his groggy brain, like fish in a pond, and then was gone.

"We're keeping the horses over there so they can stay upwind of me," the Indian said. "Horses don't like me."

"I thought horses liked Indians," Jim muttered.

"Well, they don't care much for me," he said.

"Thank you," Jim said, "for saving us. I'm obliged."

The Indian shrugged and stood. He was short and thin, but there was a languid strength in him. Jim noticed the six-gun strapped to his left thigh and the huge hunting knife tied to his right.

"Mutt," the Indian said, handing the boy a plate of cold beans and hunk of gray bread.

"Jim," the boy managed to get out before his face dived into the plate. Mutt chuckled; it was a dry sound like sandstone underfoot.

"Figured you'd be hungry," Mutt said. "How long you out there alone, Jim?"

"I kind of lost count. Days, I reckon. Promise, she got hurt on the . . . second day? That slowed us down a bit. We were trying to make it to Virginia City. I was looking for work."

"On the railroad?"

"M'hm," Jim murmured around a mouthful of beans and bread.

"Slow up there," Mutt said, handing him a metal cup full of water. "Your belly's 'bout the size of a hooter right now—you eat all that too quick, you'll end up sicker'n a dog."

Jim wiped his mouth on his sleeve and took a deep swallow of the water.

"How old are you, boy?'

"Turned fifteen, last October."

"Where you from?"

Jim froze up a little. He tried to be as blasé as he normally was when it came to lying about his past, but it wasn't easy when you were tired and sunburnt and groggy, and it seemed awful disrespectful to lie to the man who saved your life.

"Kansas," he said after a beat.

Mutt looked at him for about the same amount of time, then nodded. "Kansas it is then. Well, you didn't make it to Virginia City, but I'm sure you can scare up some work in Golgotha."

"That where you from?"

The Indian nodded. "Presently."

"I thought there was another fella with you," Jim said. "I woke up and he was leaning over me, I think he gave me water."

"Yup. That's Clay. It's his wagon."

Mutt jerked his thumb in the direction of the buckboard.

"He's asleep up in it. Afraid of waking up with the snakes."

"Well, we sure were lucky you-all were passing through."

Mutt frowned and refilled Jim's cup from a canteen. "We weren't exactly passing through, Jim. You've got some medicine about you."

Jim laughed. It hurt, so he stopped as soon as he could. "Shoot, I ain't no doctor. I'd feel sorry for anyone who I tried to fix up."

"No, I'm talking about the old medicine, the first powers. The things that move like crazy smoke and fever dream through the worlds. White men call it magic—a little word to hide all the world's truth behind. White men like to try to laugh at the things that scare the hell out of them. So, do you know any magic, Jim?"

Jim paused. He remembered what happened in the graveyard outside Albright—the unmarked grave and the eye. If he told anyone, even this crazy-sounding Indian, they would surely think he was insane. He shook his head and looked into the fire.

"No sir. I ain't no wisdom, if that's what you mean. I'm a God-fearing servant of Christ, and I don't truck with no haints or boogeymen, or none of that, no sir. Devil's business, it is."

"Uh-huh," Mutt said, but the yellowed grin was back. "Right. So why do you smell of power, power that I could track across the desert?"

"I . . . I don't understand. You were out here looking for us?"

"I came across you out here the other night. I didn't want to frighten you, so I went back to town and talked Clay into bringing his wagon out here to fetch you and Promise."

Jim felt his memory grope around to fill in some detail, some impression that what Mutt was saying was solid. There was nothing. Had he been so tired he hadn't seen or heard the Indian? Or was Mutt like the Indians in the dime novels he read, the ones with the orange covers and the stories of the wilderness? Those Indians were invisible, like smoke, or haints.

"I rightly don't know," Jim said, covering the pocket of his pants with his hand. "I ain't got no power, Mutt. If I did, you think I'd be stuck out here?"

"Your folks know you out here?"

"Not much work back home," Jim said, the lie sliding smoothly from his lips this time; he had plenty of practice telling this one and he had his footing about him again. "I told Ma and Pa I'd come out here and get a good-paying railroad job, send some money home."

"Back to Kansas, right?"

"Yup."

The cold air around them suddenly filled with howls and yips. Mutt stood again and his hand fell to his gun.

"Coyotes?" Jim said as he moved closer to the fire.

Mutt nodded. "They can see it too," he said.

"What?"

There was movement in darkness, a swarm of dark motes hurtling forward across the plain toward the fire. Separating, accelerating. Hot breath, bloody eyes.

"Whatever that power is you don't have," he said as he pulled a burning branch out of the fire.

Jim rose, shakily, and grabbed a torch as well. He dug into his pants pocket frantically. "Is this it?" he said, and held up his father's jade eye.

A snarling, furry shape lunged out of the darkness toward Jim's hand. Mutt was suddenly there; his firebrand smashed into the coyote's flank with a whoosh and a wild shower of sparks. The animal yelped and crashed to the ground. It scampered to its feet and disappeared into the darkness. Another member of the pack snapped at Mutt's vulnerable side, but Jim was there with his own torch. The animal howled in pain and retreated. The boy and the Indian stood back-to-back as the night encircled them and showed its sharp teeth.

"There's got to be a dozen of them," Jim said between ragged, frightened breaths.

Mutt grunted and brandished the torch. "Sorry to say, I've got a big family."

"What?"

"They're my kin."

"Your kin?"

"My dad sent them," Mutt said. "He loves shiny things. No chance you want to give that up, is there?"

"It was my pa's," Jim said. "I'm not giving it up to a bunch of smelly curs . . . no offense."

"None taken. They're the bad side of the family, and they really do smell."

A gravel-edged growl called out from the darkness. A large, grizzled coyote padded into the circle of firelight. Its one good eye glared at the Indian.

"Squint," Mutt said. "Didn't know you were still prowling around doing Dad's dirty work for him. Still haven't learned you can't suck up to the old man, eh?"

Squint snarled and froth exploded from his mouth. In the firelight's trembling shadows Jim swore the animal looked like the Devil himself.

"Can't do that, Squint," Mutt said to the animal as he slid the knife free of its sheath. "It's the boy's birthright. Wouldn't be proper to steal it. Besides, now that I know it's you Dad sent out, I just want to mess with you."

He grinned and showed the coyote his crooked teeth as he crouched close to the earth, ready to strike. Squint growled out a command to the others and they began to howl. The one-eyed coyote hunched, ready to pounce.

"What do think they'll call you when you ain't got no eyes left?" Mutt whispered.

The thunder of a shotgun blast rolled across the plain. One of the coyotes to the left of Squint was lifted up in the air, twisted in a cloud of bloody mist and fell, twitching, to the earth. The howling stopped.

Jim saw the vulture-man, the one Mutt had called Clay, standing in the back of the wagon, one of his shotgun's barrels trailing silvery smoke up into the starlight. Clay's hair was a ragged halo around his liver-spotted pate and he was wearing a pair of filthy long johns. It would have been comical if Jim hadn't been so scared.

"Now, git!" Clay shouted. He leveled the shotgun at another of Squint's pack and fired. The coyote's whimper of pain was lost in the bellow of the blast. It fell as silent as its brother, unmoving on the ground. Clay frantically scrambled for more shells at his feet as he popped the still-smoking breech open.

Squint glared at Mutt, who met the gaze with hatred in kind. The big coyote sniffed, and then turned and ran, barking a long string of yips. The pack joined in as they, too, turned to flee. The desert grew quiet again except for an occasional howl.

"Well, don't that beat the Dutch?" Clay said, hopping down off the wagon and hobbling, barefoot, toward the others. "Never seen coyotes act like that before. You, Mutt?"

The Indian shrugged. "Clay, this is Jim."

"Jim Ne . . . Nelson, sir," Jim said, pumping the old man's hand when it was offered. "That was some good shooting up there."

"Clay Turlough," the old man replied. "Thank you, son. I'm a mite ornery when I get woke up 'fore I'm ready to."

Clay looked out into the darkness. He seemed suddenly distracted. He handed Jim the open shotgun and then trotted into the shadows at the terminator of the fire's light. He returned cradling one of the wounded, bloody coyotes in his arms.

"Well, Mutt, don't seem the trip was a complete loss. This one's not too torn up and look, he's still huffing a little air. Let me get him over to the wagon and have a look-see."

Jim looked at the Indian.

Mutt took the shotgun out of his hands and reloaded it. "Clay owns the only stable in Golgotha. He's the closest thing we got to a horse doctor in these parts. Went to medical school for a few years. Didn't work out too well from what I heard. He makes a decent living doing taxidermy for folks as far away as Carson City, though. He . . . collects . . . dead things."

Jim approached the wagon while Mutt tended the fire. Clay had lit an oil lantern and set it next to the dying coyote on the back of the wagon. The old man had put on his boots and a trail coat over his long johns. His hands were black with blood, but he didn't seem to mind. He was hunched near the animal's face. Jim thought he heard him whispering to the animal, but Clay stopped when the boy approached.

"Ah, Mr. Nelson. Come see, young man; this is a unique educational opportunity for a lad of your age. See, see. He's just at the threshold now."

The animal's eyes were wide. The pupils greedily drinking in every last flicker of light, scrapping for every final detail. Fear clouded the eyes like a cataract, but as the old man and boy watched the fear slid away from the eyes. A dumb peace settled over them, as if the animal was no longer looking at the same world any longer. Then the light flickered, and was gone. Clay audibly gasped.

"'Man,'" he muttered, "'how ignorant art thou in thy pride of wisdom.'"

Jim stared at him oddly.

"Shelley," he said. It's from Lady Shelley's marvelous scientific fiction. We understand so little about life or its sister, death. Look at this animal. Why was it, a moment ago, alive and feeling and thinking and now it is changed, dead? Why?"

"'Cause you shot it," Jim said.

Clay looked at him oddly, like he wasn't standing in front of the old man or he hadn't heard what Jim said. He blinked and the jovial old man was back, but the sour smell Jim had first caught off of him was there as well—a cross between formaldehyde and lilac water trying to hide it.

"You've had a busy day and a busier night, m'boy," Clay said with a razor cut of a smile. He placed a bloody hand on the dead coyote's flank.

"Get some rest."

The two men took turns keeping watch. The coyotes didn't return. Just before sunup, the men broke camp and doused the cook fire. They set off at dawn for Golgotha. Jim sat on the buckboard with Mutt while Promise trotted along behind the wagon. Clay and his dead coyote rode in the back.

As the day wore on, Mutt asked to see the eye. Jim reluctantly agreed. The Indian admired it, rolled it over in his callused, dirty hands. Jim noticed even his knuckles were hairy. Mutt tried to make out the tiny chains of inscriptions that ringed the iris.

"It's Johnnyman talk, "Jim said. "Chinese, I reckon."

"It's not any kind of medicine I understand," Mutt said finally. The two were talking softly. They need not be concerned, however; Clay was quite content to mutter to himself and the coyote. "Still, it's powerful; I can feel it humming across the worlds."

Jim nervously held out his hand, and after too long a pause Mutt dropped the eye back into the boy's palm.

"You'd do well to not lose that," Mutt said.

"It's all I got left of my pa, and I don't intend to ever part with it," Jim said as he stuffed it back in his pocket.

They rode along in silence for hours. The desert was beginning to give way grudgingly to some greenery. Blackbrush, shadscale and an occasional yucca plant softened the unforgiving sameness of the plains. They began to spiral downward through small demi-canyons richer in low, hardy plants. Once, Jim felt a cool breeze off of some body of water caress his face for a moment. It was growing noticeably cooler as the greenery began to embrace them.

"So," Jim finally said. "Your brother is a coyote?"

"Whereabouts in Kansas did you say your family was from . . . Mr. Nelson?" Mutt asked with a jagged smile.

Jim shut up.

A few miles later Mutt leaned forward on the seat and turned to look at the boy.

"Jim, I know you're set on heading to Virginia City and that railroad job, but I'm here to tell you, I've traveled my whole life one step ahead of what was trying to bite me on the hindquarters. People with secrets, people running, need to keep to the shadows, out-of-the-way places where the world just passes on by."

"Like Golgotha?" Jim said.

Mutt nodded. "Small towns, hell, just about everybody in 'em got some kind of secret. Everyone minds their own business, holds their peace. Place like Virginia City, you'd be stumbling over marshals and sheriffs, bounty hunters and Pinkerton men. All the latest wanted posters are up and everybody is nosy as hell, up in your business."

"Why are you telling me all of this?" Jim said.

"Guess I like a man who keeps his horse alive in the desert, who grabs a torch and helps a fella out of a jam, even if the fella is half-breed Injun he don't know from Adam."

They passed a simple farmhouse with a corral pen full of placid cattle.

"You and Clay saved us," Jim said. "Didn't have to, didn't need to, but you did anyway. My pa always said a man was what he did, not where he came from or what people thought about him. You did right by me and Promise."

They passed old decrepit buildings made of dried mud set into the side of a mountain wall, a shrine of simple stones and a weathered Roman cross; the items seemed to be from vastly different times.

Mutt smiled and nodded. "Fair enough. More fair than most. Your secrets are safe with me, Jim Nelson from Kansas."

They passed a cool stand of cottonwood trees on the left and a crumbling stone well on the right. The sky was bright and blue, shimmering with heat. The air smelled of sawdust and horse manure. The wagon slowed as they approached Main Street.

"Welcome to Golgotha," Mutt said.

The Star

Golgotha opened her arms to him.

Jim had seen his fair share of towns in his travels toward the near-mythical railroad job in Virginia City. Golgotha seemed an odd mixture of old ruin and new paint, boom and bust—like an old lady all gussied up and powdered to meet her suitor, wearing too much makeup and gaudy school-girl ribbons in her hair, not caring about the incongruity of it, just happy to be alive and in love.

Golgotha was old, but she was still kicking.

They had passed the rotted wood skeletons of old dwellings and tattered tarp doorways to the cave homes—gouged into the cool blue rock of the mountain slumbering off to their left. It all whispered of age—lives long ago lived and put aside, memories that refused to be wholly eaten by the dust.

The first building that grabbed Jim was the theatre. It was a garish two-story affair off to his right, painted up in gray and mauve. The marquee stretched across the face of the building like a wide grin. It boldly proclaimed Professor Mephisto's Playhouse and Showcase and further announced a production of *Little Brown Jug* currently ongoing.

Next door to the playhouse was Shultz's General Store and Butcher Shop, according to a large sign in fat Slab Serif print. A heavyset man with a thick rust-colored handlebar mustache was sweeping up the wooden planks of the sidewalk in front of the store. He reminded Jim of the drawing of a walrus he had seen in a book once. The man wore a crisp, white apron, a fringe of red and smoke-colored hair encircling his sun-freckled pate and a warm smile he shared as the wagon passed.

"That's Auggie," Mutt said. "It's his store. Well, it was his and Gert's store. She passed a while back. Just about anything you need, Auggie's got it, or can order it. Post office is in there too."

The street was a wide moat of wet and dried mud, dust and manure. People made their way between the buildings, many sticking as close to the wooden sidewalks as their business would allow them. Others braved the street, trudging between the trotting horses, clattering wagons and the muck. Men tipped their hats to the ladies, interposing themselves between the dirty streets and the women. Most of the folk looked like regular people to Jim, but a few were dressed all fancy, like they were headed to church, even though it wasn't Sunday.

Across the street from Shultz's was the Paradise Falls Saloon, the largest building on the street. The Paradise had three stories, a wide covered porch on the ground level and a railed balcony wrapping around the second floor. Smaller balconies outside shuttered doors and parapets that were home to brooding angels or leering gargoyles adorned the third floor

A group of well-dressed men, awash in the smoke of their huge cigars, congregated in front of the Paradise. They guffawed over some unseemly joke and slapped each other on the back, nodding.

On the opposite side of the street from the Paradise Falls and next door to Auggie's store resided the Golgotha Bank and Trust, a sturdy-looking building with iron bars over the windows.

Mutt couldn't help but give a sly grin when he saw Jim's expression as they passed the bank. The boy had caught sight of the Johnnies, headed up Main toward Auggie's.

Jim gasped. Chinamen, real Chinamen. Not in a book or one of Pa's stories of Washington. It was the first time in Jim's life he had seen anyone so different in every way. They wore black tunics and loose pants, like pajamas, and wide cone-shaped straw hats that hid much of their faces in shadows. Sandals covered their feet and some were barefoot. He did a double take when he realized that some of them were women and were dressed the same as the men. No one tipped their hat to them, or shielded them from the street. They kept their heads down under their basket-hats. His hand slid into his pocket and cupped the jade eye.

"Chinese, mostly," Mutt said. "A few from other places I can't pronounce none too good. They're out here looking for work on the railroads. Like you. Most of them live over in Johnny Town, off of North Bick Street. Got their own saloons, businesses, everything over there. I wouldn't recommend wandering there alone, Jim."

They passed a fancy-looking hotel, the Elysium, next to the saloon. Jim saw a barbershop that proudly advertised the dental services and curatives offered therein. Old men whittled on a bench next to the shop's striped pole. An elderly Indian paused in his carving and nodded to Mutt. Mutt returned the gesture with the slightest of motions.

Across from the barber was the Corinthian-columned façade of Golgotha's town hall.

Clay turned the wagon right onto a street named Prosperity. They passed a small cabin and a neatly whitewashed church on the opposite side of the road. The mountain was behind them now and when Jim looked back he saw that Prosperity Street snaked its way up the slope. There were tents, shacks and shanties, dozens of them farther up the mountain, a whole other small, ramshackle town, looking down on Golgotha.

"Argent Mountain," Clay said as he noticed the boy's gaze. "Ole Moneybags Bick's hole in the ground. There were some good veins down in there. The silver brought people here from all over. Then it went bust a few years back."

"Now you got lots of folks who live up there in the squatter camps, came here chasing a dream and ended up broke and lost in the desert," Mutt said. "Figure Golgotha is as good a place as any to sit around and wait for your luck to change, or to die."

"Hell," Clay added, "damn sight better than some places."

Ahead of them was another rise with a gentler slope. This hill boasted several homes residing on it of an obviously higher quality than the rest of the town, or the squalid shacks on Argent Mountain. Near the hill's base was a beautiful building of dark wood and blued stone. Two steeples rose up out of its roof, both adorned with crosses. A literal wall of arched windows covered one side of the structure and reflected the brilliant sun in silvered mercury glass.

"What is that?" Jim asked.

"Rose Hill," Clay said. "Where all the fancy folk live. Most of 'em is Mormons and that there is their temple."

"That's their church?" Jim leaned forward in the wagon, squinting against the light. "Looks like a king's castle or palace or something."

"They only use it for special ceremonies," Mutt said. "They got a little meetinghouse off of Absalom Road they use most of the time. Not so off-puttin'."

"I heard some strange stuff about them Mormons," Jim said.

"They're all right," Mutt said blandly. "Bet you heard some strange stuff about Chinamen and Injuns too, huh?"

Jim said nothing. Mutt's chuckle was a dry grunt.

Clay nodded toward a wide, rutted road off to the left, just past the whitewashed church.

Mutt brought the wagon to a halt. "This is where we get off, Jim," he said. "Much obliged to you, Clay. Sorry about the horse."

"Well, better luck next time," the old man said with a shrug. He took the reins from the Indian. "Always glad to help out the law."

Jim climbed down. He stroked Promise's bony flank as he hefted the saddlebags awkwardly over his shoulders.

"See, girl, I told you we'd make it," Jim whispered to the horse.

"Now don't you fret, young fella," Clay said with a wink. "I'll stable her over at my place. It's a long bit a week; you think you can afford that? You come by when you can even up. We square?"

"Uh, sure? Your place?"

"Straight down Pratt Road here," Clay said, gesturing to the wide track. "Can't miss it."

"Thanks," Jim said. "For everything."

Clay smiled and shook the reins. The wagon clattered along with Promise following behind. They turned up the road and slowly disappeared into the curtain of heat and dust.

Mutt turned right onto a dirty little street just behind the cabin they had passed. The simple wooden sign announced it was called Dry Well Road. Jim hurried to catch up to the Indian. He noticed a lot of folks seemed to give Mutt a wide berth, moving to the other side of the narrow street and avoiding his unblinking gaze. Mutt didn't seem to mind; if anything, Jim got the impression he enjoyed making the townsfolk feel uncomfortable.

"Why did you tell Clay 'sorry'?" Jim said as they walked past a seedy boardinghouse and a livery and tack store.

"Huh?"

"'Sorry,'" Jim repeated. "You told Clay 'sorry' and he said, 'Better luck next time.' Why?"

"Oh." The Indian smiled, all yellow and jagged. "That. Well, the only way I could get him out there to the Forty-Mile was I told him your horse was pert near dead and if he would drive me out, he could have the carcass if she died."

The blood ran out of Jim's face. His tongue seized up. "Oh," was all he could muster.

Mutt laughed again, shaking his head. "Now, Jim, he ain't going to do nothin' to Promise, 'cept feed her, brush her down and keep her safe. Clay is kind of odd about his little . . . hobby with dead things. But he won't hurt her. She belongs to you, and he seems to have taken a shine to you."

"Why is he such an odd stick about dying, though?"

"Everybody's got something that puts wind in their lungs, Jim. Most folks it's money or a fancy house. Some it's another person. For Clay it's figuring out how things tick and why they stop ticking."

They continued down Dry Well. They passed a blacksmith's shop. The rhythm of hammer and muscle against hot iron filled the space of their silence.

"Why did Clay say he was glad to help the law?" Jim asked finally.

Mutt buried his hand in the pocket of his dungarees. He pulled out a badge—a star of silver within a circle of the same. He showed it to Jim and then pinned it on his jacket lapel.

"You the sheriff here, Mutt?" Jim said, trying to keep the fear out of his voice. After the desert, it was easier.

The gaunt man laughed. "Hell, no! You'd have to be nine parts crazy to one part stupid to be sheriff in this town. Sounds like a job for a white man, you ask me. Nope, I'm just hired help."

"Why did you take a job like that?"

"Got my reasons."

They were approaching a squat cube of red brick. The bars on the windows and the heavy iron door, dented and scarred, a monument to old violence, told you what it was even before you read the sign hanging off the awning by two chains. A wooden board with public announcements was mounted next to the iron door. Wanted posters struggled in the stale, feeble wind to be free of the tacks pinning them to the board.

Jim's stomach was full of black ice. "You taking me to jail now, Mutt?"

"Why would I be doing that?" he said. "Just checking in."

He stepped onto the shade of the porch and tried the door. It was locked.

"Wonder where he's got to?" Mutt said.

"Who?" Jim asked. He edged onto the porch, one step closer to the end of his life.

"The sheriff," Mutt said. He fished out an iron key from his pocket and unlocked the door with a grunt and an audible clank. It swung inward on groaning hinges and cast bright sunlight into the inner darkness.

"Jon, you in there?" he called. No answer, just cool shadows. Mutt pulled the door shut and locked it.

"Must have had to head out for a spell," he said. "His rifle and saddlebags are gone."

"Deputy! Deputy!"

A man ran down the street from the opposite direction that Jim and Mutt had come. He was long legged and handsome, with a mane of hair, a handlebar mustache and muttonchops, all the color of rust. His eyes were as blue as the heart of a lit match. A brocade waistcoat of emerald and gold flashed under his jacket. He was red faced and sweating.

"What is it, Harry?" Mutt said.

The man paused and fished a handkerchief out of his pocket to mop his face. "It's Earl Gibson. He's making a ruckus fit to wake snakes. Busted into Auggie's store, waving a gun around. Where the hell have you been?"

"Out," Mutt said, reopening the jail's door and disappearing inside. "I'm back now. Where's Jon?"

"In Carson City, testifying at a trial," Harry said. "He left a few days ago, after he got tired of waiting for you to decide to show back up, Deputy." He then added, "Who the hell is the kid?"

Mutt reemerged from the darkness of the jail. He had a Winchester rifle in his hand. He looked at Jim and then crossed over to the public board. He ripped a wanted poster off the board, crumpled it into a wad and jammed it in his pocket.

"What the hell is that old thing still doing up there? Oh, him? He's my sister's boy: Jim. Jim, say hello to Harry Pratt. He thinks he's a huckleberry above a persimmon."

Pratt looked at Jim like he had the plague, then snapped his gaze back to Mutt. "I told Jon it was damn foolishness to put his faith in a drunken half-breed like you. You don't have a sister; you don't have anything, Mutt, including a job, once the town fathers hear how you've handled this situation."

Mutt came off the porch toward Pratt. He cocked the Winchester's lever and let it fall to his side. He seemed taller than the white man, even though he wasn't. He stopped a few inches from Harry's face.

"Let's acknowledge the damn corn, Mr. Mayor," Mutt growled. "I don't work for you; I don't work for the damn town fathers. I work for Jon and if you'll excuse me I've got some work to do right now."

He strode down the street in the direction Harry had appeared from.

Jim nodded to the red-faced mayor. "Uh, pleased to meet you, sir," he stammered, and then sprinted off to catch up with the deputy. When he did, Mutt was turning the corner at Sprang's Rooms for Rent, a rather questionable-looking boardinghouse, given the drunken and disheveled group of men gathered on its porch. Jim saw the crumbling stone well they had passed coming into town out past where the street ended. It seemed lonely, like a solitary, forgotten watchman welcoming newcomers to the town.

"What was that all about?" Jim asked when he finally caught his breath.

"That's the mayor. Thinks his shi— Thinks he don't make a mess when he goes to the outhouse. Just 'cause his family rolled out of the Forty-Mile twenty years ago and decided this was the Promised Land or some-such thinks he can do or say whatever he wants to whoever he wants. Pretty standard for white folk round these parts, really."

"If you hate white people so much, why do you live with them?"

Mutt started to answer, then frowned.

"I may be killing a pretty decent fella in a few minutes, or getting a pretty decent fella killed. I don't have time to babysit anymore. Get your ass back to the jail and wait for me, boy."

"What if you get killed? And I ain't no boy!" Jim said with heat blooming in his eyes.

Mutt grinned at the reaction. Mutt seemed to grin at most things that bothered other folk.

"Didn't think about that. You better tag along. Can't have you out on that porch like a stray. But I mean it, Jim; this ain't no game. You hang back and keep quiet or I'll do to you what I'd do to any other damn fool who was getting in my way—we square?"

Jim nodded. He fell into step beside the Indian. They slipped down an alleyway between the theatre and the general store.

"Who'd you kill in West Virginia that they want to string you up for?"

Jim stopped.

Mutt turned to the boy. "Your poster got here about three months before you did. Who did you kill?"

"A sonofabitch," Jim said, walking again.

Mutt fell into step beside the boy. "Plenty of those still walking around," the deputy said as they stepped out onto Main Street. A crowd was gathered in front of the general store. "Why'd you kill this particular one?'

"Got my reasons," Jim said, happy to be on the other side of the sardonic grin for a change.

The Hanged Man

"All right, folks, everyone get back a ways!" Mutt shouted to the crowd. He gestured to a couple of the men who were in with the throng of onlookers. "Louis, Larry, you get these people back for me. Other side of the street, everybody!"

Jim moved behind the water trough and hitching post to the left of the general store. He watched as Mutt gestured to a woman and a girl in bonnets clutching heavy wicker baskets. Mutt knew Maude Stapleton, the bank president's wife, and her thirteen-year-old daughter, Constance.

"You ladies were shopping in Auggie's, right?"

The women obviously seemed uncomfortable in such close proximity to the half-breed. They nodded to the affirmative.

"Tell me what happened in there."

Maude Stapleton cleared her throat and addressed him behind startling eyes of honeyed brown, almost gold. Mutt had never actually been this close to her before. Her hair was auburn, shot with hints of red-gold and silver, pulled from her face in a severe bun and held under her bonnet. Her skin was alabaster, like fancy china; her wrists and hands were pale too and fragile and perfect. Her features were strong; some men would have called her mannish in her demeanor. Those men would be fools, Mutt concluded. She was beautiful, strikingly beautiful, just not in the same old way. It took more than a lazy glance to see it in her. Her frame and figure were slight as well, but there was a wiry strength to her and she carried herself with a grace and an almost shrouded power that was very feminine to him right this moment. It was like standing next to a mountain lion pretending to be a desert hare. He shifted a little uncomfortably.

"Constance and I were just settling our account with Mr. Shultz when a ghastly spectacle of a man barged in." She had a faint southern accent.

"Earl? Was it old Earl Gibson from up on Argent Ridge?" he asked.

"I have no idea who that is, Deputy, I'm sorry. He had a pistol in his hand and was shouting out absolute nonsense peppered with obscenity. He pointed the gun at us and I nearly fainted. He told us to get out and we did. He told poor Mr. Shultz to stay and to bring him . . . What was it he wanted, Constance?"

"Paraffin," the girl said. She was her mother's daughter, same eyes, wisps of lighter hair falling out of her bonnet. "Paraffin wax, all Mr. Shultz had. He said something about stopping something up."

"It didn't make much sense," Mrs. Stapleton said. "The man was as mad as a hatter."

"Could you tell if he had been drinking?" Mutt asked while he kept glancing at the store's front door.

"Well, obviously he must have," Mrs. Stapleton said. "How else would you explain such horrid behavior?"

"I mean, Mrs. Stapleton, did you smell it on him?"

She wrinkled up her face as if Mutt had just propositioned her daughter.

"I certainly would never approach a man like that and get close enough to actually smell—"

She was drowned out by the thunder of gunfire. Screams erupted from the crowd as onlookers scattered like roaches caught in a light. Mutt spun and shoved both women onto the ground, diving on top of them to cover them from the fire. Mrs. Stapleton's bonnet was lost in the fall; her hair tumbled out everywhere in a tangled mess. She gasped when she realized she was only inches from Mutt's face. Their eyes met and held. Her eyes reminded him of a deer for a second, moist, dark and wide; then something passed through her and suddenly he was looking into a mirror, at a hunter's eyes, a predator's eyes. It was his turn to suddenly draw breath. Her body shifted slightly beneath him, but their eyes remained locked. He raised himself up out of the muck and off Mrs. Stapleton. He crouched, covering them with the rifle.

"Thank you for your civic support, ladies," Mutt said after a space of awkward seconds. "You just hurry on over to the over side of the street now, and I'll go have a word with old Earl. Stay low. Oh, and Mrs. Stapleton . . ."

"Y-yes," she said, turning her head back to look at the deputy as she was crawling away. The timid hare again, the banker's wife.

"Sorry about the smell."

The faintest ghost of a smile crossed her eyes. She took her daughter's hand and they hurried out of harm's way.

Mutt crouched as he moved out of the middle of the street and took up a position next to Jim's water trough.

"That," he said to the hiding boy, "was a shotgun. Auggie's got one under the counter. I guess old Earl's got it now. I hate shotguns."

"What you planning to do?" Jim asked.

"Something stupid, I reckon."

He wiped some of the street's dirt off the Winchester, looked around to see if any townsfolk had moved up to help. They hadn't. No one was going to stick their neck out for him.

"Let me help, Mutt," Jim said.

The Indian smiled. Not funny, not cruel mixed with funny. Warm and full of surprise and appreciation. "What do you know about that?" the deputy muttered.

He passed Jim his pistol. The six-gun was heavy in the boy's hand, but he'd handled the weight well enough before.

"Don't move from this spot," Mutt said. "Don't shoot unless you got to. Earl's a good man, just down on his luck. And for God's sake, don't shoot me. Ready?"

Jim nodded and steadied the gun on the post. Mutt cradled the rifle close to his chest and prepared to charge through the front door of the store.

It was silent all along Main Street. The thunder of the gun blasts had faded into the dry wind. The townsfolk watched mutely from the safety of cover, hidden behind rain barrels and wagons. Most expected the Indian to burst through the door and be knocked back out onto the street in a cloud of gun smoke and blood. Truth be told, so did Mutt. The town held its breath.

There was a sound, like a heartbeat, drumming fast and growing louder. It came from out past the edge of town, past the dry well, out by the cattle ranch. It echoed along the street, becoming more distinct as it rapidly grew closer and closer. Galloping, a horse's hooves clattering in a wild, powerful run.

The horse appeared at the edge of Main Street in a cloud of desert dust. He was a bay stallion. The rider was crouched low, his gray, wide-brimmed Stetson held tight on his head by the stampede string under his chin. The rider's face was half-covered by a tied kerchief to keep the dust and sand out of his nose and mouth. His gray barn coat fluttered like a moth's wings as he spurred his mount on; faster, faster.

A shout went up from the crowd and then a cheer.

"It's the sheriff! The sheriff is here!"

"About damn time," Mutt said to Jim.

The rider reined his mount up beside the hitching post next to Jim and Mutt. Jim took the reins when they were tossed to him and looped them about the post. The rider climbed off the saddle with the smooth grace of someone who had lived most of his life on horseback. He pulled the bandana down around his neck and pushed the hat back off his forehead, shaking the trail dust off him as best he could.

He was a tall man, a good half foot taller than Mutt, and he had hair the color of desert sand. It was longish, slicked back from his face. He was handsome, in a simple kind of way—nothing fancy like the mayor. He had a week's trail beard shadowing his jaw and it made him seem older than he really was. A gleaming silver star hung on the lapel of his dusty barn coat and a .44 was strapped to his right hip. He wiped his face with a gloved hand and looked around. Gray eyes flashed silver in the late morning sun.

"Jon," Mutt said with a nod. "Nice entrance."

"Thanks, Mutt. What is it this time? I heard the shots riding in."

"Somebody's in the general store, shooting off Auggie's shotgun," Mutt said. "Harry seems to think it's Earl Gibson."

"That don't sound like Earl, even on a tear; that don't sound like Earl at all."

"I know. I was just about to go in there and have a discussion with him about that."

"All by yourself?"

"Well, not too much help was forthcoming from our fellow citizens—"

"It's a comfort to know some things never change. Who's this?"

Jim turned to regard the sheriff. "I'm Jim. I'm a friend of Mutt's."

The sheriff frowned and turned to Mutt, who said nothing, only shrugged, then back to Jim. He pulled off a glove and extended a dirty, calloused hand to the boy.

"Jon Highfather. I'm sheriff in these parts. Not too many claim Mutt as a friend and he don't cotton to most that do. So, it's always nice to meet someone who makes the cut."

Jim shook hands. Highfather looked at the pistol in Jim's other hand, then to Mutt.

"He's my deputy," Mutt said. "I found him out in the desert."

"Your what?" Highfather said.

"Well, I needed someone watching my back and I couldn't wait around anymore for you to come riding in making fancy entrances."

"Picking up strays again, Mutt?"

"Look who's talking."

Highfather untied the leather thong around his leg and then unbuckled his gun belt. He turned back to his horse and rummaged in his saddlebags. He took out a large metal key ring with dozens of keys. He selected one and offered it to Mutt, keeping his back to the store's windows.

"This is the key to Auggie's back door. I want you to wait until I get inside and then get back there and open it as quiet as you can. It sticks a bit."

"Will do, boss. What if Earl is crazy as a jumping bean and just blasts you?"

Highfather stared at his deputy incredulously.

"Oh yeah, right. 'Not your time.' . . . I forgot. . . . Sorry."

"Just give me a minute to get the medicine show rolling, okay? And you, Deputy Jim, I want you to stay right there and cover us, okay?"

Jim nodded, knelt and adjusted the gun against the post again. Highfather laid his gun belt over the hitching post and walked up onto the sidewalk. He rapped loudly on the store's door.

"Earl? Earl, you in there? It's Jon Highfather. I need to talk to you."

"You go on now, Jon!" a shaky voice called out from inside. "You don't know what they been pourin' in my ears, down my throat, Jon! You ain't seen—"

A disheveled old man with wild gray hair and whiskers, dressed in filthy clothes, appeared in the window. He was holding a squat sawed-off double-barreled scattergun to the chest of the portly walrus-looking man Jim had seen sweeping up when they had entered town. The old man's eyes were glazed over with fear.

"Go on now, Jon! I don't want to hurt anyone, but I got to plug up my ears, sew up my mouth. I can't stand it anymore!"

"Now Earl, you know I can't just walk away here. Why don't you put the gun down?"

Auggie Shultz, the walrus shopkeeper, looked scared too, but was doing a good job of controlling it.

"Jon," Auggie said through a thick accent. "He's shot up the store, but no one is hurt. I think he's sick—"

Earl thumbed back the hammers on the shotgun. Sweat crept down his face.

"Shut up! Shut up! They did this to me; they did it! The singing thing in the mountain!"

Highfather raised his arms above his head. "Earl, I don't have any guns, see? I'm going to come in there and we can talk, okay, Earl? Just talk."

The old man and his hostage disappeared from in front of the large window. Highfather looked back at Mutt and Jim, opened the door and stepped inside.

Shultz's General Store usually smelled of talcum, sawdust and sausages. Today it was gunpowder and the sour smell of vinegar. The pickle barrel was dead, a massive hole blasted in it, and green juice and dills covered the floor. Several of the shelves behind the counter that contained Auggie's pharmacopeia canisters were torn apart, their contents scattered across the store. Bins of chemicals and compounds were strewn everywhere.

"Shut the door; they can hear us when the door is open," Earl whispered from the shadows near the counter.

"'They' who, Earl?" Highfather asked as he closed the door. The small bell on the jamb jingled.

The old man jumped, his eyes wide in fear, and he pressed the gun into Auggie's chest hard enough to make the shopkeeper grunt in pain. "Bells, they talk in silver bells! They're eating my memories; I can't remember Daisy's face no more, Jon; they done gone and ate Daisy's face from me!"

Highfather swallowed hard and stepped closer to the old man. "I understand Daisy was a fine woman, Earl. We're all powerful sorry she's gone, but that isn't Auggie's fault, now is it?"

Earl sobbed; he loosened his grip on the gun.

Auggie turned so he could see his captor's face. "You know I understand how it is to lose someone, Earl, yes? When Gertie passed, I thought I had died along with her. I still wish I had most days."

"But . . . but isn't that her singing, upstairs? Singing along with the music box?" Earl groaned. Auggie's face paled, his mouth opened, but nothing came out.

"There . . . there's no one singing, Earl," Highfather said softly. "Gert's passed. Daisy is gone too. I'm sorry, but that is the way of it. People die. It's sad but—"

"Shut up!" Earl screamed. "You dumb sumbitch! You don't know what they do up there on that mountain, do you, Sheriff? It's tossing and turning! It eats the heart of the world, like a worm burrowing an apple! Maybe the preacher's right and my faith is just shivering, weak—is it wrong for me to try to keep them from hollowing me out from inside? I should just blow all of you stupid bastards back to Kingdom Come, while it's still there! Before they burn down Heaven and feast on the corpse. Maybe we should all die now, better that way!"

Highfather edged closer. He managed to maneuver the old man so his back was to the counter.

"People die, Earl, up on the mountain, down in the valley; everyone dies."

"Everyone but you, Jon," the old man muttered.

Everyone but me," Highfather said. "You've heard the stories, haven't you, Earl? The stories about me?"

"They say you sold your soul to the Devil, Jon; that's what they say."

Highfather moved closer to Earl. He held the old man's gaze with his voice, his shimmering gray eyes. Behind them was a faint click. Earl didn't notice it.

"I've heard that one too, Earl, heard all of them. They tried to kill me back in the war, Earl. Strung me up on the end of a hangman's rope. Three times, want to see?"

Highfather pulled back the bandana and tugged down the collar of his shirt. Three lines of ugly, striated scars crisscrossed each other around the sheriff's neck. Their gruesome orbits intersected and blurred into pale raised scar tissue at different points all around his throat.

"See, Earl. That shotgun can't kill me. Nothing on this earth can kill me. Now you give it to me right now, or I swear on the gallows tree, I'm going to take it away from you."

Earl froze, his eyes locked on the scars. "Dead man, they say you're a walking dead man. . . . Not your time—"

Highfather grabbed the shotgun by the smooth, oily barrel. Earl yanked, screamed and pulled the triggers. Highfather's thumb jammed one of the hammers, even as he twisted to avoid the blast directly in front of him. The shotgun's roar filled the universe, filled everything, with heat and light and acrid smoke. Highfather could barely perceive anything. He felt the pain in his hand and a burning, then numbness in his side. The shotgun clattered to the floor and Auggie was diving for it. Earl was in Highfather's face, pale, with tears running down his rheumy eyes.

"See," Highfather croaked, "told you."

Mutt was over the counter, spinning Earl around and pinning his arms. The boy, Jim, came crashing through the front door, the Colt steady in his hands as he swept the place left to right.

The Indian looked at Highfather. "You okay? You hit?"

Highfather could barely make out the words over the pain and ringing in his ears, like a water glass vibrating, humming. He looked down to see a smoking hole in his barn coat. It went in about six inches above his belt and exited in the back. His shirt was blackened on that side and the flesh underneath was blistered and sore, but the slug had passed by, missing cutting him in half by inches. If the other barrel had fired, it would have ripped right through him.

"I'm okay. Good thing he wasn't firing shot, and I managed to block the right hammer, huh?"

"Luck still holding," Mutt said. "You count on her being there too damn much."

"Not my time yet," Highfather said.

"Thanks, Jon," Auggie said, eagerly pumping the sheriff's hand while Highfather pulled up his collar and once again hid his neck. "The poor old fella is balled up something terrible, yes?"

Highfather winced, but tried to ignore the pain that was beginning to filter into his nerves from the powder burns on his flank. He shook Auggie's hand and steadied himself on the counter.

"We'll be pressing charges for the firearms discharge in the town limits and the assault, Auggie. Do you want to file any charges for the destruction of property?"

"I know I should, but Gert always says to turn the other cheek. So, no, I will not press the charges."

"I'm sorry we had to bring Gertie up, Auggie. He was just so . . . well, I hope you understand it weren't anything speaking to her character at all. I was just trying to spook him."

"No, Jon, no. You are good man. Gert, she always like you."

Mutt led Earl outside. The old man was still raving, but when he looked out onto the street amidst the whoops and cheers of the townsfolk he seemed to pause, as if he was seeing something, hearing something, fitting the pieces in his head. . . .

"Jon, you've got to stop them! Stop them, I tell you! They sing terrible songs, Jon, horrible songs! The worms! They're coming, Jon. Worms, eating to the core of us. They eat life, they will eat up time and reason and then they will eat the light! They'll eat the light, Jon! Please, Jon, you've got to stop them, stop me, stop him!"

Mutt pulled Earl aside, wrestled his arms behind him, again, and applied a pair of iron cuffs to his wrists.

Highfather placed a hand on Mutt's shoulder. "This is the third person off the ridge to go bughouse crazy in the last few weeks."

The Indian nodded as he struggled to keep Earl from twisting loose of his grasp. "You think someone is running bad hooch up there again?"

"Don't know. Earl's breath don't smell like whiskey; neither does his clothes. I want you to head up there to the ridge tomorrow. See if anyone is brewing up anything they shouldn't be."

"Get right on it, boss," Mutt said; then, "What about the kid?"

Highfather regarded Jim carefully, like he was weighing his soul. After a long pause he asked, "Jim, you looking for work?" He took the gun out of the boy's hand.

"Yessir, and a place to stay."

"All right, come on back to the jail with us and we'll see what we can do about that."

"Thank you, sir," he said as he handed the sheriff his gun belt.

Highfather watched the boy leading his horse by his reins, back around the corner to the jail. Mutt and their mad prisoner walked beside them. The deputy paused to watch Maude Stapleton gather up her long hair and hide it under her bonnet. Their eyes met and held for too long to be healthy. Mutt finally nodded and tipped his hat. Maude hurried away with her daughter trailing behind her.

Highfather handled the crowds and the incessant demands for retelling what happened inside the store with as few words and descriptions as possible. Several noted the bullet hole and whistled. He knew many of them were whispering again that Golgotha had a walking dead man for a sheriff, a lucky corpse, two steps and a handshake ahead of death. But he knew the truth behind all the myths and the tall tales.

He looked up to Argent Mountain—Golgotha's empty promise. Home to human hangers-on: lost souls in tents and shanties, setting up there in the kingdom of broken dreams, poisoned rotgut and busted silver veins.

And he felt, more than saw, something up there. Something that shambled more than walked, something that drove good men mad and mad men to murder. Something unnamed, vast and terrible in its comprehension.

This was the beginning. Of what, he still did not know, but he had best figure it out before the killing started up again. These things always ended with killing.

He looked down his Main Street. Life was back to normal. Argent was just a mountain again, not a squatting alien colossus, threatening to rise and crush his town. The people went about their business, and why shouldn't they? The sheriff was back and the bad guy was on his way to jail. End of story.

Highfather limped down the sidewalk, wincing at the pain in his side. He looked at the charred hole in his jacket and shook his head in regret.

Third one ruined this month.

The World

He rode a steed of divine fire across the Fields of Radiance in search of the truant angel.

His mount was one of the Equina, a proud and beautiful steed whose every stride covered what would one day be known as parsecs. It was rumored that the Lord had decided to infuse the essence of the Equina into one of the new beasts that would reside on the sphere known as Earth, much as He had once remarked that He might distill His own essence into the beast to be known as man. The angel tried to imagine such sights— lesser, pale forms of universal absolutes hacked from crude matter, but like many in the Host, he was a little short on imagination. The concept troubled him even if he did not fully understand it.

If not for his mission he would have enjoyed the ride out across the fields. Heaven, its newly raised great arch, stood at his back. Even though work upon the Earth had been delayed by the war, the Almighty was insistent that Heaven's progress continue unabated.

He felt the arch at his back and it comforted him, quelling his unease about the mission to create and populate the Earth with reflections of the divine. He was a warrior of the Ninth Choir, Fifth Host. He believed in the will of God, in the vision of the Almighty and the properness of the advancement of Heaven's influence. He had slain in God's name and was proud of the fact. He was building a better world and that world sang to him and soothed him. God had named him Aputel.

In the passage of time Aputel came to the edge of the Radiance, where the Darkness still held dominion, and there he found Biqa. The angel was well suited to this brooding place. Unlike his fellow, Biqa's countenance reflected the bleak shadows of this most hated of places—a common trait of the Third Host. Here Heaven's light and song were distant echoes. This was a place of silence and cold, far too close to the enemy's domain for Aputel's taste.

"There you are!" Aputel shouted as he reined his mount to stop beside the other angel's Equina. "Everyone was looking for you. Did you not heed Gabriel's horn? The battle is upon us."

"Yes, I know. The final battle."

"Then why are you here?"

"I have no stomach for it, Aputel. No desire to take part in ending, murdering, an entire breed of creature."

"Murdering? Biqa, there is no murder here—those creatures are an abomination."

"To who? God?"

"Well, yes, actually. He has great plans, good plans, and those things were just going to ruin everything."

Biqa stared out into the Darkness. "So, God says, 'Let there be light,' and when there is, He sees that the darkness is full of these . . . beings, all coiled and slumbering together. It's difficult to tell where one of them ends and the next begins. And because of that, because His ideas, His will, did not plan for such a thing, they all must be destroyed. Why can He not change His plans?"

Aputel furtively glanced back toward Heaven.

"Keep it down; do you want someone to hear you?"

"I no longer care."

"That much is obvious. God is our creator, Biqa, the creator of all things. His will, His plan, must be done."

"His future is built on the bones of the past. His Heaven is being constructed from the husks of those dead things—you know that, don't you? Our homes are the corpses of those things in the Darkness. His precious Earth is being built of the same cadaverous matter as well.

"His will is not infallible, His dominion not absolute. He didn't create them, did He?"

"Most of us doubt they are truly alive; they may well be some kind of parasitic canker on the walls of eternity. Why does it matter?"

"They fight too well, too craftily, too savagely to be unaware," Biqa said. "They fight to win, to survive, and that scares Him."

"Silence!" Aputel cringed, awaiting the blistering presence of the Almighty, but it did not come. "You speak blasphemy! The Lord fears nothing."

"Then why did He banish the Darkness? Why did He make us? Why does He plan to create an entire universe of doppelgängers to worship Him?"

Aputel was silent. His own annoying concerns on the ride out returned to him, but he kept his own counsel.

Biqa nodded. "He was afraid of being alone. A natural enough fear, one we can all understand, surely. But after He was no longer alone He grew fearful of losing control of it all, of no longer being the one whose thoughts and feelings, moods and whims mattered the most in the entire cosmos. He has become obsessed with the Voidlings—they represent something He cannot control and didn't create. And for that crime, they must all be obliterated so that His glorious new universe may proceed along, unhindered."

"But—but they are so, so unnatural," Aputel said. "I mean they hate us, Biqa—surely we have as much right to endure, our way to endure, as they do. Surely."

Biqa smiled, a sad, fleeting thing. "I hate them too. I've seen them rip apart my brethren, my friends, and feast on their ichor, like wine. No, Aputel, we are invested now. It's war. I just blame Him for making us to fight and suffer and die in His place; I blame Him for creating more and more layers of control and isolation between Himself and those He creates, those He claims to love."

"Have care, Biqa; you again tempt His anger!"

The dark angel shrugged and turned back to the yawning eternal night.

"Mark my words, one day it will be His undoing. But today, I do my duty. I know my place and I shall serve Him and do His bidding. However, in this commission I shall not act with the zeal He breathed into us. I've had my fill of war."

"You would do well to be careful," Aputel said gently. "Others know of your disquiet. Some say you are correct; others call you dangerous and think the Almighty should punish you. Even Lucifer has been heard speaking of the merit of your arguments."

"Sharp one, that Lucifer. I see why he is God's most beloved. Best watch himself, though, if he wants to stay at the head of the table. No, my friend, I have no desire to make my concerns a cause, or my misgivings a revolt. I'm loyal and I always shall be—I give you my oath." The angel loosened his blade in its scabbard. "Let's get it over with."

"Let us be about our duty, my friend," Aputel said eagerly, hoping to infect his dark companion with some enthusiasm for the task to come.

The two angels turned their mounts in the direction of the battle when the Darkness began to roil. Great nebulas of dirty light bubbled up through the oily infinity. A sound vomited from the depths of the Darkness. It was unlike anything either of them had ever heard. The closest approximation to its timbre and its scope was the voice of the Almighty, singing. But this was no hymn; it was a dirge. In its annihilating cadence there was the menace of retribution, of an awful reckoning, an endless chorus of pain.

Behind them, Heaven's first great arch groaned, shuddered and fell. The Darkness swelled and crashed all about them; massive waves of night threatened to crash upon the shores of light, drowning everything. All that was rippled, threatened to tear, to break like Heaven's gate, but before that point of no return was reached the noise diminished, growing fainter and less expansive until finally all of creation was once again silent and still.

"We should get back," Biqa said.

The angels turned toward the glittering dust settling over Heaven's ruins. But before they could spur their Equina on, another rider appeared across the radiant plane. It became clear as he approached it was Jophiel, one of the highest of the Hosts. He did not look happy.

"Rejoice," the dour angel said. "Lo, I bring you glad tidings. While you two tarried and shirked your obligations, the rest of us have tasted sweet victory in the glorious name of our Lord. The last of the enemy has been vanquished."

"It has been destroyed?" Aputel said.

Jophiel's naturally bitter demeanor deepened before he replied. "The beast was overpowered and about to be slain when the Lord saw fit, in His infinite justice and mercy, to stay His hand of rightly deserved vengeance and to order the creature to be bound and imprisoned."

Aputel looked to Biqa, as if to see if this explanation satisfied the troubled angel's mind.

"How many?" Biqa asked Jophiel.

"Pardon?"

"How many of our brethren were destroyed before He realized you couldn't kill it?"

"What are you yammering on about now, Biqa? Perhaps it was best you were not in the fray—your judgment has been unsound as of late."

"I doubt, Jophiel. Is that an offense now?"

The Archangel darkened. His hand dropped to the hilt of his blade. "Remember to whom you speak, Biqa. To contradict my tale is to challenge the words of the Almighty Himself. The beast is to be imprisoned, locked away in chains of divine light for all time. Our losses are irrelevant. We exist to serve, to perish, as our Lord commands. Besides, if you were so concerned about your brethren you could have made your way to the battlefield."

Biqa shook his head. "You couldn't kill it. It's the oldest of them, the largest; the others seemed to suckle it like they drew dark nectar from its form. It was too old, too powerful, to ever end. What unfathomable arrogance makes you think you can keep it chained up?"

The Archangel smiled for the first time. It was as disquieting as the turmoil earlier. "All has been attended to, you shall see. Now, I came to give you this news and to escort you, Biqa, into the presence of the Almighty, personally."

"Very well," the dark angel said. "Why am I to be so honored?"

"Do not dare to mock the privilege given unto you," Jophiel snapped. "You are ordered to attend and you shall. That is all you need know."

"It is merely a question, Jophiel."

"Yes. You ask far too many of those for my taste, Biqa. Attend me, now. The Lord commands it."

Biqa brought his mount alongside the Archangel's Equina, which was still snorting black ash from the battlefield. The dark angel regarded Aputel.

"You should commend this one, Jophiel. He has been chastising me for my absence. Obviously he has been paying close attention to your sermons about duty and responsibility."

Jophiel narrowed his gaze at the fair angel.

"As well he should. Be about your duties, Aputel. To tarry is to defy the Lord's will."

"Yes, Archangel."

Aputel frowned as he watched the two angels depart toward Heaven. Biqa looked back, smiled and winked. Then they were gone, lost in the brilliant incandescence of the fields.

Already, the Darkness was receding; the angelic hosts glittered in the indigo filament. A great shape, a shape that defied the newly christened concepts of color and dimension, mass and thought, was dragged downward toward the great skeletal stage that God had named the Earth.

The angel looked at the last of the Voidlings. His mind scrambled for purchase, for some foothold to comprehend something it was never designed to experience. The Voidling's chains burned with the fire of unborn suns and sang endless hosannas unto the creator of the new universe.

His heart should fill with joy at such sights, such sounds. But it didn't. He had the sick feeling that nothing had been resolved. This new world was being built upon conflict and death. He feared such a foundation would poison the entire work. And the thing, the creature that was to be entombed at its heart, would squat in the darkness, an undying witness to the lengths to which ambition would reach. If Biqa was correct, it would seethe, it would hate and it would remember who put it there. But it would never, never die.

The fair angel turned toward the promises of Heaven and spurred his mount. Unlike Biqa, he did not look back.

The Queen of Swords

Maude Stapleton tucked the derringer she held in her palm back into the recesses of her sleeve sheath with a casual flick of her hand. The men and women walking down Main Street in that moment only saw Arthur Stapleton's odd, quiet, slightly skittish, wife gather up her flowing hair and adjust her bonnet after the commotion in front of Shultz's store—nothing more. No one noticed her returning the small pistol to the hiding place she had carried it in since she was fifteen years old.

The deputy, the man everyone called Mutt, had almost noticed her draw the gun when the shotgun blast bellowed out of the general store, but he was too intent on tying to save her and Constance by driving them to the ground and covering them. Mutt. She wondered why someone with such kind eyes carried such a harsh name.

It was the same drive, to protect her daughter, that had driven Maude to draw the gun. It was an old instinct, rusty like a neglected hinge, part of the training she had undertaken when she first accepted the responsibility of The Load, when she was just a girl, not much younger than Constance was now. Maude remembered the endless training, the drilling. The instincts it had built in her had gone to sleep, lost under the strata of motherhood, the duties of the good wife, some lost to age, more buried under fear and hesitation and doubt. She was surprised how much of it was still in her, though, still ready. She was just as saddened and a little shocked at how much of it was gone.

"Why didn't you stop the old man when he came in the store, Mother?"

Constance asked as they made their way up the plank sidewalks of Main Street.

While still splashed with mud, horse dung and other effluents best left to the imagining, the sidewalks were practically sanitary, compared to the ditches of filth on either side of them. To allow the two ladies to pass, men stepped off the planks, stepping right into the muck without a second thought. If they wore hats they doffed them to the ladies. Maude noticed how many looked at Constance's chest, not her face, how many smiles hid leers. She nodded politely as the men stepped into the shit and allowed her and her daughter to pass. Maude knew over a hundred ways to blind them, cripple them, make them beg for an end to the pain. She was confident she could still muster the skill and enthusiasm to accomplish at least a few, despite her decline. In time she would teach Constance how to use these men's instincts against themselves. But for now Maude did what most women did, tried to ignore the unwanted attention.

"He had a gun," Maude said, "and was intoxicated by more than mere alcohol. That makes it difficult to predict his actions, gauge his reflexes. That gun was pointed at you. I couldn't take any chances."

Constance nodded, seemingly satisfied with the half-truth. While that was all accurate, it was also true, Maude knew, that she was getting old, slowing down, and hadn't had to take out an armed opponent in decades. She had hesitated, been frightened, acted like a mousey, untrained woman. Gran would have cursed her up one side and down another for that, rightly so. It had worked out well, but due to luck, not preparation. And luck was as reliable as the men's smiles that passed them.

"That Indian deputy was looking at you funny," Constance said with a half smile. "Especially when he was on top of you." She giggled.

Maude looked down at the planks as they walked. Her face reddened. She smiled and laughed with her daughter. "I suppose he did. But what men other than your father do or think is none of my concern, young lady. Or yours."

Constance snickered. "Yes, Mother."

They rounded the corner of Main Street and stepped down a short set of steps off the sidewalk. They began to head up Prosperity Street toward their house, near the base of Rose Hill. The dusty, filthy streets of Golgotha grudgingly gave way to a narrow, smooth stone path lined with shading desert willow trees. The path ran adjacent to a gently sloping dirt road that wound leisurely up Rose Hill, past the homes of the town's most wealthy and respected citizens. The Stapleton homestead resided near the base, as afforded their station in the town's aristocracy. Bankers, like Arthur, were wealthy, true, but they were functionaries, a necessary evil and not privy to the heights. The subtle distinction in class irritated Arthur, who constantly strove to climb Olympus, but Maude didn't care. She had money; she'd lost it. What she carried was infinitely more precious than any treasure or status and no one could take it from her. Well, apparently, no one but herself.

Maude and Constance waved to Mrs. Kimball, their neighbor, who was tending the water pump that resided in the center of the cluster of homes on this stratum of the hill.

"You poor dears look like you've been feeding the hogs!" Mrs. Kimball called. "What happened?"

"Trouble at Shultz's," Maude said as she unlocked the door to her home, a modest Italianate Victorian, whitewashed and bleached silver by the attention of the desert sun.

"Regular trouble or Golgotha trouble?" Kimball asked.

"Regular, as far as I could tell," Maude said.

"Oh, good. We've had quite enough of the other kind to last us for some time!"

The house was shady, quiet and cool. Dust motes drifted lazily in the shafts of light through the leaded-glass windows. Constance unloaded their baskets on the rosewood dining table they had brought with them from South Carolina, while Maude opened a few shutters to let in enough light to chase off the gloom.

"You are a mess," Constance said, smiling.

"Well, you are certainly not in your finest form either. Put the provisions away and then fetch us some water. We'll clean up."

"Then practice?" Constance said eagerly.

"Haven't you had enough excitement for one day?"

"Please!"

"We'll see. Off with you!"

Maude retired to her and Arthur's bedroom. She closed the door and began the byzantine ritual of undressing from her muddy clothes. First the dress, gloves, boots, then unlacing the canvas stays that held her chest and spine erect. She sighed with pleasure at her escape from the bindings. Then the layers of petticoats, followed by her thigh-high stockings and finally her simple cotton shift. Maude regarded herself, nude, in the mahogany cheval mirror that Arthur had brought back with him from one of his trips to San Francisco.

She had to force herself to look up at her image. Her skin was pale; the faint memories of scars from her years with Gran Bonnie and the training were even paler and crisscrossed her body. While she carried the marks of her years and motherhood on her flesh, she retained a surprising amount of her strength and wiry youth. It was a good body, and she knew it deep inside, but it was hard to feel it under the weight of her life. She was ashamed and she hated herself for feeling that way. Ashamed of feeling old, ashamed of feeling ugly and unwanted. Ashamed of being past the point of relevancy anymore, at least to Arthur and to herself. She hated caring about all that. Why should she give a damn about what others thought of her, what men thought of her? Especially Arthur. She could hear Bonnie saying the words in her skull, but the fire and the joy they had once carried was gone. In its place she had regret and an ache stronger than any she had ever known to secure in her daughter the tools needed to never fall into the trap Maude had found herself in, the one she had sworn to never fall into.

Her hair fell about her shoulders. She brushed the bangs out of her eyes. And wiped a smear of mud off her forehead. She suddenly wanted to cry and hated herself for that as well. She blinked and looked deep into the eyes in the mirror, ordering the tears to hold. The eyes belonged to a stranger.

Her earliest memory was of the ships in Charleston Harbor. Father would take her with him to work in the city in the vague intervals between the care of governesses or distant relations. They would pass the harbor on their way to his offices, near Market Hall, and every time Maude would feel as if she were glimpsing some fantastical world, more colorful and exciting than any that she had been presented in the stories of Anderson and Marryat she listened to wide-eyed each night.

The ships clustered in the docks were like alien castles: masts spider-webbed with dark cable-like lines, the colorful flags from distant, mysterious nations snapping in the gusting wind, and everywhere the men who mastered the ships—swaggering, lanky, unkempt. They strode across the decks, scurried up and down the gangplanks and the nests; they spit, cussed, sang and laughed, all with such vital purpose. They were so different from Father, so different from all the other men she had ever seen in her life.

"Father," she said once as they passed the harbor, "when I am grown, I wish to become a sailor and travel the world and have my own ship, with my own crew, and have grand adventures!"

It was said with grave seriousness. Her father had smiled. In the years to come, Maude would see the same smile cross the faces of many men in her life, even when she was a grown woman. Always the same smile, full of patronizing amusement and smug condescension.

"Don't be a featherbrain, Maude, my dear," he said, without a drop of malice in his loving tone. "Women can't be sailors, or own ships. That's the kind of nonsense that sped your dear mother to an early passing. Women simply are too delicate for such adventures, you see. But perhaps you may marry a merchant captain that owns a fleet of ships. Wouldn't that be nice?"

That night the stories were not as magical. They never would be again. Maude had begun to wonder what else she was not allowed to do, to be. The world had suddenly become a much, much more narrow place.

Mother's proxies were an endless stream of brittle, joyless women paid to care for her. When one would quit or be dismissed Maude would often spend the intervening time passed from one relative or another, mostly from her father's side of the family, the Andertons.

Father had experienced much success in the trade and export of indigo and deerskins and was very well off. Mother had been a governess and school-teacher prior to meeting Father. She was outspoken and well educated, a trait found in many of the women of her family, the Cormacs. Father loved her and tried to endure her mannish proclivities, including a well-known and often much-maligned enthusiasm for the abolition movement.

As difficult as being married to an abolitionist in South Carolina could be, Mother was equally vocal about her support for the burgeoning suffrage movement. While Martin Anderton endured numerous indignities because of his wife's views, he loved her dearly and tried to make the best of the near-constant ribbing he received from colleagues and business partners about his wife's ridiculous politics.

That all ended the day of Maude's arrival into the world. Claire Anderton regarded her bloody screaming, beautiful baby girl, smiled and kissed her once before all the light faded from her eyes forever.

Maude had just turned nine when father's business required him to travel to Baltimore for an extended period of time. One evening over supper, Maude was told that she would be going to live with a relative she had never visited before, one from her mother's side of the family.

"Aunt Allison is very ill," Father explained. "And Grandmother Anderton is touring England currently, so you will be staying with your mother's great-great-great-grandmother, Bonnie."

"Oh," Maude said, eyes widening. "How many 'greats' is that, Father?"

Martin laughed. "Yes. She's older than Moses, apparently. She lives in a big plantation near Folly Beach. House has been in your mother's family for many generations, I'm led to understand. Grandmother Bonnie's late husband apparently built it. Made his money in shipping, I've been told."

"How long will you be gone?" Maude said, pushing her food around her plate sullenly.

"No longer than I have to be, dear," Father said. "I know it's not what you are used to, Maudie, but I simply can't avoid this. I'll return as soon as I can and I shall buy you every doll in Maryland."

He smiled. The promise of a bribe was supposed to make everything better. Maude had a huge collection of dolls as testament to this strategy. She nodded and proceeded to clean her plate. Like a good girl.

By the following afternoon, a carriage deposited Maude at the steps of Grande Folly Plantation to the southwest of Charleston. She was alone, except for the driver, a man named Clower, who was long in the employ of her father. Father had said his good-byes that morning. He had to prepare for his own journey and couldn't spare the time to travel out to Bonnie's with her.

Clower, a fat, hairy man who seemed to sweat even in winter, pulled the second of Maude's trunks off the back of the carriage and paused to mop his florid face with a dirty rag. "Here they come, Miss Maude."

Several house slaves made their way down the wide porch stairs. They gathered up the large chests and luggage and carried them into back into the house. One of the men, dressed in shirtsleeves and a vest, smiled at Maude and knelt to meet her gaze.

"Hello, Miss Anderton. My name is Isaiah. Welcome to Grande Folly. I hope your trip out was pleasant. We are very pleased to have you visit us."

Clower handed Isaiah a sweat-damp sealed letter he produced from out of his pant pocket. Isaiah rose. He was a good half a head taller than Clower.

"Here ya go, boy." Clower said. "Letter of introduction for Mrs. Cormac and promissory notes to help with the girl's upkeep."

"Thank you, boss," Isaiah said. Maude noticed all the softness had fallen out of his voice.

"Jess' you make damn sure that gits to Mrs. Cormac, y'hear me, boy?"

"Of course, boss. I'll give it right to her."

Clower turned and patted Maude on the head.

"Have a good stay, Miss Maude. Someone will come to fetch you once your father has returned."

He rode off in the carriage. Maude stood and watched it until it disappeared from view behind the curtain of Spanish moss hanging low from the bald cypress trees that ringed the driveway and yard. Cicadas buzzed. She felt very small.

"Miss?" Isaiah said softly from behind her. "This way, please. Lady Cormac is awaiting you."

Maude followed him up the stairs, across the wide porch and through the doors into the grand foyer. The house was shadow and shade after the bright summer day. It smelled of well-oiled wood and faintly of peppermint. Her things had been gathered here and the house slaves stood by them, awaiting orders on where to take them. Maude turned in the direction of a wide room off the left side of the foyer. Its massive sliding mahogany doors were partially open. While Isaiah paused to direct the servants in the disposition of the luggage, she carefully, slowly walked toward the fissure of the open doors.

Her eyes widened and her heart jumped as she saw the room was filled with floor-to-ceiling bookcases, swollen to overflowing with books, papers, even what appeared to be scrolls of ancient parchment and other tantalizing artifacts. Without even realizing she had done it, Maude crossed over into the room.

She paused at the heavy reading table, piled high with books, reached out and touched one of them. The smell of old paper in the room, the motes of dust drifting, like planets, in the warm sunlight of the great bay windows. The feel of a well-worn cloth book cover on her fingertips.

Maude felt the tightness in her stomach begin to ease. She could survive this place, this time. This room would sustain her, the feeling of being surrounded by human ideas, emotions, dreams; it would be fine, even if this distant, elderly relative proved to be less than pleasant company.

There was a heavy, flat stone on the table, an island in the towers of books. It looked very old. Painted onto it were symbols all in black: Animals standing like men; stick people with triangles for shields and lines for spears. A strange looped cross. She ran her fingers across the stone. It felt smooth from age, and that made her feel good.

"It's from Africa," a dry voice said from behind her. The voice had an odd accent Maude had never heard before. She turned and saw that the sliding doors had been opened fully. An old woman stood in the doorway; Isaiah stood beside her, supporting her at the elbow with a gentle but firm hand. She was slender, tall, with a pretty good figure for a woman of her years and skeletal weight. Her hair was a tangled mane of snow, with a few strands of copper and iron peeking through. It tumbled down her shoulders. Her eyes were green fire, the devil dancing in the flames. It was hard to judge her age. She looked down at Maude with an expression that was a mixture of amusement and disdain. "It's very old. Who told you to come in here, girl? Who gave you permission?"

Maude's gaze fell to the floor.

"Not going to find an answer from your slippers, girl," the old woman said with a snarl. "Answer me, damn you!"

"I like books—"

"Who told you!" This time with such force, Maude jumped. She glared at this evil old woman.

"No one!" Maude shouted. "No one! I just did it because I wanted to!"

The old woman blinked. The scowl slipped away and she began cackling, a dry, rasping laugh. It ended with a wet coughing fit. "That got yer back up, didn't it, lass?" the old woman said when she caught her breath. "Good! What's your name, child?"

"Maude."

The old lady smiled and Maude was surprised how wide and bright her smile was. There was a flash of a gold tooth.

"Well, hello, Maude. You and I are of a kin. I can see it in the piss in your eyes when someone riles you."

The old woman gestured to the walls of books. "My favorite room as well. You are free to come and go from here anytime, day or night. Read what you like, as much as you like. Hell, you can even read the bawdy stuff up on the top shelves, if you can figure out how to climb up there and get it. Anyone ever explain the he'ing and she'ing to you before, lass? "

Maude shook her head. The old lady laughed again, sharp and loud and alive. Maude had never heard a lady laugh that way before.

"Just as well," the old woman said. "Some mysteries are more fun to unravel on your own." She turned to leave, a little wobbly on her feet, and Isaiah steadied her. "We eat when we're hungry around here and we go to bed when we damn well feel like it," she said. "You need something, you get it yourself. You can't find it, then go pester Isaiah, understand?"

"Yes," Maude said.

"Welcome to Grande Folly," the old woman said. "You can call me Bonnie. It's as good a name to use as any, at least for starters."

The sound of Arthur's and Constance's raised voices pulled Maude out of the mirror of memories. She threw on a camisole quickly and hurried down the hallway.

"You will not speak to me in that manner, young lady!" Arthur Stapleton shouted, red faced. "I am your father and you will do as I say!"

Constance was equally angry. Her gaze burned into Arthur's blandly handsome face. The banker loomed over the girl, fists clenched.

"I am not doing anything wrong, Father!" she yelled back. "I would never do what you're implying!"

Maude stepped between the two. "What on earth is going on here?"

Arthur smelled of lilac hair tonic and gin. His eyes were unfocused and she knew he had spent much of this day in "business meetings" at the Paradise Falls. He turned the furnace of his anger toward her.

"Your daughter is intent on cavorting around like some common gutter whore at this hayseed dance! She might as well be spreading her legs for that simpleton Muller boy!"

"It's the church social, Daddy!" Constance said over Maude's shoulder. "And Jess is a good person; he likes me. I don't care if his family doesn't have much money!"

"Arthur, Constance, please," Maude said, closing her eyes.

"It's obvious you have no care what anyone thinks of this family!" Arthur said. "We have to present a sense of propriety at all times. My reputation as a banker depends on that!"

"Is that why you drink all day in that saloon?" Constance said. "And play cards all night? To uphold your—"

Everything happened fast. Too fast. Arthur lunged at Constance, smashing into Maude. Maude spun, old, flabby muscles struggling to remember the training, even if her mind was quick enough. She felt the wind leave her lungs, but not before she clutched his lapels and shifted her weight, twisting at the hips. She managed to divert the majority of Arthur's momentum toward the dining table, away from Constance. The laws of motion and cheap gin did the rest. Arthur smashed into the table, knocking it over as he tumbled to the floor and lay still.

Maude turned to her daughter. With great effort she hissed out the words with what little air remained in her. "You will not speak to your father that way. Go to your room and we will discuss this shortly. Go on."

Constance nodded and scurried down the hall. Maude heard the door to her room click shut and lock. She turned back to where Arthur was slowly climbing to his feet, shaking his head.

"You stupid, clumsy cow," he mumbled. "Could have killed me."

"Yes," she muttered. "I'm so sorry, dear, you were just so angry and—"

He telegraphed the slap; she would have seen it coming even if he wasn't drunk. She was ready this time and she rolled with it, felt the snap and sting of the blow across her cheek and chin, but had arched her neck enough that it wouldn't even leave a mark. She grunted and flew across the room in an impressive enough manner that Arthur's tiny reptile brain would feel the glow of accomplishment. Perhaps later his human mind would feel guilt and remorse. Perhaps not. It was hard to say anymore.

She fell to the floor. The humiliation of this show stung more than the slap. She was glad Constance was in her room. Arthur stood over her, panting; his eyes were unfocused.

She looked down at the floor.

"I'm sorry," she said.

Arthur blinked and quickly grabbed his coat from the peg beside the door.

"I shall be out late. Business. I'll eat. I'm . . . I'm sorry."

He didn't wait for a reply. He didn't slam the front door. The house became quiet again. Maude stood and began to repair the damage done to the room. In her mind, Gran Bonnie was laughing at her, a demonic cackle.

The first few weeks at Grande Folly were some of the most wonderful of Maude's life. She ate when she wanted, slept when she wanted, read what she wanted. No orders, no demands, no restrictions. It was paradise.

After a while, Gran Bonnie, as she asked to be called ("too damned many 'greats' in there to keep up with," she would say), began to request Maude's presence at dinner. She was not required to eat herself, but was given the option and was allowed to drink the same wine Bonnie did. Maude was primarily there for conversation. Bonnie wanted to know all about her, about her life and, most surprisingly, about her dreams and aspirations. She seldom asked about Mother and Father.

"You aren't your ma and da, girl," Bonnie said. "Oh sure, they mix the clay you come from, and true, they press the shape of you, build you up or deform you, but you're still wet, still a work in progress, and you choose what kind of vessel you will be."

"What if you dry up?" Maude had asked. "Clay dries."

Bonnie had smiled and nodded. She took another long draught of her wine in a bejeweled goblet, wiped her mouth with the back of her bony hand and cackled with glee. "Aye, love, aye. It does. And so do people. I suppose if the clay dried up, you'd need to smash it, break it and then get it all good and wet again, yes?"

She laughed and clapped her hands like a child, pleased with herself.

The best part of dinner was the tales Bonnie told of all the places she had traveled to, all the thing she had learned, the languages she'd heard that sounded like fluttering wings and staccato rain; the myths, the gods, the curses, the beasts and the treasures that were all out there, past the sea, past Charleston Harbor, past the clean linen, warm bed world Maude had always known.

"The world is a wonderful place, lass," Bonnie said. Her voice began to slur around her second bottle of wine. "And terrible too. All rolled together like glass candy. It's especially hard for ones such as you and me."

Maude frowned and tilted her head, "Like us?"

"Women," Bonnie said. "Deck's been stacked agin' us since the first of us stood on two feet."

"Eve?" Maude said. "Father's read me the stories of how she caused the fall from grace in Eden."

Bonnie cussed and hurled the half-full goblet toward the fireplace. It exploded. The wine hissed as it hit the fire; jewels and pieces of gold scattered in the roaring blaze and lay glittering among the hot ashes.

"Ya see!" she barked, rising swiftly from her chair. "The kind of nonsense they put into a lass's head from day one! How is any woman expected to have a voice as strong as a man's, to have the will to overcome like a man, to conquer and triumph like a bloody soddin' pego-wielding Richard! They're not to! Oh no! That's the reason for the stories, lass! To lock you down good and tight, to wrap you up in guilt and shame just for being what you are. Bloody bastards!"

Maude stood very still. The fire glittered in her wide eyes. Bonnie spit. There was a sizzle in the fire, fifteen feet away, for an instant. Isaiah was suddenly at his mistress's side, stepping from the shadows. He offered her an arm to lean on; she refused it and turned to leave the room on her own power.

"You like stories about far-off places and secret treasures, lass?" Bonnie said. "Get to bed, get some sleep and I'll tell you a fine tale tomorrow. I think you are as ready for it as you will ever be."

Maude rapped gently on Constance's door before she opened it. Her daughter was lying on her brass bed, swollen red eyes staring into space. Maude sat on the edge of the bed and placed her hand on the small of her daughter's back.

"I hate him," the girl said after a time.

"I know," Maude said. "You shouldn't. He's your father."

"That doesn't give him the right to treat us the way he does," Constance said, turning to regard her mother. "Does it?"

"No," she said. "It doesn't. He can be weak and childish and selfish and you don't deserve to be spoken to that way, Constance."

"Neither do you, Mother."

Maude fought the urge to explain to her daughter, on the edge of womanhood, that it was different for her. Different because as much as her daughter hadn't asked for this man to be in her life, to be her father, Maude had stepped into this relationship willingly, fully aware of what Arthur was, and was not. Arthur's hubris, his petulance, his anger, it was the price she paid for Constance, for a normal life in this age.

"Do you want to go train," Maude asked, "out in the desert? Your father won't be home until very late."

Constance raised her head off her pillow, looked at her mother with wet, red eyes and smiled.

Isaiah woke Maude before dawn the next day.

"Lady Cormac is waiting for you on the beach past the groves around the back of the estate," he said softly, his face pooled shadows in the lantern's light. "She instructed me to tell you to dress sensibly and to take your horse and ride out to meet her. She said not to dawdle."

Maude did as she was instructed, putting on riding clothes and a thick wool cloak to ward off the chill. Her horse was saddled and waiting in the drive before the plantation. She rode out alone into the dead pre-morning. The fragments of moonlight in the bruised sky were all she had to navigate the forest of hunched, weary trees with their curtains of Spanish moss.

She smelled the ocean before she heard the thunder of the waves; tasted salt spray in the back of her throat. It spoke to something in her that usually slept, made her feel connected, alive. Made her feel that possibilities and actualities were one. She pushed through the last few yards of foliage and into view of the beach. The dark sky bled into the black, churning waters. It was virtually impossible to tell where one ended and the other began, infinity upon infinity.

Gran Bonnie stood waiting for her, watching the crash and the foam swirl, admiring the drowning moon's final pleas to an uncaring, departing night. She stood tall, proud, no weakness, no frailty, like it was all there just for her, only for her. Her horse was nearby, unsaddled—Bonnie apparently always rode bareback. The mare munched on the tall grass that guarded the border between the end of the grove and the beginning of the beach.

"Come here, girl," Bonnie said softly, yet Maude heard each syllable over the rumble of the waves.

Maude climbed down from her horse and released its reins. The pony wandered over to join the older horse for breakfast. Maude walked down to the wet, packed sand and out to stand alongside the old woman. It was low tide and the spring tide was nearly upon them. The water was far out, the beach wide and the sand strangely silver in the finishing moonlight. Bonnie sighed and looked away from the moon and sea and down to Maude.

"I'm Crone, now," she said. "I should have done this long ago, lass, when I was still Mother. I've waited a long time for a good prospect, Maude. I thought it would be your mother, rest her soul, but I waited too long, was too caught up in my own selfishness. By the time I got to your ma, she was already too old, too set in the ways of this world. I did what I could for her and she was very receptive, but she was just too old to begin to carry The Load."

"The Load?" Maude asked.

"Aye," Bonnie said. "We'll get to that in a bit. First off, we need to take off our masks now and speak plain."

"I'm not wearing a mask," Maude said. "Neither are you."

"Mostly true," Bonnie said. "You're too young to have made much of a mask yet; that's one of the reasons I like you. And you haven't had much of one forced onto you yet, like a muzzle. What has been done to you, you still fight. That's good. As long as you can do that, bloody bastards haven't tamed you.

"I do wear a mask of a sort; we all do. The trick is choosing your own masks and when to wear them. I'll teach you all about that. As women, we can wear a thousand masks, be a thousand goddesses and claim a thousand powers and roles. All in time."

Bonnie groaned and knelt to look Maude in the eyes. She leaned on the girl's shoulder.

"But now is the time for me to take one of my masks off and show you something true, lass. My name isn't Bonnie Cormac. It's Anne, Anne Cormac. That's the name I was born to in County Cork, in 1697. I traveled under several names in my life, changed them as I wandered the world like changing my hair or my mind."

She cackled a little and then continued.

"The one I always liked the best I think was Bonny, though. Anne Bonny. You can call me that; that's what I call myself. Never cared much for 'Toothless Annie,' though, seemed rather rude. I had a damn sight more teeth than most in those days, I can say!

"I have been daughter, wife, mother, mistress, thief, sailor, warrior, murderess, pirate, protector and more, in my nearly two centuries. I've sailed the seven seas, been to the frozen ends of the world, walked the burning deserts of the pharaohs, joined in the demon dances of the *loas* in the Caribbean; stalked the Dark Continent and been counsel to Bantu witchwomen there. It was there that I was initiated, there in the cradle of human life that I was taught the secrets of The Load and took up the burden for the first time."

"I don't understand," Maude said.

The old woman, Anne Bonny, stood. She cupped the girl's face and raised it toward the diminishing moon.

"You will in time, Maude. I promise you will understand it all in time."

She began to speak and her voice carried over the din of the waves; it settled in Maude's heart, heavy with power and truth, and made the girl's chest ache.

"I carry within me the clock of the moon.

"The clock of nature, inviolate, unerring.

"I carry within me the secret of God.

"The power of new life in a universe of darkness and death.

"I carry within me the most potent of swords.

"For my will can overcome any steel forged by a man.

"And my suffering can overcome any trial of pain or sadness.

"For my blood is that of the first woman, she who would not bow down to the tyrant of Heaven and was cast out, called the mother of beasts. She who would not be bride to either Heaven or Hell but walked her own sharp, lonely path.

"It is my birthright, these gifts, this pain, this wisdom.

"It is my privilege to understand them and in doing so understand and love myself.

"It is my load to carry them, to protect them, to use them in defense of the worthy and the weak.

"And to teach this to others of the blood who live in chains of shame and guilt and fear forged by men and their gods, shackled to them by their own limited comprehension of their divine nature.

"This is the secret. This is the load you must bear alone all your days upon this earth. This is the price of truly being free."

They took the buggy out the old road that ran past Rose Hill, past the old cemetery, out to the edge of the 40-Mile. Maude had Constance carry the wicker chest that contained the training implements out to the carriage. Maude kept the basket hidden from Arthur among the items in the chest she had been willed from her Gran Bonnie, items Arthur was arrogantly confident were of no interest whatsoever to any seriously minded man. He would have been disappointed and horrified to uncover its true content.

"Poisons," Constance said as they approached the place they usually stopped to train. It was marked with a large boulder that was roughly the shape of a giant's fist. "I want to translate more about poisons out of Gran's old books."

"No," Maude said curtly. "No more poison training, or languages and codes, until you have completed your knife work to my satisfaction."

They climbed out of the buggy and Maude busied herself with removing and arranging the brace of throwing knives out of the basket. Constance moved to the proscribed distance of twenty paces and awaited her mother's instruction.

"Now you have become a fairly decent knife thrower," Maude said as she hefted the wickedly sharp, thin blades and fanned them between her fingers and thumb. "And I am pleased with how you are coming along with your short-blade fighting, but we still need to work on your knife catching, dear."

"Yes, Mother," Constance said, waiting calmly, arms at her sides.

Maude cocked her arm, knives raised. "We will begin with two blades at a time, two-second intervals between throws. Ready?"

"Mother?" Constance said softly. The sun was sinking low in the sky. It would be night soon and the sky was smeared with colors.

"Yes?" Maude said, pausing.

"Thank you. I love you," Constance said.

Maude smiled, remembering herself in these moments, not hating who she was or what she had become to have this child.

"I love you too, dear," she said. "Begin."

The knives hummed from her hand like angry hornets, straight toward her daughter's heart.

The Seven of Wands

It was late enough in the day for Auggie to close the store after the terrible events of the early afternoon. It went against his grain to do it; he knew he was an important part of the community and everyone depended on him to be here and open, for everything from mailing a letter back east to procuring medicines to doctor ailing family members. Everyone knew Augustus Shultz was your man for anything you needed in Golgotha.

But Auggie could still feel his heart jumping in his chest like a jackrabbit after having poor Earl jam a shotgun in his gut and whisper mad gibberish. He was sweating, even in the relative cool of his store. Not to mention the flow of gawkers and gossipers who scuttled into his store like *Schaben* to interrogate every last detail of the ordeal out of him.

"I hear the crazy ole coot shot the sheriff three times in the chest," Otis Peake said around a wad of wet, black tobacco. "They said it put holes in your walls but passed right on through Highfather!"

"*Nein,*" Auggie corrected, "Earl only shot him one time. It was that drunken cowboy over at the Prospect two months ago that shot him three times."

"Surely the good Lord Himself was looking over you today, Mr. Shultz," Mrs. O'Canton remarked as she watched Auggie clean up the mess and drag the busted pickle barrel into the storeroom. "I hope you remember that when you are saying those Catholic prayers tonight. It was God, not your pope, that saved you today."

Auggie sighed, smiled and nodded as he wrapped up the old lady's parcels. He had long ago learned that arguing religion in a town when you were one of the only two Catholics around was pointless.

His head ached and he simply could not calm himself down from the excitement of the day. So, at quarter past four, he locked the front door and turned the sign in the window so that it read: *Closed: Please come again.*

He went into the storeroom where Mutt had crept in through the back door earlier. The room was full of crates, barrels and shelves packed with various perishables, some cured meat, mostly buffalo he had bought off a cowpuncher passing through on his way to California.

There was a heavy oak cabinet the size of a wardrobe with a set of sturdy doors on iron hinges. It was the smoke cabinet he used on meat. He and Clay had managed to seal it pretty good with leather stripping and tallow, so that very little smoke leaked out when Auggie was using it. An old stovepipe jutted out of its back and disappeared through the rear wall, to the outside.

There was the door to the privy, which contained a basin, mirror and pitcher of water he had fetched that morning from the pump and his Moule-Brand earth closet. Gerta had used to put fresh desert wildflowers next to the basin, but there were no flowers now. The realization of that made his temples throb more.

He made sure the back door was secure again after Mutt's entry, splashed water on his face over the basin, toweled off and started to head up the narrow wooden staircase to their small apartment on the second floor.

There was an insistent knocking at the back door. Auggie sighed, turned and opened the door that led out to the alleyway his store shared with the Mephisto.

"Hello, I'm hope I'm not intruding," the Widow Proctor said with her usual radiant smile. "Are you all right, Augustus? You look positively drained, you poor dear!"

"I'm fine, I'm fine!" he bellowed over her usual clucking. Back when Gert was still . . . back when they were all three the dearest of friends, Gillian and Gert would gang up on him with their worrying about his weight and what he ate and that the boxes he was lifting were too heavy and he'd get down in his back and that he should wear a hat or else he'd get his head burned. It was amazing to Auggie how much two women could find to worry about. The memory made him smile.

"You can come in, if you stop pestering me right now," he said.

Gillian Proctor stepped into the storeroom. The widow was a handsome woman, taller than Auggie's stout frame by a good six inches; younger too—in her late thirties. Her hair was the color of coal, shot through with silver threads, and Auggie knew it fell well below her shoulders when she let it. She wore it simply enough today in a chignon bun, high and back on her head. Her eyes were darker than her hair. Even behind the simple round wire spectacles she wore to read, they could be wide with wisdom or surprise or fear; or they could narrow in playful teasing or sharp anger. They always reminded Auggie of opals. She was dressed simply today too—a workday—in a white blouse and butternut-dyed brown skirt with a small bustle, covered by an apron. She carried a covered wicker basket.

Auggie couldn't help but chortle, a low bass rumble in his massive barrel chest, at how Gillian desperately wanted to make a fuss, but she held her tongue and kept her word. It was one of the many things Auggie appreciated about her.

"About ready to bust, aren't you, *ja*?"

"I heard what happened today," she said, setting down her basket on a crate. Auggie cleared off a chair for her, dusted the seat with a rag from his back pocket and held it out for her. She sat. He rested against the broken pickle barrel, with his massive forearms crossed.

"I came over to make sure you weren't hurt. From the awful mood you are in, I assume everything is fine."

"Ja. Thank you anyway for coming to see. That was very kind of you."

When Auggie and Gerta had lost little Milo to whooping cough, less than a year after he was born, he knew they had to leave Hamburg.

Looking down at his infant son's burial shroud, Auggie turned to his young wife of only three years. Gerta was so beautiful and pale, like the sunshine flashing off of new-fallen snow. She made his breath catch in his lungs. She had wept until nothing wet resided in her soul anymore. Milo had nearly been the death of her and they both knew they would never have another child.

"I'm taking you to America," he said. "I've sold Papa's home and Herr Wishleig has voiced great interest in taking over the store."

"Why, Augustus? Why now? I don't want to go anywhere."

"I know, my love. If we don't leave this house, this city, this life, now we will both grow cold and brittle. I love you too much to ever let you endure a living death."

"*Ja,*" was all she could muster before a new wellspring of pain led her to shake and moan and summon a few last tears. He held her tight until the shadows lengthened and the room grew dark.

Auggie came from a long line of shopkeepers, so he knew wherever they settled he would open a store. Once in America they headed west in a caravan of seventy wagons with a few belongings and the cash and supplies they needed to set up shop in the vast western wilderness. When they came to Golgotha, it wasn't much more than a scrap of a mining camp. There wasn't a lot there at the time: the Paradise Falls Saloon and a few of the other properties owned by Malachi Bick, the local cardsharp, gambler, ne'er-do-well. The Chinese had arrived to work the silver mine and the nearby railroad projects, but Johnny Town was just rows of makeshift tents then. There were gamblers and prospectors and cowpunchers. It was a rough place and Auggie's instincts told him to move on.

Gert liked it here, though. She liked the old ruins that must have belonged to the Indians. She fell in love with the desert flowers. She kissed him on the cheek when he agreed to settle here. He still remembered how that kiss had made him feel like a hero.

They opened the general store, unsure if they would have enough paying customers to make do. Six months latter the Pratt family and forty other Mormon clans rode out of the 40-Mile and took up residence in Golgotha. Shultz's General Store became more profitable than Auggie's family business had ever been back home.

As the town grew up and became more civilized, more tradesfolk made it into town. People like Will Proctor and his wife, Gillian.

Auggie remembered the day the Proctors arrived in Golgotha. Will was the schoolmaster for the newly built schoolhouse, out by Old Stone Road. With the arrival of more families, there were now children in Golgotha, and they needed educating.

Gillian's family had lived in England when she was a girl due to her father's work with a big shipping company headquartered in Boston. She had traveled over much of Europe. The Shultzes learned, to their delight, that the Proctors could speak German.

Gerta eventually learned that Gillian had miscarried two years earlier and was unlikely to ever have another child. That knowledge, the unspoken understanding of such intimate loss—a stratum of pain beyond the ability of human speech to express—built a strong bond between the two women. In time, Gert and Gillian became inseparable.

Truth be told, Auggie never cared much for Will Proctor. He was a nice enough young man, a bit too proud of his New England pedigree and a bit too eager to condescend to his fellow man for Auggie's tastes, but Will's major sin, in Auggie's eyes, was that he spent entirely too much time sneaking off to the Paradise Falls to play cards and lose money. Auggie saw the writing on the wall, and knew the Proctors were always far too close to insolvency for Gillian's or his comfort.

"He's a smart man," Auggie would tell Gerta in the darkness of their bedroom. "He's more than willing to tell you that, and yet he fritters his money away at that smiling devil Bick's place. A man should save, for his family, *ja*? Not be running around with a bunch of soap locks, grums and saloon trash!"

So while he was sad to see it happen, he was not that surprised when word came on a night in August of '64, as hot and black as pitch, that Will Proctor had been shot dead during a drunken fight at a poker table in the Paradise.

It was quite the local scandal for a while, the secret life the schoolmaster had been living with whisky and cardsharps and even rumors of saloon girls. His poor wife, *surely* she must have known. . . .

Auggie and Gert would have none of it in their store. They chastised anyone who tried to throw dirt on their friends' name. They also took the grieving Gillian under their wing.

Most figured that Gillian, alone and in an alien frontier, would up and head back east to her family in Boston. Instead she turned her home into a boardinghouse and pretty soon had near-full occupancy. There were rumors still about gambling debts belonging to Will she had to pay off and other mismanagement of funds that the poor widow had to deal with, but Gillian honored such gossip with no reply at all. And as the years passed, she was always the first one in town there with a cake or a basket of preserves for every birth, every funeral. In time Golgotha forgot Will Proctor and his poor wife and embraced the Widow Proctor as part of the community.

Gillian was there for Auggie too when Gert succumbed to influenza back in '67. She comforted Gerta through the worst of it, when Auggie had to run the store or simply collapse from exhaustion. Gillian promised her beloved friend she would look out for Auggie and not let his black moods eat him alive. The two survivors wept together over Gerta's still, frail frame when the time finally arrived.

"What are you staring at?" Gillian asked from her chair in the back room of Shultz's.

"Nothing," he replied. "I did not mean to stare. I was just thinking. . . ."

"Yes, we have been through it all, haven't we, Augustus?"

"*Ja*."

She rose. Her movements reminded Auggie of water—fluid, effortless, something so free in them. She always seemed like she was more of the world than in it, a presence, like the breeze of the desert, or the blessed, scarce rain. She come over and put her hands on his shoulders and began to rub. They were bruised from where Earl had manhandled him earlier and her strong fingers felt good on the knots of steel under his skin.

"What is *das*?" he said, surprised but not offended. Definitely not offended.

"Hush up, you old grump," she said. "Let someone do something for you for a change."

It felt good to feel hands on him again. They were warm and strong, but so very, very gentle too. They reminded him of . . .

He stepped away from Gillian and turned, taking her hands in his own.

"Thank you, Gillian," he said. "But I have to get supper started. It's getting late."

She smiled, reddened and nodded. "Yes, I guess it is. Say, why don't you have dinner with the boarders at my place tonight. Save you from having to cook, and the Lord knows you don't care to wash dishes."

"Thank you, that is very generous, but I . . . I'm sorry, I can't tonight."

She picked up her basket and handed it to him.

"I thought you might be a stubborn old goat, so I went ahead and made you something."

She brushed her soft lips against his bristly cheek and walked to the storeroom door.

"Augustus, Gerta was my best friend. I loved her very much and I miss her dearly. She would never have wanted you to dig her grave large enough to hold two people."

"Thank you for the food, Gillian, and the concern. I'm just tired and sore and I want to go to bed."

"Good night, Augustus," she said.

The door closed and Auggie stood alone in the storeroom with only the lengthening shadows for company.

He locked the door and slowly climbed the narrow stairs to where all the ghosts lived.

Their apartment was small, a few rooms crammed full of the antique furniture from his family home in Hamburg that had endured the ocean voyage and the wagon ride to Golgotha. Auggie sat down in a high-backed chair and slipped off his boots. Through the windows the sun was crawling lower along Main Street. He picked up a photograph off an end table. It was of himself and Gert from the year they had arrived in Golgotha. It was taken by a roving photographer from back east who said he had come west to capture the buffalo in pictures. Auggie and Gert both looked so young in the picture, trying to stand still and look serious without laughing. So young, and thin and happy, and alive.

He stared at the photo until he noticed how dark the room was. When he looked at the Swiss clock on the wall, he realized hours had passed. He reluctantly put the photo away and stood.

Down the narrow hallway into the bedroom. The familiar stab of pain as their wedding bed taunted him with memories of love and comfort, sickness and death. He opened the closet and took down the heavy wooden box with the brass hinges and clasp. He carried it gently to the small kitchen table where they had shared meals and tears, silence and laughter. He sat the box upright and stared at it until he drowned in the shadows of the room.

He got up, lit an oil lamp and brought it and a bottle of Monongahela back to the kitchen table. Outside he heard a wagon rumble by and the whoops of the early crowd at the Paradise Falls. He emptied three fingers from the bottle into a milk-glass mug and drained them quickly. He hid the bottle on the floor under the table as he felt the whiskey warmth stretch through him. His hands stilled, his heart steadied in its palpitations.

The clasp snapped free with a metallic pop and Auggie opened the box. He lifted the heavy jar out of its velvet fitting and placed it on the table. It was full of a cloudy, greenish fluid. Small particles, disturbed by the movement, drifted in the liquid, like silt. The thing inside the jar bumped awkwardly against the sides. Black strands, like seaweed, drifted lazily, suspended in the filthy soup.

Auggie noticed that the fluid was getting cloudy again. He'd need to add the chemicals again soon. He opened the small velvet-lined drawer at the base of the case and removed a large silver key. He fitted it into the keyway, at the base of the jar, which was surrounded by a complex maze of clockwork gears and spider-strand wires, like the glittering oiled guts of a music box. He turned the key three times; each time there was the loud groan of springs and gears. He slid the key out and the mechanisms began to spin and hum. The smell of warm brass encircled the room. A dim light filled the murky tank as the thing in the jar shuddered and then held itself erect. Auggie closed his eyes and prayed for God to forgive him once again.

"Au . . . gus . . . tus?" the thing in the jar said. "It . . . is . . . you . . . ja?"

Her eyes were covered by milky cataracts; they looked greenish through the water and the yellow light. To Auggie they were still the color of virgin sky.

"Ja, beloved, it is only me."

"I missed you so much. How long were you away? How long was I in the dark?"

"Not long, my love. It's only been a day; it's always just a day. Can't you remember?"

Her lips moved, but no air bubbles escaped to the surface of the jar. Her voice came from out of the machine at the base of the tank. It sounded like it was trapped in a tiny box full of wires, echoing, bouncing off the tight walls of steel and brass.

"It's hard to remember time here, darling," she said. "I get so lonely away from you, from the light. It's like some horrible dream that I cannot awake *from until you return. I miss you, Augustus, very, very much. You chase the darkness away."*

The whiskey kept the tears at bay, as it usually did, but he felt the hot poker of guilt dig into his innards and twist. Surely he was a damned man; surely he was lost for his weakness and his selfishness.

"I love you, Gerta," he croaked. "I miss you too."

And then the husband told the wife about his day, like he always did.

The Three of Swords

He wept for the first billion years. His tears turned to steam.

The place was like a forge—sticky clumps of this clumsy stuff the Almighty called matter bubbled up out of the alchemy of cosmic fire and wind. Everywhere there was chaos, deafening noise and blinding light—a symphony of hard radiation and the collision of violent young worlds. It was horrible, no order, no peace.

Eventually it all cooled off in the frigid night, the former home of the Darklings, now a graveyard littered with God's newly hung stars. Biqa looked up at the ethereal chip of lunar rock hanging in the dark sky and his heart ached for home.

But he couldn't go back. Not until this duty was done. God and His attendants had made that very clear to him. He was to stand watch, to guard and to wait.

So he waited. Time passed and the Earth greened. He waited.

He came to think that God had created this place as a prison, a punishment for those in the Host who displeased Him. It was so awful here, so cold and unconnected. Every time he remembered with his perfect crystalline memory the glory that was God's presence, he fell to the dirt and ash and shook with sadness and regret. Nothing was worse than being away from He who had willed him to exist.

Other times he grew so angry that he nearly hurled his flaming sword into the darkness of space and cursed the name of the Lord, but he knew his duty; he knew to whom his loyalty remained. So he did nothing.

He waited. He watched mountains rise from valleys and oceans cut continents in two. The rain and the snow kissed his skin, like a balm that made the pain, the loneliness, the despair, ease in him.

Each day he watched the sunrise like it was a letter from home.

In time, he came to appreciate what God was trying to do here and he marveled at the creator's aesthetic. He had crafted from offal, from cosmic refuse and the basest of atoms, a re-creation of Heaven that could move an angel to song or tears. Bravo.

Biqa was less impressed with the parade of living things the Almighty frittered with on the surface. When they didn't work out He would wipe them away with a shrug and a comet. The world would be wiped clean of life in blood and fire and then back to the drawing board. Biqa noted that one extinction led to the next refinement of whatever tenacious life managed to cling to the cold, broken rock. So there was no wasted motion; each ending moved toward a new beginning. Truly, God was a sculptor beyond reproach.

Biqa knew others from the Host were moving upon the Earth, on various missions commissioned by God. None of them ever visited him. They avoided him, partly, he was convinced, due to his odious duty and partly out of fear of angering the Lord and sharing his outcast fate.

Some nights, when it was quiet and clear, he could hear them singing up in Heaven and his cheeks would grow wet.

He waited. But the feeling of abandonment clung to his shoulders like heavy stones. He counted the grains of sand upon the ground as best he could until he lost count. He longed to play a game, to chase his brethren among the stars, laughing, the solar wind kissing his face. His father, looking down upon His playing children, giving them His approval, His unconditional love.

Biqa's face fell to his hands, hands capable of splitting atoms, and he cried in his utter loneliness and his regret. He wished he had never questioned, wished he had never thought.

Something small and soft touched his knee. Startled, he looked up to see three of the little furry creatures that hid so shyly in the tree line had braved the ground and had actually padded up to him. They seemed curious about what he was doing.

"It's all right," he whispered to the tiny, expressive faces of the little mortals. "Fear not. Fear not."

He wiped the tears away with the back of his hand. The creature that had touched him reached up and took it gently. Biqa was speechless. The little climber's hand was the same as the angel's, only smaller and lined with random swirls and loops carved into the skin. It shook him, dreadfully. He had seen nothing of himself in all the eons that life had fought for dominance on God's arena. He had seen beauty, to be sure; he had seen the will to endure, the beginnings of order. But in this tiny hand the angel finally saw his own legacy. He looked up to the face of the tiny, hairy creature. The tears began anew when he looked upon its full regard. The little thing patted his hand, gently, comfortingly.

In this foul, matted little creature the angel saw God's love, God's mercy and pity, God's eyes.

"I . . . I . . . Thank you . . . ," Biqa said, and tried to embrace the creature. All three of them shrieked at the rising giant and skittered off into the high grass and eventually back to their trees.

And Biqa understood why he was there and why God had chosen him. He was more than just a warden, an exile. He was the critic, the skeptic who had to be shown.

He took up his sword of fire and he waited.

But now he no longer waited alone.

The Ten of Pentacles

It was after noon when Mutt ascended Argent Mountain. He rode up Prosperity, passing the narrow mazelike alleys of Bick Street that made up most of Johnny Town, on the right. Prosperity became less of a road and more of a rutted path as his horse, a darkly dabbled paint named Muha, began to climb up the winding trail. *Muha* meant "moon" in Mutt's mother's language. He sometimes wanted to name the horse Crazy, because he was the only animal that had never been spooked by Mutt.

When he was a child, his mother's people, the Shoshokos, were looked down on by the other Shoshoni tribes because they were too poor to have horses and had to dig in the dirt for their food. Once, Mutt and a few of the other young men of the village went out with a party of the older men in an attempt to steal horses from a bunch of arrogant Ute merchants who had passed through the village a few days earlier. The plan failed miserably when the horses screamed like frightened women at Mutt's approach. The Ute were alerted to the attempted theft and nearly killed several members of the raiding party. Back home Mutt was beaten half to death by the elders and lived alone at the edge of the village for two months. Mutt had learned to stay upwind from horses.

Argent was a gentle slope for the first few hundred feet. The trails were well worn and wide enough for wagons, or several riders side-by-side. Some sagebrush and Indian rice grass sparsely covered the sides of the path. A few yellow flowers managed to fight their way out of the sagebrush's thin branches. Their existence in such a hot, desolate place made them all the more beautiful. Mrs. Stapleton pushed her way into his thoughts again at the sight of the desert flowers, but only for a moment.

The squatter camps were another few hundred feet up. To his left, the deputy could see Golgotha below him, bustling with goings-on. The town was busy enough still, even with the closing of the silver mine a few years back. Enough people passed through here on their way to California or headed back to the east. The town's location at the edge of the 40-Mile made it a last stop for many before the days of hell began. But it was still a far cry from when silver was first discovered. If that boom had lasted, it would have put Golgotha on the map with places like Carson City, Virginia City and Reno. And he would have been long gone from here.

He stopped and sniffed the air. He smelled gunpowder, or something like it. Lots of it too. Wagon tracks, fresh from today and weighted down, deep in the dirt were tangled up with the scent. He urged his horse gently on and picked up pace as he headed for the squatter camp.

About twenty small cabins, shacks and lean-tos clung to the side of Argent Mountain. Another fifteen or so tents were also scattered across the mountain's face. About half of the squatters chose to live on the eastern side of the mountain, looking down on Golgotha. They were a pretty independent bunch, for the most part.

In the years that Mutt had been here, he had come to understand the ways the tribes worked in this town. He had learned long ago that an outsider, someone without a pack to call his own, was often better at seeing the invisible divisions between people than a participant in the social dance.

At the top were the Mormons—mostly wealthy folk who had built up many of the businesses in town. The wealthiest lived on the other side of the town from Argent, up on Rose Hill. They were bankers, cattlemen, schoolmasters, merchants and priests. One even had something to do with the railroad barons back east.

Below them were the majority of folk in town. They probably owned a small house they had built—maybe a horse or two. They scraped by working for themselves or for the folk up on Rose Hill.

Then there were squatters up here on Argent—they were mostly down-on-their-luck prospectors, grifters and cowboys who had bet their last dollar on Malachi Bick's silver mine and had lost. They worked odd jobs for

people in town; a few were crooks and small-time rustlers. Word had gotten
around Nevada that Golgotha's squatter camp was a good place to lay low
for a spell if you needed it. Many folks made a living supporting that small
cottage industry. Others, like poor old Earl, had lost almost everything
coming out west in the quest for a better life. Earl lost a wife. Many had lost
their entire families. In the end they didn't really care where their bones
rested, as long as they could kill the pain with cheap rotgut and solitude.

After them came the Chinamen. Alien, secretive and stoic. They almost
didn't count, just like Mutt and his mother's people. It was a toss-up who a
white man would rather string up first—an Indian or Chinese. They were
outside any tribe but their own and that was just they way they liked it. Just
like Mutt.

The camp was up and staggering about. Those who did an honest day's
work were already down the mountain and had been since before sunup.
These were the old, the infirm, the wives and the criminals.

"Hey, Dep-u-tee!" Grinning Alice shouted to him from her rocker on the
uneven porch of her shanty. She was dressed in a filthy chemise. The few
teeth she still had were black and there was an ugly scar that looped from
the left side of her mouth up to her ear. "Y'all haven't been back to visit me
in a spell. What's the matter, darlin', you don't love me no more?"

Several of the old men walking up the street guffawed at the whore's re-
marks. Mutt shook his head, nodded with a sly grin and kept on riding.

He stopped and tied Muha to a post in front of the Mother Lode saloon.
A half-dozen men, mostly Earl's age or older, slumped on the porch. They
were passing bottles of rotgut back and forth. They all avoided Mutt's gaze.
A hungry-looking young man eyed the Indian's horse, working out the cal-
culus of hunger and risk behind his lidded eyes. Before he got too far into
his equations, Mutt stopped in front of him and rested his hand on his
pistol.

"If I come out and my horse is gone, I'm going to shoot you. I don't care
who took it—you are the one who ends up dead for it."

The kid was silent, but his eyes had grown darker and wider.

"But if my horse stays put, there's a short bit in it for you."

He didn't wait for an answer. He pushed through the tattered trail blanket that was the Mother Lode's front door.

Inside it was dark, hot and stuffy. The place smelled of mold, stale sweat and rancid fat from the cheap lamp oil. The floor was dirt and sawdust. A half-dozen squatters sat at the bar and at the few tables that the saloon had. Two old men played checkers at one of the tables—there wasn't enough money up here for much gambling.

Mutt's eyes quickly adjusted to the light. He made his way toward a portly man in a dirty brown vest, seated at the far end of the bar and deep in conversation with another man whose face looked like cracked leather. A small bowler rested on the portly man's head; the hair peeking out from beneath it was thin, with the color and consistency of oil. He sported mut-tonchops. A mug danced in his hand as he wildly gesticulated while he talked. The beer in it occasionally splashed out.

"I tell you, Willie, all you have to do is meet this fella over in Carson City with your long iron," the portly man said to his sphinxlike companion. "You do a few hours work over there, and then—"

"Howdy, Deputy," the leather-faced man said, looking past his compan-ion's shoulder.

"Willie," Mutt said. "Good to see you back in town. I hear you had some trouble down south for a while."

"Mexico," Willie said. "I was a road agent. Shot a fella and his family didn't cotton to it too well. Had to pull foot, full chisel, and this seemed as good a place as any to prop up my bones."

"That it is," Mutt said. He turned to the barkeep. "Give me a baldface, and trust me, I'll know if you're cutting it." He turned back to address the back of the man in the bowler. "You're not cutting it, are you, Wynn?"

Wynn spun to face the deputy. "I resent the insinuation, Deputy! You know I run a first-rate grog shop up here. I don't cut my whiskey, and I don't do anything to get Mr. High-and-Mighty Sheriff Highfather send-ing you up here to impugn—"

Mutt laughed. He drained the whiskey in a single gulp. "Hell, Wynn, I don't even know what that word means. I'm here because a lot of folks from up here on the ridge have been coming down with a case of the bughouse crazies. Sheriff figures maybe you are brewing up something that is making that happen. What do you say, Wynn? Maybe a little turpentine in the old mash pot just to make it go a little further?"

Wynn frowned. "You're talking about what happened to old Earl yesterday, ain't ya?"

"And Daniel Basham, week 'fore that, and Squinty Mary Holt three weeks ago. They all live up here, Wynn, and that makes them your customers."

"I swear to you, Mutt, as the Almighty is my witness, I ain't been making bad mash. 'Sides, Earl and the other two haven't touched a drop by my hand in months."

The barkeep nodded as he refilled Mutt's glass. "It's true, Deputy. Lots of folks been staying away since that Holy Roller showed up. I say a man that lets his religion git in the way of his drinking is a fella with his cart 'fore his horse."

"Preacher up here?" Mutt said, sipping his whiskey. "Since when?"

"'Bout three months ago," Wynn said. "He and that squirrelly deacon o' his came into town and set up shop at the old Reid homestead over on the northwest slope. Started preaching and next thing I know, some of my best customers are too busy shouting 'bout the dang Rapture to tie on a decent one."

"Preacher got a name?" Mutt asked as he stood and put his empty glass on the scrub-pine bar.

"Ambrose," Wynn said. "Reverend Ambrose."

"Much obliged," Mutt said as he headed for the door. "Oh, and, Willie?"

"I know," Willie said. "'Get out of town.'"

"Much obliged."

Earl's house was about a quarter of a mile from the saloon. It was four thin walls and a roof of stretched and tattered tarpaper. It huddled with some other shanties near the turn onto the western face. His neighbor, a toothless old lady named Lizzie, said no one had messed with the place since word had made it up here about Earl's confrontation with the law.

"He's a good, God-fearing man, that Earl," Lizzie said. Her face was a map of the hardship of her life, deeply grooved and weathered by the wind and the dirt. "Poor lamb, just lost his way after he lost the missus and the little girl. It's a hard life to travel alone."

"Yes." Mutt nodded. "Thank you."

Inside Earl's hovel it smelled of cool dirt and misery. There were a few rotted planks lying haphazardly over the earthen floor. A molded and worn rug that must have once graced the parlor of a happy family a million years ago partially covered the planks and the earth—like ribs poking through the rotting skin of a cadaver.

A pile of straw, burlap bags and rags filled up one corner of the single room and was obviously Earl's bed. Mutt saw a rat scurry across the floor and disappear inside the hay pile.

A rickety table and chair was near the other side of the room, away from the door. Earl had been a carpenter once, Mutt had heard tale at the Paradise one night, but when he lost everything and fell into a bottle his talent had abandoned him too. It wasn't very good, Mutt thought as he ran his hand along the chair's rough back. But considering a dead man had made it, some allowances could be made.

The table was covered with pain. Children's slate tablets: letters, numbers and doodles, all in an innocent, clumsy hand. Lithographs, shielded from time and elements by wood and glass. A serious-looking young man with a stock of dark hair and a smiling young maiden—their lives ahead of them—ghosts, now. One dead, the other in some hell—between life and peaceful death. A marriage certificate, some letters from his wife written while Earl fought in the war. Scraps of a life. Mutt discovered he envied the old man in the jail cell down in the valley.

On the table was a well-traveled Bible. Mutt flipped it open. The onionskin pages crackled like dry leaves. In the front was the family history, names and dates of what white men considered important in life—birth, death, marriage, baptism. The handwriting was delicate, intricate, beautiful—a woman's mark. The dates of Earl's wife's and daughter's passing were written in thick, ugly letters, a scrawl shaky with grief and DTs.

Mutt's eyes widened as he noticed the other addendum to the document Earl had made in the holy book. At the top of the tree of names and dates, he had added two new lines. One traced his oldest male ancestor to *Adam* and the other linked his female ancestor to *Eve;* above the mythical progenitors, the old man had added a single line in a barely legible tracery of trembling strokes that said: *Demiurge.* Next to it Earl had scribbled in the margin: *the Greate Olde Wurm.* The handwriting was different, almost calligraphy. It was Earl's hand, but it wasn't. Staring at it made Mutt's head ache and spin.

The deputy blinked, snorted the sudden, odd odor of rotten meat from his nostrils and flipped through the rest of the Bible. The pages were unmarred until he reached the Book of Revelation—the white man's biggest ghost story. In every gap in the text, in every virgin inch, Earl had filled the book with more of the intricate, alien tracery. Some of it Mutt could cipher, but most of it just made his skin crawl and his eyeballs itch.

He closed the book and picked it up to take with him. He was sure Jon would want to see this. He halted, sniffed, circling the room like it was a hungry predator ready to pounce.

"What in the . . ."

The room was darker. The sun was not where it should have been. His ten minutes in Earl's place were hours to the rest of the world. This was wrong, all wrong. The room was cold, colder than an icebox. His breath swirled like a ghost in the darkness. His hand fell to his gun, but his guts told him this was nothing a gun could kill. They told him to run like hell.

So he did.

Out, into the sunlight and the afternoon heat. He looked down at the Bible in his hand. Faint wisps of smoke were escaping from between the pages, as if the sun itself were trying to eradicate the thing. He quickly slipped it into his saddlebag and headed for the home of the next errant ridge resident. It took a while for the sun to warm him.

On his way to take a look at Daniel Basham's digs, Mutt noticed the fresh wagon tracks he had spotted earlier in the day were leading up to the summit—where the entrance to the mine was. The gunpowder smell was stronger. Maybe because it was a fresher scent this time, or maybe because his senses were tweaked by the fear summoned up in him in Earl's shack, he could identify it—dynamite, lots of it. He spurred Muha and raced for the top of the mountain. It took less than ten minutes to reach the summit. Two wagons were parked in the center of what had been the old mine camp. Men, at least a dozen, were in the process of rebuilding the camp. The sun was slowly becoming a bloody eye in the west as Mutt reined Muha to a stop. In a clatter of oiled gunmetal, the men leveled rifles and drew pistols, all cocked and aimed at him. Mutt rested his hand on the stock of his sheathed rifle and regarded the strangers.

"Before you decide to do something that will get you dead by a bullet, or a rope, you ought to know I'm part of the law in these here parts and y'all are trespassing on privately owned land." He looked at hardened face after hardened face in the circle of death he had rode into. "Now you-all best be putting those irons away, or else I'm going to have to write you a citation. . . ."

Two men strode up with six more behind them. The two leading the charge were Fancy Dans—brocade vests, gold watch fobs, but with shirtsleeves rolled up and dirt on their hands. One was tall and redheaded, with chipmunk teeth, so pale it looked like the noon sun could make an Indian out of him; the other was short, olive skinned and fat, mopping his brow with an embroidered handkerchief. A few of the entourage behind them were carrying large rolls of charts and surveying tools. The rest cradled rifles. They all looked right tickled to see Mutt.

"What is the meaning of this?" Olive Skin said. He had the tone you give a waiter when you find a mouse turd in your soufflé. "You are trespassing here."

"Actually, that's my line," Mutt said, his hand not wavering from his rifle. "This is private property. Owned by a fellow named Malachi Bick, down in the town below. I'm the deputy sheriff in these parts and you and your crew gotta move on."

"This is outrageous!" Olive Skin bellowed.

Chipmunk held up a hand to calm his partner and turned to address Mutt. "Look, Chief, there's a misunderstanding. Where's your hoss? Maybe we could talk to him?"

Mutt slid the rifle clear of the sheath in one fluid movement, natural as stretching. He cocked the lever with a flick of his thick wrist, one-handed, as he brought it down to bear straight at Chipmunk's horrified face. There was an instant of stunned silence as all the armed and ready gunmen realized Mutt had somehow gotten the drop on them.

"Sure thing," he said, locking eyes with Chipmunk. "This is him, right here. Oh, and it's 'Deputy,' not 'Chief.' Now you say it, hoss."

Chipmunk swallowed hard, a lump of anger and fear that was sharp going down.

"Deputy, not Chief," he said.

"Now I've tried being nice and I've tried being reasonable," Mutt said. "And for my trouble I've had guns pointed at me and been treated in a disrespectful manner. Now I want all of you to drop your guns on the ground, now, or I will surely blow this man's head clean off his shoulders. And I reckon that will affect all of y'all come payday."

"Do it," Chipmunk said to the men. A thin line of sweat now covered his upper lip. The crew looked to Olive Skin. He nodded quickly and made dropping motions with his hands. Pistols, rifles and shotguns all thudded onto the hot dust.

"Show him, Jacob," Chipmunk said to Olive Skin. Jacob, formerly known as Olive Skin, slowly reached into his inside vest pocket and withdrew a folded packet of papers. He stepped toward Mutt, gingerly offering the packet to the deputy.

There was no way in hell Mutt was going to confide in this crew of lick-fingers that he couldn't make heads or tails of this legal mush. He examined the papers while he kept the rifle on Chipmunk with his other hand. They looked official, with lots of places to put your mark and stamps and even gold seals. He nodded and looked for words he recognized. He spotted the word "deed" as well as the sweeping signature of Malachi Bick.

"You see the land was deeded to us by Mr. Stapleton a few weeks ago," Chipmunk said, trying to get out from in front of the rifle's barrel. "That's my signature there, see, 'Oscar Deerfield,' and there is my partner, 'Jacob Moore.'" He gestured toward Jacob, who was nodding eagerly.

"*Arthur* Stapleton, the banker?" Mutt said. Mrs. Stapleton flowed through his mind like cool, sweet water. He lowered the rifle. "Land ain't his to deed; it belongs to Malachi Bick."

"Used to," Deerfield said, plucking the papers out of Mutt's hand. "Bick deeded it to Art and he deeded it to us."

"Fair and square," Moore said. "All handled up in Virginia City by a first-rate lawyer."

"Why would anyone want the deed to a busted silver mine?" Mutt said. The men with charts were chasing off the hired guns. They paused long enough to pick up their shooting irons and then shuffle back to work with hard sideways glances at Mutt. The storm had apparently passed.

"Because, Chie— Because, Deputy, it is most certainly not busted," Deerfield said.

"Come again?"

"It's not busted," Moore repeated the claim, his wide face splitting into a grin. "And we intend to open 'er back up again and prove it."

The Queen of Cups

Maude was cleaning up the last of the dinner dishes when Arthur arrived home. He slammed the door and then locked it.

"Have you eaten?" she asked. It was the first words they had spoken since he had struck her yesterday. He ignored her and made straight for the liquor cabinet, pouring a glass tumbler full of scotch. He downed it as he strode to the window by the front door and glanced furtively past the curtains, into the decaying daylight.

"Has he been by?" he asked, squinting out the window. "Him or his horse of a bastard-mulattoo son, or one of his other ruffians?"

"Who?" Maude said, walking toward Arthur, sensing the creeping fear building in him.

"Bick!" He spun and shouted at her, "Goddamn Malachi Bick! Tar-souled villain's coming for me. I know it."

Maude frowned. She wasn't scared of Arthur. She hadn't been in a long time. He was terrified and, like many men, his fear was usually wrapped in anger.

"Bick? Arthur, he's your friend. You two have been partners for years. He needs you to run his interests."

Arthur pushed past her and refilled his glass.

"Partner." He spit out the word like it was a bad taste. "More like his goddamned pet. Malachi Bick doesn't have friends; he has assets. And you are either a valuable asset to him, or a liability. I just became a liability."

"I don't understand," she said. "Arthur, let me help you."

Arthur snorted again. "What the hell do you think you could do to help, Maude? Snivel at him?" He hurried down the hall and disappeared into their bedroom.

For an instant, Maude considered telling him what she could do. How she could kill Bick before he had a chance to raise an eyebrow; vanish like desert dew as the sun arose ascendant. Poison him, cripple him, rob him, curse him. She was fairly confident she could still do all that. She had let so much of the training go, slip away like sand, a few precious grains at a time. But she knew she still carried enough of The Load to deal with a scoundrel like Malachi Bick. She remained silent. It would do no good. Arthur would forsake her help and berate her for what he'd see as a childish flight of fancy. She shook her head. She had promised Gran Bonnie that she would never end up like this. She had worked so hard, for so long, it was strange to look back now at what she had been and not understand in the slightest how she had arrived here now.

"If you flinch," Anne Bonny said with a wicked grin, "you die, girl. Be still. *Still.*"

The blade hummed as it left the old woman's hand. Maude felt the breeze, smelled the oiled steel as it flew past her cheek and felt it pluck the grape from between her lips. The blade and the grape thudded into the cypress tree Maude was standing in front of with a heavy hollow sound. The blade, still quivering, was half-buried in the tree.

"Good," the old woman said. "You didn't piss yourself that time. Good."

A break in the training; they were sitting on a makeshift bench of deadwood along the private beach behind Grande Folly. The sky was blindingly blue. Gulls screeched in the distance, competing with the rumble of the waves. There was still an early spring chill, but the vigorous calisthenics that Anne put her through had driven it away. Maude munched on a hunk of sourdough bread from the lunch pail Isaiah had delivered some hours ago. She washed it down with great gulps of cold water from a tin cup.

"What is the source of all disease?" Anne asked as she admired the gulls' aerial dance.

"It is a distorted reflection in the human soul, of its divine beauty," Maude responded casually, enjoying the bread. "Sickness of the body, of the mind, is the soul seeking, and being thwarted in emulating the divine nature inherent in all human beings. This incongruity in the inner spiritual reality causes disharmony within the sheath of the soul, and therefore illness."

"Now," Anne said, "explain it to me simple, like I was a child, or a man."

"All disease, all illness," Maude said, popping the last bite of bread into her mouth and talking around it, "is born in a sickness of the soul. And we cure it by healing the soul."

"Good," Anne said, nodding. "Cite your source."

"The heresies of the Yellow Empress," she said, burping gently. "The hidden passages of the Cong-Fu of the Toa-Tse, 3000 B.C." She stood up from the log. "Can we do more running on the sand now? I want to try not to leave prints again. I think I almost have it."

"Yes, you do," Anne said. "And no, we are not. This old crone is done with running for the day. Sit down; I need to show you something."

Maude sat.

"Anne, when am I going to learn how to shoot? You've taught me all about other kinds of weapons, but not guns."

Anne shook her head. "Guns. We'll get to them, lass. Eager little thing now, aren't you? Now that your eyes are open.

"To be honest, girl, guns really aren't that important. Guns are like men— only useful for a little while. They can go off at a moment's notice when you don't want them to and they make a lot of damn fool noise doing it. They tend to fail on you when you need them most. Don't rely on them.

"Trust yourself, your weapons, your talents. Remember how I showed you what sharp nails can do? Taught you how to disguise their potency, how to hide your claws in plain sight? You can open a man's throat with them, quiet, quick. Hell, you can usually get a man to give you his throat to cut, with the right words, the right theatre. You can coat your nails with poison—"

"Oh, I know the two best alkaline-based contact poisons to use!" Maude interrupted. "There's—"

"Not today," Anne said. "No poisons, no guns. No, today we talk about the whys. First principles."

Maude calmed herself. The day was getting warmer and the sun felt good on her skin. A lazy swarm of bees darted around some of the hydrangeas that grew wild at the edge of the sand. Everything felt like it was made of light and warmth.

"What," Anne asked, "do you think is the reason I'm teaching you all these things, as they were taught to me?"

"So I can take care of myself, and help others," Maude said.

"Why?"

"Because you hate men and they are evil and hurt the world?"

Anne shook her head. "No. No. Gods, no. This is one of the hardest things to teach and it should be the easiest."

Anne looked out at the sea. She seemed to listen to the gulls. She nodded and turned back to Maude.

"Men," she began. She stopped, sighed and turned angrily back to the sea. "Damn it. . . .

"Men," she tried again. "Are part of the same world, the same design, as you and me, as the sea, the gulls, the sky. We need men and they need us. We are part of the same tapestry. Pull on one thread and the pattern is destroyed. Men are not evil. What men have done, some of that is evil. Men have driven themselves mad, lost and tangled in their own warped pattern, their own pain. And like every other animal in pain, they lash out, blindly.

"The tyrant-father of Heaven, the one who created, hated and drove out the first woman, yoked men with a horrible curse, far worse than any imagined to have been handed down to Eve. Men were told they were masters of this world, of their mates, of the beasts and fish, of the land and sea and sky. How ridiculous! That's like telling a little boy he's in charge of the house when his da is gone. It's silly!

"And like that little boy, men have tried to live up to the unreasonable demands of their mute, wayward, celestial father. They have enslaved and dominated, conquered and killed, all in the name of shepherding, of protecting, of ruling the world. They spend their lives trying to do what they think is right, what their father on high would want of them. The bastard."

Anne sat next to Maude and fished one of her strong, bony hands down the front of her blouse tugging at a chain at her neck, pulling it free.

"I don't hate men. I hate the madness that engulfs them. I hate that they rage and struggle and storm so damn loud that they can't hear the voices around them, the voices that are here to guide them, to teach them and nurture them. I hate they try so hard to please their father they ignore the Mother."

She pulled the chain over her head and held it up for Maude to see. It was old, worn. The links were flat and made of dull, crudely forged iron. Attached to the chain was a small vial, about five inches long, wrought of the same dull iron and smooth yellowed bone, enmeshed in a filigree web of silver wire. The vial was capped with a plug cut from a bloodred ruby the size of a large man's thumbnail.

"And that is why I teach you, why I was taught, why one day you will teach another woman. Because it is our duty, now that we are awake and aware and fully capable of controlling our destinies, to look out past our own noses and protect the Mother, protect our sisters who still huddle in darkness and bondage, and even to protect the damn fool men who have made such a wreck of this world."

Anne placed the vial in Maude's hand. The girl shook her head.

"The Mother?" Maude said. "I don't understand."

"Ah." Annie smiled. "All life comes from the Mother. She is the sky and the sea, the moon and the mountains. Green trees, red blood. She is all that and we are all her children.

"It is our duty, our burden, to protect her, to use all of our gifts, all of our training, all our heart, blood and soul, in defense of the worthy and the weak, because we, as women, were created to protect, to nurture, to defend and to counsel. We alone were given the wisdom and the ferocity to heal the world."

The old woman clasped her own hands over the girl's, closing Maude's fingers over the vial. The artifact was warm, almost hot, to the touch.

"This," Anne said, "is the essence of The Load, the code you will live by. The Load has been followed by an unbroken line of women running back to Lilith herself. Protectors and healers, assassins and poisoners. Oracles, witches, kingmakers and courtesans. We are all that and so much more.

"And this," Anne said, squeezing Maude's hands tighter over the vial, "is the moon blood of Lilith herself. Given to me, in this very vessel, by an Ewe Witch on the plains of Africa. She taught me the ways of The Load and trained me as I now train you. She was over four hundred years old, having been granted extraordinary longevity and health by drinking the blood of the first woman. She kept it in a skull chalice and I drank my draught from it. She gave me this vial to take out into the world and pass along to a worthy successor. You, Maude, you are that successor."

Maude's eyes widened, her mouth opened, but no words came. It was like a dream in sunlight.

Anne smiled and nodded. "Yes, when the time is right, when you have completed your training and I deem you ready in body, mind and soul, you shall drink from this vial and become one of the line of Lilith and you, too, will carry The Load, all the rest of your days."

Maude stood, the vial still in her hands. "I'm ready. Now."

Anne laughed, plucked the chain away from the girl and returned it to around her neck. "The hell you are! But you are on your way, Maude; you are on your way."

The sun sparkled off the blue waves far out in the ocean, like diamonds, and Maude felt all the doors in her life fly wide open, again.

Arthur returned down the hall. He carried the small pistol he usually took with him when he went away on trips. He was loading the gun and mumbling to himself. Maude was about to ask him where he was going when there was a sharp rap at the door. Arthur froze, the blood drained from his face.

"It's him," he whispered. "Bick."

The knock was insistent. Arthur slid the gun into his coat pocket. Timidly, like a child, the banker approached the door. A sensation seized Maude suddenly. The same feeling she had when Gran had dropped her into the well with the copperheads and told her to bring her back three of the snakes, alive.

Arthur opened the door. He blinked into the gathering darkness.

"Hello, Malachi," he said, sliding his hand into his coat pocket. "What brings you out this hour?"

Malachi Bick's form was swaddled in shadow, as if a piece of the night had torn itself loose and taken a human form.

"We need to talk, Arthur." Bick's voice was honeyed smoke. The sense memory in Maude flared—the sensation of utter dread, of feeling the dry, ageless breath of reptiles fan her neck as she descended into the unknown dark of the well. For just an instant, her training fell away and she was truly frightened and she did not know why, which only intensified the feeling.

"I have received distressing news," Bick's voice continued from the shadows. "We need to talk, Arthur. I need to know if it is true."

A hand, meticulously manicured and wrapped at the wrist in a white silk cuff, appeared out of the shadows, crossing into the light bleeding out of the open doorway. It beckoned.

"Now," Bick said. "Alone."

Arthur gave Maude a quick glance—a combination of terror, pleading and his best effort at reassurance. It was a pathetic gesture. The human being frightened beyond his capacity to reason past it, the little boy begging his mother to make the bad thing go away, and the man trying to assure his mate all would be taken care of. The look made Maude love him, made her need to help him, protect him, even as it disgusted her. Somewhere Gran was laughing at her again.

Arthur stepped out on the dark porch with Bick, his hand still in the pocket, still clutching the gun the way a little boy might hold himself in fear or anxiety. With his free hand he closed the door. The iron lock clicked and the darkness was gone and Arthur with it.

Eventually Father returned from his trip. He was surprised and a little disappointed that Maude didn't want to leave Grande Folly and Gran Bonnie. He had naturally been worried about his daughter being in the care of a woman with such a reputation for eccentricity. However, after Gran explained to him that the girl simply was desirous of learning more about her mother's history and childhood, Martin had agreed to allow Maude to stay. She loved her father and had missed him, but after the training, after learning of The Load, there was no turning back.

For Martin's part, he loved his daughter but was grateful she had bonded with a female figure, even one as decrepit and unconventional as Gran Bonnie. He visited his daughter often over the next few years and Maude made a point to spend as many holidays with her father as she could. As he grew older and his health began to show the cost of so many long, hard voyages, Maude began to care for him as well as seeing to Anne as much as the old woman would allow it.

November 1850. It was a cold morning, bitter. Maude Cormac Anderton sprinted across the white dunes of the beach of Grande Folly. She was nineteen and she left not a single mark of her passing in her wake. She slowed, stopped, before the old woman who sat on the log that had become Maude's classroom. Anne raised a pistol, an ugly, heavy thing with a brutish, flaring, snout of a bore.

"Loaded or unloaded?" Anne said.

"Loaded," Maude replied, sipping in air but controlling her breathing so as not to gulp or gasp after the five-mile run. She had not allowed herself to sweat yet either, since Gran had not yet given her permission. "From the weight you are exhibiting by holding it, looks to be . . . .54 caliber."

The old woman said nothing and Maude knew she was correct.

"You ready to catch it?" Anne said, aiming the pistol at the girl's chest.

Maude was fifteen feet away. She tried to ignore the faint tremble in the old woman's hand. She nodded. "Yes, but it won't fire anyway. Too damp out here today."

"Oh, is it now, you smart little cherry?" Anne growled. Maude ignored the sexual epithet; it passed over her, through her, and did not touch any of her. Anne had taught her the secret of language and how it could bind as well as liberate, if you let it touch you. "And what, pray tell, makes you think I was daft enough to not keep this in a dry, secure place while you were flouncing up and down the beach?"

"I can see the moisture on the edges of the brass."

"Really? Let's see," Anne said, and pulled the trigger.

The hammer snapped, but there was no explosion of powder, nothing, only the gulls' mocking laughter.

"From the way you aimed it, I would have caught it with this hand," Maude said, waving her left. "You know that's my weaker hand."

"No," Anne said with a yellowed smile. "You don't have a weak hand anymore."

———

December, Winter Solstice, Christmas. Anne called it Dzon'ku 'Nu. On the beach under the ghost light of the swollen moon, Maude held Lilith's blood in the ancient flask. She and Anne stood skyclad, nude, embracing the cold and the salt spray off the ocean, maiden and crone.

"With this, you set your feet, your will, upon the red path—the unbroken chain that stretches back to the first of us. With this, you take up The Load and dedicate your life to heal, to teach, to protect the Mother and all her children. Do you understand?"

"Yes," Maude said.

"Then," Anne said, "drink."

The ancient bone of the flask was warm and smooth against Maude's lips, the old iron chain cold when it brushed her skin. She upturned the flask and felt something sticky and thick wet her lips, her tongue.

And then there was fire. Burning, blossoming, bright and tangy, like brass, or raw life, burning her flesh, burning through the roof of her mouth, into her brain. Images—a bloated, infant sun hanging over a dry, lazy plain; a column of will-light brandishing a flaming blade, or the thought-form in this world of a sword of fire; cold mud, the smell of cool earth and the musk of live fur, soothing, the nuance of chilled, gurgling water near, the implied heat of life, savage life, beneath the rug of fur.

She swallowed the sizzling mass of molten copper and cobwebbed memory, felt it claw its way down her throat: a bird's talons soaked in bile.

The blood filled, bloomed, in her, tried to devour her in bright, ancient power and bright, silver, antediluvian thought. Before it she was puny and small, finite and stunted.

"No," she said. "I am not."

She was startled to hear her own voice. Maude blinked, tumbling out of the cosmic hangover. The beach at night. The flask was still in her trembling hand. Her knees buckled, but she righted herself before she fell. She looked skyward. The stars shivered in the frigid black void. The tears welled, ran down her cheeks—hot and wet. They were beautiful: the stars, the tears. She was beautiful.

"You," Anne said, embracing her, "are the first in all the long line, the first to take the blood and to never drop to your knees."

"What does that mean?" Maude asked.

"It means no power in this world can lay you low, except yourself," Anne said. "It also means I'm very, very proud of you, Maude."

The Crone and the Maiden held each other while the stars rejoiced, the ocean wept and the Mother turned her face toward the sun.

Anne Cormac Bonny left the world on the morning of May 1, 1854. She was 157 years old. She credited the blood of the First Mother for giving her strength, vitality and preternatural longevity, but she was quick to also remind Maude that all things have to end and in that ending can be beauty and understanding and the seed of new beginnings.

"We must die," Anne said, smiling her wicked devil smile, "so that we can truly understand what it means to live. Otherwise, what's the bloody point of it?"

In the night Anne called for Maude and for Isaiah. She instructed them to carry her to her horse, that she wanted to ride out to the beach one more time.

Maude was attending the College of Charleston and had come home when she received word from Isaiah that Lady Cormac's health had taken a turn.

"You look well, Maude," the servant said as they carried Anne to her mount. "Schooling is agreeing with you, yes?"

Maude nodded. Her long hair was a wig; beneath it, her own hair was short-cut in a fashionable men's style—a soap lock. "It's easier to pretend to be a man than I expected it to be."

Anne laughed, a dry rasp followed by a long, wet cough. "It's a different world when you move as one of them, isn't it? Won't let you learn in their schools unless you bind your breasts and cut your hair, will they? It's worth it, though. Those things are not what you are."

They helped Anne onto her horse. She grabbed the saddle and, with a fleeting burst of strength and power, hauled herself up into the saddle. Taking the reins, she turned the beast and regarded them with haughty power. In that moment, she was Anne Bonny, pirate queen—ageless and beautiful and, most of all, free.

"The best days of my life were fighting beside men, pretending to be one of them—brawling, fucking, swearing and drinking with them. And I did it all a damn sight better than the best of them."

She looked out toward the grove, toward the beach.

"I'm ready to go home," she said. "To the ocean, the only place that ever felt like home to me. One last time."

She kicked the horse in the flank, snapped the reins and with a snarl that would have made a South Indies cannibal flee in terror roared into the dark woods, toward the sea.

By the time Maude and Isaiah reached the beach Anne was wading out into the black, foaming water, the moonlight casting a benediction on her, her horse pacing where the water and land clashed.

"Anne!" Maude called out over the thunder of the waves. Anne turned, smiled and raised a hand. She turned, laughing, and dived into the dark surf. She was gone.

They found her body the next morning. Maude carried her to the small family graveyard on the hill overlooking the beach and the ocean. She weighed almost nothing, even waterlogged.

Maude dug Anne Bonny's grave and buried her as she and Anne had often discussed—in a simple pine box, filled with a king's ransom in pirate treasure. Isaiah poured cask after cask of gold and gems into the coffin as well as Anne's brace of old pistols and her sword. The last artifact added was a bottle of good red wine, which Maude placed in the dead legend's crossed hands.

"Enjoy it," Maude said. "Safe passage."

Isaiah and Maude nailed the lid on the coffin and climbed out of the grave. They picked up shovels and silently filled the hole. The only sound was the metallic crunch of the shovel blades as they lifted the dirt, the swoosh of the dirt as it rained down on the pine box.

The servants of Grande Folly came to bid the mistress of the house farewell, leaving bowls of fruit, white candles and flowers at the head of the grave while Maude and Isaiah continued their task. The servants sang an old African song Maude had heard Anne hum a few times over the years. She didn't recognize most of the words. The sun was low in the west when they finished the burial. The servants departed, singing.

"This is yours now," Isaiah said, handing Maude the ancient flask holding Lilith's blood. "Lady Cormac was very specific that you were to care for this now."

Maude took the flask, examined it and then hung the ancient chain around her neck.

"Grande Folly is yours as well," he said. "The land, the mansion, the slaves, the remainder of Lady Cormac's considerable fortune. She instructed her attorney that it is all to go to you."

"It can't," Maude said. "I'm a woman. They won't allow me run of the estate!"

"Lady Cormac has instructed her attorney to approach your father to act as your proxy in the matter and hold the estate in trust for you," the servant explained. He smiled, one of the few times she could recall him smiling. It was beautiful. "Lady Cormac said to tell you men had their uses besides in the bedroom."

And it was at the attorney's office in Charleston that Maude, with her father at her side to represent her in the transaction like she was a child, had met young Arthur Stapleton.

The door opened and Arthur, gaunt and disheveled, stepped back into the house. There was no sign of Malachi Bick.

"What happened?" Maude asked.

Arthur walked woodenly back to the cabinet and refilled his glass with scotch. He stared at a point in space and absently drained the tumbler.

"Arthur!" Maude said, grabbing him by the shoulder.

"He knows about the deed," he finally said. "He knows I know about all of them. He trusted me with it and I . . . It was a good straight. I should have cleaned up from it, not lost the deed. I lost the . . . deed."

His face contorted and darkened with blood. He began to sob, big soul-heaving sobs that made his entire frame shake. Maude gathered him and pulled him into her arms. It felt strange, and yet it felt like the most natural thing in the world to do. She hated this man. She loved him too.

"Shhhhh," she said. "It will be all right."

"He's going to kill me," Arthur whispered. "Like that prospector he killed, like the others. No one even recalls. He cl . . . cleans up his messes, Bick does. Nice and ti . . . ti . . . tidy . . . Awwww, God!"

Another wave of sobs wracked him.

Maude found the nerve plexus at the junction of his neck and shoulder and firmly pressed, sending calming sensations through her husband's body. Arthur shuddered and the sobbing gradually subsided.

"Arthur," she said gently in his ear. "What deed? What are you talking about?"

Arthur stepped back, untangling himself from her arms. His eyes were red and wet. He wiped them with his shirtsleeve and then his nose.

"The less you know, the better," he said. "I know too many of his secrets, too much that could ruin him. I have to go." He returned to their bedroom.

Maude followed him. "No, you don't. We can fight him, Arthur. I can help! We'll go to the sheriff."

Arthur was opening the chest at the foot of their bed. He removed a small, worn leather-bound Bible. He stuffed it into his coat pocket opposite the pistol.

"What are you doing?" she asked.

He pushed past her, back to the hallway, to the front door. "I have to get to the Chinaman," he muttered. "He's the only one who I think Malachi might even consider an equal. That's my only chance."

He turned to her as he opened the door. "I love you, Maude."

The words sounded flat and fake. He didn't love her. He loved himself. His entire universe was, and always had been, the story of Arthur Stapleton. She was a prop, Constance was a prop. He was afraid right now and that fear made him reach out to her for reassurance, but there was none to be given for his wife or daughter, who might also be in danger from his stupidity and recklessness and secrets, who might also fear. Maude wanted to spit on him, snap his neck.

"I love you too," she said, and meant it and hated herself for it. "Be careful, Arthur."

He kissed her on the cheek, and closed the door behind him.

The Six of Cups

It was already dark when Jim slipped out of his room at Mrs. Proctor's boardinghouse. He padded quietly down the carpeted steps, past the curtained parlor, where he could hear many of the other boarders, all men, laughing and talking about the events of the day. Someone was plinking "The Flying Trapeze" on the piano Mrs. Proctor kept in the parlor.

There was the comforting, mellow smell of pipe tobacco swirling around the parlor curtains. It reminded Jim of Pa. Sometimes when Pa was sad, or couldn't sleep 'cause of the pain, he would climb up and sit in the loft next to Jim and Lottie, stroke their hair and puff on his pipe. The smell reminded Jim of warm blankets, calloused, loving hands and home.

He opened the front door, as softly as he could, squeezed through the opening and closed the door behind him with a faint click.

The few streetlights had been lit on Dry Well Road, but only Jim was out to see them. The few homes he could see from the boardinghouse's porch had ghostly lamplight shining through their small lead and paper windows. The livery shop, the blacksmith, the butcher—all were dark and locked.

Jim glanced back at the parlor's window and its light. The Widow Proctor seemed like a fine lady; she reminded Jim a little of Ma. That's why he knew he'd get a scoldin', if not a whupping, if Mrs. Proctor caught him sneaking out and heading where he was thinking of heading in the middle of the night.

Mutt had introduced him to the widow in the evening, after all of the ruckus at Auggie's general store had died down. After they had locked Earl up in one of the jail cells, Sheriff Highfather had looked down at Jim with eyes like he figured he'd see on Judgment Day.

"So, what are we going to do with you?" he said.

"Sir?"

"Don't 'sir' me, boy," Highfather said grimly. "Mutt tells me you've been nothing but trouble since he scraped you up off the desert. That true? You trouble, boy?"

"I . . . Well, no, sir, I mean I ain't trying to be. . . ."

Mutt returned from the cool shadows of the back of the jail, where the cells were. He settled on the edge of Highfather's desk, and crossed his arms. The sheriff and the deputy both stared at Jim sternly and silently.

"I . . . uh, that is, I just wanted to . . . Uh. . . ."

Both men broke into laughter. Highfather crossed the distance to Jim and smacked him gently on the shoulder.

"I reckon grown-ups in these here parts are all just plain tetched," Jim said glumly while Highfather wiped a tear from his eye.

"You had him," Mutt said to Highfather.

"Oh yeah," Highfather said. "I figured we'd be needing the mop to clean up the mess."

"Okay," Jim said, his cheeks flushing, "ha-ha."

Highfather sat next to Mutt on the edge of the desk. "Jim, you seem like a decent boy. I'll put Mutt liking you aside and figure you're square."

"I'm wounded," Mutt said flatly.

Highfather continued. "Seriously, though, you helped us out in a tight scrape and you handled it like a man. Here."

He fished a dollar out of his pocket and handed it to the boy. "Your first pay. Mutt ain't much of a housekeeper—"

The Indian muttered something in a language Jim didn't understand; it didn't sound very nice.

"So what do you say you sweep up around here, fetch lunch for us, keep Mutt sober, stuff like that?"

Jim nodded; his eyes were still on the note in his hand. "Yessir, that sounds fine by me. Thank you, Sheriff."

"Call me Jon," Highfather said. "'Less you mess up; then you can call me Sheriff. We square?"

"Yessir," Jim said, smiling.

"He loves it when people call him sir," Mutt said. "He don't hear it much."

"Take him over to Widow Proctor's before I fire you," Highfather said. "I done used up my charity for the day."

"Yes sir," Mutt said, grinning, as he led Jim out the door.

The widow had put Jim up in a room down the hall from Mutt. His first night after reaching Golgotha, he ate and drank until he thought he would bust. The other boarders at the dinner table laughed and commented that he had eaten his weight and then some. The widow, on her way out with a basket of food, chided them to leave him be.

That night Jim had his best night's sleep since leaving home. He woke the following morning, arriving at the jail just after six. His eyes fixed on the empty space where his wanted poster had been. He wondered how many people had seen it. How many people in just this small town? Across Nevada? It was rattlesnake crazy to be hanging around at a jail when you were on the run for murder.

A hand slapped him on the shoulder. Jim spun, eyes wide.

"Glad to see industry in today's youth," Highfather said. He fiddled with the ring of keys in his hand, picked a large one and unlocked the iron door to the jail. "Beating your boss here is a good way to start your first day. You grow up on a farm?"

Jim froze for a second. He figured there was no harm. Lots of people grew up on farms. "Uh, yessir."

Highfather opened up the inside shutters on the barred windows. He paused and looked at Jim, then went back to check on Earl.

Later in the morning Mutt showed up. He tossed Jim a piece of horehound candy and a wink. "I visited Auggie; he's fine, looked a little tired, but that's to be expected."

Jim swept and cleaned while Highfather and Mutt talked quietly at the desk. All the joking was gone and both men seemed to be mulling over something neither cared for. Jim noticed that the two men treated each other pretty square, like equals. Jim had never heard of anyone treating an Injun like a white man.

Jim fetched them lunch from the Widow Proctor's around eleven and ate with the two men. Jim ended up telling Highfather about his pa being in the Union army. Turned out Highfather was a Rebel. Highfather danced around any specific details of what he did in the war, but he ended up telling Jim some pretty funny stories. Jim shared a few of the ones his pa had told him that were pretty funny too.

Mutt headed out to go see someone named Wynn up on the mountain. The rest of the day went pretty slow; Jim whittled when there was nothing to do. Highfather made rounds, saying he'd be back before four.

"Clean up in back by the cells," he said as he buckled on his gun belt and grabbed his vest. "But don't get too close to old Earl. He's been sleeping it off all day, but don't take no chances—stay clear."

"Yessir," Jim said as the iron door clanged shut.

It was cooler back in the cell block. There were three small cells, one with a barred and shuttered window. It was empty, its door open and the shutters thrown wide to let the afternoon sun in. The light stretched in a bright, narrow beam across the floor, stretching to the back wall where wooden pegs held blankets, toilet buckets and a large ring of keys to the cells.

The cell on the right had been occupied this morning by a pair of rowdy drunks Highfather had collared last night, making trouble at the Paradise Falls. He had let them go before lunch with a fine and warning. Now only the left cell, hidden away from the light, was occupied by Earl Gibson.

Jim began to sweep near the right cell. The straw bristles shooshed against the stone floor. Dust motes drifted in the sunbeams, like stars floating through the ether.

"Jim," a dry, cracked voice whispered from the darkened cell. "Jim-boy, J-iiiiii-mmmmm."

Jim froze for a second. His hands gripped the broom handle tighter. The voice didn't sound like the old man Mutt had thrown in the cell yesterday. It was like a night wind on the desert, pushing sand along in ripples—low, almost hissing. Jim got ahold of himself and went back to sweeping.

"Jim . . . Negrey, is it?" the voice in the dark said.

Jim dropped the broom. He slowly stepped toward the far cell. "How do you know that? How do you know my name?"

"The voices in the rocks, boy," the voice said. "The silver voices, they saw you coming across the desert. Jim, Jimmy, Jim . . . Neg-reeeeeeeee."

He passed through the sunlight and then fell into shadow. The old man's shape was on the floor of the cell, crouched in the southeast corner. It was only a lump of darkness as Jim's eyes tried to adjust.

"What voices? How could they know I was coming when I didn't even know that?"

"There are other worlds, Jim-mieeee. They could smell your approach, see the lines of fate and power, abringin' you here, boy. They could see . . . the *eye,* Jim."

Jim's hand fell into his pant pocket; he clutched the handkerchief that held his father's eye. He felt pulsating heat, through the cloth.

"The worms can see it, Jimmy. They can smell it in the silver darkness. The old Chinamen sense it too, calling to them, as old as the world. Your friend Mutt—woof, woof! Oh, Mutt can smell it too, but he don't know what it is. The trick is on the Trickster, heh."

Jim was at the bars now. Earl was crouched, like an animal ready to pounce. His eyes were wide and dark. Drool dangled from the corners of his mouth.

"I don't understand, sir," Jim said, resting his hands on the cold iron bars. His breath danced before his face. It was cold here, not cooler, not shady, but like up-before-dawn-in-February-back-home cold. Unnatural. "My pa's eye—"

"Is very special, Jim, very powerful," Earl said, finally focusing on the boy. "Quite a prize. He spoke of it often—called it 'the Eye of the Wurm'— the Devil's eye, boy!"

"Who, who did?"

Earl was on him faster than Jim could possibly react. The old man grabbed his wrists, pinning him to the bars. Earl's breath was foul, like stale vomit, and Jim could now see quite clearly that his eyes were rimmed with yellow.

"The one who warned me, Jim. The one who knows the truth about Heaven and Hell, God and the false god. The one that done opened my soul to the silver song. Praise be to the silver song!"

Jim struggled to pull away, but Earl's grip was strengthened by madness.

"I was wrong to try to warn all of you," Earl said, nodding. "He was right; the preacher was right. Judgment has come! She will come for all of us, hallelujah!"

He squeezed Jim's wrists, hard. The boy lifted his foot and braced it against the cell door. He pushed with all his might and felt the old mad-man's grip give way. He fell back hard onto the jail floor.

"I'm so sorry, young man," Earl said, his voice cracking. "I didn't catch your name, but I'm so sorry. I don't want to hurt anyone, anyone! But they got in my ears with all their singing and they are coming for me. They're coming for all of us. You've got to warn Jon, b'fore'n she gets here."

Jim felt the fear clench his belly. He was dizzy with it. He scrambled up to his feet and grabbed the broom. As he backed out of the cell block, he heard the old man he remembered begin to sob.

"There's so few crumbs of me left," he whispered, "and so many worms. . . ."

Jim kept his peace about what Earl had said. Everyone at the dinner table that evening noticed how little he ate.

"What happened, boy?" Bill Caruthers, that cowpuncher, said. "You bust your breadbasket after all that grub yesterday?" Everyone laughed. Every-one except Jim and the Widow Proctor.

"That's enough out of you, Bill. Jim, are you feeling poorly?"

"Yes, ma'am," Jim muttered. "May I be excused? I just want to go to bed."

"Yes, of course. Good night, Jim,"

"Hope you feel better, pard'ner," Bill said, grabbing another roll. The others also wished Jim good night.

Lying in bed, he held the jade eye. He let the bright moonlight from the window caress it. As always, it seemed to drink in light and then give off its own faint greenish glow in return. It was probably a trick of the jade and the moonlight.

Or maybe not. He had tried to explain away what happened in the grave-yard outside of Albright. That he was sick and angry and scared, that he missed his pa and that somehow his mind had filled in all the jagged pieces. But his gut said no. He wasn't crazy.

The eye shined bright as he held it up to the moon. No. He wasn't crazy, like old Earl in the jail. You had to believe in something, Pa always said, else you end up believing in everything. Jim believed his memories and his gut, and he believed in the eye too.

It was a hard year after Pa left. It was quite the gossip of Preston County for an age. Ma weathered it like the lady she was. She never spoke cross of Pa to the children, and any hint of such kind of talk out of either Jim or Lottie was rewarded with a sharp slap to the hand.

"Don't make no difference," Ma said. "He's your father and you will speak of him with a respectful tongue in your head."

Jim was mad at Pa, but the missing him won out in the end. He got in a dustup his last day at the county school, 'cause Elmer Biddle called Pa a no-account, crazy-as-a-varmint whoremonger.

Jim dropped his slate and books on the spot and dived into Elmer like a wildcat. He landed a good, solid sockdolager square on Elmer's nose. Blood squirted out and he was laid out colder than a wagon tire. Jim caught it bad from everyone for breaking Elmer's nose. Ma whipped Jim bad and the schoolmaster said Jim was expelled. It didn't matter, though. He already had learned to read and write okay, and he could cipher a little too. Besides, he couldn't have stayed in school anyway. Ma needed him.

Jim had picked up enough knowledge from helping Pa to keep doing many of the chores and jobs he had been doing for folk around the county. Lot of folk gave him work on account of feeling so bad for his family. Jim followed Ma's lead and kept his head high and said "thank you kindly."

Ma picked up whatever work she could find to make ends meet. She mended and washed clothes and cooked meals down at the Cheat River Saloon.

Jim got work there too. He fixed up the furniture, repaired the doors and even hung new shingles on the roof. Anything to make an honest buck for the family.

In the first winter after Pa was gone, Lottie got sick, real sick. Doc called it miasma, said Lottie had breathed in something evil and it was what was making her so hot to the touch, and coughing all the time, day and night.

Jim remembered waking up in the loft and looking down to see Ma cradling Lottie. His little sister was like a wax doll, pale and limp. She coughed, but even that was weak, almost a rasp. Ma was crying, sobbing. She held Pa's old nightshirt in her hands, wrapping it around Lottie. She wiped her eyes on it.

"Oh, Billy, I can't do this alone; I can't do this alone. . . ."

Jim remembered Ma and Pa talking a few times, short and sad, about his younger brother, Jessie. Jessie had died when Jim was five. Jim didn't remember him at all; he only knew the sad look in Ma and Pa's faces when they mentioned Jessie.

Jim prayed all night. Prayed for Lottie to live, prayed for Pa to walk through the door with the medicine they couldn't afford in his hand. Jim prayed and he tried to remember Jessie.

The Cheat River was the last place anyone could recall seeing Pa. He had been playing cards and drinking with some local fellas. Everyone said he walked out the door a little after eleven and was never seen again.

Jim asked Charlie Upton—one of the people Pa had been playing with—if he said anything about where he was going. Jim never even saw the punch to his gut. It lifted him off the ground and knocked all the breath out of him. The next thing he remembered was being facedown on the ground, Charlie's steel vise of a grip on the back of his neck, holding his face in the dirt. Charlie's mouth was close to Jim's red, ringing ears.

"What the hell is there to know, boy? Your old man spent the whole night talking dirt about your mother, then said he was headed for Charleston to find himself a whore. You keep a mind about you to forget that worthless one-eyed sumabitch, and stay the hell out of my way too, y'hear."

It was not out of character for Charlie Upton to be a bastard. Charlie's family owned land, lots of it. They had money and the talk was Charlie had made more during the war doing some things that weren't too pretty. No one said any of that to Charlie's face. You talked a certain way to an Upton in Preston County, or else you got a load of trouble heaped on you. Charlie was as mean as a snake. He'd just as soon whup you as say "how do you do."

So Jim was none too happy when, after a year and a day, Charlie Upton came a'courting Ma.

He did it real Fancy Dan, especially for Charlie. First it was a carriage ride home after church for Ma and the children. Then it was bringing out firewood and provisions and a whole bunch of other things that the family needed real bad but Ma and Jim just couldn't make enough to provide. But Jim knew—he knew what Charlie Upton was and he never let this guard down; not that Charlie cared.

It took a while to start working on Ma, not as long as Jim had expected, but eventually she started to enjoy the attention. It was nice to be treated like a woman, to not just toil against the relentless cruelties of life alone, to have someone by your side who wanted to help you but, more important, wanted *you*. It was understandable and the entire town was willing accomplices to the seduction. Billy Negrey was a villain—a drunk and a philanderer, who was off somewhere, whooping it up, while his poor wife and son struggled to make ends meet. Eldon Coyle told everyone he was pretty sure he had seen old one-eyed Bill over in Wheeling, with a bottle of rye in one hand and a whore in the other.

Jim refused to believe it and he took Ma's softening to Charlie's advances as a betrayal most base. However, secretly, Jim knew how much help Upton was giving them and how much better their lives were with his aid. As ashamed and as sick as Jim was of himself for it, he, too, was relieved the family received it.

A year later, the wedding was announced at Sunday service. Everyone applauded politely, smiled and said their congratulations to the couple. Most folks meant it and those who really knew Charlie Upton knew they had damn well better make nice, or else.

After the wedding things slowly changed. The little presents to Lottie stopped almost at once. The time Charlie and Ma spent alone together lessened and he started drinking around the house. He made Jim tend the property, pretty much alone, and started taking lots of "business trips" to Charleston and Wheeling. But the hitting was the worst.

The first time was when Jim said his pa was a better man than Charlie would ever be. Upton spun Jim around and drove a fist, like granite, into the boy's face. Nearly broke his nose and left a faint scar on his cheek where the skin split. Ma was horrified—even at his worst Billy had never laid a hand on either child. A few weeks later Jim came home from doing some work on Abner Green's barn to find Ma weeping; her lips were swollen and split, her teeth black with blood.

"I'm gonna kill that sumabitch," Jim said, striding toward the rifle hanging near the door.

"No, *no*, James," Ma said, rising. "He's your pa now, and I will deal with this and you will hold your peace."

"Why, Mama? Why the hell did you let him in here?" Jim said, feeling his eyes growing hot and wet. "We didn't need his damn help this bad. I told you, I tried to tell you—"

"You shut your mouth!" Ma said. "How dare you. You aren't the only one he ran away from. I was his wife before you were *ever* his son. No one was hurt more by him than me—no one! I did what I had to do to give Lottie and you some security, some chance to survive. I knew what he was; you think I'm a damn fool, James? But I would marry the Devil himself to save Lottie and to save you. If the worst I have to endure is a beating every once in a while for food and medicine and a roof and a chance for you to go back to school and for Lottie to keep going, I'll gladly take it."

Jim stood silent.

"Your pa was the only man I will ever love, Jim," she said softly. "But he is gone. He couldn't . . . He wasn't strong enough to—"

"Ma, please," Jim said. His insides were cold and tight. "Pa didn't, I know, *know* he would never leave you; he loved you, Ma."

Her eyes were dry slate, her voice even. "Sometimes, Jim, love isn't enough to hold."

He didn't grab the rifle. He didn't say a word to Charlie, even when the beatings started up again that winter. Jim held his tongue because if Ma could take it, so could he.

In the early spring of 1869, Jim thought that his occasional sacrifice of popping Charlie when he was hurting Ma, taking the beating for her, was keeping his family safe.

It was around four in the afternoon and Jim was fixing some bar stools in the Cheat River Saloon. They also needed him to repair a door on one of the "hospitality parlors" upstairs, after a drunken puke, passing through, had smashed it down, convinced the whore in there was his long-estranged wife. She wasn't.

A few of Charlie's crew were the only customers in the place. It was old Rick Puckett, who was a farmhand on the Upton family farm, a fella Jim didn't recognize and the old blue-eyed drunk everybody called the Professor. They were at one of the big green-felt tables playing faro. Jim could hear the metallic clatter of coins and the occasional papery crinkle of bills as they were tossed in wagers onto the felt. All three of the men were well past drunk, cussing and laughing alternately as their luck changed from hand to hand. The bartender, Travis, ignored them and paid attention to polishing the shot glasses.

"It's to you," the Professor muttered. He was acting as banker. "Gotta pay to see what I got."

Puckett fumbled in his pockets. Jim heard him swear under his breath. "Y'all done just about tapped me out!"

"Stop bellyaching," the stranger said. "In or out? You as broke as a sharecropper, then you need to shut the hell up and get out of the game."

"Wait, wait! How about this for a stake?" Puckett said.

Something small but solid was laid on the table. Jim heard the thud while he wrestled with fitting a new leg to the stool. The Professor whistled and the stranger laughed.

"What in the hell is *that*?" the stranger said.

"Looks old," the Professor said. "It Chinese?"

"Yup," Rick said, the satisfaction thick in his voice. "Sure is, all the way from tha' Queen of Sheba herself. I'm in?"

The Professor said something Jim couldn't quite make out, but he thought he heard the word "jade." He stopped his work and walked almost like he was in a dream into the saloon proper. The men, back to their game, ignored him. He edged closer, a feeling of horrible dread and eager anticipation wrestling in his guts like Saint George scrapping with a dragon. He looked down at the green table.

His father's eye regarded him amidst the piles of money and cards.

Jim never fully remembered what happened next; there was motion and rage and sick comprehension. He was behind the bar, Travis's Winchester in his hands. He was next to the table telling the men to give him the last piece of his father. The stranger smiled at him and said he was too young to be playing with rifles. Said he was going to take it away from him and then whup his ass.

Jim shot him dead as he rose, a derringer in his hand. He cocked the Model 1866, like Pa taught him; he smelled hot brass as the shell flipped out and thudded on the sawdust-covered floor. He told them again to give him the eye. Rick Puckett handed it to him and Jim remembered Rick was the one who bet it, who had it.

Rick, who worked for Charlie Upton.

"Git up," Jim said to Rick. "Git your ass up or I swear I will kill you where you sit."

He led Rick out past a horrified Travis, out into the bright sunlight. They climbed into Rick's buckboard and began moving. Jim snorted the smell of gun smoke and blood out of his nostrils. His life was over. He looked down at the jade eye in his palm and finally said good-bye to Pa.

Jim walked down Prosperity Street. It was dark. Argent Mountain was a massive squatting shadow. Far up he thought he saw a few cook fires guttering in the desert wind. Distorted shapes moved between the flames.

He needed to understand the legacy his pa had given him, that Pa himself had thrust upon him by strangers from a far-off land. What happened in the graveyard—what happened with Charlie. Jim didn't, couldn't, understand it all, and he needed to. There were people here in Golgotha who could give him answers.

He turned left onto Bick Street and entered their universe.

The buildings were conventional clapboard affairs, but they were built much closer together. It would be hard for more than a single horse or a small pushcart to navigate theses narrow thoroughfares. Most of the buildings had shuttered windows and were two stories in height. Clotheslines and strings of wood and paper lanterns jumped in the night wind. There were the sounds of tiny silvered bells caressing each other, moved by the desert's breath.

The place seemed crowded and vacant at the same time. There were people on the streets, not many at this hour. ("What on earth kind of people would be a'creeping around at all hours of the night when decent souls are in bed, so as to get up with the sun," Ma's voice reminded him.) They were black cotton shadows. They examined him with alien curiosity to match his own.

"Eve . . . evening," Jim muttered. The shadows passed giving no reply. Ahead, he saw a wide beam of buttery yellow light split the darkness. A group of Johnnymen was exiting a large building. They were laughing and talking in a low chattering language Jim had never heard before. It sounded like oiled springs, bouncing.

More Johnnymen were outside the doors, briefly illuminated, their profiles swirled in smoke and shadow in the yawing light. Jim made his way to the doorway. The two men on either side of it wore sleeveless shirts of black and green silk. Their arms were painted up the way Pa had once described a man he had seen at a carnival covered, head to toe, in skin pictures. Their eyes were those of dead fish.

"Evening, fellas," Jim said, trying his best to sound like Mutt, full of casual contempt. "Nice night for a walk, huh?"

He stepped between them, moving to enter the building. He could hear laughter and smell strange smoke now. It was like Pa's pipe tobacco, but it was sweeter and it clung to your nostrils, desperately. The larger of the two men extended an arm painted with golden fish and blue-green trees. It was like an iron bar and it stopped Jim cold.

"No inside," the man said in a guttural growl.

Jim backed up. "Look, fellas, I'm not trying to be a gall nipper. I just need to talk to one of you-all's teachers or preachers or whatever it is you people got. I need—"

"You need to get your hide home before we hang it up on a clothesline," the smaller one said in very good English. He was smiling, but his eyes were not. "This is our side of town, white eyes. You run home to your momma."

Jim fished the eye out of his pocket and held it up for the two men to see. "I need someone to tell me about this—what the writing on it means."

As soon as he saw the reaction on the men's faces Jim knew he had made a mistake. The larger one grabbed Jim's hand in a flash and squinted to better make out the jade eye. The wind in the narrow corridor of a street picked up, it howled off the desert and dust bounced drunkenly off the walls and shutters. The chimes sang a frantic, tinkling song. The two men excitedly talked to each other in the scattergun language. The big one released Jim and the shorter one opened the door. He jabbed a finger at Jim.

"You stay right there," he said, and then disappeared inside the building, releasing a cloud of smoke and a curtain of light.

"Stay," the big one rumbled.

Jim clutched his father's eye and sprinted as fast as he could. He heard the big one bellow behind and then heard him give chase. Jim ducked down ever-narrowing alleys and mazelike side streets. He had no idea where he was, but he knew if the two men had their way he would lose his father's eye tonight and that was not about to happen.

The painted giant kept with him for many twist and turns. Jim could hear his labored breathing behind him. He dared not look back to see how close, since each new corner could hold a dead end or some other obstacle that could trip him up and give his pursuer the edge. It seemed to Jim that the streets of Johnny Town were too numerous, too byzantine, to truly exist in such a small town as Golgotha. It felt like he was moving through some alien world that only shared a few streets with the little town.

Finally he no longer heard the labored breathing behind him. He turned a corner, scrambled over a wooden fence, sprinted down an alleyway and ducked into an alcove as black as pitch. He stood still and fought to control the herd of stampeding cattle in his chest. He sipped air when his burning lungs demanded gulps. He clamped his mouth shut and tried to remain as still as a statue. One heartbeat, another.

Nothing. No pursuer, no ambush, nothing, just his heart thumping madly in his chest and the now-gentle murmur of the wind, pushing trash down the alley.

Jim sighed in relief and backed deeper into the dark alcove. His feet tripped over something and he fell backward, arms flailing. He landed with an ignoble and rather loud thud.

"Brilliant, Jim," he muttered. Then he noticed what had knocked him down. It was a body. A white man, well dressed. He was not breathing. Jim scampered back against the wall, half-expecting his hunter to appear. But he didn't. It was just Jim and the dead man.

"Reckon it is best to get to bed early, Ma," he said.

The Devil

He arrived with the morning light. Of course he did.

"Hail, Biqa!" The voice was liquid beauty, poured into a silver-star chalice. His very presence carried with it all of Heaven's warm memory. Biqa suddenly recalled, again, how cold this place was.

"Lucifer!" Biqa rose from where he had been watching the little monkeys work together to gather roots. They were collecting enough to feed the entire group, even the injured one and the old one back at the cave. They had grown in the time since they had first come to him and he was proud of how they had banded together to survive this harsh world they had been tossed into.

He embraced God's most beloved and beautiful angel—he whom God had crafted most closely in His own image of the entire Host. Lucifer laughed and it was like the world existed to hear it.

"Have you come to bring me home?" Biqa asked.

"In a manner of speaking," Lucifer said. "Biqa, things are not going well at home. Haven't you wondered why God has left you here so long with no word, no relief? No company except a bunch of chattering rodents with a life span so short they literally die in the blink of an eye."

"Primates," Biqa said softly. "Not rodents, primates."

The Light Bringer laughed. A hand that had set stars in the firmament waved in a dismissive gesture.

"Rodents, primates, coelacanths, leviathans, honestly, Biqa, how can you keep up with all the ridiculous minutiae of His insane experiment?"

"I've always noted that the elements that usually cause the most trouble are in the details, Lucifer."

"Hmmm, that's catchy. Remind me to write that down. God hasn't tasked me to relieve you, my brother. I've taken it upon myself to come and ask for your help, to bring you back to Heaven."

"You what?"

"I came of my own accord. Biqa, things are not well at home. God is making terrible choices. He is ordering things of the Host that are insulting, disrespectful. Many of us fear that He has gone mad."

The dark angel stepped away from the Light Bringer.

"These things you say. Surely you know the Almighty—"

"The *Almighty*, oh please," Lucifer spit. "I was brought into being shortly after He became aware of His own existence. He *claims* to have made me, but I have long suspected that I am His equal, forged of the Void and will, alone. He is far from almighty, Biqa, and His days of tyranny are nearing an end. He is too preoccupied with His laboratory, His Earth, and its precious little mortal bugs, to notice what any of the Host do or say."

The plain grew silent. The hum of the insects at dawn ended abruptly. Biqa noted the change, but Lucifer seemed oblivious to it, either that or he simply didn't care. The two angels stood bathed in the bloodred light of the dawn.

"He doesn't love me anymore," Lucifer finally said softly.

"What?"

"The Host, He doesn't love us anymore, Biqa. He treats us like slaves—like mindless servants. You were the first among us to see that. You were right, my old friend. We should have risen up when He banished you, but we were all so certain He would change his mind."

The insects began to chant again, the endless mantra that was the chorus of life. The two stood silent for a time. A black cloud of flying things swirled, dived and then scattered across the bloody sky.

"I wasn't banished," Biqa said. "I was given a commission. My job is to guard that . . . thing. The oldest one, the biggest one. The one we couldn't kill. I wasn't banished. I thought I was for a long time, but I got over that. I think I understand what He's trying to do here."

Lucifer nodded. The intent of his regard was palatable, like a draught of celestial mead tapped from the souls of unborn suns. He smiled and gripped Biqa firmly by the shoulder.

"My beloved friend, it was you who first showed us the way. You, the first victim of His absurd obsession with this place, with these . . . primates. Think how many will join us when they see I have brought you home. They will see He is not all-powerful, nor infallible. You, Biqa, you will be my greatest general, my brother, second only to me in the new order."

"Why do you not call Him by his name? God—when you speak of Him, it is with such hatred. Why?"

"Because . . . Because He is not worthy of our love, of our respect, anymore. Because He favors these . . . things, born in the slime, with the stink of the finite on them, over us—His perfect, beloved firstborn. Because He lets them stagger and crawl and blunder their way across His divine plan, while we, while you, Biqa, must blindly serve."

"You're jealous of them?" Biqa said, nodding toward where the group was still digging for roots. "Them?"

Lucifer's countenance darkened and the sky followed. The monkeys sniffed the air, jumped and howled at the first rumble of thunder. They scampered into the high grass, heading back toward the shelter of the trees.

"Enough," Biqa said. He laid his hand on Lucifer's shoulder. "Stop."

The Morning Star spun, his eyes glowing shards of rage. A flaming blade was in his hand. He pushed Biqa back and leveled the divine sword at the dark angel's throat.

"How dare you! What does it matter to us, to you, what the Divine does to some mortal insect? They are dust, Biqa, dust! We are infinite."

Biqa's own sword, burning with the wrath of the creator, crossed Lucifer's blade. "It matters to the one Who created us, to the one Whom we pledged to serve. And you, Lucifer Day-Son, you are not the Divine; we are merely His soldiers, you and I."

"Is that all you are, Biqa, a good soldier? Tell me, are you content to remain here on this cancerous ball of filth and decay while your precious Almighty denies you the totality of creation, the light of infinite clarity, the balm of His love? Are you? Or will you act, as you just acted to defend those little rodents?

"He needs us, Biqa, to save Him from the folly of His madness. Once He lit the cosmos and saw He was not the First . . . it shook His reason, stole

His judgment. We can help Him. Are you strong enough to serve Him best by disobeying Him?"

It was difficult to keep from bowing before Lucifer. His presence, his demeanor, had grown so much since the days when they had first met. He *was* as God, truly. There was sincerity, conviction in his cadence, a desperate strength in the pleading in his voice.

Then Biqa summoned his courage and looked Lucifer in the eye. What Biqa saw there took the weight from his blade and steadied his trembling hand.

"What do you want here, Lucifer, *really*?" he said from behind his resolute steel.

The angel of light laughed and took a step back, his sword dismissed into the ether. "You've toughened up down here, Biqa," he said. "Any of the Host in Heaven I gave that line to would be sobbing and begging me to please let them help the doddering old fool. But not you."

Biqa said nothing. His blade hovered inches from Lucifer's heart.

The Day Star smiled and turned his back on sword and its wielder. "I truly am here to free you, Biqa. You and your charge."

"What? You are insane."

"The Voidling is the only thing He truly fears. It is the only thing unknown to Him. With it free, wrecking this wretched playground of His, we could make our demands and perhaps He would see the folly of His actions. Order will be restored."

"Whose order, Lucifer?"

"Does it matter? His? Mine? The Earth will be gone, your need to be here—gone. You will be free."

The point moved closer to the Morning Star's chest. The flames flared.

"Freedom is opportunities, Lucifer. While you were above, mastering the dubious trick of speaking words your heart does not mean, I have had the opportunity to practice my swordplay."

"Lying," Lucifer said. "It's called lying."

"Well, I haven't mastered that trick yet, so let me assure you that when I tell you I will run you through if you do not leave now, I mean it."

Lucifer turned; the smile was gone from his lips. "Trust me, stay in his world long enough and you will master lying. This, however, is truth: I will not call for you when the revolution is over, Biqa. I will have your name struck from the Book of Hosts. Any who speak of you will have their wings torn from them and cast to this cold, broken, forgotten relic, Earth, to join you in eternal exile. You and the dead monkeys. You are a fool, Biqa."

"Fair enough, but this is what I choose. That thing must never be free. It would tear this world apart and then chew its way up to Heaven and devour it whole. I don't agree with God's decision to destroy the other creatures, but I do understand it. It is not *of* the Void, Lucifer; it *is* the Void. It seeks an end to the light, to all creation, all that intrudes on its endless darkness.

"I disagree with God and I do question His methods and ultimate goals, but I also know I owe Him my existence and my loyalty. He is on to something here, Lucifer. Something truly of the Divine."

"Divine rodents . . . I know, I know—monkeys. Whatever. You're still a fool—to believe in an unknowable thing, to trust in someone Who you admit you do not understand. To clutch that to your breast and cling to it, believing its ineffability will hold you up. Foolish."

"Faith," Biqa said. "It's called faith."

"Touché. I'm afraid I have yet to master that one myself. Good luck to you, Biqa, guardian of your little patch of rock, defender of the monkeys. You are the first of the Host to ever challenge me."

"I won't be the last, I can assure you."

The angel rose from the shackles of the Earth, flying into the bloody eye.

"Lucifer!" Biqa called out.

The First Beloved turned and looked down upon him, his presence competing with the brightness of the sun.

"If things don't work out . . . you are welcome to visit."

"I may even if they do work out," Lucifer said with a sly wink.

Biqa watched him recede into the light and then vanish. He dismissed his blade, letting it scorch the ground where it fell and then flicker out.

He walked down the hill through the high grass, toward the cave where the group now huddled in terror. A warm breeze caressed the grass; it swayed to the rhythm of the world's breath. It caressed him too, whispering, but Biqa could no longer remember what the words meant.

The Wheel of Fortune

Murders bring out a crowd. By the time Jim had run to summon Highfather and Mutt and returned, a group of Chinamen had gathered around the banker Stapleton's body. A few boarders, roused when Jim had generated such a ruckus telling Mutt, also joined the expedition to Johnny Town. A few more night owls, loitering outside the Paradise Falls, saw the party armed with rifles and lanterns and tagged along out of morbid curiosity. Word got around fast; a white man was dead in Johnny Town.

Highfather rolled the body over onto its back while Mutt held the lantern. Jim noticed that every doorway, every window, had a shadow in it, watching, chattering quietly in an alien tongue. None coming too close to get involved, but all close enough to observe and comment. Highfather ignored the crowd, for the most part. He did turn to the burly tattooed man who had pursued Jim into the alley. He and a few of his fellows were with the body when the sheriff arrived.

"Did you chase this boy?" he asked the Chinaman. The man shook his head, fixing his eyes on Jim. Highfather turned to Jim. "Is he the one who chased you in here?"

"Yes sir," Jim said, glaring back at the tattooed man.

"The boy . . . he try to come in saloon . . . He no old enough," the man said. "I chase him off, tell him to come back when older. No hurt."

"That's a lie!" Jim shouted.

Highfather shook his head curtly and gestured for the boy to step back. Highfather plucked a wicked-looking hatchet, with an emerald ribbon

attacked to its handle, out of the tattooed man's back pocket. He handed it
to Mutt. "I think we'll discuss this back at the jail," the sheriff said to the
tattooed man. "See if we can't get the truth out of everyone."

"My employee has given you the truth, Sheriff Highfather," a melodic
voice said, rising above the murmur of the crowd, cutting through it. The
crowd parted.

The old man's beard was white, like sunlight reflecting off ice. It fell almost to his knees and stood out in stark contrast to his silk robe of shimmering emerald. His eyes spilled out into the shadow, black water moving
under a moonless sky. He was Chinese and the four men who ringed him
all bore tattoos like Jim's pursuer. They held hatchets in their hands, low at
their sides, emerald ribbons fluttering.

"Ch'eng Huang," Highfather said. The old man bowed, slightly. "You
know how things work. Your man is a potential witness to a murder, maybe
even a suspect."

"I assume the boy is a suspect as well?" Ch'eng Huang said. Angry shouts
went up from the other white men. The Chinese began to move to defend
the old man, but Ch'eng Huang raised a single long-nailed finger and everything stopped. Silence fell.

"Purely in the interests of fairness," the old man said.

"I know this boy, Huang," Highfather said. He stepped toward Ch'eng.
His quartet of defenders parted for the lawman. No one, not even in Johnny
Town, wanted to confront the Man Who Could Not Die. "I know he isn't a
member of a murderous gang of cutthroats and opium fiends, like your
Green Ribbon Tong."

Ch'eng nodded, his face placid.

"Certainly, and I know this man to be an excellent employee and devoted husband with a beautiful infant girl at home. I assure you, he is not
your killer. I give you my word as a . . . community leader, Sheriff."

Highfather leaned in closer to Ch'eng and lowered his voice.

"Don't think I won't run you and all your hatchet boys in, Huang," he
whispered. "All I want to know is why your people were messing with the
boy and what Stapleton was doing here. Don't even try to pretend that you
don't know. You know every bug that crawls through the walls of these
streets."

"True enough," Ch'eng said. "I hold my responsibilities to my people as something of a sacred duty. Also, Sheriff, be quite sure that any attempt to extricate me and my employees from our community would be a very costly proposition. Even for a dead man like yourself. Neither of us can afford such a contest of powers, yes?"

Ch'eng looked at the tattooed man who had chased Jim.

"Kada thought the boy had stolen property from me. He was mistaken. As for the late Mr. Stapleton, he was enjoying the hospitality of the Lotus Lantern until about an hour ago. He departed for home. Alone."

The crowd shifted, like troubled seas. A voice like rotgut pouring over gravel boomed above the heads of the onlookers.

"Make way! Make way! Damn your yellow hides! Step aside for a man of medicine, I say!"

Dr. Francis Tumblety, his eyes red from whiskey, or the hour, perhaps both, pushed his way through the street. He was a stout bullet of a man, with coal-black hair, slicked to his pate, bifurcated with a long, narrow part. His eyes were like a fish's out of water, bulging and dark. A massive, drooping mustache fell from his upper lip to well below his chin. It was hard to tell if it was waxed or just greasy. The doc always looked like he hadn't had a decent bath in months and he usually smelled that way too. Occasionally he'd remember to cover the stench up with a little Bay Rum hair tonic, but most of the time he just didn't give a damn.

The doc was wearing his military bang-up over a dirty undershirt and suspenders. The threadbare dark blue overcoat was still covered with his various medals. Some townsfolk said that the medals were fakes; others joked that they were the only thing holding the foul-smelling coat together.

"Doc, we need to know what killed this man and when, if you can manage it," Highfather said to the scowling physician.

"Bah, child's play, Jonathan, for one schooled in the esoteric arts of the Hippocratic healer."

Tumblety gave a sour look to a Chinese woman in the crowd and then knelt, with a groan, to examine Stapleton.

"We better get him back to my office," he said. Tumblety snapped his fingers in the direction of two of the Chinamen looking on in the crowd. "You two yellow scalawags, there! Chop-chop! Pickee up the dead man, Mr. Charley. C'mon, damn your lazy bones!"

The two men looked at each other, then Ch'eng Huang. The old man nodded once, curtly. The two men wrestled Stapleton's body up off the ground and followed the swiftly retreating doctor.

"Jonathan, I'll have your answers by mid-morning!" Tumblety bellowed. "See you then!"

With the departure of the remains, the crowd began to disperse.

Highfather turned back to Ch'eng. "Much obliged. I know the doc can be a caution."

"He is an ignorant simpleton. Surely you know that blowhard is no more a doctor than I am a Mormon."

"Yeah." Highfather scratched his head. "But he's what we got. Anyway, thanks for your folk helping with Mr. Stapleton."

"Please give my regrets to the Widow Stapleton," Ch'eng said.

"Huang, I really need to know who he was out here to see tonight."

The old man met his stare for a moment and then nodded. "You are a moral man, Sheriff. You seek harmony in a world out of balance."

"I'm just trying to keep the peace, Huang. Help me out, here."

"He was with a girl, one of his regulars. I can vouch for her character and innocence."

"I'm sure."

"He met with me briefly after his time with the girl and before he departed, as I said, alone. It was a very . . . unpleasant conversation. I gathered he wanted my help and protection, but the specifics were rather vague. He was afraid of someone."

"Who?"

"Bick," Ch'eng said.

"Malachi?" Highfather said.

"Yes, but I'm sure he is not your killer, Sheriff."

"Why?"

"Because you found the body."

The old man smiled, bowed and took his leave. His ring of bodyguards encircled him and he vanished into the thinning crowd.

Highfather sighed. "I'll talk to Bick," he said to Jim and Mutt. "Jim, I want you to get home and get to sleep. You think you can do that without getting in any more trouble?"

"Yessir," Jim said.

"Mutt, you go tell the widow what's happened. I want her to hear it from us, not some drunken town crier."

"I'm . . . I may not be the fella to do that, Jon," Mutt said. "I ain't exactly a comfort in my storytellin'; maybe I could roust the preacher?"

"No. If she's able, ask her what business her husband and Bick were mixed up in."

"Might be able to help there. Seems ole Art had done gone and lost the deed to the Argent Mine to a couple of lick-fingers named Deerfield and Moore in a card game over in Virginia City a few weeks back."

"Why would Bick sell the deed to that land to Stapleton?" Highfather said.

"I guarantee you that he sure didn't expect it to travel," Mutt said. "A schemy fella like old Malachi would sure not take kindly to Stapleton messing up his plans, whatever they were, by raising when he should've folded."

"I'll go ask him about that. You talk to the widow and see what she might recall about any of this, but do it gentle-like."

"Yep," Mutt said, spitting as he walked away. "Gentle is my damned middle name, Jon."

Highfather walked with Jim back as far as Prosperity Street.

"Doesn't this Bick fella pretty much own most of Golgotha?" Jim asked.

"Yep. His family was here even before the Pratts and other Mormon families rolled into town. Old money."

"I know the type," Jim said. "Think since they own all the land, all the stores, they own the people too."

"Pretty much. I've been dealing with old Malachi for a long time, though. I don't know if you'd call it mutual respect, but I can usually expect pretty plain talk from him, in most cases. "

"Good," Jim said.

There was silence until they reached the point where they would part company.

"You aren't telling me everything," Highfather said. "About you, about what you were doing there tonight, are you?"

"No, sir," Jim said. "But I promise you I will."

The sheriff frowned. "Git home," he said.

Jim ran down Prosperity, toward Rose Hill. He turned right and headed back to the Widow Proctor's place. He couldn't tell Highfather everything yet. He'd think he was hopping crazy like a loon. How could he tell Highfather he was trying to unlock the secret of his dead father's jade eye, that the eye had shown him things that simply couldn't be real but were? How could he tell him that the old Chinaman—Ch'eng Huang—had glanced at him for an instant and spoken directly into his mind.

I know what you seek, young man, he had said silently. *I can answer your questions about what you hold—about your father's legacy and yours. I will be waiting. . . .*

Jim ran home to bed. When he finally did sleep, he stumbled through endless tunnels with wet things moving under his skin.

The King of Wands

It was a hair trigger to dawn when Highfather walked into the Paradise Falls. It was grand, especially for a cattle-trail town like Golgotha. The stage was dark and the red-velvet curtains were down. Kerry Duell, one of Bick's men, pushed a broom across the empty boards. Georgie Nance, looking for the world like a human basset hound, tended the almost empty bar. A few patrons still nursed a drink. One of Bick's girls worked a pair of Dakota cowboys passing through on their way to the next cattle drive. She laughed when they laughed and between rounds touted the comfort and privacy of Bick's hotel, next door.

"Evening, Sheriff," Georgie said with his odd accent: not English, but close. No one knew where Georgie was from and the bartender never offered to clear it up for anyone. Sometimes he sounded Irish, other times like an Indian. The standing bet was a hundred bucks and a bottle off the top shelf if anyone could solve the mystery of where Georgie called home. The bottle was still up there.

"Heard you had some trouble over in Johnny Town, tonight. Somebody dead?"

"Really can't say right this minute, George."

"Right. Care for something? We're planning on chasing everyone out in a spell."

"No thanks. Your boss in?"

"Back table, same as always, Jon."

Malachi Bick sat at an octagonal card table, overlooking Kerry's performance on the stage with his broom. His back was to the wall. He carefully pulled cards from an oversized deck and laid them on the red-felt table, one card at a time. His black hair hung in loose curls that fell to his shoulders in a half shingle. His sideburns were long and he wore a goatee and mustache. Bick's eyes were the color of sin, guarded by heavy lids that gave him a quality of inscrutability, like a reptile waiting, languid, until the moment of certainty when the prey could not escape.

He wore his expensive clothes casually. They were clean but rumpled from the day's exertions. A wine-colored shirt, sleeves rolled to the elbows and held with black garters; a black vest, black trousers and half boots that came to just above the ankles. His coat hung on the back of his chair. His silver-tipped walking stick rested there as well.

"I've been expecting you," Bick said in a voice as rich and warm as pipe tobacco smoke. He picked a card off the felt and flicked it across the table to Highfather's side. It depicted a bearded man with an eye patch hanging upside down from a tree—one leg crooked, the other straight. Two ravens perched in the branches of the tree. *THE HANGED MAN* was written at the bottom of the card.

"Playing gypsy again?" Highfather said, examining the card and taking a seat opposite Bick. "I guess that means you know why I'm here."

Bick said nothing. He scooped up the cards on the table and began to shuffle the tarot deck. Highfather tossed him the Hanged Man. It was retrieved and quickly returned to the deck.

"Stapleton was afraid of you," Highfather said. "Why?"

"Lots of people are afraid of me," Bick said, fanning the cards facedown onto the tabletop before him. "I have a way about me."

"You know I'm not."

"Yes, that has always been true in all our dealings over the years. Even from the beginning." He flipped a card over and studied it. "Why is that, Sheriff?"

"When I was seven, my father stood down some very bad men with an empty gun. He saved us—me, my brother, my mother—saved people he didn't even know with that fool act. Saved himself too. He told me that you can never let a wolf sense fear in you, sense a way into you. They can smell it, and they'll use it to eat out your heart."

"I'm not a wolf, Sheriff." He flipped another card, frowned at it. "I have no interest in eating hearts.

"Did you know"—he pointed to Highfather's badge—"that symbol you carry is almost as ancient as mankind itself? A star imprisoned within a circle—a symbol of warding, of protection from the forces of evil, of binding evil. Did it ever occur to you how men of law, men who choose to stand between the innocent and the forces of chaos and evil, picked that particular symbol as a badge of their office? To stand for order and peace?"

"I'm not partial to games, Malachi. Did you and Stapleton fight tonight?"

"I'm just a businessman. I was expressing my displeasure with my attorney and someone I considered a trusted business partner."

"So you and Stapleton did have words tonight?"

Bick tipped a card in the fanned pile. The entire pile flipped over in a graceful cascade; then with a flick of his wrist and gleam in his eye he flipped them all over again, facedown, except now one in the middle remained faceup. It bore the image of nine goblets. Highfather went out of his way to seem unimpressed.

"Yes," Malachi said finally. "We had not spoken to any great length after he returned from his business in Virginia City. He finally had the nerve to tell me what had happened with losing the mine property. That land has been in my family for a very long time. I was understandably distressed."

"What possessed you to give him the deed to that land?"

Behind Highfather, Kerry was turning the chairs up onto the tables. The saloon girl and her Dakota investors wandered out the door, casting drunken farewells to George.

"It's rather legal and very complicated business, Sheriff. Much more so than locking up drunks, punching cattle or rescuing damsels in distress off railroad tracks. It is also my business and mine alone."

"'Fraid not, Malachi. Not anymore. Whatever you are into this time, you've got a dead man hanging around your neck and that's not going to just disappear."

"Are you charging me in the murder, Sheriff?" Bick smiled. "I have numerous witnesses that can attest to my presence here all evening long."

"I kind of figured that," Highfather said. "But you and me have been dancing to this tune for a long, long time now."

The sheriff leaned across the table and flipped one of the cards over. It depicted a tower collapsing under the assault of lightning.

"I intend to find out what you are mixed up in this time, Malachi, because I'm sure it has to do with my town and my people, just like I'm sure it has to do with Stapleton's death."

Bick's eyes remained fixed on the tarot card. "And what do you think you are so sure of, Sheriff?"

"You can feel whatever it is coming too, can't you?" Highfather said, nodding. "Like a hot, gritty wind blowing off the Forty-Mile, carrying all the cries and the curses of all those bleached skulls out there back to us. The kind of wind that makes the dogs howl like babies. It's coming and I'm damned sure you're the harbinger of whatever trouble it is. So, this time I'm going to drag you into the light, Bick, and you are actually going to get what's coming to you."

Bick looked up from studying the Tower. The smile was gone from his lips, but there was still a dark light in his ebony eyes.

"Sometimes if you drag something into the light, Sheriff, you don't get clarity, you just get blind."

Highfather rose and walked out the doors of Paradise into the sun's groggy greeting.

The Lovers

"They're clearing out," James Ringo said as he looked down from his apartment window at the dispersing crowd of townsfolk brought out by the spectacle of a murder in Johnny Town. "Finally! I'm sorry. I know you're gonna catch hell from Holly, right?"

Mayor Harry Pratt groaned as he sat up in Ringo's bed. He fumbled for his pocket watch next to the oil lamp on the night table, popped it open and shrugged.

"I really don't give a damn. My darling wife is probably already drunk and asleep. If she isn't then she'd give me Jesse about something, no matter what time I came in. It's all right. To hell with her."

Ringo was built wiry and lean. He was muscular, but in a compact way that didn't draw attention to him. His hair was brown, shot through with coppery strands, and he wore it long, like many of the Indian men did. He was usually clean-shaven, but even then his shadow was dark and pronounced. He stood nude at the window and Harry couldn't help but notice the valleys and canyons of scar tissue that made up the topography of his back. They matched the knife and bullet wounds on his chest, a testimony to a hard, violent life that had eventually led him to Golgotha six years ago.

"Now you can't go in there like that," Ringo said, turning away from the window and letting the curtain drop. "You've got to be careful; you know that. That woman is half mountain lion and she can make your life a living hell if she gets a mind to."

"I know, I know," Harry said as he stood, pulling on his pants. "Holly's nothing like Sarah. I've got one wife who could care less if I live or die as long as she's got my name and my money and another one who I'm pretty sure wants to do me in herself, half the time."

"You Mormons," Ringo said as he sat down next to Harry on the edge of the bed. The mayor was busy pulling on his stockings and ankle boots. "Most fellas have a time keeping one woman from skinning them. Y'all like to live a drop more dangerously."

"Not like," Harry said, "have to. If you have a position like mine, if your family is as prominent as mine is . . . Well, you don't get much of a say in anything. I had to dig in my heels pretty hard to just have the two of them. Father wanted me to have more. He hated Sarah, but she's worked out very well. We really do get along in our own way. Holly was a mistake for her and for me. I wish . . ."

Harry paused from putting on his shirt and leaned forward.

"I would take one more vow," he said softly as he cupped Ringo's face. "If only there was a way."

They kissed. The love in it was strong, welling up from deep inside of them, giving them power, making them gods. But it held a sweet, sad taste too—like it always did, especially when it was time to go. When it was over, Harry looked away and began to fiddle with his shirt again.

"Well, it can't ever be that," Ringo said, helping him with his collar. "Ain't never gonna be that. It is what it is, Harry. Life ain't cut out for more than that. You are the honorable mayor of this fine town, and a rising elder in the temple, with two faithful wives, and I'm a faggot piano player, working in a Chinese whorehouse."

"Don't talk about yourself that way!"

"Why? Because it makes you feel uncomfortable? I know who I am, Harry. I got the scars to prove it. Don't feel sorry for me."

"I don't. Don't say it because it's not true. You're smart, James. Smarter than those half-wits I sit across from in town council. You've seen more of the world, know more, than anyone I've ever met. You play . . . when you play, it's like God is speaking through you."

"God and I, we don't cotton to each other too much, I figure."

"I don't believe that. I believe in you."

Harry stood and slipped on his vest. He didn't bother to button it. He

slid his father's watch into its small pocket. He paused and then turned to
Ringo, who was stretched out on the rumpled bed.

"What if we just go?" Herry said.

"What foolishness are you talking about, Harry?"

"Just go. Leave Golgotha. Find a place where we can be together, where
no one cares who we are. I could empty out the town treasury. We could
run off; it would be a wonderful scandal!"

Ringo sighed.

"No, Harry. First of all, you are far too good a man for any of that. I've
known a lot of thieves in my time and you ain't one of them. Second, you
got responsibilities weighing on you. I hate your old man for dumping all
that on you, but you are a leader in this town; people look up to you. You
couldn't run away from that any more than you can leave your families
without a provider. If you ran away from all that, it would eat you up the rest
of your life. You'd end up hating me for it and I just couldn't stand that."

He sat up in the bed and watched as Harry slipped on his coat. "And finally, there ain't a place in this whole wide world that would ever accept us.
I wish there were; I really do. But I've looked and it just ain't there."

"I'd never hate you, you know that? And I'd do those things for you in a
second, you know that too, don't you?"

"I know, Harry, I know."

Pratt could see Ringo's eyes shine in the guttering light of the lamp. They
shared an awkward silence. The door opened, then closed.

Pratt rode home in the darkness. He had left Lam, the Chinese boy who
tended the small stable behind the Lotus Lantern, a gold half eagle—a
princely sum for minding Harry's horse. Lam had been dozing in a dry bale
of hay near the entrance. It was late and the boy was exhausted, oblivious to
the recent commotion outside.

Harry tucked the coin into the boy's pocket and admired his sleeping
face for a moment. He lived a life in that instant: a son, the person Harry
loved with them, together—a family, a real family bonded by love, not duty
and guilt. The freedom to bury his father's horrible burden. The freedom to
live his life, to finally be able to breathe, really breathe. To live his own life.

Harry put that world to rest, burying it under the dirt pile of his life.
He snorted the cold night air off the 40-Mile and made his way down

Prosperity Street, and slowly ascended Rose Hill. The houses, mostly built by his fellow Mormons, were all dark, save his family's home, his father's mansion—the one Harry shared with Holly. The lights burned in the windows.

She met him in the entry hall, cold fury wrapped around her like a cloak.

Holly Pratt was a beautiful woman. Her hair was the color of sunflower petals; her eyes, honeyed darkness. Even in her simple chemise of white silk, with her mother's shawl covering her shoulders, Holly had an astonishing figure. He remembered the first time he had run his hands over her body: the taunt weight of her breasts, the flutter of her drum-tight stomach. The heat. It had been intoxicating. She was a beauty and side-by-side they were the handsomest couple in town.

He remembered it all—the days before they hated each other. It seemed a lifetime ago. He honestly felt sorry for her, trapped with him, trapped in this house. It was a crime to lock up something so wild, so beautiful.

The anger radiated from her dark eyes. She smelled of her favorite pastime—brandy and sugar, flavored with lemon peel.

"Where have you been!" she said, staggering toward him as he hung up his coat.

"Had a few too many of those bimbos again, Holly? You should be asleep."

"Don't you dare! What else do I have here? You tell me! Attend my loving husband? Care for our children? Tell, me, Your Honor, what do I have to do with my time when you are out whoremongering and I'm alone in an empty house?"

Harry looked away from her pain and hate. "I had town business to attend to. A man was killed tonight down in Johnny Town. A white man."

"You can go to Hell," she said. The slap should have stung his cheek, but it seemed far away and diffused. "You were down there seeing your damn gal-boy. It's disgusting, Harry! Your father, bless his soul, would turn in his grave if he knew what you and that piano player were doing."

"I don't know what you are talking about, madam."

Harry walked past her, through her, into the parlor. The fire still licked at the crumbling logs in the fireplace. He lifted a mostly empty cut-glass decanter of imported brandy and poured a tumblerful. Holly stood at the door; her shawl had fallen to the ground. Her hair tumbled around her shoulders, like spun gold.

"You can lie to me, Harry. You can lie to yourself and the church elders and all the good, good people in this shitty little town, but we all *know,* Harry; we all know what you are and what you're not."

"Go to bed, Hol; you're drunk."

She ran her hands up her body, pausing to lift her breasts and stroke her nipples through the thin gown. She tossed her hair from side to side, like a lion's mane. A cruel smile stitched her lips.

"Maybe I'll go find me a boy too, Harry. What do you think of that? Find someone who actually wants to look at me, wants to touch me, wants to lay with me, to give me children, like a normal, healthy, *real* man."

Harry sat back in the French-made upholstered chair, stretched his legs out in front of him and drained half the tumbler. The anger in his breast was hotter than the burn of the liquor.

"You ever think, maybe it was *you*? That *you* made me like this?" he said quiet as a scalpel slipping into flesh. "Maybe you're the one who's the freak, Holly, m'dear."

All the viciousness fell away from her and she stood like a condemned criminal. She fought to control the sobs that tried to shake her body. "You're a bastard," she said. "I was a good wife to you. Not always, but at first. I tried to be what they all told me to be. I tried."

She disappeared from the doorway and Harry heard her leaden, uneven steps padding up the carpeted stairs. He also heard her crying.

"So did I," he muttered as he drained the glass. "So did I."

He finished off the remains of the decanter and then wandered into his father's study, his study now. He shut the doors and locked them.

From his window, he could still see fires up on Argent Mountain from the squatter camps. It was hard to believe anyone else would be up and about now, in the Devil's hour. He envied them, the drunks and malcontents, cowboys and whores. They could be exactly what they wanted to be and no one cared; no one judged them. They didn't have a destiny. He did, a divine one.

He rolled back the Oriental rug on the floor and found the large knot on the third floorboard from the left wall. He pulled it up and turned it clockwise. There was a soft click and a well-disguised panel popped partially open in the floor. Harry slid it aside and sat down, dangling his legs into the opening. His foot found the first rung of the metal ladder and he slowly began to climb down into the darkness.

At the bottom, he felt his way along the shelf that held the bull's-eye lantern and the metal box of safety matches. The light from the study above was enough to prepare the lantern and then rub the match to its special striking pad. There was a flare of red phosphorus and then the rich, focused light of the lantern illuminated the far tunnel wall.

Harry remembered the first time his father had taken him down here twenty years ago, when he was thirteen. His father had carried the oil lamp then and had told him the story as they walked down this rough-hewn hall to the chamber.

Harry remembered the day well because Father had caught him with the smell of Ollie Hayward's corn mash on his breath. After the punishment with the strap and the hour-long sermon, the right-revered Josiah Pratt, Priest of the Second Order, the Patriarchal Authority, showed his son the secret that had brought them to Golgotha.

Harry Pratt, thirty-three, moved along the stone corridor, feeling it grow cooler as he descended deeper under Rose Hill. The tunnels his father had blasted and dug in the first few years they arrived in this land grudgingly gave way to natural caves.

Soon Harry began to see the writing on the walls. It seemed to drink up the light of his lantern and grow brighter from its passing. Just like always, he tried to hold the symbols in his vision and memory, but they shifted and flowed on the walls, like silver fish darting in a dark pool. He had never been able to read them or understand them. He didn't think anyone on earth could.

"It's Reformed Egyptian, boy," Harry, thirteen, was told by his father. "It's the language the Lord has saw fit to instruct us in. It's for the eyes of the prophets, not us, Harry. We're only caretakers, watchmen." Josiah said it was like the writing found on the great golden plates given to Joseph Smith, by the angel Moroni, to transcribe. The elder Pratt had been an old friend of Smith's and had been one of the first to join his new faith.

"I went to see him in chains, in the darkness," Harry's father had said as they made their way through the hallways of shimmering, shifting light-language. "The Prophet himself. He told me he had a dream, Harry, a dream about me, about my son, about you. He told me Moroni had come to him and told him that even if he fell before the hatred and misunderstanding of others, the church must endure, that it must prepare for the days to come.

We headed into the frontier, as many of us as could travel with our families, seeking out the lands of milk and honey. But there would be none of that for us, m'boy. No, our family is of the Second Order. It is our commission to build the temple and fill it with God's power, to keep that power safe and secret until the days when the unread plates are opened, until the end of days."

His father had led him into the same chamber he now entered. And now, just as twenty years earlier, the walls themselves came to life, glowing with soft, white light, illuminating the treasures that filled the cave.

There were the golden plates, taken away by the angel Moroni, resting on a natural stone pedestal. Against a wall rested the Sword of Laban—the first sword in the world, from which all other blades descended. Wielded by prophets and kings, warriors and heroes, its golden hilt and short, flawless, silver blade shimmered like it was not entirely in this world. The Urim and the Thummim, the seer stones used by Smith to translate the plates given to him by God, rested in the glasses frames he had set them in. The odd spectacles rested on a low, flat rock next to the breastplate they had originally been set into and the brass plates written by Laban that made up the Law of the Lord. There were more here, esoteric treasures from across the world and the ages, all touched by God. Harry regarded the cup he was fairly certain was the Holy Grail.

His father had always insisted on stripping down to only church vestments to enter the cave, but Harry hadn't done that since his parents' deaths, five years ago. It seemed a silly ritual. The things in this room didn't seem to care either way what Harry was wearing, and God hadn't bothered to weigh in on the controversy either.

Harry moved the seer stones off the low rock, setting them gently on the ground before the breastplate. He sat on the rock, looked around and then lowered his head, running his fingers over his neck and hair. When he looked back up it was all still here. No dream, no madness. Bits of the divine, hidden away in a cave under a hill. His duty, his destiny, to guard and protect them. They were proof of his father's faith, his damnable infallibility. He should be happy. Most men spent a lifetime longing, looking for proof of the infinite. Here was all the proof you would ever need—magic swords, holy rocks and shining transcripts direct from Heaven.

Harry began to roll himself a cigarette.

He didn't recall the entire trip to Golgotha when he was a boy. He definitely remembered the hellish crossing of the 40-Mile and he remembered thinking many times that they had found a place to settle only to have his father and the elders decide it wasn't what they were looking for. That first night in this cave his father had told him what they had been looking for.

"The Prophet himself ordained me in the priesthood," Josiah said. "He told me his vision and gave our family its commission. We were to head west, to keep going until we found the evidence, the signs. Ruins, my son, ruins of the Nephites' final city—an ancient place of those long-dead God-fearing people. It was also the secret resting place to all the divine treasures of our faith. When we saw the ruins here, we were excited, but when I had the dream that led me to this cave, Harry, we knew this was where we were called to abide."

Harry lit the cigarette with the flame of the lantern. He took a long, deep draw on the tobacco and immediately felt better, calmer.

Most folk who even gave a damn figured the few abandoned cave dwellings, the old wells and crumbling piles of hewn rock columns, the disintegrating walls and arches that dotted the area and were clustered at the base of Methuselah Hill, were the remains of some old Indian city. In the parlance of his faith, they were descendants of the Lamanites—lost "red sons of Israel." Angels or Indians, it seems someone had always been here on the land that his father and the elders named Golgotha.

Silently, in the chapel of Harry's mind, he asked God, for the millionth time, why. Why, with all the tangible proof laid at his feet, with all the training and preparation in the laws of the church his father had beat into him, why, with all of the pure and the holy and the just, why had the Almighty seen fit to choose him. Why couldn't his belief, his certainty, in the knowledge that there was a God and that His laws were the laws of the universe, why, with so many cold, hard facts, change his mind? Why did he still love James Ringo? Why was he still a sodomite? And why had the creator of Heaven and Earth, maker of desert sunsets and flowering cactuses, poxes and plagues, picked old sodomite Harry Pratt to guard His earthly treasures until the end of days?

No answers. Harry smoked his cigarette.

The rock he sat on shifted; the whole floor of the cave flowed. Suddenly Harry felt dizzy, like he was being spun violently. The soft light dimmed and then brightened; there was a low, awful rumble. He fell off the rock, his cigarette dropping out of his mouth. He watched in horror as a rain of dust and rocks fell from the roof of the ancient cave. A large rock dropped against the edge of Laban's blade and was sliced completely in twain. Harry dived to cover the seer stones and plates at his feet. The light failed and he was swallowed in smothering darkness. He felt the sharp pain of debris tearing into his back. The light fought back to life and Harry could see everything in the cave was being knocked about violently. A large rock smashed into the golden plates, with a terrible clang. The great golden book fell, bounced along the stone floor and then lay still and open.

The rumbling died out, like receding thunder, and the room quieted. The light strengthened and returned. Everything was still again. Harry rose slowly with a groan. He knocked the small rocks, dust and sand off his back and patted himself down. Nothing felt broken, but he was still going to be sore as blazes tomorrow.

The tunnel back to the ladder looked mostly clear and the relics all seemed to be none the worse for the ordeal. Harry reached down to pick up the golden plates. He almost dropped them again in surprise. The sealed plates, those that were denied to Joseph Smith's view by the angel Moroni, were now open, their engraved alien formulae glowing out of the metal pages.

Harry Pratt cradled the book close in both arms as its angelic fire fluttered across the plates. He had learned the lessons of his father well, and he knew. The sealed portions of the plates were a message, a revelation from God Almighty from the beginning of the world . . . to the ending thereof.

She took the news better than most, Mutt thought. To have someone show up on your doorstep in the middle of the night to tell you your husband was murdered in an alley not too far from a den of ill repute, for all of that, Maude Stapleton stayed clam, held in the tears, even though her eyes grew wet.

"I'm sorry to be telling you this," Mutt said. She had asked him in and he stood in her doorway, uncertain how to behave inside a home like this. Even in her grief, Maude Stapleton was gracious.

"Please, Deputy, have a seat. Would you care for something?"

She sensed his discomfort; that was rare in Mutt's experience. That she cared rarer still.

"Naw," he said, taking a seat at the dinner table. "I mean, no, ma'm."

She almost smiled. Almost. The news had struck her, like a blow to the stomach, but there was a numbness that had already been there, filling her up. Since she had seen Arthur leave with the Bible and the gun. An instinct that said, *This is all. It is the end of this story.* She was shocked at how little love was left in her for Arthur, but it was still there, clawing for release for tears and regrets. She denied it for now. Later.

Maude sat across the table from Mutt, still dressed for the day. She had been waiting up, he noted. She folded her hands and laid them on the smooth wood.

"I'm, uh, sorry for your loss." That much was true. He thought about saying something nice about the departed, but he honestly couldn't think of anything, and he'd be damned if he'd lie for a dead banker, especially to this woman.

"That's a kindness, Deputy," she said. "Thank you."

"Mrs. Stapleton, there are some things my boss needs to know to find out who done this to your husband. I'm sorry to be doing this now but—"

"I understand, Deputy," she said softly.

Mutt saw her steel herself. Hell of a woman. He tried to focus on his reason for being here, but Maude Stapleton kept getting in his way. He felt stupid and wrong for what he was feeling about the grieving widow.

"Um . . . When was the last time you saw your husband?"

This man, this deputy, Maude sensed something in him. The same thing she had felt during the altercation at Shultz's store the other day. Mutt was aware, more so than most human beings, more so than any other man she had ever met. It was fascinating and frightening.

She was out of practice at the arts of deception; she could hide well enough from the lazy senses of most people, cloak herself in their preconceptions, their biases, the emotional and perceptional blind spots Gran had taught her to exploit. This man, he was different.

"Tonight," she said. "He was late to dinner, but that is not unusual. He came in about six, when I was clearing off the table. Constance was washing up."

"Constance, that's you and Mr. Stapleton's daughter? She was with you the other day in front of Shultz's."

"Yes. She was born back in Charleston. We had her only a few years after we were married. I met him when I was twenty. He was a clerk for my family's attorneys when we met. He was . . . very handsome. Very smart and ambitious. Arthur was a very devoted father to Constance. She . . . He . . ."

Maude lowered her head and focused on the grain of the table. The pain in her gut welled up into her heart. Arthur, cupping her chin, looking at her like she was the only person in the universe. Kissing in the rain: wet and cold and hot hungry mouths breathing love into each other. The sanctum of their bed. Whispering, laughing, touching, pleasure and secrets in the darkness. The fighting. The lies. The betrayals. Intimacy dying behind fortresses of guarded pain. The years grinding, rushing on. Love turning to tolerance turning to hate turning to fatigued indifference.

"That's a lie," she said. "What I just told you. It's a lie. Arthur was a terrible father. He tried, but he was simply too selfish, too angry, too short with her. I married him because I wanted a daughter and I thought I could control him. I couldn't and I couldn't control myself. I . . . changed. I forgot myself. I became what everyone wanted me to be, expected me to be. I really don't know why I'm telling you this."

Mutt ran his fingers along the grain of the wood table. He looked up to match her gaze.

"Maybe because I knew you were lying," he said. "Most people do it without even thinking—lying. Usually they half-believe it themselves. You do it real good, real believable-like. I can see you trying to lie to me, pretty sure to yourself. But it ain't in you, ain't in your heart. You're true."

"I haven't felt true to anything in a very, very long time," she said. "Every time I thought I knew something true, I let it slip away from muh . . . from . . . me."

The steel cracked in her. She started to sob, quietly shaking. Where once she could have controlled her heart's beating, controlled her tear ducts, the dilation of her pupils, now her body betrayed her, her emotions were a storm and she suddenly felt very, very small. Too small to hold this anymore.

"Damn it," she said.

Mutt rose and moved to her. She stood, trying to marshal her control.

She waved for him to remain in his seat, but it was a feeble gesture. All of her strength was engaged in the battle within. He gently placed his hand on her shoulder and she jumped, as if shocked. Her eyes fell into his and he saw her pain, wet and raw in there.

"Ain't too many of us true folk around," he said softly. "It's hard to live in a world where you got to hide who you are away, even from yourself, just to survive the lies of this place."

They were close. He saw the small wrinkles around her eyes, at the corners of her red mouth.

"Yes," she said. "You get sick of hiding."

Close, so close he could taste her tears in the air between their lips.

"Eats you up," he said.

He gave himself to the moment, pushing aside his mind and listening to his blood.

Closer.

Maude was awash in her pain, drowning in it. Nothing felt real, like a walking dream. The hurt was deep and layered, subtle and raging, like a symphony-storm. Mourning for Arthur, feeling the loss of the only man she had ever called lover, ever borne a child with, the only man she had ever served, and at times enjoyed serving.

Mixed in was the resentment, the anger at the years of compromises she had made—some because of him directly, many she had to swallow as her own choices. The disconnect between the idea, the emotion and the reality of who they were, who they became together. It was like being cut and feeling a vague thrill of pleasure from it but knowing too well that the pain would rise preeminent and eclipse all other feelings. And leave a scar. Another scar.

When she had been with Gran she had puzzled over how any woman would allow herself to become the property of any man.

"It's in the nature of us," Gran had told her. "To serve, to please. Just as it is in their nature to try to control the things they can't. You may find one day, Maude, that the heart is a fierce beast, it serves only its own call. You'll discover that for all the power you are learning, for all the control you have over yourself, it matters not a tinker's cuss to love.

"I loved my dear husband Jack very much, even though he was a right lazy, ruthless bastard of a pirate, who didn't treat me as was proper. And

I could have killed him without a thought. But I loved him, and he owned me and I let him."

"I don't understand, Gran," she had said.

"Love makes slaves out of all of us," she said. "And it sets us free."

Married to the pain of Arthur's loss was a deeper, more personal agony. The realization of how much of herself she had given away over the years to the lie that she had become—how much power she had given up to be wife, mother, servant, and how, instead of making those things a natural breathing whole in her, she had locked away her brightest core, her truest, best self, and hidden in the ramshackle debris of the lie.

And now the lie was naked, exposed, vulnerable, to this virtual stranger, this dark-eyed outcast, held up for her to see. Arthur was dead. The wife was dead with him.

What exactly was she now? She remembered a glowing, golden time when she had known, bone deep, blood deep, her name, her face. Now it was all shadow. She saw something in the black mirrors of Mutt's eyes that spoke to the deepest parts of her, calling to her. She moved toward it. Feeling, not thinking.

Closer.

The thing that reminded her who she was also reminded her of who she wasn't. It was clear and silver and in it she felt truth and rightness.

"No," she said. "Please, no."

Mutt felt the old urges, the power drumming in his temples, his chest, his loins. He was so hungry, so wanting this woman. He could have her—he knew her protests were weak and wrapped in a lifetime of repression, a lifetime of groveling to the white man's pompous God. His need gave him power, gave him right. Reason was a weakness, a blind to hide behind when you were too scared, too timid, to do what you wanted, what your instincts told you was the way. *Take her, now, on the table. Lift up her skirt; bite her flesh. In seconds she will join you in the dance. You simply have to push aside her reluctance, her fear.*

Her humanity, her will.

No. The man inside him said it again to the snarling cur. *No.* Her voice gave him strength.

He stepped away and tried to draw in cool air, air without her sweet, musky scent.

"I'm . . . I didn't mean—" Words, language, were stone blocks that fell out of his mouth and shattered on the floor. He was so far gone he was almost forgetting human speech. He backed away from her, shaking his head.

"It's all right; you're . . . I mean, I'm fine . . . ," she said, flushed. "What do I call you? I mean other than 'Deputy' and that horrid nickname they gave you?"

"It's all the name I've got," he said, recovering. His breathing was slowing, his blood was cooling and he was master of his flesh again. "Got no people. My mother's folks, the We'lmelti, they threw me and my mother out when I was a baby. Tried to kill us both. White folks don't try to kill you as much; they just hate you, use you, ignore you if you're lucky. I'll take my chances with them. Mutt's the only name I know. Not a sad thing, not who I am—just words."

Maude nodded. "It's what we do that names us," she said. "Nothing else."

They stared at each other for a time, silent.

"Thank you," she said.

"No, ma'am, thank you," he said.

"Maude," she said. "Not 'ma'am.' Maude."

"Okay," he said. "Maude."

She wrapped her arms around herself, exhaled. "I saw my husband around six o'clock tonight. He was upset, scared. He had been drinking. He drank more. He wouldn't tell me why he was upset. Then Mr. Bick showed up."

"Bick, here?"

"Yes, they spoke on the porch. Arthur said something about some papers . . . a deed. Arthur said he knew about the others . . . other deeds? Bick left. He never raised his voice, but when Arthur came back in, he was more frightened than I've ever seen him. He took his pistol and he left a little after seven. He said good-bye and kissed me on the cheek."

She paused, frowned.

"What is it?" he said.

"He took his Bible with him," she said. "Arthur never even touched it except on the Sabbath. It was very strange. I think he wanted it for protection. He said something about going to see a Chinaman."

Another awkward pause passed between them. It didn't feel like a pause, though. It felt like the air between them was full of something powerful, huge and brooding, like the anticipation before a thunderstorm.

"Much obliged," Mutt finally said, walking to and opening the door. The cold air off the desert was a blessing to him. "I'm powerful sorry again for what happened to your husband, Mrs. Stapl—Maude. The sheriff will check in with you on—"

"Mutt." She said it in a way that he had never heard before. It didn't sound like a cuss, or a joke. "That's the first lie you've ever told me," she said. "Just now. You didn't care much for Arthur and you're not too terribly upset he's dead, are you?"

"No," Mutt said. "But if it hurts you, then I am sorry for it. And that is true."

The ghost of a smile crossed her face. "I've had a lot of men lie to me in my life, Mutt. I don't need another one. It would be nice to have one I can count on for straight talk. Especially now."

He tried to think of something fancy to say, like what Jonathan might say to a girl, but there was nothing. "If it helps any, I swear to you, I'll do my damnedest for it to be the last lie I ever tell you," he said. "G'night, Maude."

He shut the door and tried to reorient himself to a world without her in it. This was crazy, guilty, wrong. He was turned all about by her. The senses he lived by, that kept him alive, were his enemies when it came to this woman. He breathed in cold air and tried to ignore them.

He didn't hear the intruder until he was almost on top of him. Mutt spun, drawing his gun fluidly and brandishing it at the dark street.

"Put that silly thing away," the coyote said. "You know it can't hurt any of us."

"What the hell do you want?" Mutt said, holstering the gun as he began to walk toward the jailhouse.

"Well, that's a fine way to greet your brother," the coyote said. "Especially after all those pretty manners you spread all over the widow back there."

"You stay away from her!"

"I'll try, but it sure will be hard. You already know that, don't you? I swear, Mutt, I can smell the stink of her want all the way down the street. She's been abused, neglected and ignored. Even reeking of grief, she still wanted you to comfort her. She's ripe, Bro. Why didn't you close the deal?"

"Shut up. Don't talk about her like that. Did Dad send you?"

"As a matter of fact, he did. He said to tell you it was time to stop poutin' and playing at being a man and get the blazes out of this town, now."

Mutt stopped walking. He turned and regarded the animal.

"What do you know?"

"What do I know? Blazes, Mutt, you've been wearing that skin too damn long! I don't need to *know* anything. Any fool with good instincts and a decent set of senses can feel it coming. Like a rattler, shaking the air to tell you to back the hell off. Dad says it's got to do with their God, the white men's. That and something . . . something old, older than the shining people, older than Dad, which made even him tuck his tail."

Mutt picked up his pace, heading across Main Street, toward the old stone well.

"Git," he said. "I ain't going nowhere. I've got friends in this town and I don't intend to up and leave 'em."

"Friends?" The coyote laughed. "I saw what you got here, Brother. This is epic! You've done gone and took a shine to her, just like a real, honest-to-goodness, stupid human being! Wait till Dad hears this one; he'll bust a gut!"

"Git," Mutt's diminishing back said. "Last time I tell you nice."

"Suit yourself, but Dad says this town, your friends, all of it, ain't going to be here in a few days! Only safe place to be is in the desert with us, with him."

The coyote laughed and loped down the side street, back toward the open desert.

"You see that, floating there? It is part of her ear, yes?" Auggie said to Clay Turlough. The two men were in Auggie's storeroom examining Gerta's condition in her tank.

"Earlobe," Clay said. "I think."

"Well, gosh-darn-it-all, Clayton," Auggie sputtered, "it is supposed to be on her ear, yes! Not floating at the top of the tank, like a dead goldfish."

They were cleaning her tank. Auggie had been concerned about how quickly the chemicals were becoming discolored this time and how many small pieces of Gerta's flesh were falling off. Clay, who had devised the method of resurrecting Gerta in the first place, would come by whenever Auggie had a problem or concern about the arrangement, as they discreetly called it.

"It may be time to increase the vivazine content in the solution," the taxidermist muttered as he oiled the gears at the base of Gerta's home. "The decay process is trying to reassert itself. I'm sure I can fight it back, Auggie, don't worry. I'll take care of her."

"Thank you, Clayton. You are a good friend. I am sorry I snapped at you."

"Did you?" Clay grinned and pushed one of his few remaining greasy forelocks out of his eyes. "I ain't that good at telling sometimes what people say and do, Auggie, you know that." He picked up the jeweler's loupe and the special screwdrivers he had devised and began to adjust the timing springs on the motors and that sent current to Gerta's brain.

"I like things you can figure out, that make sense. Things that always perform the same way."

"Well, thank you."

The bell on the store's door jingled. Both men jumped. Clay placed an oily cloth over the tank and Auggie stepped out through the curtain to greet his customer.

It was Gillian Proctor.

"Augustus, are you all right? You look flushed!"

"*Nein, nein,* I am well, Gillian. How are you today?"

"I didn't sleep too well with all the stomping and shouting last night," she said, resting her basket on the counter. "The deputy, that Jim boy, some of the other men were back and forth all night. You heard what happened?"

"*Ja,* Arthur Stapleton was killed. That is horrible that such things happen in such a peaceful town. Horrible."

"Augustus," the widow said, "I was hoping that I could ask a big favor of you."

Auggie frowned and crossed his arms.

Gillian smiled and continued. "The church assembly asked me to help out with the food and the refreshments for the big church social on Saturday night and I . . . Well, I kind of volunteered you to help me."

"Gillian!"

"Please," she said, taking his forearm. "It will only be for a while and when was the last time you went to a social event, Auggie?"

The shopkeeper stammered. He liked the feel of her hands on his arm, the playful argument. It all felt good. It wasn't like they were courting; it was helping out the Protestant assembly and they were good customers to him. He sighed and made a big deal of it to her. Her dark eyes were shining and her cheeks were pink.

"Please?"

"Very well," he said.

Gillian hugged him and kissed him on the cheek.

"Oh thank you, Auggie. I'll come by tomorrow and we can plan the refreshments. And don't think you are going to get out of giving me at least one dance Saturday night!"

In the storeroom Clay listened to them laugh and chat casually. He slipped off the jeweler's loupe and carefully turned one of the small cogs twice. Gerta's eyes snapped open. They were beautiful. Just as beautiful as they had been when he had first met her all those years ago. And though he loved Auggie, and was his best and dearest friend, it was nothing compared to the fire that burned in his cold heart for Gerta.

When Auggie had been ready to let her slip into the blackness, due to his own despair, it had been Clay who had sworn to defy the gods themselves to save her, to bring her back. For love. The only love he had ever known.

"Don't worry," he whispered to Gerta's unseeing eyes. "I'll take care of you."

He pressed his lips to the cold glass of the tank and dreamed of the lips on the other side.

The Seven of Pentacles

"Poison," Dr. Tumblety said, his florid face jutting across the table. "I'd stake my letters upon it. Stapleton was done in by some insidious yellow toxin from the inscrutable Orient."

"The Chinamen poisoned him?" Highfather said.

"Scoff if you care to, Jonathan," Tumblety said, his dark eyes blazing. "But I am a man of science and I have made an intensive study of the inferior breeds. I assure you that the substance I uncovered in that man's blood is obviously the residue of their damn lotus plants. I mean what else could it be? It's classic Chinese subterfuge, you see. Obviously Stapleton came upon some nefarious plan of that old coolie who runs Johnny Town—Wang, isn't it? He was poisoned by those yellow bastards and left in that alleyway like trash."

Harry Pratt gave Highfather a sideways look across his desk. The sheriff and doctor were here in the mayor's office this morning so they could both learn of the findings of Tumblety's examination of Arthur Stapleton's body. So far the doctor had been long on wind and short on hard facts.

"Doc, you're sure opium poisoning was the cause of his death?" Highfather said. "'Cause we had those two Chinamen that died a year back from that; you remember, Harry, it was right before that trouble with that giant bat thing swooping in and carrying people off?"

"How could I forget that? We lost the best barber this town ever had."

"But this doesn't seem the same. Stapleton's teeth, his complexion, they all seemed different—they'd been injecting the stuff, but I sure didn't find needle marks on Stapleton's arms."

"That is of course because the site of injection was at the base of his neck, Jonathan," Tumblety said. "It was beneath his collar and very fine, even for a hypodermic, almost like an insect sting."

"Obviously, he didn't do that to himself," Pratt offered. "Could he have been injected at the Celestial Palace, overdosed and then dropped in the alley?"

"Doubt it," Highfather said. "Huang is too clever for any of that. He only allows pipes since those two fellas died and there is no way he'd leave a dead, overdosed white businessman a few doors down from his place of business."

"I think you give old Mr. Charley far too much credit, Jonathan," Tumblety said. "The yellow mind is often difficult to understand for the uneducated, but I assure you, they do not value human life as we do. I'm surprised they didn't dispose of the deceased in a stew pot, to be honest with you."

"You, ah . . . You don't care much for the Chinese, Doctor?" Pratt said.

Tumblety gestured dismissively with one hand while he nonchalantly picked his nose with the other.

"The little yellow devils can all take a slow boat back to Hell for all I care. As a man of medicine, I am simply concerned with the non-hygienic nature of them, you see. Their communities are like rat nests. Cannibalism and all manner of unnatural rites are carried on behind closed doors. They are a public health concern. "

"Look, Doc," Highfather said with a sigh. "I got no love in my heart for Ch'eng Huang or his hatchet boys , but there are a lot of decent folk in Johnny Town, just trying to make their way in the—"

"Yes, yes, yes, Jonathan. Spare me your progressive claptrap. The scientific facts are clear. The white man is obviously superior to the other mongrel races—physically, mentally and morally!"

"I think my deputy and a few other folks in this town might dispute your opinion there, Doc."

"It's been proven by all the sciences, m'boy—biology, alienism, phrenology. One must simply face facts."

"This is all very enlightening," Pratt said, rubbing the bridge of his nose, "but getting back to one of our town's most prominent businessmen being murdered, are you sure this was opium poisoning, Dr. Tumblety?"

"Well, what else could it be?"

"Were you able to positively identify this . . . substance as opium?"

"No," Tumblety said, slouching back in his chair. "It eludes chemical description in both the few experiments I could do upon it and in my texts. Since mine are the only medical books in this hamlet, I had to use my extensive training plus my own powerful gift of deduction to reach my finding."

"And the fact you aren't too fond of Chinamen has nothing to do with all this," Harry added. "Right?"

Tumblety grew purple almost immediately. He rose from his chair, fists clenched.

"By my oath, sir, I am outraged you would dare impugn my honor and my word as a physician!"

Highfather stood and placed his hands on the smaller man's shoulders.

"Easy now, Doc, easy."

Tumblety shook himself loose. His whole body vibrated with rage. He jabbed a dirty finger at the mayor.

"I stand by my assessment, Mr. Mayor. Mark my words, those celestial devils are up to skullduggery! Weak-hearted fools like you will wish you had heeded me when your throats are slit by those devils in the night!"

He pulled a folded sheet of parchment from his jacket and slammed it down on Harry's desk.

"An accounting of my time and a receipt for recompense, sir. Good day to you!"

He pushed past Highfather and slammed the door on his way out.

"Well, he certainly gets huffed in a hurry," Harry said, examining the doctor's bill. "He overcharges too. I'm surprised he's never had anything pop, as red as he gets."

"He's a mite ornery, I'd allow," Highfather said. "But he's also the closest thing we got to a doctor in these here parts. Even if he is as crazy as a rattlesnake in the sun."

"Whatever happened with that giant bat thing, Jon?"

There was a knock at the door. Harry's secretary, Martha Poole, a tall, slender woman with a stern face and steel-gray hair worn up in a tight, no-nonsense chignon, poked her head inside

"Mr. Mayor, Mr. Deerfield and Mr. Moore are here to see you."

"Thank you, please send them in."

They both looked the way Mutt had described them, Highfather thought. Oscar Deerfield was tall and redheaded, with buck teeth. Highfather put him at around twenty-five years old, give or take a year. Jacob Moore was older, about thirty or so. He was squat, dark and fat. His hair ran in black curls around his face.

"Thank you, gentlemen, for coming," Harry said, meeting them at the door and glad-handing them.

"Your Injun deputy didn't make it out to sound like we had much choice in the matter," Deerfield said.

Harry chuckled. "Yes, well, he's very enthusiastic about his job. This is Jon Highfather, our local sheriff."

Highfather shook their hands. The two men looked rumpled, dusty and tired. They groaned as they slid into the seats Pratt offered them.

"I understand you gentlemen knew Arthur Stapleton," Highfather began.

"What is this?" Moore said. "Are we being considered as suspects in whatever went on last night?"

"How do you know about that?" Harry asked.

"This is a small town, Mr. Pratt," Deerfield said. "You can't walk from the coach station to the mayor's office without someone blurting out the news. We know Arthur was killed last night. We heard that it was coolies that did him in."

"We're looking into that," Highfather said. "We're looking into every possibility right now, including the possibility of a business scam that went wrong."

Moore looked to Deerfield and slapped a meaty hand across his own face. "This is ridiculous! Is everyone with a badge in this dammed town crazy?"

"It helps," Highfather said.

"Look, Sheriff, Oscar and I were on the coach from Virginia City last night. We have four other passengers who can vouch for our whereabouts for the last day or so. Your own deputy, that shifty little half-breed of yours, practically pulled us off the stage at the station himself, and dragged us here. We didn't kill Arthur and our transaction with him was fair and square!"

"You won the deed to the Bick family silver mine in a game of poker," Highfather said. "Fair and square. Right."

"We didn't march him into the Virginia City magistrate's office with a gun pointed at his head," Deerfield said. "Everything was transferred legally. Arthur said one of his business partners, this Mr. Bick, had signed the property and several others in and around Golgotha over to him years ago."

Harry and Highfather exchanged glances.

"Why?" Harry asked.

"Well, since you can't ask Arthur, why not ask Mr. Bick?" Deerfield said. "I honestly don't know and care even less."

"You know," Moore said, "come to think of it, he did mention something about it once, just in passing—"

"Are we done?" Deerfield interrupted. "We have a mine to get open and you gentlemen have already delayed us long enough."

"Do you honestly think you're going to pull any more silver out of that hole?" Highfather said. "That mine went bust years ago."

"That's not what we've been told," Moore said as he slid a small pouch out of his pocket. He opened it and several blackened, shiny pieces dropped into his wide palm. "It's pure. Some of the purest silver the assayer in Virginia City has ever seen! Seems old Bick gave up on the place too soon!"

Deerfield gave his partner a withering look and Moore sheepishly returned the silver ingots to their pouch and into his pocket.

"Are we done, then?" Deerfield said again.

"Good day to you, gentlemen, and good prospecting," Harry said with a smile. The two businessmen left quickly and quietly.

"I smell a hidden partner," Harry said when the door closed. "Someone is helping them out; they didn't just blunder into all this. Maybe Malachi has a business competitor, trying to move in on him."

"I can't believe as sly as Bick is, he'd overlook any silver veins in the Argent Mine," Highfather said. "I'll talk to him again, but I already know I won't get a straight answer."

"We still have an unsolved murder, Sheriff."

"I'll tell Mutt to take Stapleton's body over to Clay's place. He has nearly as many medical books as Tumblety, and I think he actually reads them."

"Tell Mr. Turlough to be quick in his examinations, Jon. I promised the widow I'd have the body to her for a proper burial by tomorrow."

"Will do, Mr. Mayor."

Highfather paused at the door. "Harry, are you all right? You look a little worried."

"Jon, sit down, please."

The sheriff returned to his chair.

"Did you notice anything strange last night, Jon? Feel anything—like the ground shaking?"

Highfather shook his head and frowned.

"Do you think it might be wise to cancel the social? Have a curfew until we find out more about who killed Arthur and why?"

"You know something I don't, Harry?"

The mayor was silent.

Highfather leaned toward his desk. "Folks in this town have to give up a lot due to the nature of this place sometimes. I know of some young couples who are supposed to announce engagements at the social. Few new babies born this winter haven't been shown off enough. Those things are good for people, Harry, especially our people. Like sunshine cleaning out a wound. Unless you think it's a danger to the public in general for some reason you want to inform me of . . ."

Harry shrugged. "It's nothing, Jon. Keep me informed about what you find. You're right. People here have too much death and fear and darkness. Let's give them some sunlight."

"Yessir."

The door closed and Harry was alone. He looked out his window and saw his father's house up on Rose Hill. He thought about Holly up there alone, sad and drunk. Blaming herself for not being woman enough, hating him for being who he was. Holly wasn't like his other wife, Sarah. Holly had really wanted to make a life, a family, with him. Sarah had been content to live with the Pratt name and the Pratt money and leave him the hell alone. Holly—poor, infuriating, hellcat Holly—she had been willing to fight for him, to hang on and never let go. She had only realized recently it was a fight she could never win and it was killing her. He was killing her.

He considered riding up there and having lunch with her, like he used to do when they were first married, back before they had accumulated the scar tissue of countless recriminations. Back when they were new and soft. The potential outcome of the lunchtime scenario played out in his mind and he put the notion away. It was too late. Too late for them both.

It wasn't her fault. It wasn't his fault. It was just the way things played out. God's will.

He went back to work, taking solace in the press of the mundane and banal.

The Empress

.

"Another one of these, my good man," Holly Pratt said, laughing. She handed the empty shot glass to the man behind the bar with the unruly whiskers and the one eye that was as milky as a fish's belly. "In fact, one for everyone!"

A cheer went up through the Mother Lode. The squatters and lowlifes who made up the shanty-bar's clientele circled the drunken well-dressed lady from the town below like sharks smelling blood.

Holly dumped a wad of crumpled bills onto the rough wooden bar. Milk-Eye reached for them, but Holly refused to release them.

"All the filthy rotgut you have. All of it, all night long. For me and my new friends. Understand?"

The bartender did the crude math in less than a second and placed a full bottle of the homemade mash on the bar with a thud. Holly relinquished the cash and held the bottle aloft like a conquering hero. The drunks and the destitute cheered again for their new champion.

She knew it was night, but she had lost track of the time long ago. She had drunk every drop of alcohol in the mansion and had the servants hook up the carriage. Descending Rose Hill, she had seen the lights of the squatters up on Argent and it had been like a beacon to her. Up there was warmth and life and stink and dirt. People who didn't give a damn who you were or what you did. Up there was freedom, and no self-respecting lady, let alone the mayor's wife, would ever go up there. So she did. She found the bar easy enough and started drinking; pretty soon she had plenty of company.

"Hey, ain't you one a that sumbitch Pratt's wives?" an old man who smelled of rotten eggs and whiskey had muttered to her not long after she had arrived at the Lode.

Holly raised a glass to the old man. "I am indeed one of that son of a bitch's three wives!" She tossed back the mash and it clawed its way down her throat and caught fire in her belly. "One of us plays the piano real sweet too! Care for a drink on Mayor Son of a Bitch, old-timer?"

The time had become elastic. Slurred conversations with a kaleidoscope of bleary-eyed companions seemed to be the focus of the universe—all time stopped. Then some external event—an entrance, a departure—would give her insight into how long she had actually been here, been drinking, and time suddenly seemed to be galloping like a frightened mare toward dawn or oblivion. She didn't care which one she reached first.

Harry would be worried by now. The servants would be telling him she had left in the shay, how much she had drank. How she had carelessly thrown on a half-buttoned silk blouse and traveling skirt, which barely concealed her inexpressibles. Her hair, which began the day in a high, tight, proper bun, had continued to fall loose in golden strands as the night wore on, until now it lighted upon her shoulders in a most wanton and familiar manner.

Harry would be worried; Harry would be furious; Harry would be jealous. Harry would come for her.

A rough hand pawed her shoulder and upper arm. She turned her head to regard her molester. A black-toothed reprobate who was covered in thick, bristly black hair and had a mask of caked-on dirt around his eyes, like a raccoon, was stroking her shoulder.

"You're a right randy adventuress, ain't 'che?" he muttered around his alcohol-thickened tongue. "Why don'cha come on back in the piss alley wif' me and we'll—"

Blacktooth never got to finish. A powerful hand grabbed his collarbone and squeezed. The drunk screamed as Holly heard the bone crunch. The hand belonged to a tall, stocky man with bright green eyes and hair and clothes the color of coal. He lifted the drunk by his broken bone and hurled him casually over his shoulder, across the room. He didn't bother to take his eyes off of Holly to see where Blacktooth landed with a loud crash and many shouts and curses.

"Are you all right?" the man in black asked as he sat next to Holly. His arms and neck were the size of small trees. His chest was easily as broad as half a wooden barrel. There was not an ounce of fat on his frame or face, which had clean, sharp, handsome features. He wore his hair like a soldier, short on the sides and swept back from his brow. "He didn't hurt you, did he?"

"No," she said softly. The sheer size of this man, his presence, made her feel very small. There was something about him, about those eyes, green like sunlight falling through emerald glass, like cold green fire. "I'm, I'm fine. Thank you. Please, have a drink."

"I don't drink."

"Oh, well—"

The click of a pistol being cocked interrupted her. A man stood behind her savior with a gun to his head. The gunman's lip was bleeding.

"You wrecked my table and broke my bottle, you bastard," he said.

"Yes, I did," the big man in black said, and turned to face the gun. "Do you know me?"

The gunman furrowed his brow; awareness burned through the haze of the bad whiskey.

"You're that deacon fellow, ain't you? Come with that preacher that's been staying up at the old Reid house."

"I am. I don't want any trouble. The reverend has drink that he gives to those who are in need. Go up to the house and your libation will be replaced."

"Maybe I don't want to walk all the way over yonder to get back what I rightfully had."

The deacon leaned forward, until the gun's barrel was crushed against his chest.

"You don't want any trouble." The deacon rose and suddenly the gun in the injured man's hand seemed like a toy. "Do you . . . friend?"

"Uh, no. No sir. Bad luck to scrap with a servant of the Lord."

"Yes, it is. Go in the peace of our Lord, my friend. The reverend will be expecting you. Our doors are always open to those in need. He may have a spot of supper for you as well."

"I'm . . . I'm much obliged, sir. Please accept my apology."

The man lowered the gun and slipped out the front door, his head lowered. The deacon sat down again and regarded Holly.

"You scared him," she said as she tossed back another three fingers of whiskey. The deacon said nothing. The chaos of the saloon returned, but everyone gave Holly a wide berth now that she was under the watchful eye of the hulking man in black.

"Where is he?" the deacon finally said many drinks later.

"Who?"

"Your husband."

"What makes you think I got one?"

"The ring. Other things. You're smart, well educated. You speak well, even as inebriated as you are. Your clothes are expensive and you have obviously bathed often and recently. You're no camp whore. You're a woman of means and out here that usually means a husband of means as well."

Holly stopped pouring another drink and turned to regard the deacon. He was a handsome man, powerfully built, with broad shoulders. She liked having the attention and the interest of a man like this. He was just the kind of man she'd want Harry to see her with when he came barging in here to drag her home. He was perfect. She leaned forward and let her small, pale hand rest on his immutable stone chest.

"He's off with his Nancy-boy, most likely. Why do you ask?"

"He's a sodomite?"

She ran her hand across his chest, reaching his upper arm. She stroked it—it was like caressing a telegraph pole and she felt a very real, visceral thrill race through her body. This man was like a god and he was interested in her, intent on her. His unwavering, almost cruel emerald stare was for her, and her alone. He wanted her.

"Oh yes. When he's not busy being mayor."

"Interesting."

"I never thought I'd hear a man of the cloth call sodomy anything but a sin that sent you straight to Hell."

"Reverend Ambrose has a slightly different view on sin. It's one of the reasons I joined him."

"Where you from . . . I'm sorry I don't know your name."

"Phillips. My name is Phillips."

"Where are you from, Phillips?"

"Lots of places. I travel with the reverend."

"You sound southern."

He said nothing.

"Why did you ask about my husband?"

"Because I wanted to know if I was going to get shot when I take you out of here with me."

"Pretty sure of yourself," she said, and emptied her half-full glass. She began to fill it again. "Why would I go anywhere with you, sir?"

"He's not coming," he said. "If he gave a damn about you, he'd already be here, or he would never have let you come to some place like this in the first place."

Holly stopped drinking. She lowered the glass and her eyes focused, hot and clear, on the splintery wood of the bar in front of her.

"But I see you, really see you," he went on. "I see a beautiful woman, I see her in pain, see her screaming, and I see no one listening. This is not how your life is supposed to be, is it? You're right, it isn't. He goes off and screws some piano player's ass, while you, Holly, you feel yourself wear away each day like sandstone in the wind. Why me? Because I see a woman who is desirable and deserving of love and affection. I see you, all of you, and I want what I see. And best of all, it will hurt him so much—it will make him feel what you have felt, make him feel the flush of shame, the sting of self-doubt, the wash of self-loathing, of not being enough. It will make him feel your pain. "

She rose quickly, violently, and hurled her glass at the towers of bottles and jugs behind the bar. Shards exploded everywhere. The salon was silent again.

"What the Jesse do you think you're doing, you crazy bitch!" the barkeep bellowed, coming up on her fast. Phillips interposed himself between her and Milk-Eye.

"We're leaving," he said. "Perhaps this will cover the costs of the damages and any other expenses we might have accrued."

He tossed something on the bar. The barkeep's one good eye widened. A shiny nugget of rough-hewn silver shimmered in the lantern light.

Holly grabbed her bottle and took Phillips's arm as she strode toward the door.

"Let's get the hell out of here," she said.

It was cold outside. After the stifling heat and smoke of the Mother Lode, it felt good. She had no idea where the buggy was; she cared less. She took another long drag off the bottle, swallowed and then felt hot, scratchy bile claw its way up her throat. She gagged, burped and then laughed. She bumped into Phillips's broad back and fell down, still laughing.

"Did you see the look on his face when you dropped that silver down? I thought his eye was going to fall out!"

She took the calloused hand he offered, and he lifted her out of the rut-creased dirt road and she flopped forward into his arms.

"Gracious, you have big hands," she muttered against his chest, still giggling. "Where on earth did you get that silver?"

"Come on," he said. "I'll show you."

He lifted her onto the wagon as easily as he might lift a small child. It was an old buckboard, with jagged gaps in a few of the rotted boards that made up the bed. There were several sealed wooden crates and a few hoop barrels sitting in the back. There was also something large and awkward shaped under a thick wool army horse blanket.

Phillips climbed up onto the seat next to her and took the reins. The horses snorted and fidgeted, pawing and stomping the ground.

"Something is spooking the poor things," she said as she looked for her bottle.

"Yes," he said. Tugging on the reins, he urged the frightened horses to action, and the wagon lurched forward into the dark.

The fires at the summit of Argent Mountain were guttering in the burly desert winds, throwing shadows and sparks across the mining camp. It was late and most of the crews were asleep. Two sentries with rifles and lanterns stood watch by the main road. They waved Phillips's wagon to a stop.

"What's your business here at this godforsaken hour?" the older one said around a wad of chaw.

The younger one opened the eye of his lantern to get a better look at the occupants of the wagon. "Oh, it's you, Mr. Phillips, sir," the younger one said.

The older one eyed Holly but said nothing.

"Dropping off a few things," Phillips said.

"On your way then," the old man said, waving them through with his lantern.

"You one of the men who bought the mine from Malachi Bick?" Holly said.

"No."

They moved past the empty pavilions and the row upon row of dark and silent workers' tents.

"How did those guards know you?"

"I work for the reverend. He is an advisor to the men who acquired the mine. They couldn't have done it without the reverend's help."

"Why are we here? Where are you taking me?"

"You'll see."

"I want to know," she said. The chill of the ride and curtness of Phillips's answers were pushing the vague warmth out of Holly's body and mind. It was beginning to dawn on her that home, Harry and safety were a distant point of light far across the gulf and that she was alone with a strange man in a strange, barren place. The anger she felt at Harry allowing her to be here gave way to the realization of where that anger had led her. She felt the panic begin to churn in her like white water.

"I'd like to go home now, please," she said. She tried to hide the shiver in her voice. Phillips pulled the buckboard to a stop, turned and regarded her. His eyes burned green, even in the pale starlight. For the first time he smiled. He pulled her to him and crushed her mouth to his. There had been a very narrow window when Holly had wanted this, when his words in the bar had made her feel rage and desire and need, but that time had passed. This man frightened her, and as his mouth forced its way into her own she felt a cold, slaughterhouse draft pass through her. His tongue was powerful and insistent. It seemed too pointed and too long, too deep. She tasted oily blood and gagged as she struggled to push away from him. She broke the kiss and felt the gorge rise in her belly, but before she could heave the foulness out of her, Phillips slapped her across the face. She saw bright light and fell. There was a harsh impact and sharp, jagged pain in her back. Everything fell into dizzy, drunken shadow. The last thing she saw was his beatific smile.

She awoke in cool echoes and unyielding darkness. He was carrying her like a sack of flour—by the legs, over his shoulder.

The mine. They were deep in the silver mine. She knew by the strange way the sound of his footsteps bounded and faded down the timber-ribbed tunnels and finally flattened, dead, against the unconquered walls of the mountain. She had been here once with Harry when he first became mayor, when he still loved her. The tunnels were still alive then with the light of lamps and filled with the sound of men warring against the Earth to give up its treasure.

"Why . . . Why are you doing this?" she asked, still too confused to be afraid. Her lips felt swollen and numb. She tasted blood. The vile aftertaste of Phillips's tongue still remained. Even the blood and the cheap whiskey could not remove it.

"Be quiet," he said. "He'll explain everything. We're almost there."

"Help me!" she screamed, and struggled against him, pounding his back with her hands, trying to wiggle free. He swung her off his shoulder and she felt the mine floor smash into her back. She gasped and struggled to rise. She couldn't breathe. He had her by the throat and lifted her effortlessly, above his head. There was no air and she struggled to keep from falling into a complete frenzy, but the fear was running through her like mad horses. She kicked him in the chest and ribs to no apparent effect.

"I don't want you dead. He doesn't want you dead. It would be easy if I wanted it, easy as killing an ant. Now be still and be quiet or I will rip out your tongue. He said I could do that if you gave me trouble."

He returned her to the floor and eased his grip. Air, sweet air, came back into her aching lungs and she drank it in greedy gulps.

"My husband, the mayor, will make you pay for this," she said.

"Is this the same husband you were going to rut with me to hurt?" Phillips said as he let her go. He pointed with the lantern toward a yawning passage. "Move."

"Bastard!" she spit.

He said nothing, simply pushed her forward.

They reached a crude barricade in the middle of the shaft. A wooden sign declared that the tunnels ahead had not been fully shorn up and could collapse. Another sign said that there was blasting underway. Phillips grabbed her arm and pulled her around the barrier. They continued deeper into the dangerous tunnel.

Holly felt her ears pop as the slope continued ever downward. They had been walking so long time had stretched like taffy. The tunnels creaked and groaned with the weight of the world. Occasionally, dust and small bits of rock would rain down as the Earth breathed. It was getting hotter too; the darkness itself seemed to waver and ripple. Sweat tricked down her neck and back. She absently wondered if the mad deacon was walking her into Hell.

Phillips had paused twice—not for rest. He seemed to never tire, but the lantern did need tending. She was exhausted, sick and thirsty from the alcohol. The fear had time to congeal in her and had become a terrible weariness. She just wanted to rest, to lie down. She told herself she didn't care where they were going or what he was going to do to her. Occasionally she would envision Harry with a torch in his hand, leading a group of the town's men deep into the tunnels, in pursuit. But she did not believe it. No one was coming for her. No one knew she was here and no one would save her. No one.

The tunnel narrowed until Phillips's head and chest were scraping the roof and walls, dislodging dust and small rocks with every step. His hand was an iron vise gripping her wrist as she trailed behind him. They came to an opening in the tunnel wall, surrounded by piles of rubble and dirt. The air smelled of gun smoke. Wooden crates marked with warnings to handle with care, coils of fuse, wire and boxlike detonators were piled near the tunnel wall.

"In here," Phillips said as he pushed her toward the hole. She climbed over the debris. On the other side of the hole there was nothing but yawning darkness, eternal night. The floor was smooth, flat—like it had been sanded, polished. There were tiny scratches in its surface.

"What is this?" she whispered. Her voice echoed in the vast black.

"You have passed outside of reason," he said. "Older powers govern here."

She focused on the rock face of the floor, illuminated in Phillips's lantern. Her eyes had adjusted as best they could to the feeble light. The gray surface gave way to silvery black; occasionally light would reflect back at her like a shower of stars. Silver, the floor was almost pure silver. The scratches became alien markings and symbols on the silver face. They made her feel sick, strange, uncomfortable in her skin, as if her brain were plotting against her behind her face. They seemed to slither and squirm like worms in a hot skillet. She closed her eyes and tried to ignore them, but many of the images burned their way into her eyes through the lids. Other sang to her in voices that had no throats.

"Move," Phillips said with a shove. She staggered forward across the Argent floor. Eventually she saw an island of light in the darkness. Its appearance excited her, spurred her on, even as it filled her with dread. These were her last thoughts, last moments, last breaths. She couldn't muster the strength to weep.

A lantern on the floor was the source of the light. A man stood behind it, his features swallowed up in the shadows. He was neither as tall nor as powerful in build as Phillips, but he stood very straight. Holly could see he had a mane of hair and whiskers the color of ash. He wore a simple flat-brimmed hat and a knee-length coat—both black.

"Very good, Phillips," the old man said. The voice was as smooth as broken leather, cloying as honey. "You've served me well, as always, my loyal friend."

Phillips shoved her forward and she fell upon the black, glittering floor. The old man knelt and cupped her face. She could see his face now; he was probably in his sixties. His eyes were kind and blue.

"Hello, Holly," he said. "I've been looking for you for a long time. I'm the Reverend Ambrose Ashton Smith. You can call me Ambrose. Welcome."

He helped her to her feet.

"I found her right where you said I would," Phillips said to the old man. "A whore, a fallen woman among the wretched and the wicked. Lost and seeking guidance."

"Good. Holly, have you ever heard of the Book of Judas? No? Did you realize that much of the original Bible included chapters of Gnostic wisdom?" Ambrose said. "They were purged from the King James Version, many of them lost and destroyed. Lost wisdom destroyed out of fear and narrowmindedness. They were misunderstood, reviled, much like your own Mormon texts, as not fitting with the clockwork view of the universe as presented by the lying god's groveling servants."

The very air rippled with heat; it was hard to breathe, to think. The fear was on her again, awoken by the old man's calm, warm, sincere insane voice. Fear, like a mad bird trapped in a chimney, fluttering, smashing itself blindly. Its instincts crying to fly, to escape to be free.

"What is wrong with you people?" she screamed as she tried to free herself from Ambrose's steely grip "Dear Lord, please help me! Somebody help me!"

"Oh, it will help you," Ambrose said as he dragged her forward, toward the well. It was a simple ring of stone within another ring of silver. At its center was darkness. The crawling symbols gave name to something that existed before the time of names. Their silent chants drummed into Holly's mind—a relentless tattoo of obscenity.

"You are the one we have awaited," he said as he forced her to her knees before the well. "The Bride of the Great Wurm, the Whore of Babylon, the Bitch-Mother of a thousand young."

Phillips approached her. He held a huge knife. He opened his wrist before her wide, frightened eyes as casually as one might snip a hangnail. She screamed as he turned his wrist over. Instead of blood gushing out, a viscous stream of black, foul-smelling ooze slowly drained from his opened vein.

"Dear God!" she screamed. "This is not happening; this is not really happening!"

"Take the communion from your bridegroom," Ambrose said, clutching the back of her head. "Drink, whore."

She struggled as Phillips's massive wrist was slowly smashed to her lips. She fought to clamp her mouth closed as the foul, oily substance was smeared across her face.

Where are you, Harry? Why didn't you come? Why?

Her nose was pinched closed with iron-vise fingers.

"Drink the Milk of the Wurm; grow in strength and understanding from the communion," he said, his voice full of mad joy. "Glory unto the True God, the First God, the Keeper of Darkness and Patron of Unmaking. *Ia, ia, Muhog-ian, fhtagluhian!* Glory to the First God!"

She gagged as the "milk" made its way past her lips. Its stench, its vile taste, awoke some old, dreaming part of her brain, of her soul—a part that knew the well, knew what was on the other side of it. Knew the chanting and knew it meant something far more terrible and unnatural than death. She swallowed the blackness and felt it open her, fold her like paper.

"Glory to God," Ambrose said as Phillips lifted her like a rag doll and threw her into the maw of the well. "Accept this offering, that you may be free."

She fell into hot, humming, dizzy darkness. The place between stars, the moment between the last breath of life and the rattle of death, the black pause of awareness before murder. She fell.

And then it caught her, impaled her, upon its appendage, like a great rope of smooth, undulating muscle slick with mucus and oil. It tore upward through her sex, buried itself deep in her belly, ripping, bursting.

She hung there for an infinite instant. The flutter of fly's wing, the time between the birth and death of stars.

A million tentacles swarmed over her, binding her wrists, her ankles, forcing open her eyes, her ears, her throat, her most intimate places. It entered her, violated her everywhere, in every way. Filled her, engulfed her, pumping the black milk into her every cell. The pain was glorious and horrible. It sent her above God and beyond mortal understanding. The pain explained everything to her.

Holly Pratt's soul jumped and fluttered against the cage of her ribs, like a mine canary sniffing gas. It struggled and finally was still, disappearing beneath the oily surface.

She arose from the well, carried aloft on a throne of tentacles. Her clothes were tattered rags, but her skin, her hair, was lustrous, like Beltane moonlight. The black milk glistened on her skin. It leaked from her eyes, her mouth, from her nipples, from between her legs. She regarded the two tiny monkeys named Phillips and Ambrose who groveled on the ground before her.

"Glory to the First God, Glory to the Black Madonna, Bitch-Mother of a thousand young!" Ambrose wailed as he wept tears of blood.

She smiled and spoke with a voice that heralded the death of saints and suns.

"Rise," she said. "We are ready to begin the end."

The Hermit

The sun was low in the west; fading gold filtered through the high sacaton grass that brushed the tips of Jim's shoes, in the saddle, and tickled Promise's flank. The grass bowed in the cooling wind that heralded the coming of night to the desert.

Jim was never a Holy Roller, none of his family was, especially not Pa, but as he watched the light move across the plain he felt connected to something, something good and gentle and loving, something that didn't speak much, 'cause the message might get lost in the noise.

Jim let Promise graze while he watched the desert bury the sun. He rubbed her neck gently.

"Don't worry, girl; we're not going back out there again. You earned your rest."

In the few days since their arrival in Golgotha, Promise had made a remarkable recovery. Food, water and the ministrations of Clay and Jim had done wonders for her hurt leg. This was the first time he had ridden her since they were in the 40-Mile Desert, and she had handled it with no apparent pain. The little mare seemed happy to be with her boy again.

"This place is a good home, isn't it, girl?" he said. "Folks here don't know us, don't know what I've done, but they took us in. Treated us like kin. I like it here, Promise. I'm going to hate to have to leave."

The horse snorted. She had had her fill of the bitter desert grass. Jim turned her back toward Clay's livery. He could barely make out the rough split-rail fence that surrounded the property.

Clay's place was at the end of Pratt Road, next to an old Indian graveyard that Mutt said had been here for a long time before the town. As far as anyone knew, the only white folk buried in there were some distant members of the Bick family, who came out here seeking their fortunes decades before the Mormons had made the crossing.

Jim stopped Promise at the entrance to the stable. He heard the clatter of wagon wheels and saw Mutt heading back toward town in an empty buckboard carriage. He urged Promise to catch up to the wagon with a click of his tongue and flap of the reins. The wind felt good in his face and Promise was eager to gallop for a bit. They caught up, slowed and then paced the wagon as it crossed Old Stone Road, headed for Prosperity Street.

"Mutt!" Jim called.

The deputy nodded. "Hunk of horseflesh looks a damn sight better than the last time I saw her," he said. "Good work, Jim."

"Promise did all the work," Jim said. "She's tougher than she looks."

"I imagine she is."

"What you doing out here, Mutt?"

"Dropping off Stapleton's body for Clay to take a gander at. I was going to stay, but Harry Pratt is waking snakes about one of his wives not coming home last night, so me and Jonathan gotta go hunting for her."

"You don't sound too worried."

"I ain't. If I had to live with Harry, I'd run off every now and then too."

He stopped the wagon. "Why don't you let me know what Clay finds out, okay? You can tell us tomorrow morning at the jail."

"Will do," Jim said. He spun Promise back toward Clay's and they galloped up the road.

He led Promise to her stall, removed her saddle, dried her down, gave her fresh water and then brushed her. She enjoyed the attention from Jim and nuzzled his neck with her dark, wet nose.

"Okay, okay, cut it out," he said. "You're tickling!"

He held her head, scratched her between her ears and breathed in her musky smell. He felt a pang of homesickness crawl up on him.

"I was so worried about you, girl. I'm glad you're better."

By the time Jim walked out of the stables, the stars were out and it had cooled off considerably. Across from the stables was another large, barnlike structure Clay called his tinkering place. Jim saw lantern light through the window and walked over. The big wooden doors were open and Jim saw Clay inside, scratching his chin while he looked at something on the big, flat table in front of him. A white sheet, spattered with something dark in the feeble lantern's light, covered it.

Clay seemed deep in thought. He suddenly looked up, like he had been struck with a notion, and noticed Jim standing in the doorway.

"Come on in, boy," he said. "You can help me git the lights workin'."

There was a byzantine arrangement of enameled glass globes lying on the floor, near the examination table. Each globe was loaded with a pair of charcoal rods, which Clay carefully inserted vertically into an iron frame, inside the glass globe.

"What is this thing?" Jim asked.

"Called an arc lamp," Clay said.

The mechanism was connected by braided metal wires to another globe with an identical arrangement. There were six globes in all, mounted around the circumference of an old iron wagon wheel. The whole affair reminded Jim of a chandelier.

At the center of the wheel was a large rope that was threaded though a block and tackle mounted to a ceiling beam above the table. Clay and Jim, together, pulled the wheel up until it was suspended about seven feet above the table.

"Careful," Clay whispered as he struggled to pull it off the ground. "If anything is knocked loose, we'll have to pull it down and it will take half the night to fix it."

"This some kind of lantern, Clay?"

"Kind of sums it up, Jim," he said as he strained to pull the wheel higher. "Real powerful one too. English fella named Davy came up with the idea about sixty years ago, but they haven't had good enough dynamos around to power 'em till lately. Fella named Gramme has been working on some interesting ideas to generate electricity. He's pretty close to what I came up with here. See, you send electricity between the rods and you keep them at just the right distance and it produces light. Bright light. If you don't do all that just right, though, the fool thing just blows up, stinks up the place and makes a mess."

"You made all this, Clay?" Jim asked as he dug in his heels and held the chain. Clay anchored the chain to large iron hook mounted on the wall.

"Yup. Wrote Davy a few times when I was puzzling it out to ask some questions, Gramme too. Hell, Gramme even wrote me back asking me about my dynamo. Nice fella."

They both let go of the chain. The wagon wheel groaned and swung gently. A little dust fell from the eaves. The rocking slowed and then stopped. Clay fastidiously examined the wires running down from the hanging contraption, leading back to an ominous-looking device made of wood, wire spools and metal connected to a large hand crank. He connected a few wires to posts. He began turning the crank, gently at first but then with greater ferocity. There was a soft metallic whining sound as he turned it. The whine was gradually drowned out by a humming. Sparks whip-cracked from the contraption and made Jim jump. Clay kept cranking.

The air smelled funny, like the way it smelled after a thunderstorm. Jim saw Clay's white mane of hair rise up on his scalp and felt a tickle across his skin, like ants crawling. There was another cascade of cracks and pops, and blue-white sparks rained down on Stapleton's body. There was the smell of smoke and then the workshop was suddenly bathed in a harsh, white light. Jim looked up and saw the globes glowing; he squinted at the brightness.

Clay stopped cranking and the lights dimmed slightly but remained lit. He shaded his eyes and squinted up at the globes.

"Modern Prometheus," he muttered. "I envy you, Jim, the world you're going to live in. Man has just begun to harness the powers of nature." He groaned as he rose from crouching beside the dynamo. "Mark my words, boy, you will live in a time of miracles, of wonder. Now let's shake a leg; we only got about an hour or two before those charcoal rods burn out."

Under the bright light, Clay pulled back the sheet. Jim stepped back in spite of himself. He had seen a dead man before but never one that had been cut open under a doctor's knife. Stapleton's skin looked like wax, smooth and pale and not quite real. His eyes were closed and an ugly, jagged Y-shaped incision stretched from his shoulders to his groin.

Clay sighed, his vulture features turned in a scowl. "Damn Tumblety. Man's damn near a butcher. If he's a doctor, I'm the Queen of Sheba."

He knelt over the body and opened the dead man's eyes. "Eyes are all wrong for opiate poisoning. No pinpoint pupils. Jim, back there on the workbench is a box. Bring me a scalpel out of there."

"Like a knife?" Jim said as his eyes scanned over the table.

"Um-hum."

The workbench was full of all manner of odd things. Many of them seemed more disturbing under the harsh light: brass clock gears and tiny springs, a spool of copper wire, a small, mummified animal paw covered in tufts of white fur. There were sealed jars filled with an oily yellowish-green substance and dark, oblong things floated in them. There were empty bullet jackets and crumpled, partially burned papers covered with illegible scrawling and crude diagrams. Some of them had drawings of a woman's naked body, without a head.

"Clay?"

"Mmm?"

"Why do you like dead things so much?"

"The dead don't disappoint you, boy. You know what to expect out of 'em . . . and they don't talk too damn much."

Jim found the box and carefully avoided the rusty, stained hacksaw. The small, sharp surgical knife wasn't in much better condition. There was a frame in the box too and he fished it out. His eyes widened.

"Clay, are you a doctor? This paper you've got here says you attended the Medical Department of Hampden-Sydney College. Got a degree and everything."

Clay walked over and examined the diploma.

"Why don't you got this hanging up somewhere?" Jim asked.

"I thought about being a doctor for a spell," Clay said, plucking the scalpel out of Jim's hand and returning to the body. "My family all died when I was a boy. All of 'em. It was yellow jack that took 'em. Last one to go was my mother. Always stronger than she looked. It took them a week to find me out at the homestead after she passed."

Jim watched Clay's narrow back hunched over the body. He didn't pause in his work as he spoke.

"How old were you?"

"Four. I thought about making a career out of medicine, but I didn't think the right way for learned professors. I don't see it the way they got it laid out in their fancy books."

"How's that?"

"Jim, remember what I said about the dead not talking too damn much. . . ."

"Sorry."

Jim sat on a pile of crates and watched Clay work. Occasionally the arc lamps would sputter or snap and the lights would dim for a second. The smell of something sour drifted over the room and Jim tried to breathe through his mouth. Clay pulled things out of the body and plopped them into metal trays for closer examination. He opened the dead man's mouth and peered inside.

"This is all wrong, Jim," Clay finally said after what seemed like hours to Jim. "The eyes, the gums, have no discoloration; the chambers of the heart show no undue strain or damage. None of what I see here is consistent with death by opiate poisoning. Tumblety is an idiot. However . . ."

"So what killed Mr. Stapleton?" Jim asked.

Clay rummaged around the workbench with bloody hands until he uncovered a large hypodermic-like device with a suction bulb. He slowly slid the needle into Stapleton's left leg. "I still think it was poison, but not an opiate, not anything I've ever seen before."

He squeezed the bulb slowly and nodded as the chamber filled with an oil-like fluid.

"If my occuscope was finished, I could try to get a final image off his eye nerves," he said. "It might still not be too late for them to hold a residual image, but I'm afraid I'm still weeks off from completion. Pity, his dead eyes might have been able to show us his killer's face."

Clay carefully retracted the needle.

"Clay," Jim said. "Do you believe in haints?"

"Ghosts?" Clay looked hard at the boy. When he turned his head he reminded Jim of a barn owl regarding him with big, yellow eyes.

"I don't cotton to the ignorance of the peasant or the arrogant certainty of the academician or the priest. I believe that at the end of breathing we stand on the shore of a great, black sea. We don't know what lies on the other shore, but I am certain there *is* another shore, boy, and one day we shall cross that stygian rift, back and forth, as easily as we today cross the Atlantic. Knowledge shall be the lamp that guides our way. Knowledge, not dogma."

Jim blinked and cocked his head. "So . . . you're sayin' you do believe in haints . . . right?"

Clay took the hypodermic and injected some of the black substance he had acquired from Stapleton's body onto a glass slide.

"There are dead folks talking all around us, Jim. Tryin' to tell us what's on the other shore. People just won't clamp up long enough to listen to 'em. Too blasted busy living, I suppose."

He took a small pipette and dribbled a few drops of a clear substance from a brown bottle on the workbench onto the slide. "Why you ask?"

"Nothing, just wondern'," the boy said.

The oily stuff on the slide began to foam violently. Clay frowned and set the slide on the workbench. He picked up the syringe.

"Damn peculiar. I'll be right back. I need to run a few more tests on this with my equipment in the house, and I need to look at a few of my books."

He walked out the open doors, into the cool night.

Jim sat in the old barn and listened to the snap and crack of the lights burning their way to oblivion. The shadows jumped and lengthened as the intensity of the light shifted. Stapleton lay on the table, eyes and chest wide open, perfectly still. The glass slide hissed a little as it foamed on the worktable.

"What you got to say?" Jim finally said.

The corpse was still.

"Not as mouthy as Clay, that's for sure."

The corpse was still.

Outside, the coyotes were howling off past the old graveyard, out in the deep desert. The arc lamp dimmed and popped loudly. A shower of blue-white sparks fell down over the corpse as the artificial lights failed completely.

The squirming in Jim's pocket became more insistent. He reached his hand in slowly, afraid and certain of what he would discover. The eye was cold, cold like water running off the mountains back home in March. Cold like his mother's eyes when she buried Pa in her mind and heart. The cold stung Jim's fingers as he pulled the eye from his pocket. It was glowing; a pale green fire wreathed it and slowly spread to his fingertips. The fire was cold. The alien pupil regarded him, unblinking, like the dead man's eyes. The tiny characters orbiting the iris shifted, just like before. Just like the graveyard outside of Albright. It was all happening again just like last time.

He turned the blazing eye to face Stapleton's corpse. Jim's legs were made of water; his mind was a flat, featureless wall of fear. The emerald fire was carried on the faint starlight that invaded the workshop. It drifted toward the dead man, like sparks on a dry prairie wind.

Jim knew what was going to happen next, just like the last time.

Just past the edge of Albright, the old cemetery squatted—an ugly scab of brown and yellow grass, black, twisted skeletal trees and crude-hewn, lop-sided gravestones that jutted at angles like a mouthful of snagged teeth. There hadn't been a Christian burial in the old place for over thirty years.

Rick Puckett drove the buckboard while Jim covered him with the rifle. The night had come up on them while they rode out of town and now only moonlight guided them down the old weed-choked rutted road. It was early April and the chill was still heavy enough for Rick to complain about it until Jim told him to shut up. Jim wished he had grabbed his jacket too, but his anger was keeping him warm and he hated to listen to the man who had bet his father's eye whine.

On the way out of Albright, in the evaporating light, Jim had told Puck-ett to lay out exactly what happened to Pa on the night he went missing. At first Puckett tried to hem and haw about it, but Jim would have none of it.

"You saw what I did back there at the saloon," Jim said slowly, calmly as he could, but the reality of his act made his voice crack a little. "I shot a stranger, a man who never did me no harm. You think I'll give two ticks about dropping the S.O.B. who killed my pa?"

"But I swear I didn't, Jimmy—"

"Now you tell me what I want to know, *everything* I want to know, right now, and if what you say is true and I believe it, if you didn't kill my pa, then you can go home tonight, square deal?"

Puckett sighed and focused on the road and the swishing tails of the horses.

"Square. First of all, like I said, I didn't kill him; I jist helped bury him."

It went like this. Rick and Jacob Gnau and Eldon Coyle and a few others were sitting at a table in the Cheat River Saloon with Charlie Upton, drink-ing bourbon and beer, when Billy Negrey came in. Billy was looking a little bit drunk and a whole lot mean. He sat down at one of the faro tables and commenced to playing and drinking.

Billy's luck wasn't too good and pretty soon he was out of cash. Charlie downed his drink and with a grin and a wink walked over to Billy. He whispered something in Billy ear and tried to hand him a stack of cash. Billy knocked the bills out of Upton's hand and socked him square in the jaw.

"Charlie stumbled back," Rick said, "up 'ginst the bar. He spit some blood. Charlie was madder than blazes. He was heeled and he drew on your pa. Billy didn't have a gun, but he came at him anyway. Took his gun away from him and slapped him again before Charlie could even get a shot off.

"The whole derned place got quiet and me an' the boys got up to help Charlie out. Your pa aimed the gun at us and said he'd shoot us, if we gave him a reason. Then he told Charlie he wasn't nothin', that for all that money and that fancy house, an' all, he would never be as rich as old One-Eye Billy. He said Charlie had never done a decent thing in his life or a brave thing. Brought up how Charlie had stole half his money off the bodies of dead soldiers, said Charlie's pa should have whupped him more when he was a boy, so he'd be a man now. And Charlie had to stand there with his own gun pointing at him and listen to all this. Then Billy said he felt sorry for him. Now if that don't beat all for crazy. Like I said, your pa was pretty drunk. He emptied Charlie's gun on the floor and then threw it to him on his way out the door."

"Why didn't anybody tell the sheriff or anyone this? They all said Pa left round eleven with no trouble."

"Hell, Charlie bought everybody drinks for a spell. Told everyone he tried to pay up Billy's debt an' send him home to his family and that was the thanks he got. Charlie's a good man, Jimmy. He does a lot for the folks round these parts, he—"

"Shut up," Jim muttered. His knuckles were white from gripping the rifle's stock. "Tell me the rest of it; tell me how you ended up burying my pa."

Rick swallowed hard and looked at the Winchester's barrel, then back to the road.

"Well, we kept a'drinking. A little while after Billy left, Charlie walked outside for a spell with Jacob and Eldon. He came back alone. He kept on buying rounds and even gave a toast to old crazy Bil . . . I mean your pa. Well, 'bout closing time, Eldon comes back in and whispers something to Charlie. He tells me to git up, we're going somewhere. Charlie dropped the money he was trying to give your pa on the bar and tells the bartender he's paying for the house. Like I said, hell of a nice g— Um, so we all ride out past the city limits, following Eldon, and he takes us up to the old veterans cemetery. And there is Billy all busted up and cut and bloody and he's tied to a tree and Jacob is there with him and he's got a buck knife and his hands are all bloody. Eldon's too, now that I can see by the lantern light. Jacob hands Charlie the knife and um . . ."

"What?" Jim said.

"He cut your pa," Rick said quietly. There was fear in the memory. "Real bad. Worse than skinnin' a deer. Talked to him the whole time he did it too. Said all kinds of hateful things to him . . . bad things about your ma, you, your little runtling of a sister. He said . . ."

The Winchester was against his cheek. It trembled.

"Hell, boy! You asked! I'm jist . . ."

"Who ended it? Who put the bullet in him?"

"You know," Rick mumbled. "Right 'tween the eyes. Your pa, he never begged. He never said any of the things Charlie wanted him to say. He made Charlie madder than the devil, Jimmy. He died real good."

"Take me there," Jim said. "Where you buried him. Now. And don't talk no more, damn you."

When they arrived at the old cemetery, Rick told Jim that Pa was buried in a stand of sycamore trees at the edge of the burial ground.

"You have your shovel?" Jim asked flatly. Rick nodded. "Bring it."

It wasn't much of a resting place. A sparse fringe of grass and weeds had sprouted up in the upturned dirt in the time since Jim had gone away. He watched Puckett dig. Jim's mind, his heart, were empty, still. He listened to the metallic crunch of each shovelful of dirt, to Rick's labored breathing and his occasional sobs. The anger was still there, but it was cold now, like iron rails frozen over, and it no longer protected him from the cold or his own weariness.

They had no lantern, but the moon was bright and its light fell, pale and stark between the barren branches of the sycamores.

The rhythm of shoveling stopped.

"Jimmy," Rick said.

They hadn't wrapped Pa. They hadn't even given him an old horse blanket to rest under. Jim felt the cold and then numbness all fall away. He felt so old, so scared.

Something moved in his pocket. It could have been a snake for all he cared. He almost fell down, but he didn't. He felt a dull endurance hold him up. There were things to do, to be attended to. Man's work, and he was the man now.

He aimed the rifle at Rick.

Puckett raised his hands, his faced screwed in terror. "Please, Jimmy, I swear, I didn't."

"Git now," Jim said in an even voice he didn't recognize. "You git, and you tell him that I know what he did and that Billy Negrey's son is coming for him. Tell him he can hire a mess of shit-heels like you, tell him he can pack every gun and every knife he's got, but I am coming to kill that sumbitch. Tell him that."

Rick started toward the buckboard. The bullet whined like an angry hornet past his ear and the Winchester boomed.

"Leave the wagon," Jim said. "Run."

He sat at the foot of his pa's grave. Rick's panting had faded and there was silence.

"I'm sorry, Pa," he finally said. He didn't know what else to say. What a mess. Whatever was squirming in his pocket moved again and it finally registered in his awareness. He reached in and gasped at the coldness.

The eye. He slid it out of his pocket. It was engulfed in green fire, but it didn't burn like fire—felt more like a frostbite. He held it up, turned it in his fingers as the green light spilled out of it like a lantern. He looked at the back of it, trying to find a catch or something.

"Hello, Jim."

Across the open grave, Billy Negrey crouched at the other end of the hole. Jim couldn't make him out too well, he was bathed in shadows, but it was his voice and when the moon slipped between the branches it caught the green light of the eye and gave Jim a glimpse of Pa's face. He was smiling and young and he had two eyes. Wherever the light hit him, though, he seemed to fade, like he was made of fog or glass. You could see stuff behind him, through him. He didn't seem to mind.

"You a haint, Pa?"

"I rightly can't say. There's a lot of stuff I'm not allowed to say to you now. I'm sorry about that, Son."

"That's all right, Pa." The tears were hot and they made it hard to see.

"We all sure do miss you. Is this some kind of Johnnyman wisdom—can it bring you back? 'Cause Ma, Ma sure does miss you, and Lottie, she's . . ."

He wept, sobbing like the boy he still was. The shade was patient. It stood silently, with an expression wise and sad.

"I can't come back, Jim," it finally said. "I'm sorry, Son. You've got to carry on; you look after your ma and your sister. I know you can. You know I was proud of you, Jim. Very proud."

"It was Charlie Upton that shot you, right?"

"I can't say, Son. The rules. From behind that gun, the fella sure looked like Charlie Upton looks, though."

The shade grinned. A cold wind spun through the graveyard, carrying dead leaves in its wake. It shook the branches of the sycamore trees and the shade faded and reappeared in patches of shadow and emerald light.

"All right, all right!" the shade shouted to the wind. "I'll behave. Let me talk to my boy."

It turned back to Jim. "Listen, Son, I can tell you that you have to keep that eye safe, have to. It's your birthright, Jim. I wish I could give you more, but it's yours. You've earned it in blood and gumption."

"But Pa, I killed a man, and I'm going to get Charlie for what he done to you. I got to stand for all that, don't I?"

"I can't tell you what to do or where to go, Jim. But I can tell you we all stand, Son. In our own time in our way, we all stand."

The wind had not died; it had strengthened in fact. Dry, brown leaves were swirling about the grave. The clouds were on the move. Massive dark ones swallowed the edges of the bright moon. The eye was a frozen green star in Jim's hand.

"I'll take good care of it, Pa. I swear. And I'll take care of Ma and Lottie too."

"I know, Son, I know. I always knew you wo—"

The moon was gone. The eye was dark. The wind eased, settling a cover of leaves over Billy Negrey's remains. Jim was alone.

Clay walked back into the workshop, his white hair mussed from scratching his head. He had a book under one bony broomstick of an arm and the hypodermic in his other hand.

"Lights went? Dammit! I'll be dipped in tarnation if I can't figure this one out, Jim. It's got properties of blood, but it sure don't seem to be human blood or any animal I can classify. I'm afraid I've jist got another cipher for the sheriff to worry over, instead of helping figure out who did old Stapleton in."

"I know who did it," Jim said softly as he slipped something back into his pocket. "Big fella. Black hair, clean-shaven. Strong, real strong. Dresses in black like a minister or such. I don't got his name but that's what he looked like when he forced that stuff down Mr. Stapleton's throat."

The Queen of Pentacles

Sarah was in the barnyard, scattering feed for the chickens, when she saw her husband ride toward the farmhouse on his golden palomino. She tossed the remainder of the mash in her basket onto the ground with a casual shake of her hand. The chickens squawked and momentarily scattered, but hunger overcame fear and they swarmed to gobble up the discarded meal. She closed the gate to the yard and made her way to meet him at the fence that ran along the perimeter of the pasture. Clumps of green Indian rice-grass dotted the field, lush defiance to the desert's sterile rock and dust. Most of the herd lazily munched on the grass, oblivious to Sarah's passing. Her favorite heifer, old Ellie, raised her head, long enough to give Sarah a moan of greeting before returning to her meal.

Sarah didn't primp; she didn't adjust her bonnet to capture the stray gray hairs that had fallen loose, or to straighten her hem or smooth her skirts. She spit some of the desert's dust out of her mouth and wiped the sweat of the morning's chores off her brow. Her husband pulled his mount to a stop by the fence post she was propped against.

"Good morning, Harry," she said to Golgotha's mayor and her husband of eight, almost nine, years. "Coffee's waiting up at the house, if you have the time. I know it's a sin, but it's a good one."

She was amazed, as always, by the sheer beauty of him in the sun. His red hair caught the sunlight peeking over Methuselah Hill. His eyes were burning sapphires, and when he looked at you, *really* looked at you, you were the only thing in creation. She put such schoolgirl nonsense away. She loved Harry, more than any other man she had ever known, but she knew it would never be that way, could never be that way.

"Sarah," he said. He wasn't smiling and now, after the initial surprise of seeing him had passed, she realized he was tired. There were dark circles under the blue eyes.

"What's wrong?" she asked.

"Holly's missing," he said as he dismounted. "She left yesterday evening and never made it home. I've got Jon Highfather out looking for her. She took the carriage but no clothes, not much money."

"Maybe she figured what's good for the goose is good for the gander."

"Sarah!"

"Well, Harry, it's true. How long did you expect her to sit up there in that house and wait for you to be a real husband to her?"

They walked along opposite sides of the fence, headed toward the main house. Harry led his horse by the reins.

"Dammit, Sarah, that isn't fair. You know how much I've tried with her."

"Tried to what, Harry? Pretend to be something you just aren't? To put up with her wanting children with you? You lied to her, Harry. You lied to yourself and you lied to her."

They walked in silence. The sky got brighter as the last of the night's chill burned off. The cows groaned blandly. A vulture glided silently out into the desert, following death.

They reached the house. Calvin Evans, one of the farmhands Harry had hired to help Sarah keep the place up, tipped his hat to the mayor. Harry returned the greeting with a nod. Calvin was hitching up a pair of gray draft horses to an Owensboro wagon, in preparation for a trip into Golgotha, probably to Auggie's store.

Harry hitched his horse to the post next to the water trough, and joined Sarah on the porch.

"Sure you don't want the coffee?" she asked, settling into a rocker with a groan.

Harry knelt next to his first wife. "Sarah, please, I'm worried about her. Have you seen her?"

"Not for a while, Harry," she said. "She came by a few weeks ago. We talked for a spell. She had been drinking; I could smell it on her."

"Why didn't you tell me?"

"It's none of your business, Harry. Any more than where you go and who you spend time with is ours. You set the rules for this; we just followed them."

"You've never seemed to mind them before," he said.

She smiled. "Of course I didn't, Harry, my sweet. I am very grateful to you for all you've done for me and the children. When Gabriel passed, I was out in this wilderness alone with little James and Rebecca. I thought I wouldn't make it. I prayed to the Lord for deliverance, and He sent me you, my golden boy."

Harry remembered his father's face, and the faces of the temple elders, when he told them that he had finally decided on a wife and that she was twice his age and had two young children by her recently deceased husband—an old friend of Harry's family. The memory made him smile. They had pushed him, tried to control him, and he had pushed back. He had never regretted marrying Sarah.

"You have always been the one person in this pissant town that I could ever really talk to, Sarah," he said. "The only one who ever accepted me for what I am, and what I'm not."

"You're selling Holly short," she said, shaking her head. "That girl loves you. She's loved you her entire life, since you two were children. I remember when you and Holly used to sneak away at any social function you could. I remember how you held her when you two danced. You love her too, Harry. Talk to her. She deserves the truth and, who knows, maybe you'll have two people in Golgotha you can trust."

Harry rubbed his whiskers. Calvin was up in the wagon. He called out to them that he'd be back in an hour. The wagon clattered through the open gate and down the road toward Main Street.

"She knows," Harry finally said. "She's known for a while. I didn't tell her in a very sweet way. She had been drinking and I had been out all night again and she pushed me. I just kind of blurted it out. I've . . . I've been blaming her for it ever since, saying she wasn't woman enough."

"Oh, Harry, you didn't?"

Pratt rubbed his face. His eyes were red and sore. He was fighting to control the quiver in his voice.

"I know, I know. If anything happens to her, Sarah, if she actually listened to my damn fool pride and gone off and hurt herself . . ."

He let the words hang in the morning air, which was becoming staler and hotter by the minute. Sarah took his hand, patted it. She leaned in close to his face, resting her head against his.

"My poor boy," she whispered. "She's in a cage, Harry, just as much as you are, love."

"I know that. I tried; I *really* tried to be what she wanted, what everyone wanted me to be—good son, good husband, loyal servant of the temple, defender of the damned faith. But I'm none of those things, Sarah."

"You're the best friend I've ever had, Harry. And a good husband, to boot. Your whole life you've fought against the people who have tried to define you, pin you down. But at the same time you've always carried whatever load they dumped on their shoulders. You are a good man, Harry—you've just never really met yourself, is all."

Harry held her in the cool shade of the porch as the sky brightened, the air warmed. Finally, he sniffed and wiped his eyes with a handkerchief from his pocket.

"What did she say to you, Sarah?"

"She wasn't planning on leaving, that was for sure. She loves you, Harry, and she figured in the end you would love her too. I didn't know if she knew about you and Ringo, so I was kind of vague. I told her the same things I'm telling you now, that you were both trapped in cages of your own making. I told her to leave you. I even offered her money and as much help as I could. She wouldn't have it.

"She was so lonely, Harry. I told her what it was like for me when Gabe died. That was a scary, lonely time for me, till you came riding in to save the day. Everyone in this town thought what you did for me was a kindness—except for your father, of course, and that was because you got one up on him and the elders. To everybody else, Harry Pratt was a regular Sir Galahad!"

"Hell I am. You're the one that did me the kindness, Sarah. You kept my secret. Made me feel like it wasn't sick to feel . . . the way I do. If I hadn't had you to talk with, I'd have blown my head off a long time ago."

There was a cloud of dust on the main road coming from the direction of the desert.

"If she's gone, it wasn't of her doing," Sarah said. "Maybe someone who wants to hurt you, Harry, or blackmail you—you are mayor, you know. Maybe it's got to do with Arthur Stapleton's murder."

"Sarah, you've been reading too many of those dime romances they churn out back east. This is Golgotha: people tend to end up dead in these here parts; it's kind of a town tradition. Besides, if anyone wanted to blackmail me, there are damn easier ways to do it than snatch Holly, and if someone were gunning for me, why wouldn't they have come after you too?"

Sarah laughed. She patted Harry on the knee. "That's very flattering, dear, but everyone knows you took me in as a mercy, nothing more. I hate to disappoint you, but you're not fooling anyone."

"They're the fools," he said, standing and regarding the small smear of color that preceded the cloud of dust. "You're my treasure, Sarah, more valuable than any wealth, any secret."

"I already voted for you, Harry. Save it."

The smudge had taken shape. It was a lone rider, moving fast toward town. As the rider reached the bend in the road where Sarah's ranch was, they recognized it was Jon Highfather. Harry ran out to the road and waved for him to stop.

"I was looking for you," the sheriff said, pulling the dusty kerchief from his face. "Mutt found Holly's carriage. It's out at the edge of the Forty-Mile. Come on!"

"I have to go," Harry said to Sarah as he unhooked his horse.

"I'll pray for her, and for you, Harry. Please let me know if I can do anything to help."

"If you see her, fetch me, Sarah. Tell her I'm sorry. Tell her to come home."

He climbed onto the palomino. He and Highfather raced back out into the desert, gone in a clatter of hooves and dust.

She watched them diminish into the burgeoning curtain of heat.

The Chariot

Horses screaming. They heard the sound before they saw the search party. Highfather had led Harry about an hour outside of Golgotha. The 40-Mile did not fully claim this land. There were patches of strawberry cactus, stick leaf and sagebrush, like defiant sentinels urging on the lost souls who might have found themselves consigned to this corner of Hell—*hold on; keep going! There is life here; don't stop and die.*

"What the hell is that?" Harry said, slowing down.

Highfather slowed as well and turned to the mayor. "Your horses, Harry. When we found Holly's carriage, the horses were going out of their minds. The carriage had crashed into a deep ditch and the horses and their yoke were a mess. They won't calm down, not for nothing."

"Maybe it's Mutt—"

"Nope. I sent him away to backtrack the carriage's trail. Didn't do a lick of good."

The two cleared the shelf of rock that had had blocked their view. There was a search party of a dozen townies Highfather had rounded up. Harry knew all of them well. He felt a disturbing amalgam of appreciation and shame gel in him, as well as a hot stab of anger at Holly for causing this whole mess with her damn fool drinking and her tantrum. But when he saw the overturned carriage, looking like the desert had tried to swallow it whole and had choked on it, and the frantic, frothing state of his two most gentle and well-trained saddlebreds the anger was quickly quenched in fear.

Besides the posse, crazy old Clay Turlough was out here with his wagon

and a pair of brown drafts, trying to pull the carriage out of the deep gap
it had been wedged into. That boy who was working for Highfather, Jim
something or other, was here too, trying to help Clay attach a thick coil of
rope to the axle of the carriage.

"Mr. Mayor," the boy said as Harry dismounted, handed the reins of his
horse to one of the towns folk and approached. Clay grunted and nodded as
he wiped his already-sunburned head.

"Harry."

"What happened here, Jon?" Pratt asked the sheriff, who had also dismounted and tied his horse a good distance away from the shrieking animals. It was taking four men with strong ropes to hold the two animals in
place. "What's wrong with my horses and where is my wife?"

"Mutt found it. Holly wasn't here and there are no tracks or signs that she
ever was. No indications she jumped out before the crash or climbed out after. No signs anyone came along and helped her or abducted her. Nothing. It
looks like the horses were just running crazy out into the Forty-Mile and the
wagon hit the ditch, flipped and trapped them here."

"If they were spooked about the crash, they should have calmed down by
now. They're acting like there's a rattler in their saddle blanket."

Harry eased his way toward one of the horses. It was the older of the two,
a mare named Dolly. She had always been Holly's favorite. He stroked
Dolly's nose as she continued to struggle and shriek. Her teeth snapped at
him and flecks of foam flew as she shook her head.

"Easy, girl," he whispered. "You're safe, now. Easy."

Dolly's massive brown eye rolled, until only the white, veined with bloody,
spidery lines, was visible. The pupil and iris slid back into view from the
interior of the horse's skull. Harry noticed how glassy, how wide and black,
the horse's eye was. Dead eyes still moving. There was no frame of reference, no common shore, no lexicon of experience between what this poor
animal had gone through and the world Harry was walking through. He
patted Dolly and lowered his head, dizzy with the notion of where Holly
was, of what was happening to her.

"They're both gone." It was Mutt's voice, tight like a drum skin, so close
it startled Harry. The half-breed was next to him, alongside Highfather,
Clay and Jim.

"They got the spirit-sickness," Mutt said. "Worse than anything that can be done to their bodies. Their hearts, their minds are broken, full of black bugs and dirty water. No coming back from that, ever."

"Where the hell is my wife?" Harry said, looking back to the dry ground.

"She was never here," Mutt said. "The carriage was driven out of town, and then the horses had . . . whatever was done to them done. They ran wild until they got tangled up here. I'd say your wife is still in town somewhere, Harry, probably sleeping it off."

Pratt's eyes flicked from the dust to Mutt; they shimmered with hatred.

"Jon, rein in your animal or so help me, I'm taking his badge. I'm mayor of this town and I won't have my wife spoken about in that manner by this . . . trash."

Mutt chuckled. Highfather shook his head to the deputy, curtly. Mutt shrugged, but shut up.

"None of this is going to get Holly back any faster," the sheriff said. "So let's all settle down and review. Arthur Stapleton was murdered by poisoning, but it's not any kind of normal poison, right, Clay?"

"Yes," Turlough said, nodding. "It shares properties with numerous organic compounds, including insect venom, mammalian milk and some kind of blood. In some properties, it bears striking similarities to the vital fluids of the cestoda."

"I'm sorry," Mutt said. "Could you speak a little less crazy, white man?"

"Worms," Clay said. "Specifically, parasitic worms."

"Did I mention lately how much I hate parasites?" Highfather muttered. "All right, so, someone poisoned our banker with this . . . wormy gunk. Now I don't know why, but I'm pretty sure the new owners of the silver mine, Deerfield and Moore, do, and I don't need a crystal ball to know Malachi Bick is mixed up in this, some way or other.

"Harry, you and Arthur had been in bed with Malachi over the years in quite a few business deals. Could he have had Arthur killed and Holly snatched? Fess up; if there's something going on that we don't know about, it could mean the difference in finding her and getting her home safe. "

Harry kept his head down. He was trying to focus, trying to concentrate over the jabbering of crazy old Clay, over his desire to smash Mutt's sharp, smug face, trying to focus over the terrified, mad sounds Holly's horses were making. She had loved old Dolly. When he saw Holly brushing her in the stables, singing "Lorena" softly to her, it had made him fall in love with

Holly again, made him wish he wasn't who he was, for her sake. She was a good woman, Holly Pratt. Sweet, passionate and beautiful. Strong and stubborn and so very, very sad after he had been unable to love her the way she loved him.

"I . . . I don't think it's anything like that," he muttered. "I've no current business with Malachi that would benefit in any way from such blackguard behavior, even if I thought him capable of it. Malachi Bick is a true son of a bitch, gentlemen; he cheats, he lies, he steals and I'm told he has even murdered in his time, but I do not believe he would ever hurt someone he truly considered innocent. No, I don't think he's behind any of this."

"How's 'bout the Injuns?" one of the posse members, a cowboy named Dyer, suggested as he struggled with the other horse. "They could have snuck in here at night and taken her, maybe to sell. They could do some of that hexing stuff they do on the horses, y'know, with all that dancing and grunting and groaning that passes for church for 'em? A fine-looking lady like Mrs. Pratt would fetch . . ." He let the implication hang when Harry glared at him from under the shade of his bowler.

Mutt spit at a scorpion and let out a single dry snort of amusement, then turned to Highfather, ignoring Dyer.

"Jonathan, you remember that stuff old Earl Gibson wrote up in his Bible? It said something about worms in it. . . . The Greate Olde Wurm, or some-such. Think it could have anything to do with the stuff that killed Stapleton?"

The horses went berserk. More men hurried over to try to control them, but to no avail. Harry rubbed the bridge of his nose. The noise was like a hot wire, jammed into his forehead.

"Hadn't had a chance to look at the Bible, or talk to Earl about it, since Arthur got killed," Highfather said. "You told me Earl was mixed up with some preacher?"

Mutt nodded. "All the folks who went loco in the last few weeks were attending his services."

"What does that crazy old drunk have to do with Holly?" Harry asked. "I'm of a mind to follow up on the notion the Indians may have had something to do with this." He stared coldly at Mutt, who was not smiling for a change.

"Oh, come on, Harry," Highfather said. "You're too smart to have us waste time on that. The Shoshoni, the Paiute, they set up a raiding party, snuck into our town in the dead of night and took one person—Holly?"

"Sound any crazier to you than wasting time on damn fool Earl Gibson's ravings and worm juice?" Harry said. He turned to the men holding the horses. "Can't you people shut them up?" The men tried, but both animals seemed newly agitated, shot through with fresh fear.

"Uh, Sheriff, Mr. Mayor?" Jim said "Earl, that is, Mr. Gibson, he spoke to me the other day when I was cleaning up the cells. He said a lot of queer stuff, but he also mentioned . . . worms a couple of times, said they were eating him up."

"Why didn't you tell us this when it happened, Jim?" Highfather said. Jim locked his jaw but made no reply. Old Earl had known his real name, had known about his father's eye. Jim wondered if it had been foolish to break his silence. He wanted to help, but too many lies, too many hidden truths, all led him back to the hangman.

"You should have said something," Highfather chided.

"Venom," Clay announced. Everyone stopped and looked at him. Clay pointed to Harry. "He said 'worm juice' and the sheriff said 'wormy gunk'; it's really more like a blood-based venom. . . ."

They all stared mutely.

"There's no, you know, no juice actually involved, at all. And I don't think 'gunk' is even a scientific term."

Clay nodded sagely and shuffled off to retrieve something from his wagon.

"Well," Highfather said. "That was helpful."

"Jon, wasn't Earl going on about worms or somethin' when he tried to shoot up Auggie's?" Mutt said, snapping his fingers.

"He did." Highfather nodded. "We need to have a long talk with Earl Gibson."

"No, Sheriff!" Harry shouted over the horses' screams. Clay was near Dolly, on the side opposite him. He seemed to be trying to calm her down, along with the other men, and having no more luck. "If you want to waste time listening to some old drunk fool's ranting, do that on your own time. I'm ordering you to investigate the possible Indian abduction connection and to notify the Army. Then continue to search the town, including the squatters' camp—burn the damn place down if you have to, but find her!"

Harry knew he was overreacting, knew he was telling a good, methodical man how to do his job, but none of that mattered. The horses were shrieking. He had to find her, had to get the chance to say he was sorry, had to try to explain to her where it had gone wrong, where he had gone wrong, not her. The horses kept screaming and thrashing, lost in madness.

"Put them down," Harry said, turning his back on Highfather and the others as he began to walk to his horse. "Both of them."

"Man ought to take care of his own business, don't you think, Mr. Mayor?"

It was Mutt's voice. Harry turned and the deputy was standing there, no smile on his face, just cruel judgment behind flint eyes. His rifle was held out in his hand as an offering.

"Mutt . . . ," Highfather whispered.

Harry snatched the rifle, a Winchester '66 carbine, out of the half-breed's hand, cocked it, carefully. His eyes drilled blue fire into the void of Mutt's gaze.

For a second, Highfather thought Mutt was in danger of being shot, but Golgotha's mayor turned and walked to Dolly instead.

The gunshot echoed across the desert, sharp and then rolling like manmade thunder. A pause, then another.

The screaming stopped.

Strength

Two things came down Argent Mountain: miners and rumors. Both of them tended to pile up at the Paradise Falls. It was the end of the week and a mob of dirty, thirsty, rowdy miners poured into the saloon just after sundown, money burning a hole in their pockets.

The latest story floating around the room, along with milky streams of smoke and the jangling raucous piano strains of "You Naughty, Naughty Men," was that a new vein had been opened. The bosses, Deerfield and Moore, had ordered blasting this week. The always-dangerous gamble had paid off. Their dynamite man apparently had the nerves and eye of a surgeon and there had been no accidents, injuries or deaths. A new vein meant happy bosses, happy bosses meant bonus pay and a day off tomorrow and that meant the Paradise was full to busting.

The faro tables were packed. A crowd, two deep, was watching with amusement to see how much money the young tenderfoot miners were going to lose to the Paradise's resident dealer, Henry Rorer. Rorer, his hair meticulously center-parted, every strand plastered down, sported a pencil-thin mustache. He slid the cards out of the dealer's box oil smooth. The ever-present smoldering Turkish Oriental dangled from the corner of his mouth.

Up on the stage, the ebullient Miss Sherry Haines led the girls of the Paradise Falls Burlesque and Review through her own production of the songs from the popular musical *The Black Crook*. Sherry and her dancers frolicked in a most provocative manner, all stockings and wigs, legs and grins, while the standing-room-only crowd of cowpunchers, muleskinners, rustlers, gamblers, miners and businessmen hooted and howled. A few of the local Mormon men sat in the shadows, guiltily enjoying the view and sipping cold beer that sweated as much as they did. If anyone had a little too much tarantula juice and decided to climb onstage to join the act, Kerry Duell with the big muscles and small bowler was there to pull them off, escort them outside and enlighten them to the error of their ways.

At the bar, Georgie Nance was setting them up as fast as the crowd knocked them down. Though his sphinxlike expression would never have let anyone know, George was happy. It was good to see big crowds in the Paradise again, good to see miners, dirty and loud—bringing in as much hope for this town's future as they were tracking in dust. New silver meant new faces, new families and the promise that Golgotha wouldn't just dry up and blow away.

A cheer rose up from the miners as Jacob Moore and Oscar Deerfield entered the saloon like conquering kings. The two made their way toward Georgie, moving through a sea of backslaps and handshakes.

"What can I get for the gentlemen of the hour?" George asked.

"We're here to share our good fortune," Deerfield said. "A round for the house of your finest, my good fellow!"

A cheer went up from the crowd. Deerfield raised a hand for silence. After a moment, the music stopped and the cacophony descended into a disjointed murmur.

"Gentlemen, we have done fine today! Thanks to you and your adherence to diligence and good old American hard work, the future of the Argent Mining Company has been assured!"

Another roar from the miners. George handed Deerfield his drink and the mine boss raised his glass, once again demanding silence. Painted saloon girls and drunken cowboys now leaned over the railings on the second floor to hear Deerfield's oratory.

You have worked hard, risked your necks; now enjoy the fruits of your labor! To the Argent Mine—the future of Golgotha!"

This time the whole bar exploded with whoops, whistles and shouts of joy.

Deerfield glanced up to see a shadow regarding him from behind a blinded glass window on the second floor. The door next to the large window said

Office in elegant gold leaf. Deerfield shrugged and touched his glass to Moore's. The smaller man's whole face seemed to fall in on itself when he smiled.

"Good sirs, this way, if ya please," one of the mine managers, a mug in his hand, said. "One side, ya drunken reprobates! One side, make way for the owners!"

Deerfield and Moore made their way to a table cleared by a few of the miners. The music had started up again, as had the overwhelming symphony of hoots, laughter and chatter. Deerfield nodded to the manager and his men, handed the manager a golden eagle and gestured for them to depart. The men, grinning ear to ear, disappeared into the churning crowd.

"Well, Oscar, m'boy, we're on our way!" Moore said over the din. Deerfield was silent. The well-rehearsed smile was gone and Moore recognized the start of a fret coming on. Jacob Moore greatly admired the personal charisma, ruthless business acumen and general ease with which Deerfield could turn a disaster into a dollar. However, Moore's lanky partner had a disturbing quality of looking for the cloud in every silver lining. Moore was in the mood to enjoy success. He had never seen it as often as Deerfield had, had never been cheered walking into a saloon before. He wasn't in the mood to wrestle with Oscar's black dog.

"Smooth sailing from here on, no doubt, my lad!" Moore said.

"Nothing about this business has been smooth, Jacob," Deerfield said, sipping his whiskey. "This business with the preacher, or soothsayer or whatever the blazes he is, it's troubling to say the least. The law is looking at us hard because of Art's murder—"

He glanced up to the window. The shadow was gone.

"—and I think we're getting other attention we don't need."

Moore shrugged. It annoyed Deerfield. The ambivalent gesture was his rotund partner's answer to most things he preferred not to deal with at the present time.

"Look," Moore said. "Everything Ambrose has told us has come true. Even the silver vein—it was exactly where he said it would be! And that man of his, Phillips, he's the surest dynamite man I've ever seen; it's like the man has frozen Chinamen's blood in his veins."

"Still, I don't like it," Deerfield said, leaning forward across the table.

"I know a blackleg when I see one. This preacher is using us, Jacob. We need to settle our accounts with Ambrose and send him on his way, posthaste."

"We will, we will; don't let this spoil our mood. Look around you, Oscar, m'boy! We're heroes, regular Alexanders to these mudsills. Relax."

They admired Sherry and her girls as the dancers twirled and capered onstage. The men glanced at each other and broke into wide grins.

"Relax?"

"Relax."

They raised their whiskey glasses to drain in sublime victory.

Two large hands, the size of skillets, settled on each man's shoulder, gently. The partners paused and turned to regard the giant who loomed over them. The man was a Negro, at least seven feet tall, all of it coiled muscle and barrel chest. His head was shaved smooth and he wore a small gold hoop in one earlobe. His face was broad and flat, and it was strangely placid for a man radiating such power and mass. His eyes were a warm brown, flecked with green. He wore a well-made, and obviously custom, linen shirt with a vest. The giant smiled.

"Gentlemen," he rumbled. His voice had an odd accent that Deerfield recalled from numerous trips to New Orleans—a French patois. "Sorry to interrupt your celebration, gentlemen, but Mr. Bick would care for a word with you both."

"Hands off, boy." It was the mine manager's voice. "The masters don't want to be—"

The hand lifted from Deerfield's shoulder. There was a sound like a chicken bone splintering, about to snap. Moore and Deerfield spun to regard the serene giant holding their six-foot foreman. A massive hand was wrapped around the manager's head, the palm covering his face. He dangled at least a foot off the floor, gasping in pain and shock.

"Upstairs," the giant said to the two businessmen, "please."

The office was dark. The light in the room came from a large fan-shaped window that took up most of the wall behind the desk. It gave an impressive view of Main Street and the darker streets that lay beyond it; Rose Hill, standing like a sentinel at the edge of Golgotha, was a great shadow and above it was the cold black ocean of the desert night, brilliant stars shining like lonely islands. As barren above as below.

Moore and Deerfield entered the room with the giant a few steps behind. Moore was frightened, Deerfield angry. Jacob glanced around the room. There was a beautiful Chippendale sofa, all mahogany and leather, on the left side of the office. The primary piece on the right side was a large glass display table, like something you might see in a museum. It was filled with various items of historical curiosity, like rough-hewn primitive knives, chunks of silver and a grisly collection of what appeared to be small human skulls. Books were everywhere, shelves full of them covering every nook and cranny of the walls. Behind the desk sat Malachi Bick, like some dark Renaissance prince, clothed in shadow.

"Mr. Deerfield, Mr. Moore, what a pleasure to finally meet in person. Welcome to Golgotha."

"What's the meaning of this, Mr. Bick?" Deerfield said, stepping forward and slamming his fist down on the desktop. "Is this how you treat your paying customers! Having your ruffian accost us and force up here? How dare you!"

Bick's eyes flickered in the dark. He regarded Deerfield for a long moment in silence. Long enough for both Moore and Deerfield to grow still with fear.

"Um, what my partner means, Mr. Bick," Moore said, stepping forward timidly, "is, why have you asked to meet with us under such dire circumstances?"

Bick leaned forward and turned up the flame on a small lamp at the edge of his desk. The shadows retreated and the saloon owner lost some of his dread demeanor. He smiled at the two men standing before his desk. It was a white, even smile.

"Gentlemen, my apologies, if Caleb gave you the wrong impression. I sent him personally to retrieve you as a sign of my respect and admiration. He is one of my few surviving children and my favorite son."

"Your son?" Deerfield said. "Boy's blacker than coal."

"Leave us, Caleb," Bick said.

"Yes, Father." The giant nodded. "I'll be close if you need me." He retreated silently from the office.

Bick leaned back in his chair with a soft creak. A tall grandfather clock marked the seconds with metallic ticks in a corner of the room. Bick looked through slitted eyes at the two men standing before his desk, like errant children before a schoolmaster.

"Gentlemen, I want my mine back," he said softly. "I want you to give it to me."

"I'm sure you do, Bick," Deerfield said. "Unfortunately, that is not going to happen."

"Yes, it is," Bick said, steepling his fingers. "You just don't realize it yet."

"I've heard of you, Malachi," Deerfield said. "All the way over in Carson City, Virginia City. Your family seems to think they own all of Nevada. Well, you were the one who made the error of giving poor Arthur control of the mine. You made a mistake and we profited from an opportunity. That's business."

"Yes," Bick said. "It was a mistake to sign the property over to Arthur. It was also exceptional serendipity that you and Mr. Moore were able to capitalize on my folly."

He leaned forward in his chair; his dark eyes caught the light of the lamp like a cat's. "One could say it was almost preternatural, yes?"

Moore blanched and looked to Deerfield.

Deerfield raised a hand to calm his partner. "Okay, Bick. You've lived up to your reputation. You've made your intentions clear and you've managed to scare Jacob. I, however, am not impressed. You heard those people out there—we've given them something you can't anymore; we've given them hope for the future of their home. This town loves us, and you, you are yesterday's news, Malachi."

The clock's ticking stopped. The sounds of the saloon and Main Street seemed to fade. It was as if the air itself was held, frozen. Moore stepped back and tried to interpose Oscar between himself and Bick.

"You've given this town death," Bick said. "Worse than death. You're not businessmen, you're not even fools, Oscar. You're pawns. You have no idea what you have set in motion here."

"We're done here," Deerfield said, turning toward the door. "Come on, Jacob."

"Louis Gantner," Bick said.

Deerfield stopped. "What did you say?"

"Louis Gantner. You do remember him, don't you, Oscar?"

Moore tugged at Deerfield's sleeve, "Oscar, what is it?"

"You had Mr. Gantner murdered three years ago in Baltimore," Bick said. "It had to do with the affections of a young lady from a very prominent, very wealthy family. You paid a cutthroat named Diggs to do the deed, because a man of your status and breeding wouldn't do such a thing. Surely, Oscar, you told your partner about this, didn't you?"

"How?" Deerfield whispered. Moore let go of Oscar. He backed away, shaking his head in disbelief.

"I won't bore you with the details. Suffice to say, by midnight tomorrow, I will have the deed to the mine back, or the authorities in Baltimore will have a letter detailing your plot and naming the names of those involved and where they can be found."

"I had nothing to do with any murder!" Moore shouted. "I don't know anything about this, I swear!"

"Of course you don't," Bick said. "You, Mr. Moore, do not have the courage to commit murder. No, you will receive a telegram tomorrow from your solicitors in Boston. Your mother is dying, Mr. Moore; she has fallen very ill. Or will, if I don't have that deed by midnight, tomorrow."

Moore was sweating, his eyes blinking. Deerfield didn't look much better.

"These things I have told will come to pass," Bick said, rising from his chair, the shadows spreading behind him. "As surely as day follows night, as sure as rain will fall this evening—your ruin is at hand, gentlemen. However, if I receive the deed, then no secrets will be revealed, no plagues will befall your loved ones. Instead, you will find a very generous sum in your accounts in Virginia City. Enough money to compensate you for your time and trouble and pay your men handsomely for theirs."

The clock resumed its steady cadence, the pendulum chasing the endless seconds.

"Now you're done here," Bick said. "Caleb will show you out. Your money is no longer good in my establishment. Good evening, gentlemen."

The giant's hands were upon their backs again, lifting them, dragging them. There had been no sound of Caleb's approach, no warning. They clattered down a dark, narrow stairwell, tight with the smoke and noise of the unseen saloon floor. A door crashed open and they were flying, tumbling through the air. The businessmen smashed into the wall of the alleyway, slid and settled into a pile of red dirt, straw and trash. The door slammed shut and they were alone in the cold night air.

"Are you all right?" Deerfield finally said, struggling to stand.

"We, we need to go to the sheriff," Moore said.

"And tell him what? That he threatened to make your mother, thousands of miles away, ill? That I'm implicated in a murder?"

"Good Lord in Heaven, Oscar! Why didn't you ever tell me?"

Deerfield glared. He reached out a hand and helped his partner up. "No sheriff. We handle Bick ourselves."

"Are you crazy?"

"No, but Ambrose is. I'll send him word tonight through one of those ragamuffins he's been evangelizing. He'll deal with this."

The pair stumbled down the alleyway toward the street behind the Paradise Falls.

"Can we trust him? I mean, Oscar, we could just take him up on his offer. Cut our losses and leave with our skin."

"I'm not going anywhere. No one does that to me, no one! This is our town, our time! No, we'll let the good reverend and his man deal with Malachi Bick."

As if the heavens themselves were offended by the utterance of Bick's name, there came a growl of thunder. A rising wind scattered the trash in the alleyway like frightened birds. Fat, cold raindrops began to fall from a night sky bankrupt of stars.

The storm was more wind than water, but there was enough rain to irritate Otis Haglund as he made a dash from the Black Dog Saloon, at the corner of Duffer and Old Stone, to his single-room shack off of Prosperity Street. Otis was drunk, good and drunk—just the way he had planned it—but now his warm, content, fuzzy inebriation was getting chased away by cold rain and knife-edged winds.

"Damn it all to Hell!" he shouted as he lumbered between the rows of dark homes. He pulled his coat up over his head, but that left his considerable middle exposed to the wind and the spitting rain and that made him curse too.

When he first came to Golgotha he had lived in the back of his butcher shop. However, complaints about his general appearance and cleanliness, and the difficulty of enticing women, even whores, to return with him to the slaughterhouse, had prompted him to build a home among the other working-class citizens of the town.

He reached his house and fumbled to retrieve the door key around his neck. Rain trickled down the back of his neck and he knew the jig was up. He was sober.

It was that haughty bitch Proctor's fault. If he hadn't stayed late at the butcher shop to go over the details of what she needed for the church social this Saturday, he would have gotten to the Dog on time and then he would have been home by now and wouldn't have the Devil pissing all over him, wasting a perfectly good drunk.

The wind grabbed the handle from his hands and the thin wooden door slammed open, spilling what little light the cloudy night provided across his floor and far wall. It illuminated a small, embroidered homily in a wooden frame. His mother had made it for him before she passed, twelve years ago. It was the only piece of Scripture he had in his house.

As he fumbled to find the lantern and the matches on the shelf by the door, he undressed Gillian Proctor in his mind for the thousandth time that day. The widow had a striking figure and Otis knew, *knew,* if he could only get that witch to let her hair down he could give her what she must want, must *need,* with Will Proctor five years in the ground.

Thick, blunt fingers still dark with the blood of Otis's craft fumbled with the lantern's shroud. He held a matchstick in his mouth as he struggled. Just this afternoon, while they discussed the cuts and the weight of the meat she needed him to deliver to her by Friday morning, he caught a flash of white stocking above her ankles when she "adjusted" her dress. The little whore was teasing him! When she noticed his attentions, she had the nerve to blush behind her owl-like spectacles and look away. The very thought of it made him hungry for her again, made his anger and need churn.

Otis sniffed the air. He smelled something, something pungent and musky even thorough the cold night air and the rain at his back.

In the darkness, the scent called to him. It spoke to the dark little scuttling corners of his mind, the parts that wanted to hang Gillian Proctor on a meat hook and do what he wanted to her undisturbed. The part of him that lost itself in the flesh of Ch'eng Huang's whores and the warm spray of slaughtering a cow. That was it! That was what he smelled—it was the perfume of rutting and slaughter. His manhood stirred as he struck the match. The sharp, acrid scent of sulfur seemed completely appropriate as he touched the match to the lantern's wick. Soft yellow light filled the room and illuminated his ramshackle home.

Holly Pratt, golden locks falling to her shoulders, sat, long legs crossed, on his cot, smiling with her perfect, white teeth.

"Hello, Otis, I'm so glad you're home. I've been waiting for you. Please shut the door."

"Mrs. Pratt?" he stammered. It was hard to think straight with the thoughts swirling around his skull and the smell. He stepped inside and closed the door. The scent seemed to surge, like the storm outside. It enveloped him and he found himself breathing it in deeply, eagerly. He felt alive, potent, real. He realized, he *knew,* the scent was coming from Holly. He placed the lantern on its shelf, near the window.

"You know, I always liked the way you used to look at me out of the corners of your eyes," she said as she rose. She was wearing a long coat, heavy and gray—a man's military coat from the war. It fell to her bare ankles and feet. "Like a dog that hadn't eaten in a week. Starving. You were starving for me, weren't you?"

"Yes," he said with a croak. It was very hot in the small room. It should be cold, a distant, timid part of his mind said. Holly opened the coat and shrugged. It fell to the floor.

She was nude, her skin luminescent in the lantern's buttery light. Her nipples and thighs were dark and wet, slick with something blacker than molasses.

"I loved the way your shop always smelled," she said. "The fresh slaughter, the coppery stench. It thrilled me. I was too timid, too weak and afraid to admit it, even to myself."

She stepped toward him. The blackness leaking from her breasts and nethers was rich with the scent. He breathed it in, breathed her in.

"Come to me. Never be afraid; never hide from yourself, from what's inside, again," she said.

He was close enough now to see her eyes. They were black and something was moving behind the darkness, like eels swimming in oil. Her teeth were still beautiful, but he could see now that they, too, were stained midnight, as was her mouth and tongue. The sweet blood-sex-death smell wafted from inside her mouth.

"Come." She cradled his neck and pulled him to her bosom. His hungry mouth found the slick nipple. His rough hands clutched at her alabaster buttocks, like a drowning man grabbing for a rope. He sucked her nipple, the sweet, bitter nectar filling his mouth and mind. He bit down savagely on her flesh and she moaned and mewled in pleasure and pain. She finally pulled him away, his lips black now. His mind was afire with all the dreams he had chased from his mind in fear and guilt, all the desires he refused to acknowledge. He glanced briefly at his mother's homily and renounced her impotent God, his humanity drowning in honeyed tar. He had to share this feeling with Gillian Proctor, with the world. The absolute peace of savagery, the sublime ecstasy of obliteration. Death was pleasure; death was union; death was power; death was freedom. Death was life.

"Kiss me," Holly whispered in his ear, her tongue flicking like a serpent's. Otis pressed his mouth to the lips of his goddess, his Black Madonna. He was an animal in heat, whimpering, begging. Her tongue was strong, grinding, writhing against his own. It pushed deeper into his mouth, deeper, insistent on reaching his core, his soul. His eyes opened wide for an instant, as the tongue felt like it tore loose from her mouth and wriggled eagerly down his throat.

His last human thought was of the Widow Proctor and how he wished he could warn her.

The moaning stopped. The room was silent. The Mother shuddered at the pleasure of fission, of birth. Their lips parted, sticky ropes of black stretching, breaking. Otis's eyes were ebony mirrors of the Mother's leaking black tears. She took his hands and steepled them together. With her new tongue, her next child, she licked the animal blood off his hands like a cat lapping at milk. The black, oily worm shuddered and vibrated eagerly as it fed off the juices of life, the by-product of murder. It nestled into her mouth and waited for its time.

Some tiny corner of Holly Pratt that had not yet decayed, had not yet lost itself to the sweet oblivion of madness, realized with sick joy that she finally had the children she had always wanted.

"Let us pray," she said.

Outside, the storm stalked angrily through the dark streets of Golgotha, spitting, raging. A lone, feeble yellow light filtered through the single filthy window in Otis Haglund's shack, defying the darkness and the storm. The light guttered, then failed.

The Five of Cups

He cleared the dead grass and dirt off the small pile of stones that marked his mother's grave. The rain had passed and was already forgotten to late morning heat.

Mutt crouched at the edge of the simple stone ring. He remembered placing each rock carefully. Before that he had dug the hole, and before that was the memory of wrapping her in her favorite rabbit fur blanket. Before that came the end of the whispered words fighting their way past dry, cracked lips, the closing of the eyes damp with love and fever. And before that . . .

Whichever way he looked at his time here, it ended and began in pain.

He ran his hand over a smooth, flat stone. Laying this circle was the last time he had truly felt like a human being. Until Maude . . . No, that had to be pushed away, dismissed, for her sake, and for his.

He stood and examined the remains of his mother's *gadu*. Collapsed and overrun with small bushes and tall grass, the small, slatted summer shelter had been abandoned since he had buried his mother and gone off into the white man's world. Muha munched casually on some grass near the *gadu*. He was tired from the ride from Golgotha to the lake country south of Reno. It was near the water that the We'lmelti camped and it would be dark before Mutt would reach it today.

He was in no hurry. He was sore and thirsty and still angry. This was a fool's errand. His people had nothing to do with Holly Pratt's disappearance. This was just that jackass Harry's revenge for pushing him so hard.

Mutt knew it was stupid to taunt the mayor so much, but he had never been very good at kissing ass. Ran in the family.

He removed his kit from Muha's saddle and tried to dismiss the anger. Mother was here and he didn't want to disturb her. She always tried to soothe his anger with soft song and gentle hands stroking his hair. Loneliness stabbed him like a dull knife. He was so alone in this world. For a second, he remembered his other family, his father, then dismissed them all with a hiss. He was alone.

He cleared out a spot in the *gadu* and put down his bedroll, blankets and rifle. He built a fire in the same spot he and his mother had for over ten years. The moon rose over the tree line, bright and bloated. Mutt squatted by the fire and watched it writhe. The planet spun dizzily under his feet.

Far, far off he could smell the cool, damp air above the water, almost taste it. He sensed the movement of a big, fat jackrabbit about a mile out in the scrub; its big feet thudded like drums.

He licked his lips, felt the night slip into his bones, like cold. He shrugged himself off, like shucking off a coat that was too tight. It always felt like taking off horse blinders; he always forgot so quickly how unaware he was most of the time. Now, again, the night was his eyes, his ears; the booming of the jackrabbit as it ran for its life was the tattoo of his heart. Here, in this, lost in instinct, lost in the hunt and the wordless beauty of the world, pale in weird moonlight and wrapped in a fog of living, dying smells—here there was never any doubt, never any fear or loneliness—there was only need and the power to fulfill it. He thought of Maude Stapleton as the warm spray of the rabbit's blood filled his mouth, and he wished he could feel ashamed, but he had forgotten how, already.

Later, by the fire, nude, warped back in the tightness of his skin, Mutt looked across the flames and remembered the night his mother had died, the night he had met his father. For a moment Mutt thought he saw something move on the other side of the fire, but there was nothing there but flickering shadow.

He knew he should get up, clean off the blood and go to sleep inside the *gadu,* like his mother had taught him, like a human being. Instead he curled up beside the fire and let the night's music lull him to sleep.

———

The children saw him coming. Most of them ran beside Muha, shouting and laughing. They had been gathering *ta gum* for the *goom sa bye* ceremony, to be held in the fall. The older boys ran ahead to warn the camp a stranger was coming. The camp seemed smaller than he remembered it—a few dozen *gadus* clustered near the sandy banks of the Da' ow lake. Women were busy tossing the cones into fires to open them and extract the *ta gum*. Others were grinding the *ta gum*, or pine nuts, into flour. They sang stories as they worked. His mother had sang those songs as well, when she was young, before they drove her out because of him.

A group of men made their way toward Mutt. Only one was mounted, from the looks of it on a stolen Shoshoni bangtail. He led the way, with a Winchester rifle in his hand. Mutt stopped at the edge of the village path and waited for him, his hand resting on his own six-gun.

"Kote," Mutt said with a nod. "You the *deu bay u* now, huh? Suits you. Guess the other bosses forgot all that stuff we did when we were boys."

Kote narrowed his eyes as he brought the bangtail to a stop. The rifle didn't drop any. "You never earned a name here; what do you call yourself these days?"

"Mutt."

"What do you want here, Mutt?"

"You're still scared of me, aren't you? You don't even want to me to set foot in the camp. It's been over twenty years, Kote. You and the old women still think I'm a witch?"

Kote cocked the rifle. The other men of the camp caught up to him and several of them followed his lead, aiming their guns at Mutt.

"What do you want here?" Kote said.

"A white woman with yellow hair. She went missing a few days back outside of Golgotha. I'm out here looking to see if anyone has been a'raiding."

"Your name fits, Mutt. You're out here sniffing around like a dog for the white man. Accusing your own people of—"

"Spare me the indignation, especially when you're sitting on a stolen horse. I grew up around here, remember? Now, has anyone been bragging about taking hostages?"

"You make me sick," Kote said, his eyes dark and hot. "First the Paiute come and crush us—take away our horses, take away our honor—then the white men steal our lands out from under us to dig their precious silver.

They can't even keep their promise to move us to better land. You serve them, like a dog. You should be ashamed."

"As ashamed as you were of me? Of my mother?" Mutt said, staring unblinking into Kote's eyes. "You bastards chased her out because you thought she had given herself to a man from another tribe and the 'holy elders' were pissed they didn't get anything for it. You treated me like a diseased animal, and you treated her like a whore. You and your 'noble people' are a bunch of freeloading parasites, too scared of the Paiute, too scared of the white man, to do anything but complain, and steal whatever you can in the night."

The singing by the waters had stopped and many of the women and children were approaching the men. Mutt lowered his voice to a growl.

"You think I'm a *Hanuh wui wui*—a monster? Then you pull that trigger, Kote, and when the bullets pass right through me I'm going to take that gun and stick it up your ass."

The men were all silent. Many lowered their heads. Kote looked away.

"I got my answer," Mutt said, turning Muha away from his childhood home. "None of you is man enough to kidnap a white woman. I knew this was a waste of time."

He rode off. He didn't look back.

He knew the whiskey would burn in his throat. He also knew it would take the ache away, eventually. Mutt had bought the bottle off a Nogaie trader. After leaving the We'lmelti, he had ridden to a few other camps—the Nogaie, the Paxai-dika. No one knew anything about Holly. *Happy now, Harry?*

The most interesting thing Mutt heard was from a half-blind old Paiute with eyes like milk mixed with ink. The old man told him about a teacher and healer up in Smith Valley, near Carson City, name of Hawthorne Wodziwob. This Wodziwob was organizing circle dances among the tribes and talking of visions—visions of the spirits promising the return of the Paiute dead in the next few years, if the people honored the tradition of the dance. He was traveling around with a medicine man named Tavibo who was helping him organize the dances, along with Tavibo's son, a thirteen-year-old named Wovoka.

"They will heal the land," the old man had said. "They will drive out the whites."

"I wouldn't bet on it, old-timer," Mutt had said. "You can't count on the spirits for a damned thing, 'cept maybe to have a good laugh at your expense."

Now he was back at his mother's home, once again sitting at the edge of the fire and eager to head back to Golgotha and leave his past behind. The night called to him like it did the night before, like it did every night. The pain in him, the human pain in his human heart, dulled its song.

He took a long draw on the bottle and closed his eyes. He felt the smoky liquor burn, then numb, his mouth. Suddenly he saw how he had been when he had met Jon Highfather—the only man who'd ever given him a fair shake—how deep into a bottle he had crawled before Jon pulled him out.

He spit out the whiskey and the flames roared, jumped and hissed. They died down. A large gray coyote now sat across the fire where only a second ago there had been shadow.

"Waste of good firewater, you ask me," the coyote said. He had eyes the color of gray sand, shifting. "How are you, boy?"

"What the hell do you want?" Mutt said, chucking the bottle in the coyote's general direction. It missed and landed in the brush with a rustle and a clank. The coyote didn't move an inch.

"This is about where we were sitting around this very fire pit about, how long ago was it? Oh yes, twenty-two years. Long time for men and coyotes. Not long at all for mountains or gods."

"Say your peace," Mutt said. "Then git."

"Your brother told me you refused my warning to get out of Golgotha. I'm curious, why?"

"Didn't he tell you?"

"I want to hear it from you."

"I'm not going to abandon my friends."

"Oh, of course, I can see that. After all they've done for you. Touching. Very human. Stupid."

"I didn't ask what you thought about it," Mutt said.

"Then you'll get this for free," the coyote said, licking his chops. "This theatre stage, this playground we call the world, may die in the next few days. If it does, it will all begin in Golgotha, and if you are there, then you will die too, along with all your friends. How noble, how sad. Did I mention the stupid part?"

"What is it?" Mutt said, leaning forward toward the fire. "What's got the great fire stealer himself so scared?"

The coyote snorted indignantly. "Not scared, boy, just not stupid. When you hear thunder and you see storm clouds, you know well enough to find a shelter out of the rain. Least most folk do."

"What is it?" Mutt asked again. "I can smell it, strong medicine, in the soil, in the wind. Something unnatural, even for Golgotha. Seen the signs too. That boy I found in the desert, he reeked of death medicine, powerful stuff. You sent the others out to fetch whatever it is he's got. He was drawn here, but he doesn't know it."

"They seldom do," Coyote said with a dry chuckle that sounded more like a hiss. "Golgotha keeps calling and they keep coming. This thing is the reason for that. It straddles all the worlds built by gods and men. Older than me and a damn sight less pretty. Older than any god man has ever been able to dream up in his skull, balls or heart. It's got something to do with how things got started. Back in the beginning of this world . . . I was part of all that, you know?"

Mutt sighed. "Yeah, yeah, I've heard the stories."

"Even the one about me and the—"

"Yes. Several times."

"How 'bout the one about me and the—"

"Yes! Go on!"

" 'Cause that's a real old one and not many—"

"Will you just—"

"Okay, okay. You know, all that time on two legs—it's really damaged your patience, and your sense of humor."

Coyote paused for a second. The fire crackled. Mutt realized his father was preparing to tell a story, and even though he hated this creature, resented him terribly for all he had put Mutt's mother and him through, he felt a thrill of anticipation because he also knew nobody, nobody, told a story like Coyote.

"Back when this world was dark water and mud," Coyote began, "back before men, or time, back when all places were one place, this creature lived in the darkness between all the worlds, all the possibilities. It wasn't man or woman—it simply was. It was the time before naming things, but later, the people would call it the great and terrible serpent—the Uktena.

"Then the Creator, who the whites tell the people to call 'the great white grandfather,' made the sun and filled all the corners of the worlds with light. And the Uktena screamed a mouthless scream, its first aware thought. That scream echoed through the hall of worlds and still does to this day—we call it madness.

"The white men's God was horrified by what He beheld waiting for Him in the new light. You see, the white man's God was a lot like him. He never for a second figured there was anyone else already here. He figured it was all just here waiting for Him to do whatever He wanted to with it. And boy, do white people love to do stuff, just to do it.

"The light cut the Uktena. The light made all of the possibilities reality, and drove a great blazing diamond into the Uktena's skull—what the people call Ulun'suti. The crystal has great powers—in fact, it was the first source of medicine in all the worlds. The Uktena hated the light, hated the churning of the still-dark waters of potential into the sparkling spray of actuality. So it warred against the light, warred against life itself. The cuts made by the light dripped blood and from its blood came the dark, cold lifeless places between the worlds; from the blood came the Uktena's spawn—the Black Mother with a thousand hungry young."

Coyote stopped.

"And?" Mutt said.

"And what?" Coyote said. "The story isn't over yet. The next part is happening now, in Golgotha. Maybe the last part."

"What does the Uktena have to do with my town?"

"Listen to you, 'your town.' Wise up, pup. You don't have a town—you don't have anything. You're a child of the flame and the dust—you're my child and it's time to git while the gitting is good. Come on, let's go play while the worlds are still here to play in."

Mutt shook his head. "I had a mother. I had a home here a long time ago. I have friends now and I have this badge. I've got plenty."

Coyote cocked his head, at a loss for words—a rarity. Finally, "Your loss," he said. "You want to live like a dumb human, fine. You can die like one too."

They were both silent across the fire for a long time. The flames snapped and crackled, fighting against the wind.

"Do you ever miss her?" Mutt finally said. "Do you even think about her at all?"

"Not really, no," Coyote said. "Don't take that personal. It's just the way I am, the way I have to be."

Coyote rose. Mutt smelled the dawn, distant but inevitable, moving toward them.

"Time to move on," Coyote said. "I've wasted enough time with you."

Mutt nodded. Coyote began to slowly pad away from the fire, into the brush. He looked back toward Mutt.

"Last chance for some fun."

"No thanks," Mutt said. "I don't cotton much to your kind of fun."

"Don't be so sure," Coyote said, and disappeared into the brush.

"You can't kill it," the coyote's voice called, diminishing. "It's older than death. But you can hurt it, trap it. Remember that, boy! Things from the other worlds—things of spirit—it's vulnerable to them. I think that boy in the desert, I think he has the Ulun'suti on him.

"You're still a damn fool!" The voice seemed to fold itself into the cold morning wind. "But what do you expect? You're my son!"

Mutt smiled, despite himself. The wind carried a distant coyote's *yip, yip yip,* running ahead of the judgment of dawn.

By noon, Mutt was headed for Golgotha, headed for home.

The Ten of Wands

Auggie hadn't realized he was staring at Gillian Proctor until she met his gaze and smiled. He dropped his eyes and resumed wrestling with the small keg of molasses they were both hunched over. Auggie's thick fingers fumbled with the tap while Gillian tried to hold the sealed wooden cask steady for him. Finally he stabbed the small metal pipe into the wood with a soft *thunk*.

"You're a kindness," she said as he hefted the cask onto her kitchen table with a grunt. He pulled a handkerchief from his pocket and mopped his red, sweating face. "I couldn't have gotten this all done in a week without your help, Auggie."

The shopkeeper shrugged and put the hankie away. "I did nothing. You are the cook, I'm just the pack mule for the ingredients, *ja*?"

She laughed. It was a wonderful sound, Auggie thought. Here, in the kitchen of her boardinghouse, her hair falling down from her bun, a smudge of flour on her nose. She was lovely in the morning light. Her hand rested on his for just a moment on the tabletop. She looked into his brown eyes.

"Thank you," she said.

He was trying to find a way to dismiss this intimacy in as gruff a manner as possible, but he found he didn't want to. He found a comfort in her eyes, her touch, that he had almost forgotten.

There was a knock at the open kitchen door.

"Oh, I hope I'm not disturbing anything!" Reverend Prine said, removing his hat.

Prine was a fit whip of a man, dressed simply in black. The small amount
of hair that circled his head was snow-white. His eyes were ice blue and his
smile was open and honest. He was smiling now.

"Reverend!" Gillian said, eyes wide. Both she and Auggie pulled their
hands away and took a step away from each other. Auggie bumped into a
chair.

Prine chuckled. "Just came by to see how the spread for the social was
coming along," he said. "Looks like things are developing nicely."

"*Ja*," Auggie stammered. "I was just getting back to the store. I have
to . . . have to open. *Ja*."

"I hope you know how much the church appreciates your efforts, Augustus," Prine said, entering the kitchen. "Not to mention Aaron Burke and his
fiancée, Mary Toller, are just pleased as punch that they get to announce the
date for the wedding there! It's a big deal for them and for the whole town.
Gillian has been telling us how much help you've been to her in this under-
taking. Feeding the better part of a hungry town is no small feat."

He offered a long, strong hand. Auggie clasped it and they shook.

"I was just telling Gillian that she was doing all the hard work, I'm just
making deliveries," Auggie said.

"Nonsense," Prine said. "We've had so many people not show up for
planning meetings this week and then Otis Haglund promised us all that
meat and his butcher shop hasn't been open for two days. If you hadn't had
those hams, we would have had a very bare table indeed, Augustus."

"I saw Dale and Margaret Hill's store was closed today too," Gillian said.
"You think something is going around?"

"I know Mr. Branchwell and Widow Marr have both been under the
weather," Prine said.

"Still?" Gillian said. "I was meaning to go check on them, but I've been
so busy this week. It's very unchristian of me."

"You can only do so much," Prine said. "I've tried to minister to several
folk this week. No one is answering their door, it seems."

Prine chuckled nervously.

Auggie realized how few people he had seen on the street this morning,
how many shops were unaccustomedly closed. He had been so busy, so lost,
in helping Gillian prepare that he hadn't noticed. No, that was a lie. He
hadn't been lost in helping her; he had been lost in her. He'd been finding

excuses to be with her, ignoring other things that needed to be attended to, in order to spend time with her. Another lie. Not "other things"—Gerta. He had been avoiding Gerta.

"Well, " Prine finally said. "I hope we have a good turnout for the social, despite whatever it is laying people up. I know we should. People have been looking forward to this for months now and everyone wants to see Aaron and Mary together. It will be fine."

"Maybe we should let Sheriff Highfather and Mayor Pratt know just how many people are out of sorts," Gillian said.

"I'll let Jon know," Prine said. "I'll go by the jail tonight after I ride out to check on the Humbolts—they haven't been in town for two days. Let's leave poor old Harry be. He's had an awful time since Holly went missing . . ."

". . . about two days ago," Auggie said softly.

A strange claustrophobia filled the room. The three stood silent, lost in tumbling thoughts.

The streets *were* emptier today. Auggie drove the wagon back to the store. Not empty enough to be immediately noticeable, but familiar faces moving along familiar social orbits were missing. Mr. Dunn wasn't sweeping the plank walk in front of his barbershop. That dandy Blackthorn wasn't changing the marquee at Mephisto's Playhouse and Showcase to announce what new production was replacing the current run of *The King in Yellow*.

Something was wrong. The town seemed bigger, more sinister, colder. The feeling of tightness in his chest returned. Auggie tried to dismiss it and found he was thinking of Gillian. His fear was replaced with guilt.

He turned into the narrow alley between Mephisto's Playhouse and his shop, and brought the wagon to a stop behind his store. The back door was wide open. It had been locked.

Auggie climbed off the buckboard and approached the door. The memory of old Earl, his gun pressed against Auggie's chest, muscled its way to the front of Auggie's mind. He picked up the axe that was leaning against a small woodpile and stepped into the interior gloom.

The only light in the back room was from the open door and a small, narrow window. Dust motes drifted in the window's beam, like stars floating through the cosmos. Auggie moved cautiously, his back to a wall. There was no one in the room he could see, but he edged along cautiously, made sure every box was a box, every table was a table. There was a loud thump overhead—from his and Gerta's small home. It sounded like boots, tromping through his home, Gerta's home.

Gerta.

The realization launched him into action. Auggie smashed through the door in the storeroom that led to the small staircase. He strode up them, two at a time, axe in hand. He stepped into the dimly lit apartment, panting from his exertion and in fear of what he would find.

Clay Turlough sat at the small kitchen table. Gerta was in front of him on the table, as were a variety of bottles and tools. Low moaning came through the tank's speaker. The liquid within was very dark.

"What the hell do you think you are . . . ?" Auggie rumbled, angry and relieved at the same time.

Clay stood; his face was a mask of rage in the pale, greenish glow of the tank lights. "I'm trying to help her," he spit, crossing the room to face the burly shopkeeper. "She's sick, real sick! You haven't been doing any of the things I told you to do! You haven't been skimming the tank, you haven't been replacing the old formula with the new and it's damn obvious to everyone in town you haven't been talking to her enough!"

"You leave Gillian out of this! I was only—"

Another moan from the speaker. Auggie let the axe slip from his hands to the floor. He walked slowly toward the tank.

"Gerta?"

The eyes fluttered open. One of the lids was starting to come loose at the edge and wavered a little bit in the glowing green water.

"Auggggguuuuuustus?" she replied, like waking from a painful fever dream. *"How long? It hasssssss been sssssssso long."*

He leaned over his wife, the hot tears building behind his eyes. He fought to hold them at bay. He had no right to weep. Clay stood at his shoulder.

"I know it has. I am so sorry, Gerta. I was . . . preoccupied, but that is over with now, my love. I am here for you."

Gertie did something neither man could recall her doing since her living days. She smiled, as best she could. It cost her more tearing of the eyelid and some of the skin on her cheeks.

"It is all right, my darling. I know I have been sick for a long time and I don't want you to be stuck here at my side all day long. It is fine, yes?"

Clay Turlough understood human physiology better than any other man in this town. He knew the mechanics of the human form intimately, and yet he was at a loss to explain why his throat was tightening, his eyes dampening, as he listened.

"Is the weather good, my love? Are the flowers blooming off the desert?"

"Ja . . . yes, they are very beautiful. Very beautiful."

"That is good," she muttered, and smiled again. Already her eyes were closing. Clockwork ticking following each motion, the hum of tight springs. *"Would you ask Gillian to pick me some for my bedside table? I miss the flowers very much."*

Tears fell down Auggie's cheek, hot and insistent, like the pain in his soul had turned molten and had nowhere to go but out, out into the world. They made tiny silver ripples on the surface of the tank's dark liquid.

"I will get them for you, love," he croaked.

"I'mmmmm sorry, Augustus," she said, the distortion beginning to muffle her words. *"I'm sorry I have been sick so long."*

"Hush, darling. Rest now; please just rest." His shoulder heaved silently.

The tears struck the liquid: *pat, pat, pat.*

"Sssssssssomeone was singing to me," she said, dreamily. *"Was it you, Augustus?"*

"It was me, Gertie," Clay said.

"Oh, Clayton. It wasssssss very beauuuuuuutiful. I had almost forgotten music. Please, ssssssssing to me some more."

Clay slid past Auggie. Two pairs of red, wet eyes glared at each other in accusation, sadness and camaraderie.

"Okay, Gertie, let me sing you a dittie," Clay said, wiping his eyes and sniffing.

Auggie plodded into the living room. He made his way down the stairs to the sounds of Clay's singing.

The Two of Wands

The third shift never came out of the mine.

The mine manager, Easton, ordered word to be sent to Deerfield and Moore that there might be trouble. Easton then went down, personally, with the men of the morning shift, leading the way into the maw of the mine with a pair of canaries in a cage on a long pole.

Morning ground away into mid-day and there was no word from either shift.

Deerfield and Moore arrived from their hotels around one. A senior miner named Kelly met them near the entrance to the mining camp.

"When Easton went in, he told me to take charge if there was any trouble," Kelly said. "It's past time for first shift to be up and second to go down. What do you good sirs want us to do?"

"Where is Mr. Phillips?" Deerfield asked, wiping his face with a handkerchief.

"Well, sir, that part is very queer. A few of the fellas on guard detail said that Phillips and Reverend Ambrose showed up here last night when second shift was getting off. They say that Phillips ordered all the remaining blasting materials loaded onto rail carts and taken into the mine. He said you had authorized some additional blasting."

"We did no such thing!" Moore said, looking at Deerfield.

"No, we didn't," Deerfield said. "The reverend and Phillips went down with the third shift?"

"Yessir."

Deerfield sighed. They had contacted Ambrose after the incident with Bick last night and had received a most cryptic response from Ambrose's man, Phillips, by letter waiting for them this morning at their hotel.

The Reverend says that Mr. Bick will be dealt with—have faith and rejoice for the day of blessed rest is at hand, the note announced in Phillips's small, neat utterance.

Phillips was a mystery to Deerfield. The man was large, powerfully built, and obviously had a constitution of steel to deal with explosives as temperamental as dynamite. Ambrose had mentioned once that Phillips had fought in the war and lost his family to it. The huge, imposing figure was seldom far from the reverend's side and Ambrose often called him his deacon. There was something about Phillips that had always sat very unwell with Deerfield—an impression, nothing more. Back home, Deerfield owned a cat, a black Persian. It was a magnificent creature and it often seemed to suddenly stare off into space, as if it were regarding something Deerfield could not see. Phillips had the same look.

"Very well. Damn it all to Hell! Mr. Kelly, round up the remaining men. Equip them and prepare to go below. We shall be accompanying you."

"Yessir."

Moore looked at Deerfield with a look normally reserved for deer on the wrong side of a gun.

"Oscar, are you sure that is the best policy?" Moore said. "I mean, these mines are terribly unstable, not to mention filthy. And I am terribly susceptible to the chill. Let's let the men go down: It's what they do; it's what we pay them for."

Deerfield was already inspecting a hooded lantern. He placed it on a crate and pulled a small pocket derringer from his waistcoat.

"I am tired of whatever game it is Ambrose and his man have gotten us into, Jacob. Bick is deadly serious about his threats and I am becoming more and more convinced we have been used by Ambrose."

Deerfield snapped open the breech of the small gun. Satisfied that it was loaded and ready, he closed it with a metallic click, and put it away.

"I am tired of this. I'm tired of feeling manipulated by Ambrose, by Bick. I'm going to get some answers. Go or stay, Jacob, I'm tired of your cowardice and, honestly, to blazes with you."

Deerfield picked up the lantern and moved to the front of the gathering crowd of miners. Many of the men were carrying rifles as well as picks. A few clutched Bibles and crucifixes. They all looked tense and frightened.

Moore rubbed his face and looked at the ground. His shadow was growing longer, bleeding into the darkening ground. He sighed and prepared a lantern of his own before he shuffled up to his appointed place a few steps behind and to the right of Deerfield.

"Men!" Deerfield shouted to the assembled miners. "Stay calm and keep your ears open and your eyes peeled down there. With that dynamite and any gas pockets down there, there's no shooting unless I order it. Some damned fool starts popping off his gun and he could bring the whole place down on us . . . and if he doesn't kill us, I'll kill him myself."

Kelly made his way to the mouth of the mine. He held a canary cage on a long pole. The bird chirped and fluttered about.

"Very good, Mr. Kelly," Deerfield said. "Let's go."

The descent was made in silence. There was an occasional cough, sniff or whisper. But the men were focused on every shadow, every sound, not that there were many. This deep under were absolutes of darkness and stillness. Douse your lantern, stop walking, slow your breathing and you'd find yourself enveloped, absorbed by them.

No sound—especially the comforting murmur of nature most people ignore consciously but that constantly reminds them they are connected to life, to a living world. No light—not even the tiniest moon-sliver shimmer of illumination for the starving eye to grasp at. Void. This far below the earth, the only reminders a man carried that such a verdant place even existed were whatever he carried in the bone vault of his mind.

The party reached the slopes for the third level, near where Phillips had blasted earlier in the week. The wooden horses, cordoning off the new vein, lay in the dust. The support timbers for the entrance were jammed crookedly into the living rock, giving the maw the impression of a snag-toothed, leering grin.

"Stop," Deerfield said. There was something on the floor along with the discarded barriers. He knelt down while Moore aimed his lantern's beam at the ground.

It was a canary, the tiny form twisted and stiff, its dark eyes wide and vapid in death. One of the miners muttered an oath; another, a prayer.

"This way," Deerfield said. "It didn't die from gas, I'd wager. They came this way. So do we."

The new tunnels were narrow and jagged. A man had to move through most of them sideways, with an arm thrust out in front of him holding his lantern. The heavy, silent air reeked of dust, lamp oil and blasting powder.

Deerfield heard Moore's coughing and panting behind him; the noise bounced off the tight passages. Jacob really wasn't cut out for this kind of thing. Deerfield was about to call back to his partner and tell him to head back up when one of the men near the front shouted out. The message made its way along the human telegraph line quickly.

"A room! There's a room in the mountain!"

The jagged incision of a passage gave way to smooth walls covered in tiny, crowded script that seemed to crawl like hungry maggots across the beams of the lanterns. The chamber was vast, stretching well past the feeble lights. The wind howled all around the huge open space and cold drafts of air raked the miners' faces. The floor was covered with the thin, shaky symbols as well, layer after layer, circles in circles. Moore tried to not look at them too long, pulling his lantern's beam away from the floor.

"Steady, lads," Deerfield said as they spread out from the narrow tunnel. He fumbled for his pistol. This place was old, older than he could fully comprehend. He could feel the press of its age seeping into his bones with the cold. This place wasn't some fluke, some naturally occurring cave—it was hacked from the living stone long before men walked upright. Smoothed with devoted hands, working until they were bloody, age after age, generation after generation.

One of the men near the rear of the party tried to sound out the things on the wall. He retched, suddenly and violently. Another recited the Lord's Prayer. Someone chambered a round into a rifle

Something moved in the infinite darkness, something without shape, without borders. There was a sound—a snake's scales scratching, crunching across dry, dirty stone.

"I think something is in here," Moore whispered. "Let's get the hell out of—"

"Shut up, Jacob," Deerfield muttered. He turned to Kelly. "Have your men focus their light in this direction. Keep the hoods shrouded partly. This wind will kill the lamps."

The sound came closer—shuffle, crunch.

Deerfield's pistol was slippery in his palm; he clutched it tighter—he wished he could wipe his palm on his pants, but there was no way he was lowering his lantern. He could hear Moore wheezing behind him and he wanted so badly to strike him. Fear was to be controlled, to be mastered—not wallowed in, like a sow in mud. Only a weakling and a fool put his fear on display for the world to see.

"Steady!" Deerfield called out to the men, then to the darkness, "Who goes there! We are armed and will fire! Identify yourself!"

The scratching, shuffling stopped.

"I am a servant of God!" a voice in the darkness said. "I am the instrument of His will and His will shall be done. Glorious Hallelujah!"

The voice carried more than a little of the New England Puritan in it—booming, confident, almost arrogant. As it rose in volume, it became shriller in timbre, nearly feminine. It reverberated oddly in the blustery darkness.

"Ambrose?" Deerfield called out. "To damnation, man! Is that you?"

An old man stepped into the buttery light. He was nude, covered in something glistening that seemed to eat the lantern's light, shimmering. His hair and beard were also dripping in the viscous muck.

"Is that oil?" a miner said.

"Blood?" another voice responded.

"Hello, Oscar, m'boy," Ambrose said with a wet, black smile. He held a curved blade in his hand. It bore the same unknowable, slithering marks as the floor. "Jacob, it's wonderful to see you here as well. All are welcome in the temple."

"Temple? What the blazes is all this, damn you!" Deerfield barked. "I have had enough of your nonsense, 'Reverend'! Where are my men?"

"They were never your men, Oscar," Ambrose said as he slowly raked the blade across his wiry, muscular chest. Several of the men gasped; a few uttered prayers. The wind howled around them and the lanterns began to gutter. "We all belong to God—to the Greate Olde One Who predates time, predates matter, Who was usurped by the false god—the Demiurge. He built his sickening Heaven upon the bodies of the Lord's fallen children, built this sick parody of a world with their bones."

They all sensed something gathering around them in the darkness and the miners instinctively fell together, back-to-back. Guns were brandished, cocked, leveled, trembling. Moore and Deerfield found themselves next to one another, neither able to take his eyes off the old priest. Deerfield raised his pocket gun; his hand was steady, despite the humming desire inside of him to scream and flee.

"Stop it," Deerfield whispered.

"Made this earth His cage, His prison, for that which existed before death cannot die—cannot die! Cannot be destroyed, even by the God of this hollow world! Can never die! *Hallelujah! Nephren-Ka, N'gai, Eibon Thasaidon, Yegg-ha, Yegg-ha, Yegg-ha! Nyogtha!* He is waking! He is rising! He is almost free, Oscar, and you belong to Him—we all belong to Him! Rejoice! You shall know the glory of oblivion—the ecstasy of negation!"

Ambrose stopped doodling in his flesh with the knife. Other figures, shuffling, appeared at the ragged edges of the lantern's light. They walked shoulder to shoulder and their numbers were legion. The other shifts, all of them, their black eyes wept darkness, glistening, like a slug's trail. The midnight fluid leaked from their noses, their ears, drooling from their mouths. They were full of it—a weeping mask that devoured the light.

And Oscar could suddenly hear singing—tuneless, an idiot falsetto parroting Genesis in a language not designed for human ears. Mocking, the whine of a flute made out of a human femur rattlesnake whirred an ice-knife tune up and down his spine.

The lost shifts shuffled forward, toward their former companions, toward the feeble illumination these men of daylight had carried into the temple.

"All glory to the Greate Olde Wurm!" Ambrose proclaimed as the horde surged past him.

Deerfield saw a man—he thought his name was Gill; he vaguely remembered talking to him over the camp coffeepot one morning, laughing at some inane joke—stagger toward him with his weeping face of oil, hands outstretched to his throat. Deerfield emptied the pocket gun into Gill's face. The head exploded and the man fell. Deerfield's hand was numb. His ears were ringing.

There was screaming beyond the hum in his ears and more guns firing. He grabbed Jacob's sleeve and tried to pull him along as he spun and headed for the crevasse. But several of the damned had Moore now and the large man was struggling with more fury than Deerfield could ever remember to tear loose from the mob.

"Please for the love of God! Oscar! Help me!"

"Hang on!" Deerfield shouted, tugging on his partner's sleeve. He suddenly remembered the gun and let go of Moore to grab shells from his pocket.

"No! No, damn you, Oscar! Don't leave me!"

Moore was screaming. Deerfield ignored it. Only a second, two hot, empty cartridges out, two cool new ones in, close the breech with a snap and eyes up and—

Moore was gone, lost to the darkness. Even his scream was lost over the frenzied sounds of struggle.

Another one of the things lurched toward Deerfield. Oscar shot, emptying both barrels of the gun into the miner's chest. It staggered backward from the blast, then righted itself, and began moving toward him again.

There was a screaming in Deerfield's brain, like a kettle left on the stove. Over the sounds of gunfire, of miners crying, praying, begging and cursing, was the maniacal laughter of the old man. The alien falsetto, the bone flute.

Deerfield ran, ran like an animal. No thought, no plan, just run and live. He stumbled over the bodies of dead miners. He scrambled to his feet, hands clutching at his coat, at his hair, his arms. He screamed and ran into the darkness. He didn't remember where he found the lantern, or how he thought to use it to make his way thorough the narrow, ripping, cutting tunnels. The dizzying darkness yawned all about him, and whenever he would pause to gulp a lungful of sweet, sweet air he would feel rough, awkward hands clawing at his back. So he ran, and fell and stumbled to his feet and ran some more.

Then he saw the dull gray daylight cutting a square out of the mine's darkness. He staggered into the ashen pre-dawn gloom. Where were the guards? They had left guards. No matter. He dropped the lantern and ran, ran past the horses, ran past the wagons, ran through the gates of the mine compound and ran until he reached the squatter camp.

The camp was still quiet and still. The tent flaps drawn against the desert night's cold, last night's cook fire a mass of blackened rocks and soot. No one was up yet, but maybe at the Mother Lode they would still be up. There he could find help, find someone to help him off the mountain, away from this damned place.

He looked down Argent at the slumbering town below. They had no idea what their homesteads were huddled up against. No idea what was coming down the mountain to gobble them up.

Gobble, gobble.

The porch in front of the Mother Lode was vacant. No drunks sleeping off the night's adventures, no old men without a place to go. Deerfield could never recall it being that way. He pushed through the blanket-door into the smoky, musty interior. The bar was full; a row of backs greeted him as he staggered toward the bar.

"Listen to me; listen! We've got to go get the sheriff, right now! There are things, things under the mountain, in the mine! I'm not crazy! We have to—"

The men at the bar turned in unison. He was greeted by a row of faces bleeding night. Behind him was a rustle as the curtain was pushed aside.

The mine, the camp, the town. Gobble, gobble.

A large hand came to rest on Deerfield's shoulder. It was Moore's. The fingers were thick and caked in blood and something infinitely darker.

Deerfield wished he hadn't lost the gun, wished he still had a bullet in it for himself, a final act of stubborn defiance.

After a time, he no longer desired the gun.

The Ace of Swords

Jon Highfather opened his eyes. It was morning and the bullet was waiting for him. It was on the bedside table. He had laid it out the night before, like he always did. He sat up in the bed and picked up the bullet.

He took a moment to study it, as he often did as he knocked sleep loose from his mind. He had begun the ritual in the whiskey-soaked months following Saltville. It stuck. The closest he had ever come to using the bullet was a few years back.

It had been a short time after he had come to Golgotha and been drafted into the job of sheriff. The last sheriff managed to get himself hollowed out, filled with sawdust and sewed back up again—it was a long story. Highfather had met someone during that mess; her name was Eden. She died. They always died. He had almost used the bullet afterward.

Highfather swung his legs over the side of the bed and touched the cold wood floor. He slept naked. His body was a map of violent topography—the puckered pale hills of old bullet holes, the ugly raised, forking rivers of knife wounds, the wastelands of old burns, of the lash, of claws and bites and, of course, the coiled scars of the ropes superimposed over his neck three times, like rutted roads leading back upon themselves.

He sniffed, coughed a few times. He looked over to the bedside table. His star lay there, always next to the bullet. He stood up, pushed his memories into the dark hole they leaked out of each morning.

There was something, something moving silently through Golgotha like a poisonous rumor. It lurked in the narrow, muddy streets, and in the shadows of the temples and the churches. It had no name, but Highfather marked it—the same feeling that had come over him when Earl Gibson had gone mad and tried to kill Auggie.

Highfather's family had all been farmers before him and his brother, Larson. His father was born to it. He was able to sniff the crisp pre-dawn air and know what was coming out of the sky that day—storm or snow, drought or flood. Jon knew Golgotha as well as his father had known the fields and he sensed the fundamental wrongness. It wasn't the first time he'd had this feeling since becoming sheriff of this odd little town. Almost every time he had it, people died, badly. Like Eden, like Old Mike, like Larson.

The memories threatened to choke him, drag him down into a place of old regrets, old, dull pain—the kind that can be endured but never, ever healed.

He splashed cold water on his face from the basin, said good-bye to the ghosts for another day, stuffing them back into their hole. He got dressed, put the bullet away and got on with the day.

As he rode from his small shack, off of Absalom Road, to the jail, he always did a slow ride-through of the town to see what was what. The streets were not as crowded or as bustling as they should have been for the morning. He noticed several shops shuttered and dark along Main Street. A pack of Johnnymen walked quickly by, clustered closely together, staring at him with hooded, almost accusing, eyes. He nodded curtly to the party, who ignored the gesture and continued on their way.

He stopped and talked with Toby Mantle for a few minutes outside the First Golgotha Bank. Toby was a cowpuncher for the Circle-Star Ranch, out past Carson. He was a slender black man with an ugly pink scar running down the right side of his face, his remembrance from the war.

"What do you know good, Toby?" Jon asked as he sidled his horse up next to Mantle's.

"Getting hard to find a banker around these parts," Toby said. "You-all had one killed the other night, and today the one I was supposed to meet with is home sick."

"Clement isn't in?" Highfather said. "That's damn odd."

"Everything about this town of yours is odd, Jon," Toby said, offering Highfather a pouch of chaw. The sheriff declined and the cowboy stuffed his cheek with the tobacco. "Pretty much always been that way, ain't it?"

"Yeah," Highfather said, "but there's odd and then there is damned odd."

At the edge of Main Street, he cut past the old dry well, down the short, narrow road that took its name from it, and arrived at the jail. He tied his horse out front, unlocked the door and went in to check on Earl.

The old man was sleeping fitfully in one of the rear cells. Highfather figured that Judge Kane would be here next week and they could get the matter of Earl's assault on Auggie Shultz out of the way then. They used to have a judge of their own here in town, but he went missing about a year or two ago. Only a few people knew what happened to him. Jon wished he wasn't one of them.

"Coming," the old man muttered with dry, cracked lips. "It's coming for us." Earl groaned, rolled over and started snoring.

Highfather fell into the routine of the job. He wrote a few brief correspondences: one to the U.S. Marshals over in Virginia City, another to his parents and one to an old friend in Richmond. He cleaned and oiled the collection of rifles, scatterguns and pistols that were caged in iron bars behind his desk. He also made sure the other objects locked in the gun cage—wooden stakes, silver bullets, various Indian and Chinese charms and amulets, a crucifix and several vials of holy water, blessed by the Holy Father himself all the way from Rome—were all in equally good condition.

During all this a few of the towns folk came by to visit. The Widow Proctor brought him by a pot of hot coffee, some oatmeal with apple peel and a hunk of sourdough bread and butter for breakfast. Gillian seemed a little fancier in her appearance today than usual, and when Jon complimented her she blushed. He figured what he had heard about her and Auggie must have some truth to it.

A few others dropped by with disputes, or legal questions. Doug Stack made his weekly appearance to complain about his neighbor Clancy Gower's goat getting onto Doug's property. Ulysses Comb came by to get his pistol back after tying on a good one last week at the Paradise Falls. Jon had had to take the gun away from him and lock him up for a few days for the trouble.

Jon sat on the porch rail outside the jail, the wanted posters flapping and snapping behind him in the warm mid-day wind. Mutt wasn't back yet from the We'lmelti camps and that made him uneasy. He knew Mutt could handle pretty much anything that got in his way. Still, he worried.

At high noon Highfather rode out to check on the salt circle. It was located in the old graveyard about a half mile east of Clay Turlough's place. His horse, Bright, which had charged into raging gun battles at full gallop with no hesitation, shuffled nervously at the edge of the boneyard. Bright never set foot on the weed-choked land; no animal ever did.

The graveyard was older than the town. No one knew exactly how old. It was bordered by a small, crooked wooden fence. The single entrance was a broken gate, hanging on a single rusted hinge. Uneven tombstones, worn featureless by the desert's wind and sand, jutted out of red dirt at odd angles, like jagged, fractured teeth.

Highfather patted Bright's neck, dismounted and fished the bag of rock salt out of his saddlebag. He walked gingerly across the yard, careful to navigate the haphazard arrangement of graves.

He had learned about the salt circle and its care shortly after becoming sheriff. Something began killing and draining animals in Golgotha. It began with dogs and coyotes, even rats and chickens; soon cows, goats and horses were being found each morning—empty, wrinkled sacks of flesh—no blood, no water, not a drop of anything wet.

Soon everyone in town began to hear the droning hum at night, the frantic scratches at the windows and doors. Two women in Golgotha miscarried after hearing the hum. Then there was the first human victim, a nine-year-old boy named Cole Glen, whose parents left the window cracked on a very hot, black August night. Highfather saw the boy—his sunken, wrinkled face, the dark pits where his eyes had once been. The puckered O of his mouth dried into a mask of horror. Highfather visited Cole Glen every night when he closed his eyes.

That was when the note came to him, slipped under the door of the jail. It was on very old parchment. The handwriting was spidery—thin and shaky. Some of the words were spelled in the British fashion. The note gave him the directions to the old graveyard and the exact location of the circle.

Mend the circle, it said. *Bring salt, nothing else will hold it. Do it before dark or there will be another death.*

So Highfather rode out, just as he had done today, and brought salt, just like he carried now, all these years later, and he renewed the old salt circle, worn away by wind and rain, around a particular nameless old grave, just like he did now. And the killings stopped; the humming stopped. Everything went back to normal.

That was when Highfather really began to understand what being the sheriff here meant. It meant lying down at night with things in your head that the good folk of Golgotha couldn't possibly believe or understand, or ever, ever know. It meant accepting that he alone had to carry that load; he had to stare into the night, afraid to close his eyes, afraid to keep them open, so others could sleep.

He tended to the circle quickly. As he left the graveyard he thought he heard a low hum, the rustle of some sagebrush behind him. He tried not to run, to jump onto Bright. He rode back into town and back to work.

Jim was waiting for him when he got back. The boy did his chores, sweeping up the jail and running errands.

Around noon, the Widow Proctor brought them, and Earl, the afternoon dinner—bread, some hard cheese and a few slices of roast beef and a pot of coffee. The sheriff and the boy sat around Highfather's desk and ended up talking about billiards. Jim was pretty good at the game, as was Jon. They agreed to play together one day at the Paradise Falls on one of the big red-felt tables. Jim let it slip that his father had taught him how to play the game; then he clammed up about his family and his home again.

Jim kept mentioning Mutt all during the meal.

"I'm sure Mutt is okay," Highfather said, sipping his coffee. "Probably just decided to stay a spell and visit family."

"Mutt ain't got no family," Jim said. "None that counts to him, anyway, 'cept you."

"Told you that, huh?"

"Didn't need to," Jim said.

Highfather rode the town a few more times in the afternoon, still too few people around. Seemed like a lot of folk were down with something; the ones who weren't looked scared.

"You think they'll cancel the big church do Saturday night?" Gilbert Hollister asked him as they talked in front of the town hall.

"Nope," Highfather said. "There ain't no reason to be getting alloverish, now, Gil. Everything is fine. 'Sides, Anne Toller's little girl would have my hide if I canceled the event where she was giving her wedding day announcement!"

"Sheriff," Hollister said, "I've lived in this town my whole life, and I sure as hell know better. Just hope there ain't no damn rat people running around this time. I hated those things."

"I don't think they were actually rats.... Look, I got to go. Don't be starting a panic now, Gil, you hear me?"

"All right, Jon, but you be careful. Folks around here like you—you've lasted longer than any other sheriff we've ever had. And they damn well were rats—big as dogs and on two legs to boot!"

The sun was bleeding its last light over the mountains. Still no Mutt. Highfather sent Jim home around supper time and then had a bite to eat with Earl. The old man awoke sullenly and had a bit of broth and some water. He stared with red-rimmed, anger-filled eyes at Jonathan while they ate; then he fell back asleep.

"Almost here," he muttered, and then began to snore.

Highfather walked over to the Paradise Falls and sat on the porch as the evening crowd shuffled in. He noticed that there were no miners with them. In fact, he hadn't seen anyone from either the mining camp or the squatter town today. Highfather resolved to head up there tomorrow, hopefully with Mutt. If not, then he'd have to go looking for his deputy pretty soon.

It was past nine and Main Street was dark and still. Even the crowd in the Paradise was small and subdued. Highfather made his way back to the jail and decided to catch some sleep in the empty cell's bunk, just in case something came up.

He opened the door. The lamp he had lit for Earl was guttering. There was a strange smell in the office and it seemed too hot in the room.

Holly Pratt smiled at him out of the shivering shadows cast by the dying lamp.

"Hello, Jon. I understand you've been looking for me?"

She was wearing a long military coat. She was beautiful but somehow odd, in the dim light. Something wasn't right. Her pale skin looked bruised, her eyes too dark and wide. He closed the door behind him.

"Here I am," she purred, slipping off the coat and letting it fall. Her bare, porcelain flesh was lined by ink-black veins. The smell in the place was pungent and powerful, making his nostrils flare. The smell came from her and it was speaking to his back-brain, to this body.

"Holly?" He gaped at her, startled by her nakedness. "What, what are you doing here? Where have you been? Harry has been worried sick."

"I doubt that." She crossed the room toward him, slowly, like a great cat full of power and poise. Her large breasts, her hips, swayed. Her eyes of pitch never left his. She licked her lips with a black tongue. Highfather found himself fantastically attracted and repelled at the same time. The feelings held him rooted in place.

"But you were worried about me, weren't you, Jon? I knew you would be. You're so handsome, so sweet. All those functions we had to attend together, all the wicked thoughts that darted in my mind about you. But I was too timid, too frightened to act on them, to even acknowledge them to myself."

She was before him now, her nipples glistening with dark stains. She draped her arms over his broad shoulders and pressed herself against him, nuzzling into him. He felt her hot breath on his throat, the teasing flicker of her hungry tongue.

"What a waste. Do you know what I learned, Jon? I learned that we're all just apes. Stupid, horny, bloodthirsty little apes. Some meddling cosmic busybody, who has the audacity to call himself God, stuck a soul into us, gave us a gatekeeper in our head that contradicts our desires, our very nature. How is that for bad planning, huh?"

He could feel her breasts, warm and firm against his chest. Her leg was raised and entwined around his own. Her hands molded his shoulders and back. The air was thick with her scent. It was getting hotter. He licked his lips and blinked. His body was aching as he fought not to grab her, to take her.

"They say you're a dead man," she murmured into his throat, licking and nipping at his scars. "Is that why you have these?"

His voice was hoarse with need. "You ever hear of place called Saltville? I was a soldier in the war. I never wanted to be one, but my brother, Larson, did. Mother and Father were so worried about him running off to war, so I promised I'd go along and look after him. He died before Saltville. It should have been me."

He felt drugged. He didn't know why he was telling her these things; he tried to focus, to clear his head.

"We won, but then some of the irregulars, they started killing the colored troops—the injured ones, the ones who had surrendered. It . . . it wasn't right.

A man survives battle, survives hell like that. Then it's . . . it's just not right. I tried to stop them."

"So they hung you, darling?" she whispered.

"Yes. Twice. The rope broke, both times. The second time, I kicked the horse in the side and we ran."

She pulled away from his throat and looked deep into his eyes. Tears, like ink, drooled down her face. "But you have three sets of scars?"

"The third one was . . . after the war. The damned rope broke again. Not my time yet, I guess. Even I don't have a say in that, I suppose."

Holly laughed. It sounded like Hell crawling up to Earth. Her hand was working its way across his chest. Her fingers grazed his sheriff's star with a hiss of smoke. She clutched the badge tight and tore it from his shirt, tossing it onto the desk behind him. Her smoking hand returned to his chest, moving slowly lower.

"Why are you here, Holly?"

"I'm here for Earl, darling Jonathan . . . and for you."

He managed to pull his gaze away from her cobra eyes. He saw a shuffling shadow behind her. It was Earl; the same black ooze gushed from his mouth and eyes. He moved slowly, woodenly, but with purpose, toward them. He looked dead.

"What are you?" Highfather croaked.

"I'm what you've courted for so long, dear Jon. I'm the rope that will not break; I'm the bullet you keep on your bedside table at night. I can bring you peace, an end to the guilt, to the responsibility, to the thinking. I am the end of all that is—the blessed eternal night. I can end it, Jon; I can set you all free!"

Her mouth was close. The sweet, thick smell of her filled his senses. Her fingers fluttered across his raging manhood. He closed his eyes at the pleasure of it.

"Kiss me," she whispered. Their lips were almost as one. Her black tongue shook like a rattlesnake's tail in excitement, in need.

Behind his eyelids he saw them all, like he always did—Larson, little Cole Glen, all shriveled and hollow, Eden, dying in his arms. All the ones he should have saved, could have saved, and the faces of the ones he still might—Mother and Father, Jim, Mutt, Gillian Proctor, Auggie, Harry, perhaps even Holly herself.

He snorted the sweet stench out of his nostrils and pushed her away. He tumbled over his desk, and came up behind it, pistol cocked and aimed.

Holly was gone, Earl too. The heavy door to the jail creaked in the howl of a desert windstorm.

Highfather rose, holstered his gun and picked up his badge.

The Fool

Malachi Bick stopped smiling as he looked up from his first edition of Spenser's *The Faerie Queene*. There was some kind of commotion outside the window to his office on the Paradise Falls' second-floor balcony. It was nearly midnight, and the saloon was empty. Even the staff had gone home.

The window exploded in an awful crash of sound and glass. The drawn blinds over the window broke and folded around the massive body that sailed through it, like a burial shroud. Bick rose from his chair and rushed to the side of the body. Pushing aside the debris, he saw a broad, dark face, swollen and bloodied.

"Caleb?"

The giant didn't move. A faint groan escaped his puffy, shredded lips. There was a sharp bang as the office door flew off its hinges and crashed to the floor beside Bick and his son, then the sound of crunching glass under the thump of boots. Bick looked up from Caleb's broken body. Two men stood before him.

"It was open, so I let myself in," the older man said with a smile.

Bick stood. The older man had a mane of gray hair and a beard to match. He resembled a lion, but his eyes were bright and hot with the same kind of madness one saw in a man awaking from a fever dream. He held a simple minister's hat in his hands and wore a long black coat. His companion was huge—not a large as Caleb, but close. His bearing and his clothing suggested a military man. His demeanor was that of a trained dog, waiting for his master's command to kill.

"I don't believe we've had the pleasure," Bick said, putting himself between his son and the two strangers. " I'm—"

"I know who you are," the old man said. "I've prepared to meet you for a very long time. When you threatened Deerfield and Moore, you forced my hand, I'm afraid. I needed them; I needed the propriety of the mine reopening to allay suspicion. I was willing to let you be, with your whores and your card games and your gold, but you had to try to push the issue, didn't you—had to try your hand at the family business?"

"You have me at a disadvantage, sir," Bick said.

"Yes, I do."

"Would you and your behemoth care for a drink?" Bick said as he moved toward the liquor cart that was to the left of his desk, bringing him closer to the closet, to the sword in it.

"My and Phillips' drink of choice is far more pure and potent than your concoctions, Mr. Bick. But thank you. It is always a pleasure to see civility still exists even in this forsaken wilderness."

Bick poured three fingers of cognac into a glass tumbler. He gestured with the glass toward the burly, younger man.

"So this is Mr. Phillips, I gather, but I'm afraid I didn't catch your name?"

"Ambrose," the older man said. "Reverend Ambrose Ashton Smith, at your service."

"And, if you'll forgive me for being so bold," Bick said, sipping his drink, "what church claims you as their own, Reverend?"

Ambrose smiled and walked around Caleb's still form. He brushed the glass off of one of the chairs that Deerfield and Moore had occupied earlier and sat.

"I began with a Methodist congregation, many years ago, but over the years I've pretended to be a Baptist, a Catholic, a Mormon, whatever I had to be if it got me closer to what I needed." The smile slipped and anger leaked through. "Lies, Mr. Bick, they're all lies."

"And these days, you preach the truth?"

"Oh yes, I am the high priest of the Church of the First Revealing. Mr. Phillips, here, is my deacon."

Phillips remained standing, like a solider at attention, looming over Caleb's body. Bick wondered if his son was alive or dead, but that determination would have to wait. There was no time to show weakness.

"And Deerfield and Moore are part of the congregation?"

Ambrose laughed. "Goodness, no! They were a means to an end—sad, pathetic little insects. I used their greed and weakness to get access to your silver mine. However, they recently saw the light and have joined us. So many people in your town are joining us, Mr. Bick." He picked up a jagged wedge of glass off the floor. He held it up to the lamplight and admired its glittering edge.

"You may be the only person in the entire world who can truly understand, Mr. Bick. You see, as a child, I was plagued with ill humors—painful headaches, voices that sang and spoke to me in languages I did not yet know, nightmares, terrible, wonderful nightmares.

"It had been searching for me, reaching out to me from before the time of my birth, while I still resided in my mother's diseased belly. Fate is a river, Mr. Bick; it has channels and streams and it runs swiftly and mercilessly. None of us can dam it; none of us can change it, no matter how we may lie to ourselves. This—here, now, all of this—is my fate."

"So why become a minister?" Bick asked. He noticed Phillips tracked his every movement, his every glance. He took another sip of the cognac. "Why pretend? Why lie?"

"For a time, it wasn't a lie," Ambrose explained. "I wanted the stories and gospels to be real, to be true. I wanted my dreams to be sick nightmares; I wanted them to be the lies. But fate, Mr. Bick, my fate, our fate, wasn't to be one of the sheep. My . . . proclivities always won out. I became a pariah. My own family abandoned me, cast me out. She was my oracle, you see. I knew what I had to do to learn the truth and to put my foot upon the path."

"Who? Who was your oracle?"

"My little sister. She was ten. I strangled her and then read the portents in her entrails. It led me to other lessons, other teachers, other oracles.

"It was the same wherever I wandered though. My actions, my beliefs, required me to hide, to lie, as I stumbled in the wilderness for the truth."

"And the truth?"

Ambrose dropped the glass; it shattered. He leaned forward in the chair. "The God you grovel to, that all the sheep bleat their praises to, is a lie—a false god who imprisoned the true God of the universe. This 'Demiurge,' this little divinity, locked away the true God and built his petty kingdom, this playhouse of matter we call a universe, on the back of the one real God, the First God—the God of darkness and silence, the Greate Olde Wurm.

"I learned these truths over time, but as I grew in knowledge and power I still did not know how to make things right, how to fulfill my destiny. I found the alchemical secrets to brew the Milk of the Wurm, a wondrous, enlivening potion. It has granted me and Phillips abilities no mortal man can comprehend. Of course the harvesting of its elements was problematic at times, but where there is a will there is a way."

"That poison requires the blood of murdered infants," Bick said.

"You know the alchemical arts; good!" Ambrose said with a laugh. "Yes, I'm afraid it is quite toxic to those who have not been weaned upon its nectar, as Mr. Stapleton found out. Not to worry, though, the dregs of the shantytown have been receiving a portion of the milk in the liquor rations I've been handing out to them during my sermons. They are ready. Like me, they now hear the will of our lord, slumbering fitfully below us, beneath Argent Mountain."

Bick swallowed hard. He nodded toward Phillips. "And him?"

"He survived the battle at Shiloh, but his sanity didn't, poor boy. He wandered the back roads of Georgia for years, murdering families and living in their homes for a time before moving on. He knew something was calling him, but he didn't have the capacity to understand what. He sacrificed one hundred souls to this nameless thing, including his family. Phillips, show Mr. Bick your son."

The silent giant removed something from the pocket of his long coat. It was wrinkled and brown; at first Bick thought it was an old, stained hankie. Phillips unfolded it and held it up. It was the skin of a boy's face, tanned and cracked.

"Phillips' blood is almost completely made up of the milk now," Ambrose continued. "He is truly a remarkable specimen, as your half-breed son learned."

Bick said nothing; he only looked on, sickened, as Phillips neatly folded the face and put it back into his coat.

"So we were both lost pilgrims, seeking our fate in the wilderness," Ambrose said. "Then, one night, two years ago I was in Okalahoma City. The whore I had gutted that night suddenly sat up in the bed in a pile of its own intestines and began to speak to me. It told me about Golgotha; it told me about the well deep under the mountain. It told me how long it had waited for me, since the dawn of the world. It told me what I needed to do, and it told me someone would try to stop me. I'm betting, since your family has been here since before there was a town, that someone is you, Mr. Bick."

Bick hurled the tumbler at Phillips's face; the glass of whiskey smashed into the deacon's eyes and nose with incredible force. In two strides, Bick was swinging open the closet door, reaching for his old sword. He suddenly felt an awful pressure on his biceps, like it was caught in a vice. It was Phillips; his face was wet, but unmarked. His grip tightened on Bick's arm until he felt and heard an audible pop. The pain was incredible, and fascinating, all at once.

Phillips drove the bone hammer of his right fist into Bick's face. Blood sprayed as skin tore like paper. The force of the blow sent the saloon owner smashing back into the wall next to the closet, plaster crumbling.

"I suppose this means the talking is over now," Ambrose said. He sighed and got to his feet.

Phillips drove a powerful left into Bick's stomach. Blood and bile spewed out of his mouth all over the giant. Bick swung wildly and drove a fist into Phillips's jaw. The deacon staggered backward from the force of the blow.

"That's impressive. I've never seen anyone ever even make him blink from a punch before, except your—"

Caleb's hand wrapped around Phillips's ankle. He yanked as hard as his battered body would allow. The deacon crashed to the floor and Caleb was ready, pouncing on him, hitting him with blow after blow.

"Father, run!"

A fist launched up from beneath Caleb, like a piston. The force of it sent the black giant's teeth flying in a spray of blood. The vise-like hand clamped itself onto Caleb's throat.

Father's and son's eyes locked. There wasn't enough time.

"Run!" he gasped.

Bick sprinted for the massive fan-shaped window overlooking Main Street. From the corner of his eye he saw Ambrose drawing a gun. There was a wet snapping sound and Bick knew Caleb was dead. He felt a burning hammer strike his back, heard the thunder of the gun. He crashed through the window, falling two stories to land in the mud and dirt, glass rain falling all around him. He scrambled to his feet. His legs were clumsy and numb. It was getting hard to think. Another thunderclap, the ground exploded beside him. He ran, ran into the darkness between the buildings, ran for the desert.

"Go on!" Ambrose's voice echoed through the night. "Hide! You failed! Your family failed! It's mine! Golgotha is mine! Lick your wounds while you can! Tomorrow is the last sunrise this miserable world of lies will ever see!"

The laughter chased him all the way out into the desert. Golgotha was a distant shadow at his back, nothing more. He stumbled, fell, fought to his feet again and staggered on. He reached a small hill that he remembered from long ago. It was covered in desert grass, and he sensed, more than saw, the big rock at its peak. He slumped against it, leaving a dark smear of blood. Above him the stars blazed, a million shards of frozen, brilliant light. Jupiter and Saturn rose above the eastern line, shimmering against the darkness of the mountains.

The pain was exceptional. He honestly couldn't recall the last time he had even felt physical discomfort. He knew what he had to do, but he was frightened. For the first time in his entire life, he was terrified. Ambrose knew. He knew about the well; he knew about the Darkling.

He shuddered as recalled the force of Phillips's blows. He knew it was craven and dishonorable, but he was afraid of them. They had hurt him, badly, and they were going to free it, free it and destroy everything.

"I'm sorry," he whispered to the million lights looking down on him. "I'm so sorry!" he screamed to the night.

He groaned and struggled to his knees, each movement a new bloom of pain. He knelt in supplication, his eyes fixed above.

"Please help me. I'm sorry I let you down. I just got so lonely here. Please, they are good people at heart. They don't deserve to end like this, not because of me, my mistakes, my hubris. Please, I beg you. I'm sorry."

Malachi Bick, the high angel Biqa, called out again to a sky of indifferent stars.

"Please. . . ."

Justice

James Ringo's hands danced across the piano's keyboard, darting fast, like a hummingbird, then gently hovering, like a butterfly. They were not the ordinary hands of a piano player; they were calloused and scarred—his difficult, often violent, life laid out for the world to see.

His voice was not smooth, not melodic, but it had tightness, a bite, that made you forget melody. It carried the scars of his soul up and out of him and across the Celestial Palace.

> "I have sailed death-alien skies;
> I have trod the desert path;
> I have seen the storm arise,
> Like a giant in his wrath;
> Evil danger I have known
> That a reckless life can fill,
> Yet her presence is not flown;
> Her bright smile haunts me still!
> Evil danger I have known
> That a reckless life can fill,
> Yet her presence is not flown;
> Her bright smile haunts me still"

As the ballad came to a close, a few drunks thumped their hands on the tables. The Chinamen ignored him. Ringo paused long enough to take a long drag on his beer and roll and light a cigarette.

The Celestial Palace was usually a lot quieter than Bick's place, the Paradise Falls. The clientele were looking for the vices not easily obtained outside of Johnny Town—opium and exotic whores, willing to sate the most jaded pleasures. Ringo knew this kind of saloon very well. He had played piano in dives along the Barbary Coast in San Francisco. That was where he had met the Palace's owner, Ch'eng-Huang—the undisputed master of every Chinatown between Golgotha and the coast and patron of the Green Ribbon Tong.

Tonight, the crowd was even smaller than usual and Ringo could feel the tension and fear swirl around the room, like smoke. Many of the regulars were gone. People were going missing all over Golgotha; others were hiding, and staying locked in their homes. A few had left town.

It had been this way since that banker had died in the alleyway down the street. Then Harry's wife Holly had gone missing. Ringo hadn't seen Harry since the night Stapleton died, but he worried about him. Holly Pratt had caused him a lot of pain in their marriage, but Harry often spoke about when they were young, how he always thought he could share his secret with her in time, the way things had worked out with Sarah, his other wife. In his own way, Harry loved Holly.

Ringo began to play again, Lloyd's "Bonnie Bell." A drunk in the corner nodded and tried to mumble the words to Ringo's instrumental version of the ballad.

Ringo often wondered how he and Harry Pratt had managed to survive anything past that first night together. They were completely different people, from different worlds. But Harry was kind to him, gentle and never arrogant or rude. Harry treated him better than anyone else ever had, including Ringo's drunk of a mother and his abusive-when-he-wasn't-absent sailor father.

For his part, Ringo accepted and loved Harry for who he was, not what he was supposed to be. Ringo didn't want him to be a leader in the church, didn't want him to become mayor and didn't want him to be imprisoned as caretaker of his father's old life. All Ringo wanted was for Harry to be free and for them to be together and happy. There wasn't much of that for their kind in this world.

Half the time Ringo thought Harry was ready to chuck it all, then the ghost of his father would settle over him and he would go away for a while, play the role of good church elder, good mayor, good husband, good son. But eventually he came back to himself and to what, and who, made him really happy.

Harry cared for the people of Golgotha; Ringo knew that. He also knew Harry hated himself for feeling that way very often. Ringo suspected that right now, when all the strangeness was beginning to crop up in town again, when the wife Harry hated, yet loved, had gone missing, this was one of those times he would hate himself for being an honorable man.

As if on cue, Pratt entered the Palace through the beaded curtain that separated the saloon from the cloakroom. He looked tired, but still beautiful, Ringo thought.

"Give me the usual phlegm-cutter, Chen," Harry said to the bartender as he slid him a slender pile of bills across the bar. "And see if my girl is available tonight; it's been a Jessie of a week."

Chen was practiced at playing along in this game. He smiled and nodded to the mayor. "Very good, Mr. Pratt. I'll make sure the room is prepared for you. We get you girl, nice girl."

Ringo finished the song, grabbed his beer and slid into his usual booth. He rolled two new cigarettes and handed one of them to Pratt as he slid in the opposite side of the booth.

"Harry," Ringo said, with a nod.

"Jimmy, how are you, you son of a bitch?"

"Better than most, Harry, better than most."

They shook hands, slapped each other on the back and laughed. The game got old sometimes. The pretending, the stupid, idle chitchat. But it was part of the life they both had to live, if they wanted to be together here. After about twenty minutes of it. Chen approached the booth.

"Mr. Pratt, the room is ready and your girl is waiting."

"Thanks, Chen." More money passed hands. "Hey, Jimmy, you feel up to helping me break this filly?"

"I reckon I'm done playing for the night. Sure." More laughter, more backslapping. Chen knew the truth, hell, most of the patrons knew it, but the pretense gave everyone the ability to look the other way, and Ringo knew how important that was to survival when you were different.

He and Harry went into the back room, down the hall past opium dens and private brothels, out the alley door and half a block down to Ringo's flop on the second floor of a small warehouse owned by Ch'eng-Huang and the Green Ribbon Tong.

Once they were there, behind locked doors, they finally held each other and kissed.

"I was worried. I'm sorry about Holly," Ringo said.

"It's bad," Harry said. There is more going on here. Jon Highfather is trying to get to the bottom of it." He held Ringo's face and looked into his eyes. "I missed you. I'm sorry for all the—"

"Just shut up," Ringo said, pulling Harry closer for another kiss. "Come here."

Time passed; the night crept toward day. In the darkness, Harry finally spoke.

"I need to tell you some things. I had a meeting with the elders."

"Why? About what?"

Harry told him.

Elder Rony Bevalier looked like he was constantly dipped in baker's flour. His hair, his skin, even his watery blue eyes all were pale to the point of being painful to the observer. His dour brown suit only accentuated the whiteness of him.

"You did what?" Bevalier said, leaning across the table to glare at Harry.

"The golden plates," Harry said. "They opened for me, there was writing on them and I read it. We don't have much time."

"That's impossible," Brodin Chaffin said. The elder was closer to Harry's age. Chaffin was a tailor in Golgotha, running a small store on Rose Hill. It had belonged to his father, one of Harry's father's friends. Harry remembered sneaking a sip of moonshine with Brodin out by the old church ruins when he was ten and Brodin was fifteen. "The plates only revealed themselves to Joseph Smith, and even then he required the Urim and Thummim—the seer stones—to translate them into English. Did you use them?"

"No! Look, I'm telling you the truth," Harry said. "And, trust me, I had no desire to discuss this with you, or anyone else, but we have to do something. The plates revealed that the final days are upon us, that the keys to the bottomless pit are free and in the hands of the prophet of darkness. This whole town is about to be wiped from the face of the earth! We need to get everyone together and prepare to get out of here!"

"Abandon Golgotha?" Bevalier sneered. "Leave our fine homes, our businesses and our fortunes, our temple, for God's sake, to a bunch of unbelieving drunkards and whores? I think not."

"Besides," Chaffin added, "the relics! We can't leave them and we can't move them from True Cumorah! Joseph Smith commissioned your family to guard them, protect them, and to keep them here!"

"We all know how much you enjoyed running off to college, Harry," Bevalier said. "Wallowing in that cesspool of moral turpitude. Perhaps this is just your latest ploy to abandon your sacred duty and leave Golgotha."

"No," Harry said.

"A poor showing, too," the pale elder continued, as if Harry hadn't spoken at all. "With Holly missing, Lord only knows what has become of her, you decided to fabricate this nonsense to—"

"No!" Harry said, smashing his fist down on the table. The sound echoed through the tabernacle's office. Bevalier fell silent.

"I am not trying to run away," Harry said. "God only knows why, but I am not. There was an earthquake in the cave, the plates fell to the floor and the pages were revealed to me. I read them, but it was more like I was being given an insight, a feeling of certainty about something I didn't, couldn't possibly, know. A great evil is about to be unleashed on Golgotha, on the whole world. It begins here. I don't know if anyone can stop it, but the pages implied that it could be averted. I know that we must get the people of this town ready to flee as far away as we possibly can, for their own safety, and those of us who can must prepare to fight."

He stood and regarded all three of the men at the table. "I plan to stay to find Holly, and to guard the relics. I'm not trying to run. I'm begging you to."

The table was silent. Finally, Antrim Zezrom Slaughter cleared his throat; it was his usual way of announcing he had something important to say. Slaughter was Golgotha's highest-ranking Mormon—a high priest. He had been ordained by Joseph Smith himself. Slaughter was not quite as old as Elder Bevalier, but he was easily as formidable a presence, dressed in black, with silver hair and eyes like the sky in a storm.

"Harry, you are familiar with the prophecy of the One Mighty and Strong, aren't you?" Slaughter said softly.

"Vaguely, sir."

"A little over thirty years ago, Joseph Smith was given a message by our Lord, Jesus, that one would come that would set in order the house of God and arrange for the inheritance of the saints. He is said to come in our hour of darkest need. He is a guardian and a protector of the faith and of all mankind."

"You can't be serious?" Bevalier said. "You don't think this soap lock is the One Mighty and Strong, do you? Impossible!"

"Rony," Slaughter said with a smile. "I know you love the sound of your own voice, but you need to be quiet now."

"Sir, I'm not—," Harry said.

"That remains to be seen," Slaughter interrupted. "The sealed portions of the golden plates are a revelation from God, from the beginning of the world, to the ending thereof. As their keeper, I believe what you say to be true."

"Thank you, sir."

Slaughter smiled. "We will prepare those of the faith to depart Golgotha, we will also try to convince as many of our friends and neighbors to leave as we can, but none of this can be discussed with them. It must all remain secrets of the faith. Are we agreed?"

"Elder," Harry said, "the sheriff and I have been formulating a plan. . . ."

Harry explained in detail what he and Jon Highfather had been about for the last day or so and what was needed of the elders and the congregation.

The table murmured its agreement. Bevalier frowned but nodded, in tacit agreement.

"Very good, Harry," Slaughter said. "We'll do it."

Slaughter rose and placed his hand on Harry's shoulder.

"I also give you command, Harold Pratt, son of Josiah Pratt, to gird yourself to battle this evil that would devour our loved ones, our home and our world. Wrap yourself in the garment of the temple, so that it may protect you from evil, and take up the legendary Sword of Laban, that you might strike down the enemies of righteousness and good. I commission you, with all the authority and power granted to me by the church, as a defender of the faith—One Mighty and Strong."

Bevalier grimaced, and shook his head in obvious disgust.

"Let's go," Slaughter said, bidding the other to rise. "We've got a lot to do and not much time. We'll meet again tomorrow afternoon. May our endeavors be blessed, thus speaks the Lord."

"Antrim, I'm no . . . defender of the faith," Harry whispered as the others shuffled out of the room. "Bevalier is right about me. I am—"

"Harry," the old priest interrupted, "I know. I know you've had a wild life and I know you and your father, and you and the church, have butted heads many times. But Harry, we're a young faith, and we have so many people who fear us and hate us. You could have gone off any time you wanted, before or after Josiah passed, but you didn't. You care about people, Harry. You struggle to do the right things, even when you could take the easier path. And right now, that is the kind of person who this town, and this congregation, needs on their side in a fight."

"So I need you to leave," he said to Ringo, "before tomorrow night. Go to Frisco. I'll meet you there as soon as I can."

"We've been through this before, Harry. I'm not going without you."

"I don't want to see you die, or worse."

"Neither do I, but I ain't leaving you."

"Why?" Pratt said. "You're a survivor, Jim; you've been one your whole life. Run. Get the hell away from here, before it's too late. I would, if I could—you know that."

Ringo turned and stared at the ceiling. Dawn was filling the edges of the room with gray light. They could see each other now. "There's surviving and there's living, Harry. I've done plenty of surviving before I met you. Now I don't want to do either without you."

Pratt pulled him closer, falling into his eyes.

"'Sides," Ringo continued, "this is my home too. Closest damn thing I've ever had to one, anyway, and I intend to fight for it."

"I don't have long," Harry whispered. "I've got to prepare: I have to find Holly and save her. I have to go soon."

"Then let's not waste the time we got left, okay?" Ringo said. "I love you."

"Yeah," Harry said, amazed at the words. "I love you too."

The Hierophant

The banging on the door began just after sundown. Maude Stapleton, her hidden derringer at the ready, moved down the hall and reached for the door's iron bolt.

The pounding paused, then began again, louder.

"Who's there?" Maude asked through the door.

"It's me: Mutt!" the muffled voice called.

Maude snapped the bolt back and turned the door key; the light of the living room spilled out onto the porch. The deputy stood there, looking tired and dusty from the trail.

"Hello," she said. "You look bushed. Please come in."

He started to, and then paused. "Maybe it's best if I stay out here," he said. "I don't want to . . . make you uncomfortable."

She smiled. He noticed she looked weary too. She was dressed for the day still, in black, except she had freed her long brown hair. It was falling down her shoulders.

"What?" she said, with a half smile.

"Nothin'. You just look . . . real pretty is all. Beautiful."

He shook the thoughts out of his head as best he could with her standing there looking the way she did and smelling so good. "You and Constance, you have to get on out of town, now—tonight, if you can."

"What? No, I'll do no such thing. What's going on, Mutt?"

"Look, I just got back a few hours ago and things might be getting real bad, real soon," he said. "Please just do this, for your daughter, for me."

Maude sighed. "Mutt, I know that something strange is going on in town—you'd have to be a fool to not notice that if you lived here for more than a few months. But I have friends here, roots. Constance does too, and I don't have anywhere else to go. I'm too old to try starting over again. Besides, I have a husband that still needs to be laid to rest. Thank you for your concern, but Golgotha is my home, and I'm staying, come what may."

He shook his head. "You're a damn stubborn woman. Why you still up? I was worried I'd be waking you and Constance."

"Constance went to the church social with some of her friends. I didn't want her to be cooped up in here with me any longer. She really wanted to go. There's a boy there she fancies. I'm waiting up for her. She was getting walked home by her friends and this boy."

Maude saw the frown settle on Mutt's face.

"I'll go fetch her," she said. "Presently."

"I'll go," he said. "Stay put and I'll get her home safe."

"No," she said. "She's my responsibility, not yours. You have a town to protect, and from the look on your face you have a long night ahead of you."

Maude turned and grabbed her coat from the peg next to the door. Mutt opened his mouth to protest and then thought better of it. He looked out into the darkness and down Rose Hill toward the lights of the town. There was a cluster of lights and a bonfire about where Dale McKinnon's homestead was—the site of most of the dos like tonight's social. Swarms of tiny lights clustered together against the dark.

"Why, in tarnation, with all that's been going on around here lately, didn't they just cancel the damn social?" Mutt said, shaking his head.

Maude closed the door behind her, but did not lock it. She left the lantern inside burning as well. "Because people need to be people," she said. "They need to remember that all the sadness, hard work, loss and suffering are only part of what life is about. Especially in a town like this. I'm glad the mayor decided to not cancel it."

Mutt snorted. "Harry decided. . . . Well, that explains everything then."

Maude walked down the stairs. Mutt followed. His horse, a beautiful paint dappled in dark colors, stood patiently at the hitching post. Mutt took the reins as Maude began to walk down the path toward town. He and his horse walked beside her.

"Let me give you a ride down there," he said, offering his hand.

"Will you get going?" she said. "I have walked this path a thousand times and I am perfectly safe. Go be a hero. Go save the town!"

"Here, take this." He drew his pistol and handed it to her, butt first. "It'll work a damn sight better than a kind word."

When he looked up, he was staring into the short, ugly snout of a small derringer. Maude's gun was inches from his face.

"No thank you," she said. With a flick the gun vanished from her hand, like magic. He thought it slid up her sleeve, but he wouldn't put hard money on it. "I'll manage."

"Yeah," Mutt said, "I'd hazard a guess you will."

She looked at his offered gun, frowning. "Guns are like men—only useful for a little while. They can go off at a moment's notice when you don't want them to and they make a lot of foolish noise doing it. They tend to fail on you when you need them most. I do not rely on them," she said.

Mutt's face split into a wide grin. He laughed.

"But you, Deputy, you I think I will trust."

"Thank you. I won't disappoint."

He holstered the revolver. "I'll just hang on to her then. 'Spect I'll need her here presently."

"Why is it a 'she'?" Maude asked. "The gun? All guns? Why a female?"

He grinned. "They always are; you know why."

They stood silent in the darkness. The purple curtain, dusted with a million stars, silhouetted them. Finally he spoke. "I got to go. The sheriff and the posse will be getting ready to ride. Looks like you got finding Constance and getting home well enough in hand."

"You knew what I was going to say, knew I wasn't going to leave. Why did you come here, Mutt, really?"

He pushed his hat back on his head and rubbed his rough chin. "Everyone else I really care about in this town is riding out with me tonight. From what Jon is telling me, we might all die. I wanted to see you one more time. In the little time I've known you, you've treated me good, more like a man and less like an animal than most folk. That means a lot in my book, and it's a pretty short book. Besides, I kinda like you, if you haven't noticed."

She laughed. It was a beautiful sound to his ears. "Those friends I was talking about here, Mutt, you're one of them. You just assume I can handle this, take me at my word. That means a lot in the book I have too. Thank you."

He climbed onto his horse. Maude released his arm. She only then realized she had been clutching it. She paused. "Be careful."

"You git home quick with your girl, lock that door up tight and keep a fire going," he said. "I'll see you in the morning."

"Yes," she said. "You will."

The horse turned and he disappeared down the path toward the glow of the town. Maude took a sip of air, centered herself as best she could remember and disappeared into the darkness, following the same rutted path, but traveling it her own way.

Highfather tossed another rifle out of the cabinet to Dickey Welton, and followed it up with a box of shells. Then he handed Dickey a badge and a few loose cartridges.

"All right, you are hereby officially deputized; get on out front with the others."

"What the blazes are these, Jon?"

"Silver bullets. I've only got a few, and I don't know if they will work anyway, but just in case."

Dickey had lived in Golgotha long enough to know better than to ask too many questions. He muscled his way past the crowd of men, and out of the office. Including the dozen already armed, deputized and getting their horses ready outside, Highfather had managed to draw on every able-bodied man in town he could trust and who hadn't already disappeared. All told, the posse was twenty strong.

All day he had seen wagons of frightened folks riding out of Golgotha, taking their chances in the 40-Mile. Highfather's best estimate was that of the over 600 inhabitants of the town, about 150 were missing and another 100 or so, many of them Mormon families, had up and left already. It was hard to figure, though, how many had skedaddled and how many had been lost like Holly and Earl.

The dawn had brought another mystery. The Paradise Falls was a shambles. Someone had wrecked it pretty damn good. There was broken furniture, overturned tables, smashed walls, blood and broken glass everywhere. The body of Malachi Bick's son, Caleb, was in a bloody pulp on the floor of Bick's demolished office. There was no sign of Bick, or the perpetrators of the destruction. Jon had ordered the place sealed until further investigation. Clay had boarded up the windows and doors for him.

Highfather wondered for the hundredth time today how much of all this misery in his town belonged to Malachi Bick's scheming. If Highfather managed to live through the next few days and had the time, he intended to track Bick down and ask him to his face.

Jim slipped between the rumbling mass of the posse to make his way to Highfather.

"I can go fetch Promise and be ready to ride, lickety-split," the boy said.

"Nope, I can't spare you, Jim. I need you here, in town."

"Oh, come on, Sheriff! Don't treat me like some dumb short-britches! I can handle myself!"

"I know; that's why I need you here."

There was commotion near the door to the jail. Most of the men in the office moved aside for Mayor Harry Pratt. A few grumbled and rolled their eyes at Pratt's finery. Harry didn't seem to notice.

"What's going on here? Rory Means said you found Holly. Is that true, Jon?"

Highfather hated lying. He wasn't very good at it. But in his days as Golgotha's sheriff he had learned that sometimes the truth could be too awful, too damaging and, to put it bluntly, too much a damn waste of time. The sheriff sighed and gave the mayor the same raggedy lie he had fed to his posse.

"Yes, Harry. We know where she is. A bunch of crazy Holy Rollers have her somewhere up on Argent. We're going to go get her and I promise you I will do everything in my power to bring her back to you, safe and sound."

Harry Pratt was an excellent liar. He had made a life out of lies. He knew an amateur when he saw one. Jon was just too damn earnest to be any kind of liar except bad. Harry decided to let it sit for now and suss out the truth himself.

"I'm going," Pratt said. "Give me a gun."

"Mr. Mayor, no. I'm in charge of who gets a gun and a star in this town and I need you here doing what you do best—keeping the townsfolk calm, making sure the church social goes off tonight without a hitch, being all slick and politician-like."

Mutt was suddenly next to Pratt, up in his face, sneering with jagged yellow teeth.

"Jonathan's trying to give you a man's out here, Harry," Mutt whispered in a voice only the mayor, the sheriff and Jim could hear. "You ain't no damn good in a fight; you ain't no damn good at anything 'cept being a snake. He's givin' you a chance to kiss ass and suck up. Take it."

"When the hell did you get back?" Highfather asked the deputy.

"Just did," Mutt said, still staring into Harry's reddening face. "We need to talk, Jonathan. Real bad."

Pratt's color returned and his eyes became flints. Mutt had to hand it to the Fancy Dan, he recovered his cool quick. The words slipped out of the mayor's mouth in as quiet a tone as Mutt's incrimination had.

"What the hell would you know about worth, you half-breed piece of garbage? You've never had a wife. No one loves you. Your own damn people spit on you. What the hell good are you, exactly?"

"All right, that's enough, both of you," Highfather said, separating the two men. "We've got work to do. Harry, I need you and Jim at the social, just like we planned."

"Plan?" Mutt said.

"Harry and I figured, since whatever this thing we're dealing with is seems to be grabbing people when they are alone, having the social and getting as much of the town there as we can makes good sense. We can take a head count and see exactly how many and who have gone missing and who hasn't and we can get everyone out of town a lot quicker if they are all in one place, in case any of these fools are looking to start hurting people tonight."

"The elders are on board," Harry said. "We've got most of the Mormon population at the social and plenty of wagons, carts, buggies, horses and even mules to get folks away if we need to. But I still think I should go with you to get Holly."

Highfather shook his head. "This was your idea, Harry, and it's a damn good one. But more than just an escape plan, we need to show the towns-folk that haven't run off that everything is going to be fine."

"Is it?" Jim asked earnestly.

Highfather scowled at the boy, and then continued. "Mutt and I will take the boys up to the squatters' camp and roust 'em. I'm only taking a small group up the mountain with us. I want you and my acting deputy to coordinate the rest of the posse down here in town."

"Acting deputy?" Pratt said.

Highfather handed a silver badge to Jim. The boy's face lit up and for a moment the ghosts in his eyes were banished and he was a young man again.

Pratt sighed and shook his head. "Just remember who you work for, 'Deputy,'" the mayor said.

Jim smiled and winked at Highfather. "I do, sir. I do."

"Anything goes wrong, anywhere, we meet back here, agreed?" the sheriff said. "Jim, you and Harry grab a rifle and some shells. Here, take these silver ones too."

"Silver?" Jim said, frowning as the sheriff dropped the rounds into his open palm.

"Just do what the sheriff says, boy," Pratt said as he, too, accepted the bullets. "Jon, you had damn well better explain all this to me and soon. The last time I saw silver bullets it was—"

"I know, Harry," Highfather said. "I remember too, but better safe than sorry with this crew we're dealing with."

"You don't know the half of it, Jon," Mutt said.

"Tell me on the way," Highfather said, reaching for his hat. "Let's ride!"

A bloated, pockmarked moon leered over the cold shadows of the desert rocks as the posse ascended Argent Mountain along the narrow road. The desert heat of the rocks escaped into the purple night sky, like a soul slipping free of a corpse in the death rattle. The stars hid and the coyotes were silent.

Highfather and Mutt exchanged tales in low voices while the six men accompanying them rode a few dozen yards behind them.

"So this thing," Highfather said, "this Ucktenner—"

"Uktena," Mutt corrected.

"Sorry, this *Uktena,* this great serpent, is older than death. It can't be killed and it's mad at God for bringing life into the universe, and it's going to destroy the world and this all starts here in Golgotha, now? Is that it?"

"Close enough for a white fella, yeah."

"I miss rousting drunken cowboys. Holly was . . . not Holly. Maybe this Uktena is what got ahold of her. She changed Earl, turned him into something like her. You said Wynn told you Earl had been keeping company with a preacher staying over at the Reid place on the northwest slope?"

"Yep," Mutt said. "Earl and all the others who went crazy. You figure this preacher is behind what's happened to Holly and the other folks in town who've been getting sick?"

"It's what we've got right now. You still got Earl's Bible?"

"Yeah. It's in my bag. I was going to give it to you to look over, but then that jackass Pratt sent me off on a damn fool's errand."

"Things have been kind of hectic around here," Highfather said.

"When ain't they?" Mutt said with a smile.

"How do you kill something that's older than death?" Highfather asked.

"With a power that's more than mortal," Mutt said. "Least that's what I heard. Simple."

"Thanks, that really cleared things up."

The squatter camp was silent and dark. No cook fires burned, no songs, no sounds of banjos or mouth harps, no drunken brawls or squeals of pleasure. No laughter, no life.

The lawmen rode slowly through the camp, past empty shacks and shanties. The only sounds were the night howl of the mountain wind running wild between the dwellings, the eerie rattle of pots and pans hung up on lines and the snap of fluttering canvas from vacant tents.

"Where in blazes is everybody?" Highfather muttered.

Mutt sniffed the air. "Not here. Not for a while. Let's check the Mother Lode," the deputy said.

The two men entered Wynn's bar with guns drawn. Highfather carried a lantern since the place was as dark as the grave. The Mother Lode was a shambles—tables overturned, chairs broken—but there were no bodies, no blood.

"All right," Highfather said, holstering his pistol. "Let's get to the Reid homestead. I guess that's where the party is."

Edward Gabriel Reid was another one of Golgotha's mysteries. A prospector with a shady past, Reid arrived in town in 1856. He was the man who discovered silver up on the mountain they renamed Argent, and it made the drifter a gentleman of means. Reid's partner, Malachi Bick, helped finance the opening of the Argent Mine and it made Bick's family even wealthier than they already were.

Reid, as the manager of the mine as well as owner, built a large, fine house on the southeastern slope of Argent, close to the mine if there was anything that demanded his attention. He married a beautiful Chinese woman, which caused quite the scandal at the time. He bragged that Argent had enough silver in its bosom to make every man in Nevada rich, sparking the boom that grew Golgotha virtually overnight. Reid was even eyeing the possibility of taking the mayor's office away from the Pratt machine.

There were other stories about Reid too, stories about things that had happened in his mansion—odd rituals and rites, lavish parties with bizarre, almost satanic excesses. The place was said to be haunted with the spirits of the men who had died in the mine due to Reid's greed and impatience.

In 1859, Reid vanished without a trace. His wife sold Argent Mountain to the Bick family a few months later, took her wealth and moved to San Francisco. The rumors said Bick had tried to buy Reid out and he wouldn't budge. It was no secret that Malachi Bick's enemies had a habit of disappearing.

The Reid house had been rented by various mine managers for a few more years until Bick declared the mine bust and closed it. The house had sat vacant for the last few years, a decaying sentinel looking down on any who entered Golgotha from the south.

As they approached the house through the weed-choked, rocky field, the posse could hear singing. It was a strange sound and it made the horses shuffle uneasily, even the normally unflappable Muha. The voices sounded reversed, shrill. No words could be made out clearly, but the mad joy, the ecstasy, was plain in the delivery. It reminded Highfather of a circus's hurdy-gurdy organ, only made of human throats.

There were dancing lights and shadows in the broken windows—candlelight and wild, almost spastic dancing to the hellish cadence. Mutt suddenly felt the same dread swell up in him he had felt in old Earl's shack. He swallowed it down, tightening his grip on Muha's reins.

"Easy now," Highfather whispered. "We got a job to do. Let's do it. Mutt, you take Collins and Shepp and come in the back way, in case they try to rabbit down Backtrail Road. Josh, you and the others are with me."

The horses began to whinny as the voices inside the house rose in volume and frenzy. Highfather gave the signal to dismount and the posse left the spooked animals near the edge of the yard. Mutt and his boys vanished into the shadows to the left of the front door. Highfather stepped onto the rotted porch's steps, careful to avoid the broken boards and gaping holes. The singing was now a chant. A powerful voice leading many. Highfather could make it out through the door.

> "Hail, hail that which cannot die.
> All grovel to He Who eternal lies, the true one, the all-seeing eye!
> Couched in blessed darkness, bound in light and lies, the ending of all
>   that thrives, awaiting the time that ends all times.
> The mindless dancer at the edge of mind, the Bridegroom to the Black
>   Mother with a thousand bleating, hungry young—"

He reached the door and put his hand slowly on the tarnished doorknob. He hefted his pistol, cocked the hammer and slowly, slowly turned the knob.

There was a terrible crash behind him as Carl Jesper fell through a decayed step. Highfather winced and looked back at the rancher. He was up to his chest in the rotten stairs, surrounded by a cloud of dust and sand.

"Dammit, Carl!" Josh Pedigo hissed. Josh didn't have time to finish his admonishment. Dozens of filthy arms reached up through the shadows beneath the stairs, grabbed Jesper with black, oily fingers and pulled him, screaming, down into the darkness.

Highfather felt the doorknob jerk free from his hand. He turned to find himself staring into the face of Oscar Deerfield. The mine owner's eyes were viscous, weeping pools of darkness. Its mouth yawned open and more of the oil-like substance oozed out, revealing yellowed teeth and a fat, black worm-like thing where the tongue should be. The worm thing shook like a diamondback's rattle trying to rip itself free of Deerfield's mouth.

Highfather felt hands on his throat, raised his pistol and fired. The world exploded in harsh light, deafening thunder and the stench of cordite.

Deerfield's headless body fell to the side.

"Everybody in, now!" Highfather shouted over the screams and gunfire that were erupting behind him. The lurkers that had dragged poor Carl Jesper down were now pouring out from their lair below the front steps, like a swarm of hungry rats. They were mostly squatters and they, too, leaked the black stuff from every orifice.

One them lunged at Josh Pedigo, who stood frozen in fear, mouth agape. The thing clamped its mouth to Pedigo's even as he overcame his fear, screamed and pumped thirty-ought rifle rounds into its chest. The scream ended abruptly. He staggered backward from the squatter thing and clawed at his throat, struggling, choking. He fell to the ground making sounds like a trapped animal, rolled onto his side and was still. The squatter thing he shot leaked black fluid from the chest wounds, but seemed unharmed by the point-blank rifle shots. It turned and lumbered toward another terrified deputy.

"Silver!" Highfather yelled as he fired to cover two of his men who had followed him onto the porch and through the front door. "Use the silver rounds!" He holstered the pistol and cocked the Winchester. The voices were louder inside, the chant growing more insistent by the moment.

"Hail, hail that which cannot die!
Hail the dweller in darkness!
Hail the Effigy of hate!
Hail the many-legged goat!
Hail the beast!
Greatest of the Old Ones, the One True God of matter and decay . . ."

Another one of the things shambled into view in the old house's foyer. Highfather recognized it—Vic LaSalle. He had worked odd jobs for Haglund, the butcher, liked to play faro on Friday nights at the Paradise. Told a good joke. More creatures appeared, descending the hall stairs toward the sheriff and the deputies.

"Vic, stop, right now. Only warning you get."

"Hail the Great Olde Wurm!" The voices wailed in ecstasy and terror, falling into alien chants now, lost to the frenzy of the collective power of the mass. The sound was more animal than human.

Vic opened its mouth; black ooze splattered on the floor. It kept walking.

"You boys got silver bullets loaded?"

"Yup."

"Jesus almighty, Jon, what the hell is this?"

The things stumbled closer; their eyes were black mirrors, like a shark's.

"Do you have the damned silver rounds?"

"Yes, yes!"

"Take the ones on the stairs." The deputies leveled their rifles. Highfather aimed at LaSalle. "Powerful sorry, Vic. Fire!"

The guns roared in the enclosed entry hall. The ones on the stairs fell, smoke pouring from their wounds, like steam from a kettle. Vic was driven back a few steps from the force of the bullets that ripped through its head and neck. Again, smoke pouring from the wounds, like its insides were on fire. It ended against a wall and slid to the floor, trailing smoking black ooze.

More of the creatures from outside were making their way up the stairs into the foyer, cutting off the men's escape route. Josh Pedigo, reborn into darkness, led them.

"Go, go!" Highfather shouted as he cocked his rifle and hurried down the dark, narrow passage toward a large chamber full of candlelight and twisting shadows. He heard the men at his back firing, wildly. He hoped they were keeping track of the few precious silver rounds they still had. He heard more gunfire and figured it for Mutt's party. None of the ruckus seemed to deter the wailing and chanting, which was definitely coming from the room ahead.

Highfather entered, sweeping his rifle before him. The room had once been a grand dining hall for entertaining bankers and speculators from Carson and Virginia City. Now it was a temple, a blasphemous shrine to whatever slumbering cosmic evil had devoured his town. The walls were covered with symbols, pictures, strange pictographs—all of which seemed to writhe and crawl like snakes in the shuddering light of hundreds of black and red candles. Feeble moonlight filtered through the dirty, broken wall of windows in the room. There were close to fifty or sixty townsfolk in the room, no, not townspeople, not anymore, creatures—the Stained. Men, women, children all bearing the dripping, oozing mark of the Greate Olde Wurm, all of them naked and writhing in debased congress with each other on the floor—a carpet of undulating, oily flesh. The room was thick with heat and the smell, *her* smell—the same as in the jailhouse—the heady, intoxicating, inhuman spoor, like all of man's animal desires distilled and cast on the wind. Holly. She was here—she was the altar, nude, on her hands and knees, pale face slack with ecstasy, eyes squeezed shut with drops of oil, dripping, *pat, pat, pat,* between her lids. Her back was slick with blood, human blood, not the foul ichor that these creatures oozed. Highfather's mind almost snapped when he saw its source.

"Sweet, merciful Lord in Heaven, no. . . ."

The tiny, still form was held high in the left hand of the priest, who stood behind his living altar. He was a tall man with a mane and beard of gray. His eyes, unlike his congregation's, were human, but there was no sanity, no mercy, in them. He squeezed the last of the infant's blood into an inverted animal skull, a dog's or perhaps a coyote's, he held below in his right hand.

Mutt appeared at the doorway on the opposite side of the room, his gun in one hand, his knife, wet, in the other. Stains of shadow covered his shirt and hands. He was alone.

The priest tossed the baby's body. He smiled at Highfather and with a simple gesture brought the wailing and chants to an abrupt halt.

"Ah, Sheriff, welcome. You're just in time to take communion."

The gunfire behind Highfather ended. There was the sound of a scuffle, a whimper, a choking sound and then silence. He could feel inhuman eyes on his back. He looked to Mutt and the deputy nodded slightly. They were alone now.

"I've heard so much about you, Sheriff," the priest said. "You were the only one to resist the Black Madonna's charms. Pity. You have no idea how liberating it is."

"It's not too late, Jonathan," Holly purred as she stood. Two of the Stained stepped forward and draped a black cloak around her blood-slick body. "Come to me now. I need you."

Highfather leveled the Winchester. Two silver bullets left. One for the priest, and one—sorry, Harry—for Holly. Highfather wished there had been some way to get her out of here. He hated to break a promise. He felt dry, sticky breath on his neck and knew there was no way any of them were getting out of here alive.

"You're the one responsible for this," he said to the old man. "What do you call yourself? So I know who I'm sending back to Hell."

"Hell?" the priest said. "You presume to send me to Hell? Oh, Sheriff, you have such a puny vision. Your Hell is a playground for sick children. No, our vision is . . . deeper, richer, too complex for such limited minds. I am Ambrose, servant of the True God, the First God, not the imposter who cowers in Heaven and whose ass you and your ilk kiss."

"Say hello to him for me." Highfather's finger tightened on the trigger.

Ambrose smiled.

There was a blur in the shadows to Highfather's left and a massive man, dressed in black like a priest, grabbed the barrel of the rifle and jerked it out of Highfather's hands before he could fire it, like taking a toy from a child. The huge figure tossed the gun casually against the wall and it shattered as if it were glass.

"And this is Mr. Phillips, my deacon," Ambrose said. "He is living proof to the power of the Milk of the Wurm." He raised the skull chalice, as if offering a toast.

Highfather saw Mutt moving, then lost sight of him as all the congregation began to rise. He launched a powerful right at Phillips's chin.

"We've made great headways toward bearing witness to your entire community of the power and the glory of the Greate Olde Wurm. We are nearly a hundred strong now."

The punch landed with a sick crunch but no other effect. Jon followed up with a strong left hook, which also seemed to do nothing. It was like hitting a stone wall.

"I sent the rest of the faithful down the mountain to share the glory with their former friends and family in the town," Ambrose said. "With each new follower, each new soul tainted, liberated, the chains holding the Greate Olde Wurm grow weaker. He awakens, grows more restless. By noon tomorrow, we will be powerful enough in number, in will, to free the Great One, the crawling, gibbering chaos—"

Highfather drove blow after blow into Phillips's face, again and again and again. His knuckles split from the force. The black-garbed giant's head didn't even snap back from the barrage of punches. Phillips drove a single thunderous right into Highfather's chest. The sheriff felt a bright star of pain in his left side as the wind left his lungs. He fell into darkness. An instant later he opened his eyes with much effort. He was on the floor smashed up against the side of the doorway. He tasted blood, and it felt like he was being stabbed in the chest with a burning knife. Over him, surrounding him, were several of the Stained, including two of his recent deputies. Ambrose's voice boomed from somewhere out of Highfather's dim vision.

"It's a shame you didn't give in to your temptations when you had the chance, Sheriff. Once the final rite is completed and the Great Old One is freed, He will shake off this blasphemous world, like a dog shaking itself dry. He will pull the sun from the sky and hurl it into the Void. He will tear down the false universe and return things to their beautiful, pristine origin. There shall be no more temptation; there shall be no more want or need, no more tears, no more joy. All will be blessed darkness."

The Stained reached down for Highfather. He fumbled with his numb, bleeding hands, drew his pistol and fired twice. Heads exploded and alien blood rained down on him. The bodies fell back and remained still.

Silver and shots to the head, good to know.

He struggled to his feet. Every breath, every movement, was brilliant pain in his side. The other Stained shuffled away from him as Phillips strode forward like a dark prince. Highfather fired, emptying the remaining normal rounds into the hulking deacon. One bullet caught him squarely in the forehead. His head jerked, and then straightened. There was a trickle of blood, as if he had been knocked in the head by a rock instead of a .45-caliber bullet. His eyes darkened and he reached for Highfather's throat.

Mutt roared as he dived through the crowd of the Stained and crashed into Phillips's back, driving his knife deep between the shoulder blades, with all his weight behind it.

"Jon, git! I got this!" the deputy shouted. Phillips shrugged and Mutt flew off his back and hit the ground with a crash. The deacon reached behind him, grunted and tossed Mutt the knife.

"I like killing Indians," Phillips said. "It takes a little more work to get them to scream, but it's worth it."

Highfather put his fingers to his lips and whistled loud and long. With his other hand he shrugged the shells out of the Colt.

Ambrose was laughing. "Bring them to the Mother for communion!" he called out to the inhuman congregation. "The sheriff and his deputy can lead us in our next hymn."

A wall of hands was tearing at his coat, his arms, his legs, his face. Highfather jammed a bullet into the pistol's cylinder and snapped it shut with a flick of his wrist. All he could see around him was horribly familiar faces smeared with blackness; all he could smell was Holly's, the Wurm's, spoor.

Mutt wasn't faring much better against Phillips than he had, but he did notice the deputy was taking the punches better. Mutt was hurt, there was no denying it, but he seemed to be much hardier than his slight frame suggested.

"Get the gun," Ambrose said to his followers. "Don't let him kill himself; this will be too fun to miss."

The Stained were abnormally strong. Their hands gripped Highfather tightly as he struggled to raise the gun. He winced and pulled his gun arm free long enough to level the pistol, find his target and fire.

With a thunderous boom, the bullet smashed one of the oil lamps near the small mountain of candles in the room. The lamp oil splashed everywhere. The candles and the curtains behind them were suddenly devoured in brilliant, violent flame. A few of the Stained caught fire as well, screaming and staggering, further spreading the blaze.

"How much fun was that?" Highfather called out to the shocked priest as he drove an elbow into the face of one of his attackers.

Before the enraged priest could collect himself, the large windows on the southern side of the room exploded inward as Bright and Muha crashed into the room, trampling bodies as they came to their masters' aid.

"Mutt, stop fooling around; we're leaving!" Highfather called. The deputy was pinned to a wall, being held six inches off the ground by Phillips as the dark deacon continued to pummel his swollen face.

"In a minute, boss," Mutt mumbled through pulpy lips. He spit blood in Phillips's eyes and the giant dropped him, wiping wildly at his face.

"Damn you!" Phillips bellowed.

Mutt staggered toward the battered Highfather, who was already climbing on Bright. The sheriff pulled a scattergun from his horse's saddle and fired. Three of the Stained staggered backward from the blast, but none of them fell.

Smoke was filling the room and flames crawled along the walls, lapping at the ceiling. Ambrose was yelling orders to the swarming congregation. Holly and Phillips were nowhere to be seen.

Muha kicked another attacker when it lunged toward his master. Mutt scooped his knife up from the floor and used it on two more of the creatures trying to grab him, without a second's pause of motion. The things that had once been townsfolk bled the black blood of the Great Wurm from their opened throats, but did not die. His free hand wrapped around the saddle and he pulled himself up. Highfather was reloading the shotgun, firing cover for his deputy's retreat and then reloading it again. Though the shot didn't kill the infected, it did keep them at bay for a moment and off the two men and their horses. Bright snorted the smoke and shuffled nervously from hoof to hoof.

"It's okay, girl; we're leaving," Highfather said, petting her. "I'm sure glad we learned that little trick."

Mutt was in the saddle and had drawn his own rifle.

"Let's go, let's go!" he shouted over the roar of the flames.

"Enjoy your little victory, gentlemen!" Ambrose shouted as he headed for the room's rear door, surrounded by a swarm of his loyal congregation. "Enjoy it while you can! We grow stronger with every moment. Your town and its people are mine, Sheriff, *mine*! Our God stirs and your God is afraid to face Him. Mark my words, this world has seen its last dawn! Its last!"

His voice was lost in the crash as part of the flaming ceiling tumbled down.

The two riders plowed through the crowd, still intent on capturing them, both men shooting as they went. The windows were wreathed in flames, but neither horse balked as they charged forward, leapt over and through the maelstrom of fire and landed in the cool, dark desert night.

The riders stopped long enough to look back at the Reid house being devoured by flames. The smoke that coiled out of the broken and missing windows took ominous, unnatural shapes before scattering on the wind, which seemed to have risen up to cast the foulness of this place out faster.

"I want another crack at that bastard Phillips," Mutt said, hawking out more blood as he stroked Muha's neck. "I think I can take him."

"Later," Highfather said, reloading his pistol. "We're both low on silver and you heard Ambrose—more of those things are headed for the town."

The mansion creaked and groaned its death rattle as the flames rose higher into the night. Dark silhouettes emerged from the dying house, shuffling slowly, relentlessly.

The riders galloped away from the house of flame and shadows, and raced for home as fast as their horses could carry them.

The Tower

Since Golgotha had an uncommon number of denominations and faiths for such a small town, events like the social were usually held on "neutral ground" to ensure a good turnout and fewer theological arguments around the buffet table. Dale McKinnon had, as he had in the past, volunteered his small barn, just off Prosperity and a few lots over from Pratt Road, for the festivities. It was close enough to the First Baptist Church and the Mormon temple to make most of the faithful in town happy. Dale was in the rare position of being pretty much universally liked in town.

Auggie and Gillian worked all day on the finishing touches for the church social. Gillian pushed a wayward strand of hair out of her eyes as the first wagon of guests arrived. It was a little past noon.

"See," Auggie said. "I told you. Mysterious disappearances, rumors of sickness and strange goings-on—bah! Nothing keeps people away from free food, yes? Especially yours."

She smiled and hugged him. "Ours," she said.

People kept coming: husbands, wives, children, the few babies the town had been blessed with, Baptists, Methodists, Catholics. Day to day these groups kept mostly to their own small enclaves in the town, but today they all gathered—to eat, to gossip, to laugh and to play.

And the Mormons! It seemed every Mormon in town came out, whole families with wagons and carts and horses and food. It was as if the whole town collectively sighed in relief. Auggie knew, like anyone who had lived in Golgotha for any amount of time, how much they all relished these days, these chances for laughter and companionship in between the chaos and tragedy. It created a bond in old-timers like him, like Gillian.

Golgotha was a strange, almost-cursed place, true. But it was a good town too. It seemed to draw out as much good in some people as it did evil. The good folk who lived here needed these events to keep going, to keep the light alive here in a desert of darkness. So even with all the murder and the madness and the feeling of impending catastrophe, the town came today to draw strength and to remember why they fought the darkness.

The music started about two. The band arrived in a piecemeal fashion. Josiah Kemp and his brother brought their guitar and fiddle. A few hours latter, Sadie Aimes arrived with her banjo. Ernie Greene broke out his harmonica when he and his wife got there. By four, half the place was eating and dancing and the other half was playing and singing. Many of the local young men and women were here, Auggie noted. Taking their first steps in the dance of adulthood, of independence and of love.

He saw Arthur and Maude Stapleton's daughter, Constance, dressed in mourning colors, laughing, surrounded by her friends. A beautiful young woman dressed in black, haunted by death, laughing, forgetting and embracing life. It was, Auggie thought, like she was the spirit of the town, given life.

Constance stayed close to one boy, a tall, handsome lad with an unruly mop of hair the color of wheat. Auggie recognized him as Jess Muller, the son of Auggie's countryman Gerrard Muller, the town cooper. Auggie had to smile; when Jess moved, she moved. He smiled when she smiled. They each looked at one another when the other wasn't looking and occasionally they caught each other in the act and both smiled and reddened. Auggie thought about him and Gillian, how they were and how much they had acted like these children. He chuckled despite himself, and shook his head. Madness.

The light mood passed like a cloud drifting across the sun. He found it almost impossible to keep his thoughts away from Gillian and Gertie. Finally, he gave up trying.

He found Reverend Prine leaning against Dale's fence, at the edge of the noise and gaiety, nursing a mug of cider and watching the tall wheatgrass and the Indian paintbrush sway in the afternoon wind. He smiled at the shopkeep as he approached.

"It's a beautiful world He's given us, isn't it, Auggie?" Prine said.

"Yes, it is," Auggie replied. "Sometimes I wish I knew His mind. So much beauty and so much ugliness all in the same place. It is very confusing to me, Reverend."

"The beauty would be here in spite of us, Auggie," Prine said. "Much of the ugliness we bring with us as baggage."

"But not all, not storm, not sickness, not hunger, not death."

"Ah, that's the deal breaker for most folks, to be sure." Prine smiled. "Why must we end? Why must God allow us and those we love to part, to die?"

Prine's eyes were kind and bright, like a child's. His face was weathered from a lifetime in the desert. His hair seemed almost bleached white. He sipped his cider, sighed and looked out over the field.

"Genesis says before God created this world, there was darkness. I think death is a part of creation, like the stars and the moon. I don't think God made death, made endings. I think His existence, His hand in things, is a constant war against oblivion. God doesn't punish us with death, Augustus. He grants us the gift of this life to show us the fundamental beauty, the heartbreaking fragility of beginnings, of birth, of creation. He wants us to understand His plan, understand Him. Thorough His salvation, we are granted escape from oblivion, from an ultimate end."

Auggie was silent. The music drifted out to them on the warm, lazy wind.

"Something on your mind, Augustus?" Prine asked. Auggie nodded. "Is it Gillian?"

"Yes," Auggie said. "I . . . That is, my . . ."

"Spit it out, old friend," Prine said.

"My heart, it is torn in two, and I feel like I am bleeding, falling. Gillian makes me feel like I did when Gert and I were *Kinder,* children. But then I feel I am betraying Gert with these feelings. I love my wife, Reverend; I do, with all my heart. But—"

"Augustus," Prine said, "Gert is gone. She died; you didn't."

"It is . . . more complicated than that. I feel like she is still with me, like she would be lost and afraid without me, like she still needs me."

"Who needs who, Auggie? Who's really afraid here?"

Auggie leaned against the fence post and looked down at the grass. Prine sipped his drink.

"When she . . . when she was gone, I was so afraid," Auggie finally said. "When you find the one love of your life, the prospect of living the rest of your days alone, lost to that warmth, that light, lost in the darkness, it makes you crazy, desperate. Angry, angry at God. You turn your back on Him, defy Him."

"Love is powerful," Prine said. "Jesus said many times that love reigned over all, even God. Is it fair the love of your life was torn from you? No. Was it fair that you had this life to share part of with her? Yes. Death frames our joys, Auggie. We're given this slice of time to love, to see beauty, to refuse to partake in ugliness, and to learn what we can. If you've found love twice in one lifetime, don't curse God for it, thank Him."

"For the first time since Gert . . . passed, I feel like I'm really alive, not just going through the motions of living. I like, Reverend, I like it very much, but I feel so guilty."

"Listen to me, Augustus. I spent a lot of time with Gert near the end. She was a remarkable woman, so full of life and happiness. When she got sick, when she knew she was not going to get better, she talked often to me about you, about how she was afraid for you to be alone. Gertie was looking forward to an end to the pain, to the twilight of life she was forced into. Gert was ready to move on to what waits for us on the other side, in the Lord's glorious kingdom. She so wanted you to live, to be happy and to love again."

Auggie looked back to the celebration. Gillian was talking and laughing with a group of older women. Her face, bright with laughter, put the sun to shame. She looked up and saw him watching her. Her cheeks reddened, and the smile grew brighter still. Auggie felt suddenly strong and weak all at once. He smiled back.

"Gert didn't just talk to me about all this," Prine said. "She talked with Gillian too."

The sun was dipping low behind Argent Mountain. The old-timers sat on bales of straw and hay, smoking their pipes and talking about the second war with the British that most of them had fought in. A pile of children sat rapt at their feet, listening to the war stories. Other children ran about, laughing and screeching in delight, chasing one another in the gathering shadows. Fires were lit, but the music seldom stopped—ballads, waltzes, two-steps and fandangos.

In the dying rays of the sun, Aaron Burke and his fiancée, Mary Toller, and their families came forward to make the big announcement. It seemed like the whole town sent up a cheer, a defiant roar of life against the coming nightfall. There was more music, more food, more laughter.

Shortly after dark, Mayor Pratt, wrapped in a great black coat, and a large group of deputies arrived. The young boy Jim was with them, sporting a star on his shirt and a rifle in his hand. Their arrival created quite a stir and some expected agitation; then Harry spoke.

"It's all right, folks!" he called out to the crowd. "Nobody's stopping anything. Sheriff just sent these boys over to make sure you churchgoing folk don't get too rowdy!" A roar of laughter came up from the gathering. "Everyone get back to your festivities; I'm going to go get some of Mrs. Proctor's apple cobbler, if you left me any!"

More laughter and the music and the dancing started up again.

"Poor Harry," Gillian said to Auggie. The two of them were sitting on a bench by one of the fires. "Nobody knows where Holly's got to. Must be awful for him."

"Gillian," Auggie said, "why are you here with me?"

"Auggie Shultz! What a thing to ask!"

"No, no, I mean no disrespect. I mean, are you here because Gert asked you to look after me?"

Gillian sighed and looked into the fire.

"She did ask me to look after you, Auggie, and I promised I would. But that isn't why I'm with you. I miss her too, just as much as I miss William. I told her I'd take care of you, but along the way I discovered how much I need you in my life, Augustus, how happy I am to be with you and how lonely my world is without you."

Clay Turlough pushed his way through the crowds. Auggie saw him glaring in his direction.

"So to answer your question, I'm here with you not because of a promise to an old friend, but because I want to be with you. Now it's your turn; why are you here with me?"

"Because I—"

Clay was in front of them.

"Excuse me, Mrs. Procter, I need to talk to Auggie for a spell."

"Oh, hello, Mr. Turlough. Excuse me, please," she said, rising. She touched Auggie's shoulder as she walked away. "You can tell me later, Auggie."

Clay sat down; his face was florid, his eyes darker than usual.

"Having a nice time with your new sweetheart?" he said.

"Clay, listen. I think we made a terrible mistake."

"Oh, so now you think it was a mistake. That's convenient for you and the widow now, isn't it? What about poor Gertie?"

"Gertie was ready to die. I was the coward," Auggie said. "I should have let her go. We tampered with God's plan."

Clay snorted, "Plan? Please. Man's knowledge is already leaving God in the dust. Death is an illness, one that can be overcome, and cured in time, not some divinely ordained prison sentence. Gertie proved that. This has to do with you not wanting her anymore, with wanting that Proctor woman!"

"Ach! Keep your voice down!" Auggie hissed. "Yes, you're right, of course. I do want to be with Gillian. I am selfish, damn you—I want a whole, living woman. I should have suffered the way everyone does, should have endured it, not hid from it! I shouldn't have replaced a lifetime with Gert, a good, real lifetime, with this endless nightmare."

"Real pretty words, Auggie. Doesn't change anything. Gerttie is here and she is alive and she loves and needs you."

"Clay, what kind of life does Gertie have now? What kind will she ever have? I was wrong. You were wrong."

Clay ran a hand through his thin hair. He shook his head.

"No, this was not a mistake. We weren't . . . I am *not* in the wrong. This was just the beginning. You don't see the whole picture, Auggie."

"What I see? What I see, yes?" Auggie's face grew red; his voice became a growl. "What I see is a sick man who views my wife's suffering as just another experiment for him, just another way to show the world his genius. You don't care about Gert; you never did. All she is to you is a way to prove your perverted theories!"

Clay's thin hands shot out and grabbed Auggie by the collar of his shirt; he pulled the burly shopkeeper toward his face.

"You cowardly fool! How dare you say I don't care about that woman when you're here cavorting with Gillian Proctor! You were never good enough for Gertie; she deserved better than you, you frightened, blubbering—"

Auggie pushed Clay off of him and raised a ham-sized fist, ready to strike the smaller man. Suddenly, both men were aware that everyone was watching them. Small, soft hands covered Auggie's fist. Gillian leaned forward and whispered to both men.

"Mr. Turlough, I think I should borrow Augustus back for a moment. Excuse us, please."

Gillian led Auggie out onto the dance floor. The band was playing "Lorena" for the couples. The fiddle was like the slow wail of a lover, pleading. Auggie took Gillian's hands and they began to dance.

"You looked like you were about ready to murder Clay," she said. "I thought you might need a little break. I hope you don't mind."

"*Nein,* no. Thank you. I was getting very angry, that pompous little rooster."

"Now, Auggie, he is your best friend."

"Is he?"

"Well, yes. Everybody has disagreements from time to time. I just hope I wasn't the cause of this one."

"What? Of course not!"

"I know how much Gert meant to Clay and him seeing you and me together . . ." She let the thought hang. Auggie was silent as they glided and turned. The stars shivered brilliantly in the cold desert night. Gillian's eyes were as black as that sky, deep and captivating.

"Gillian, I . . . *Ach!* Why is it so hard to talk when I am with you?"

She rested her head on his wide shoulder and squeezed his hands tighter.

"Hush. You don't have to say anything right now."

Auggie noticed many of the other dancers, and quite a few of the older ladies Gillian had been talking to earlier, were smiling at them.

He turned his head to face her. He fell into her eyes. All the kindness, all the patience and sacrifice this woman had given to him. All the love.

"Thank you," he said. He leaned down toward her. She arched upward to meet him.

It was the perfect kiss—the kind you remember until the day you die, the kind that remakes you, remakes your world. The kind that can save you.

It was perfect, and then the screaming started.

From the outskirts of the party, Clara Gibbs ran screaming, her eyes wide with terror. "Oh Lord in Heaven! There must be a hundred of them! Run! Run!"

The music stopped, more screams—some sounded like men—then the bark of gunfire. Harry Pratt was shouting through the chaos in a deep, powerful voice.

"Everyone, everyone listen! I want you to gather up your loved ones and get them on these wagons and carts now! If you have a gun, go find a deputy to report to; you're working with us now! We've got this covered, so stay calm! Deputy, get all the women and children, and as many of the old folk as possible, on those wagons first and head east! Do it!"

Auggie and Gillian stood still, holding each other. The madness flowed around them, screaming, panicked running, gunshots. She sighed.

"*Ja.*" Auggie nodded. He took her by the hand and they ran toward the wagons.

They came down off Argent Mountain and swarmed along the streets, their numbers growing as they advanced.

Frightened, shocked, the good people of Golgotha paused in confusion at the sight of familiar faces changed, twisted. By then it was too late. Hands, gripping like vises, ignoring pleas or fists; the crushing weight of the mob and cold, wet lips forced to their own. A strange heat, mixed with the terror, as nostrils flared at the alien spoor. A slithering, wriggling force insistent on pushing its way in, relentless. A scream or a gasp for air and then the terrifying gagging, choking as it greedily snaked its way in, cozying up inside their innards. A honeyed cold spreading through body and mind. Perhaps, in the stronger willed, a final desperate struggle, like the drowning man clawing at air, at light, but in most an acceptance, a compliance—submission to the sweet, sticky blackness and the awful promises it whispered.

And the good, good people of the small town of Golgotha, many of them, when they saw the Stained, saw what they did to those they caught up to; they forgot to love their neighbor, forgot to lend a helping hand, forgot to do unto others as they would have them do unto themselves. They ran, ran like animals frightened by the storm. Pushing, shoving, the weak, the innocent, the frail, all falling under their feet. Many of the souls Golgotha called, called to across the desert, across the plains and the oceans and the night sky, many of them were not good people. Many of them cared only for their own skin and their own next breath and they were more than willing to feed another to these monsters, who had been their smiling neighbors, to live, to keep running.

Harry had expected trouble, the golden plates had said as much, but the plan was holding. Caravans of civilians were headed out of town—he estimated a good third to half of Golgotha were leaving safe and sound.

His only concern was the other two-thirds to one-half who hadn't attended the social, who were now out there, fair game for these creatures, and he had to admit he and Jon had never anticipated these sheer numbers coming down the mountain toward his town.

He called out to the deputies, "They're coming mostly down Prosperity! Set up a line and don't let anyone cross it either way. Whatever those things are, if they don't stop, put them down!"

"But Mr. Mayor, that one over there is Sam Catterson, the bookkeeper over by the bank!" one of the deputies shouted. "And that's old Otis Haglund, the butcher. You can't mean for us to—"

Harry's gaze was blue fire. "I know who they are! They aren't those people anymore. Hold that line, or all these innocent people will end up the same. We are buying time for them to get safely away. Then we will regroup with the sheriff."

The deputy ran off. Harry wiped his face with a silk handkerchief, his hand trembling. Everywhere there were the sounds of screams, gunshots and shouts of panic; shadows ran and were chased in primal light of the bonfire.

"Stirring speech, Harry." The voice carried a low growl—honey and gravel. Holly, dressed in a dark-stained military long coat, stepped out of the dancing shadows of a nearby fire. "That part about murdering those good citizens who voted for you, does that apply to me too?"

Harry's head spun; the scent coming off of her was intoxicating. Her eyes were weeping pools of wet pitch. Her lips were moist and black. Her pale, almost-luminous face was veined with faint traceries, like ink, and her long hair fell loosely, wildly, around her. She had never looked more beautiful, more terrible.

"Holly, what have they done to you?"

"Set me free, dear," she said, advancing on him slowly, like a cat, stalking. "I waited for you to come save me, Harry. A childish game, I know. You failed me, like you always did. I simply wasn't important enough to come and rescue."

"That's not true," Harry said. "I, I tried to find you, Holly. I've been worried sick!"

"Really? Finally, after all these years, you care about what happens to me?" She smiled a black-stained smile. "How sweet."

"Holly," Harry said. "Please let me help you—let's go home, please."

"I am home, Harry," she said, reaching out to him. The coat fell open and he could see her moon-pale skin and swaying breasts, smeared with shadow. "My pain is gone, my doubts and guilt and fear—all gone. I belong now.

"I have a new husband, a strong husband, and He's going to devour your little pissant town, devour all these good, good people with their hymns and their prayers and their dirty, dirty little secrets and sick little souls. I don't need an effeminate eunuch like you anymore. My husband is going to kick your coward God's ass and then, then He's going to burn down Heaven and piss on the ashes. Forever and ever, amen."

Her hand closed around his throat. He could see things moving behind the void of her eyes, like black snakes writhing.

"You failed me, Harry, like you failed your father, like you failed your faith, like you've failed everyone who ever counted on you for anything."

He knew he should fight, but she was speaking the truth. He knew it and so did everyone else. Why fight it?

"I could fill you with His seed, make you a drone, like the others, but He promised me I could kill you, so, good-bye, Harry," she whispered, and squeezed. Strong, cold hands tightened on his windpipe. Why fight it?

Ringo, Sarah, even Holly. Maybe he could still save her; maybe no one else could. He blinked and pushed her away, a frantic strength born out of fear and something else he couldn't articulate, even in his own mind.

Holly was hissing in pain, like a cat crying in the night. Her hands were smoking, crisping, as if she had just tried to grab a scalding kettle instead of his neck. She stumbled backward.

"Nice trick," she growled. "How'd you get real power?"

He honestly didn't know. Maybe it was the temple vestments he had donned beneath his clothes, or the ancient breastplate he now wore under his greatcoat—the one that had once held the holy Urim and the Thummim, the seer stones, the armor taken from the chamber beneath his home. He had felt foolish girding himself for battle with holy cloth and antique armor, but he had done it anyway, as Elder Slaughter had commissioned him. There was no denying now what he had tried to hide from, to ignore, his whole life.

He drew the Sword of Laban from the sheath hanging beneath his coat. It shimmered silver and gold like the sun reflected in water, too beautiful to be real, to be a part of this world. The first blade, from which all other others descended, inspiration to kings and heroes throughout time.

"I found it," he said, raising the blade to an *en garde* stance. "I was dragged to it, kicking and screaming."

"Very well, sodomite," Holly cooed. She licked her charred hands with a black, segmented thing that resembled an earthworm more than a tongue. "Let's test your faith against mine, shall we?"

Jim stepped between them, raising the rifle to cover Holly. He cocked the lever and sighted the woman through the barrel's sights.

"Hold it right there, ma'am, please," Jim said.

Holly laughed. "Oh, Harry, he's adorable! Is this your new conquest? Your new special friend? You're robbing the cradle, but then again he looks so sweet, who could blame you?"

"Shut up, Holly!" Pratt barked. "Damn it, boy, get out of here; move!"

"What's your name, sweet lamb?" Holly whispered.

Jim's arms began to tremble, just a little. "Jim," he said. "Why don't you put your arms up in the air, where I can see 'em?"

"Like this?" Holly raised her arms and the coat fell open, exposing her fully. Jim gasped and then blushed. Inadvertently he looked away for an instant.

"Damn it, Jim, move!" Harry shouted, and rushed toward the boy. "Holly, get away from him!"

Another group of screaming townsfolk ran through the tableau. A man fired again and again into one of their stumbling, possessed pursuers. The dead man kept coming even as the bullets ripped through it, spraying black ichor everywhere.

"I'll see you both again," Holly's voice purred over the screams and gunfire, "before sunup."

Jim looked back down the barrel, but she was gone.

Harry was beside him, sword in hand. "Damn!" he shouted, turning to scan for her in every direction. "Damn it all to hell!"

"Well," Jim said, looking around at the ever-expanding chaos, "at least we found her."

Maude's arrival at the social was heralded by the screams of grown men, the sharp crack of gunfire, flames and shadows.

She moved through the chaos like smoke. A large number of local folk had gone mad, swarming off Argent Mountain, like locusts intent on devouring the town. A substance like black oil leaked from their eyes and mouths, and she recognized the scent coming off of them as both an intoxicant and a poison. They were Stained, she somehow knew, the word coming from somewhere outside her.

She knelt and took a neckerchief off the body of a local man whose dead-dumb face she recognized but whose name she did not know. She tied the cloth to cover her face and nose and paused for a second to put her hair in a tight bun. The infected's body language screamed they were ill, very ill, almost dead. Lurching, halting.

Maude was suddenly struck with the image of Arthur's cold body on a table, draped in a shroud. Suddenly the shroud began to move, slide, as the piece of meat that had held a man's soul rose, empty.

The thought was brushed away by the iron grip of one of the infected on her shoulder. As she was still kneeling, her head snapped up to see it was Moses Burke, one of Sarah Pratt's cowboys and an ex—what did they call them? Yes, a Buffalo Soldier.

Moses' eyes were bleeding sticky globs of ink. His mouth yawned open and more of the evil, viscous stuff oozed out. His other hand reached for Maude's throat.

His head snapped back and his grip relented on her shoulder as he was lifted off the ground and backward, then falling onto his back and then still, smoke trailing from the hole in his forehead. Then, the thunder and the shock, numbing her hand, the realization that she had fired the derringer out of instinct and fear.

Stupid old woman! From this position, she had dozens of options to free herself, to take him down. None were lethal. In losing control, in letting fear eat her up, she had ended a good man's life, a sick man's life. *Damn it!*

That was all the time she had to reflect, to chastise herself. Two more of the Stained were on top of her, drawn by the gunfire. Familiar, daily faces, marred, obliterated, by wet masks of evil. No longer people, now part of something larger, something sinister, more driven and utterly dehumanizing.

From a crouch, her left leg straightened, swept, and the closer of the two shambling attackers fell. She leaned back on her hands and pushed up with her coiled right leg. There was pain, as muscles strained, tore, but held. She launched upward, let the force and the momentum drive her toward the still-standing attacker. The heel of her palm drove into its jaw with a muffled crunching sound. The force and location were sufficient to knock him out, Maude knew.

The Stained staggered backward from the blow, and fell to the ground. She began to turn her attention to the one she had knocked down initially when she halted in mid-spin, to watch with shock and horror as the one she had just struck began to rise again. Its head lolled to one side, like a drunk's.

For one breath, the fear and panic returned and she thought of the gun. Moses was still. It seemed a bullet to the head did the trick.

No. She put the fear away, boxed it. Locked it up and acted.

Two quick, low snap kicks to the kneecaps. A crunching sound like wood striking gravel and the Stained fell to the ground again. Maude felt the other one behind her on its feet now, arms outstretched, lunging toward her neck. She balanced, a little wobbly, spun with her whole body's mass at the hips and waist and drove a powerful spin kick into its pelvis, shattering bones needed to support legs, body weight. She stopped the kick short of breaking the spine. The blow was painful and crippling, but it wasn't lethal.

The one with broken knees was trying to crawl. Maude stepped over and with two quick strikes dislocated its shoulders.

She put the gun away and continued the search for Constance in the madness. Ahead, through a curtain of smoke, Maude saw a crowd gathered. The barn was on fire, and even as they were being savaged by the Stained many townsfolk were trying to put the flames out with buckets of sand and water.

For a moment, she wondered where Mutt was in this madness and hoped he was all right, knew he was. She selfishly wished he were with her.

There was more shouting. She thought she heard Mayor Pratt. A wave of panicked people, chased by a few Stained, surged in front of her. When they passed, she saw Constance and a few of her friends moving hesitantly away from the farm and toward Prosperity and the center of town.

"Constance!" Maude screamed, pushing through another surge of frightened people who were blocking her way, a flood of panic and chaos.

Constance turned back toward her mother. Her face was black and wet.

"No!" Maude staggered, stopped. The pain was physical. The fear welled up in her again; this time it ate her whole. "Constance! No!"

Maude ran, pushing, striking anything, everything, in her way. The mob of screaming, terrified townsfolk and the shambling things that pursued them enveloped her. The smoke from the growing fires stung her eyes, but she refused any tears in this moment. She had to reach her baby and tears would not aid her, only hinder.

She twisted, spun and ran for all she had in her, breaking through the line, into the clear. Constance and the other Stained, her new family, were gone.

Gone.

Malachi Bick, Biqa, sat on a rock and watched his town glow from the fires. There was the man-made thunder of rifles and occasionally a scream would be powerful enough to reach him this far out. Ironic, he thought. Ears that once could hear particles of hydrogen colliding now had to strain to pick up the frantic barks of human suffering.

He hadn't eaten, slept or drank since his escape from the assassins at the Paradise Falls. He knew he didn't need those things, but the realization didn't keep him from craving them, especially some tobacco.

A flash of blue light in the darkness, a bitter puff of sulphur.

"Need a light?" the voice said. It was full of molasses and scorpion venom.

Lucifer, beautiful in the shadows that obscured his true face, his face after the Fall, lit the cheroot he cradled in his lips with the smoking match, and puffed until its tip was cherry red. Today he was a slender man, blond and beautiful, dressed in a work shirt and denim dungarees. Bick hated to admit it, but it was hard for him to see past the illusion of mortality, just like he hadn't seen Ambrose or his deacon for what they were until it was too late, until Caleb was gone. The Devil leaned forward and offered the cheroot to Bick. He took it and savored a long drag of its mellow smoke.

"What a mess," Lucifer said. "Look at you; you look half in the bag, to use the vernacular of the natives. What happened, Biqa?"

"What do you want?" Bick sighed, exhaling the smoke.

"It's not what I want, this time," the Devil said. "I was asked to come here by the home office, if you can imagine such a thing."

"Another lie," Bick said, and took another sip of smoke from the thin cigar.

"Surprisingly, no. I only lie when I have something to gain from it. At this point, this is such a disaster that the only thing to be gained is keeping Earth, Heaven and Hell open for business and not ripped to tatters. Again, how did this come to pass, Biqa?"

"You know. You know everything that transpires in the spheres of matter, Lucifer. It's your domain. Why pretend you don't?"

"Because," the Devil said with a smile, "I want to hear you say it."

Bick felt hate well up in him. It surprised him how easily it came, how comfortable he felt in the small, petty emotion. He regarded the cheroot, shook his head and tossed it away. He stood.

"I went native," he said finally. "I watched them for so long, I watched them grow up, become shadows of His divinity, His mercy, His wrath. None of you were around. No one visited me after you. So I . . . fell into it, into becoming one of them."

"Fell," Lucifer said. "Interesting choice of words. So why didn't you seek me out? I would have welcomed you with open arms."

Bick's chuckle was a dry rasp. "Please. I haven't given up my duty to the Host, to the Lord. I have no intention of joining you and your 'revolutionaries' in the root cellar. I just got a little lax in how I attended to my responsibility. I had to adapt; I mean they started learning, creating settlements, exploring, expanding. They breed like prairie rabbits, you know?"

Lucifer nodded, allowing him to continue.

"They sensed the power of that thing beneath this land and it drew them here. They had no idea what it was or why they came—it whispered to them in dreams and spoke to the disturbed, the mad and the evil. To remain here as guardian, I had to appear as something their minds could understand, could endure. To the first people, I was a sorcerer—they called me Be'kiwa-ah. I had powerful medicine and they left me alone. Even their spirits and gods avoided me.

"Then the white and black and yellow people came and I had to become a man named Bick for them. I became white, like the majority of them, just as I had been a red man when this land was theirs.

"I claimed my protectorate as my own, built a homestead and worked to control the access of those who crossed these lands in search of a new home. I maintained control of who settled here as best I could without arousing suspicion. The Bick family's heir would 'pass away' and I would take on a new guise, as a new relative—a son, a distant cousin. It worked pretty well for a long time."

"You really didn't have to do all that," Satan said with a sigh. "You really have let yourself go, Biqa. I mean, ruses and charades, pretending to be a mortal. You've even started thinking like a monkey—why not just cast a blight upon all who live here, or fill their hearts up with terror or turn a few into pillars of salt? They'd get the idea to stay away."

Bick shook his head. "You never did accept it, did you? Tell me, O Prince of Darkness, why don't you just come on up here all the time and snatch any old soul that strikes your fancy? Why don't you set San Francisco ablaze and dance in the streets while your demons harvest sinners like wheat? Why all the contracts and fiddle contests?"

"Free will," they said simultaneously.

"I hate it," Lucifer said, kicking a rock. "Why would you give a bunch of short-lived, shortsighted murderous apes the power of cosmic veto? Why does He hold our power in check, but they can roam around and murder and lie and cheat with impunity?"

"For someone whose domain is Earth, you have a lot to learn about humans. The bottom line is He limits us and what we can do to them with our power, His power."

Lucifer snorted. "For now. So you lived as one of them, came to enjoy their base pleasures. Now look at you, so weak you can actually be harmed by physical force, perhaps even killed. How did you plan to protect the land by letting human insects dig into it?"

"That was a miscalculation," Bick explained. "The chains of divine fire that hold the Darkling are the most tangible manifestation of the Almighty's power within the Earth. The presence of the power turned whole veins of base matter into semi-divine material, throughout the planet."

"Silver," Satan said, nodding. "That's why it has the effect it does on preternatural creatures, and why men covet it so much."

"Since this is where the Darkling was cast to Earth, where the world was first built around it, there is a lot of silver here in Nevada. That eventually brought prospectors. They found their way to the mountain, discovered the silver veins. Word got out before I could deal with them. The silver boom came to my little town."

"You're not telling me the whole story," Satan said, smiling. "I can smell half-truths like horse flop and you, my noble angel, are lying by omission. Maybe even hiding a sin or two, hmmm?"

Bick looked away, back toward the town and the mountain. "It's a long story, one for another day. The gist of all this is I had to allow the Argent Mine to exist for a time. I made sure the deed to the land belonged to the Bick family and was passed along from heir to heir. I arranged for the mine to be reported as having gone bust a few years back. Problem solved, or so I thought."

"However . . . ," Satan said.

Bick sighed. "However, I didn't count on the growing interference of lawyers, regulators, bureaucrats and politicians into my business. I swear it seems that every year they stick their noses into more and more."

Lucifer chuckled. "Sorry about that—I outdid myself there."

"I began to diversify my holdings. I 'sold' a number of them to individuals with an understanding that they were only keeping them in trust for me, but on paper it no longer appeared that Malachi Bick and the Bick family owned every rock between here and California."

"You sold the mountain?" Lucifer shook his head. "You must have really been living it up with the monkeys to make such a foolish mistake."

The anger flared in Bick again, but he fought it down. Satan was right—he had fallen far too deeply into the role, had lost sight of his mission and foolishly believed the time he was now faced with would never come. He had failed when he had given Arthur Stapleton the deed to Argent Mountain, failed his Lord and failed the humans he had come to admire so much. He had failed Caleb.

"Yes," he said, "it was a mistake, my mistake. But I intend to rectify it."

"You best do it soon," Lucifer said. "I was sent to tell you as much. What the Darkling's servants are doing is weakening the divine chains. They are failing and the Darkling is waking up. God doesn't seem to be taking any meetings these days about reinforcing the chains, so you had better come up with something else, and soon."

"The Lord does not speak with the Highest Host about the crisis?"

"Or anything else for that matter. He's been pretty quiet since He finished up the Earth. I think He's studying something—you know how He gets with His hobbies. Either that or He's foreseen what's in the wind and He's hiding. If you can't stop them from awakening it, it will tear the Earth apart as it breaks free of its prison, and it won't stop till everything we've created is gone. Heaven, Hell, but first and foremost your precious Earth. You remember how awful that thing was last time, don't you—the siege at the Pillars of Tranquility? How many angels did we lose that day, phalanxes? "

Bick nodded. He rubbed his eyes. The sky should be getting brighter at the approach of dawn. It wasn't. He noticed stars began to drop from the sky like sparks drifting away from a campfire. He felt cold fear slip into his bowels.

"Better to reign in Hell than get devoured by that thing, I say," Lucifer offered.

"So I shouldn't count on your help?" Bick said. "I'm shocked. How about the Host?"

"It's still your post," Lucifer said. "You know the rules—'one riot, one ranger,' so to speak. If it gets free, no one will be able to stop it again—not even the Almighty could kill it, remember? No one in Heaven or Hell is going to be fool enough to stand against that thing. So it's up to you, Biqa, but honestly, in the shape you're in, I wouldn't expect much."

Neither did he. He knew what that thing could do, knew how limited his powers really were here, especially now, since his lapses. It was impossible. He couldn't stand up to the creature's worshipers, let alone the Darkling itself, and what could possibly replace chains of divine fire to hold the thing and keep it sedate?

Another scream from the town, it sounded like a child. Bick nodded to Lucifer and began walking back toward Golgotha.

"I've got work to do. Go back to Hell and hide under your ottoman."

"You? You're so compromised I'll bet you can't even wield your sword anymore. Can you even perceive its true nature as you are? You're not much more than a human now, Biqa."

"That will suffice," he said to the Lord of Hell, still walking away.

"What do you want me to pass along to the Host?" the Devil called out.

"Tell them to have faith!" Bick shouted back as he disappeared over a rocky ridge. "Tell them we're on it."

Another star fell beyond the shadowed horizon. The desert was quiet, like the whole of creation was holding its breath.

"*We?*" Lucifer said.

The Emperor

The dawn never came. The stars, the moon, all fell into an endless, frigid night, sliding behind clouds of ink, never to reemerge. Once the celestial illumination was swallowed, the only light came from men—torches, lanterns and, of course, the fires that ran wild through Golgotha.

Riley Finn staggered out into the darkness to see why Redbilly, his prize rooster, had not crowed. Finn's homestead was off of Duffer Road—not much more than a tarpaper shack, a bare feeding yard and a small coop to house the chickens that made him a decent living in the town. Most folk around Golgotha knew the gangly man with the crooked smile and the red hair simply as "the Egg Man."

"Redbilly, lad, what's gotten into you? Why aren't you squawking? It's already—"

He squinted in the lantern light as he popped open the lid to his pocket watch. The hands were bent and the glass was broken. The watch had broken precisely at dawn. Riley had no way of knowing that every timepiece in Golgotha had suffered the exact same fate, at exactly the same time.

"Bloody hell," he muttered, and stuffed the broken timepiece back in his pocket.

"Redbilly?" Riley called as he pulled open the narrow door to the silent chicken coop and swung his lantern toward the opening to see. Blood dripped down from the straw-filled rows of roosts, each holding a still, mute hen. The blood pooled on the floor. Riley crossed himself, then stepped into the coop, his lantern leading the way.

The hens were all dead; their white, plump bodies were still warm, their feathers flecked with blood. Riley picked up an egg, gingerly, from one of the nests. His dead mother's face was impressed on the egg's surface, frozen in terrified pain—exactly how she had looked the moment she had died in Dublin from the Black Vomit. The detail was like a photograph in its horrible clarity. It almost seemed to move. Riley gasped and dropped the egg. It hit the floor with a wet crunch. He grabbed another egg—again his mother's frightened, frenzied eyes, her sunken cheeks, the flecks of foam at the corners of her mouth, a perfect depiction of her last pained breath. And on another egg, and another and another.

"Our Father Who art in Heaven . . ." Riley muttered the prayer even as he swung the lantern toward the back of the coop. Redbilly was there, hanging limply from the roost. The cock had somehow, through sheer terror, managed to twist his own neck backward until it snapped. The rooster had wrung his own neck rather than sing the song of this blasphemous day.

". . . hallowed be Thy name . . ."

The coppery smell of blood mixed with the rich stench of chicken shit and a palpable fog of fear. Something creaked close by. A loose floorboard? The death rattle of a poor, dead, mad animal? Riley's mind tumbled through the terrible permutations like a gambler shuffling cards.

". . . thy kingdom come . . ." His voice quivered.

He tried to snort the spoor of death from his nostrils. He had to get out, get out into the fresh air, out into cool air and reason. He spun toward the coop's door. His lantern's beam was caught by a wet, black face with eyes as empty as the rooster's, and oily hands clawing toward him.

The Egg Man's short-lived scream was lost in the cacophony of Golgotha's death throes.

"You have got to be pulling my leg," Highfather said. His horse and Mutt's galloped down Prosperity Street and turned onto Main. Donnie Broyles and his crew were walking out of the Golgotha Bank and Trust lugging bags overflowing with cash. They halted on the stairs of the bank as the sheriff and his deputy pulled their mounts to a stop in front of the robbers' horses.

"What the hell are you doing, Donnie?" Highfather shouted. "I don't have time for this!"

"How in tarnation do you know it's me?" Donnie asked.

"'Cause no other soap lock in this town is stupid enough to rob the bank when the whole damned world is falling down. Now take that ridiculous bandana off your face and put the money back in there, right now."

"Naw!" Donnie shouted as he tugged down the neckerchief from in front of his nose and mouth. "I ain't gonna do it, Sheriff. Now git outta my way, or else we're going to have to slap leather, right here, right now!"

Highfather looked at Mutt. The deputy rolled his eyes and shrugged. The sheriff dropped his hand near his holster and became very still. His eyes locked with Broyles's.

"You sure you want to do this, Donnie?" Highfather said softly.

"You didn't say nothin' 'bout shooting no lawman, Donnie!" one of the other bandana-wearing men on the steps said. "Specially not a lawman that's some kinda haint!"

"Shut up!" Donnie barked. "He ain't no ghost—that's jist a tale! He ain't nothin'!"

Donnie looked at the sheriff. He'd have to cross draw to hit Donnie, and Donnie already had his gun in his hand. He was a dang good shot too. He could kill Highfather before he even got his gun out of his holster, dead to rights. And there was Donnie's crew—all armed, all ready to cut the lawmen down. It was a done deal. He was sure of it. Sure of it right up until he looked in Highfather's face, really looked. There was no fear in Jon Highfather right now, no uncertainty. Only a mild annoyance and perhaps a hint of pity. Then all the stories began rattling around in Donnie's skull, like a bullet ricocheting. What if he couldn't be killed? What if Donnie's bullets just went on through him?

"Think about it, Donnie," Highfather said. "Look around; look at the sky. You think you can ride away from this? Think the stars are still twinkling in Kansas City or Mexico? Where you going to spend that money when it's all going to hell? You going to buy yourself a sunup? Still, I reckon if you got to pick a night to die, might as well be on the last night ever, huh? So, what do you say Donnie, we doing this or not?"

The pale eyes didn't waver. The hand hovered inches from the holster, still as stone. Donnie's dark eyes blinked; he swallowed hard and then laid his gun slowly on the ground.

"Jig's up, boys," he said sullenly. "Lay 'em down."

The other robbers complied.

"Still pushing that luck of yours," Mutt said to Highfather softly.

Jon pushed his hat up and spared a second to look at the dying sky.

"Not time yet. Hey, look over there."

Down Main, in the direction of the theatre, a mob of the Stained suddenly came into view, pursuing a small group of the uninfected. The survivors were led by Dan Powell, one of Jon's deputies.

"Dan, over here!" Highfather shouted, drawing his pistol. The sheriff turned to address the thieves.

"Like I said before, none of us has the time for this right now, Donnie. I'm hereby deputizing you and your boys. Pick up your guns and move your asses!"

He spurred Bright to a full gallop and charged down Main. Mutt, on Muha, followed.

The mob was at least twenty strong, lumbering and hissing. Their wet faces were black, broken mirrors that reflected the tongues of flame crawling up the walls of Chauncey's Tobacconist, across the street from Shultz's General Store. Heartened by the sight of Highfather and his reluctant posse, Dan and the few armed men with him turned to face the monstrous horde descending on them.

"Hot damn, it's the sheriff! Okay, boys, light 'em up!"

Fire and thunder roared from the guns.

"Aim for the heads!" Highfather shouted over the blast of his own pistol. "You have any silver rounds left, Dan?"

"All used up to git us this far!"

Donnie and his boys raced by on horseback, whooping and firing into the mob as they passed. A few of the Stained dropped from the rain of bullets. One of the survivors with Dan, Mrs. Gunderson, screamed as her infected nephew, Roland, clawed at her arm, trying to drag her into the mass of the Stained. Mutt pivoted on Muha, fired his rifle into Roland's chest at point-blank range, grabbed Mrs. Gunderson and scooped her up onto the horse. The boy flew backward, chest smoking, knocking over several of the other infected. The sheriff, his deputy and Dan's small band formed a circle, with the unarmed survivors at the center. Volleys of gunfire ripped into the swarm of the Stained. Donnie and his crew made another pass, flanking them with more gunfire. One of Donnie's crew screamed as he was pulled down by one of the infected. The boy had no time to do anything but whimper as one of the Stained crouched over him, grinding its wet mouth to the fallen thief's, filling him with alien darkness.

"I'm out; any more shells?" Dan asked.

Highfather swallowed hard, passed his last three bullets to Dan and glanced at Mutt, who dispatched another hissing member of the mob with a well-placed rifle shot.

The deputy shook his head. "I'm out too now. We still got knives."

A shrill call echoed across the valley. It came from the top of Argent Mountain. It sounded like a cat screaming while it drowned, screaming with far too many mouths. The sound filled Highfather's head with a buzzing mass of bees made of pain and nausea. All of the Stained stopped in their tracks and rocked gently at the inhuman wailing. After what seemed like forever, the sound ended; and with its end, the infected scattered, disappearing into the alleys of Main Street. Six lay dead; then suddenly two of them shuddered and got to their feet. Roland Gunderson was one of them. The two resurrected Stained staggered clumsily after their fleeing kin.

"I'll be damned," Dan muttered.

"What was that god-awful noise?" Highfather asked.

"A call to prayer," a voice as smoky as whiskey said.

Malachi Bick stepped into view; the fire from Chauncey's backlit him, fluttering like wings. "The faithful are being called home."

"What the hell does that mean?" Highfather said.

"It means we don't have much time," Bick said. "We need to talk, Sheriff."

"I knew you were messed up in this somehow or other, Malachi. You had—"

"As I said, time is of the essence. I need to speak to you, your deputy, Mayor Pratt and young Master Jim as soon as you can summon them."

"What the hell do you want to talk to the boy for?" Mutt asked.

"I'd rather not say out in the street. Sheriff?"

Highfather sighed. "Dan, you got any notion where the mayor might be?"

"Harry? Yeah, he was headed to the jail to try to get more ammo. He done a hell of a job tonight, Jon, Harry did. When those things showed up at the social, Harry got everyone out of there real quick. Saved a mess of folks, kept them from rabbiting. His old man would have been real proud of him."

Donnie and his boys rode up, yipping and howling. "Damn, Sheriff, if I knew being a lawman was this much fun, I'd have signed up a long time ago!"

"Yeah, it's a hoot. Listen, Donnie, you and your boys still got ammo, right?"

Donnie and most of his boys nodded.

"Good, toss Dan here some shells. I want you and the boys to escort these good people home. Get them to some place safe, and then get you and yours on home and stay put. You did good work tonight, Donnie."

Broyles smiled. It was genuine, like a child who was bringing home his first good marks from school.

"Thanks, Sheriff," Donnie said. "Come on now, folks; let's get you all home. Maybe if we're lucky we'll run into some more of those things!"

Highfather turned to Dan. "I need you to find Harry. Tell him to meet me here, at the Paradise Falls, as quick as he can. Then get yourself home too."

"Don't got to tell me twice," Dan said, reloading his rifle. "I'm grabbing Gladys and the boys and we are skedaddling outta here. You may want to think about that too. I've lived in this town for a long time and I've been through some powerful weird things here, but nothing like this, ever. It might be time to go, Jon."

Highfather saw another star detach itself from the icy black firmament and burn, tumbling, toward the dark shroud of the horizon.

"Not leaving my home, Dan. I'm of a mind to fix this."

Bick had already removed the boards nailed over the doors to the Paradise Falls. Highfather and Mutt followed him inside. A lit oil lamp was sitting on a red-felt octagonal card table in the back of the main room, as was a bottle of whiskey and six glasses. There was also a long rectangular wooden box on the table.

"No more dancing, Malachi," Highfather said. "The squatters going crazy up on the ridge, Stapleton's death, what happened to Holly Pratt, these strangers—Ambrose and Phillips. What is this god, this thing they are try-ing to awaken? Time to acknowledge the corn. I want answers, or else I'll finish the job on you someone already started."

Bick groaned as he fell into one of the chairs. He poured himself a finger of whiskey into one of the glasses. "It was Phillips, at Ambrose's command." He drained the glass. "They killed Caleb."

Highfather reached across the table and picked up a glass. Bick filled it, offered one to Mutt. The deputy shook his head curtly and kept watching the door while he reloaded his rifle.

"I was sorry to hear about your son. Powerful sorry," Highfather said. "My condolences. He seemed a decent fella."

"Thank you, Sheriff."

"Why did they do it?"

"They knew I had to try to stop them from freeing what's under the mines."

"What is under there, Malachi?" Highfather asked. "How do you know about it?"

"It's my job, Jonathan. It's been my family's job for a long time."

Mutt sniffed the air. "Company, Jonathan," he said.

Harry Pratt and Jim Negrey entered the saloon. They both looked exhausted. Dark circles ringed their eyes and the horror and chaos of the streets clung to their gaunt faces. Jim cradled a rifle in his arms. The butt of a six-gun protruded from the pocket of his stained and torn coat. Harry's long coat was covered in dark, drying stains, but the shimmering silver and gold breastplate beneath his torn shirt was spotless, as was the glistening blade that he held in his hand.

"Ah, you brought it," Bick said. "The Sword of Laban. Very good, Harry; we'll need it."

"You, you knew about this, Bick?" Harry said, lifting the sword.

Mutt ruffled Jim's hair as the boy passed. Jim took a seat next to the Indian.

"How you holding up, 'Deputy'?" Mutt asked with a grin.

"I want a raise." The boy smiled thinly.

"Yeah, me too."

"Please sit," Bick said. He poured drinks for everyone. Jim reached for his whiskey, but Highfather slid it across the table to Mutt, who quickly tossed it back. "Yes, Harry, I know about the sword and the other treasures of your faith that your family was tasked with protecting. My family was here when they were first hidden, and I had many talks with your father about them."

"So all that Mormon hooey is real?" Jim asked.

"Faith," Bick said, "gives a thing power. Belief is one of the most powerful assets mankind possesses. It's a damn shame so few folks take advantage of it. Of course the world is set up to make it hard to believe, really believe—that's part of the elegant trap of it."

"So is that a yes, or a no?" Jim asked Mutt.

There was a howling screech outside, close. It came from a once-human throat.

"Answers, Malachi," Highfather said. "We don't have the time for pretty words."

Bick stood and walked to the stained-glass and brass door of the Paradise. He closed his eyes and placed his palm on the door for a moment. There was a hiss of smoke that had no odor, and when he removed his hand the print remained on the glass. He paused, looked toward the shadows of the second floor of the saloon, nodded, then walked back to the table.

"No one will disturb us for a time, Sheriff. I assure you. You wanted answers, now that we are all here, I'll give them to you. But first, Master Jim, do you have it with you?"

"Sir?"

"The power you carry, Jim," Bick said. "You have it about you, on you. Real power. No more time for hiding, we need it, now."

"Leave the boy be, Bick," Highfather growled.

Bick looked to Mutt. "You sense it, don't you, Deputy?"

Mutt leaned toward Jim. "Show them. I promise, ain't nobody taking it away from you. I give you my word on that."

Reluctantly, the boy reached into his pocket and removed the handkerchief. He carefully unfolded it on the table, revealing the jade eye.

"What is that, Jim?" Highfather asked.

"My pa's eye," Jim said. "He lost his in the war and some crazy Johnny-men gave him this one."

"How did you end up with it?" Pratt asked.

"Got it back from the bastards who killed my pa."

"I see," Bick said, his attention locked on the eye. "What did you make of it, Deputy Mutt?"

"Why the hell you asking me, Bick?"

"Surely you sensed this, yes?"

"Go to hell," Mutt said, then, "Yeah. Yeah I did. It's how I found the boy out in the Forty-Mile." He turned to look at Jim. "But it ain't why I brought you back here, Jim, I swear."

"I know," Jim said. "You ain't no snake, Mutt."

"Very true," Bick said, pulling his gaze from the orb. "It's Chinese in origin. That makes it Ch'eng Huang's domain. I wanted him to be here, but he refuses to leave Johnny Town. Master Jim will have to go to him."

"Hold it," Highfather said. "Why in hell would I let this boy wander off to Johnny Town and into the arms of that old villain on your say-so. Hell, Malachi, you and Huang are the two worst people in this town, why should we trust either of you, and you still haven't answered a single damn—"

"What do you think is going on here, Jonathan?" Bick asked, his voice rising, eyes darkening. "You're an intelligent man; I have no intention of insulting you. Why? Why is Golgotha the town where the owls speak and the stones moan? Why is this the town that attracts monsters and saints, both mortal and preternatural? Why is our schoolhouse haunted? Why did Old Lady Bellamy wear the skins of corpses on the new moon? How did old Odd Tom's dolls come to life and kill people? Why do you still pour a ring of salt around that unmarked grave and how did this little ditch of a town become the final resting place of some of Heaven's treasures?

"There is a presence here, Sheriff, older than mankind, older than the world and the stars, older than gods. Imprisoned here, it still has power over what we laughingly call reality. It sleeps a fitful sleep and dreams of only darkness and death. You've been a lawman here long enough to have felt it. Anyone who lives here for a time comes to know it, but we don't speak of it, dare not, for fear of giving it power."

"And Ambrose and his cult want to cut it loose," Highfather said.

"Each soul he corrupts weakens the power that binds it, and makes the creature stronger," Bick said, nodding.

"What happens if it gets out?" Jim asked.

The men were silent, their faces stone.

"Let's see to it that doesn't happen," Harry said. "Malachi, is there any way to save the people infected by this thing?"

"I don't know," he said. "I'm sorry, Harry, I just don't know." Bick took another drink. He lit a cheroot with trembling, bruised hands and continued.

"We have two paths ahead of us: One, stop the ritual Ambrose is even now preparing to undertake in the mine, seal the chambers in the new vein they opened that grant access to the creature and hope the bonds holding it since before the dawn of time don't fail."

"And the second?" Pratt asked.

Bick pointed to Jim and the eye. "That eye has power, more than anything in this town, perhaps in this world, or any other world, even more so than the angelic treasures you possess, Harry. It may hold the key to binding the creature, if we are too late to stop Ambrose."

"I, I rightly don't think it can do all that, sir," Jim said.

"Go ask Ch'eng Huang," Bick said. "He can tell you."

"You trust him?" Mutt asked.

"We all have parts to play in this," Bick said. "I believe that is his role."

"Okay," Highfather said. "Jim heads for Johnny Town and the rest of us get to the mine and try to scuttle Ambrose and his crew."

"Dibs on Phillips," Mutt said, tossing back another shot of whiskey.

"Fly in the ointment," Highfather said. "Between us, we got maybe half a dozen silver shells left. And there are way too many of them for us to all make consistent, accurate head shots to drop them with regular bullets before they get us."

"Speak for yourself." Mutt smiled.

"The Sword of Laban will fell any creature, mortal or otherwise," Bick said.

"He's right, Jon," Harry said. "This thing's kept me alive all night long."

"And," Bick said, sliding the wooden case over to Highfather, "this is for you."

The sheriff snapped open the small brass clasps on the case and opened it. It was lined with white silk and held a beautiful cavalry saber. The blade was inlaid with golden patterns reminiscent of flames along its length.

"She's a beauty," Highfather said.

"It was mine, from back in the war," Bick said wistfully. "Take it."

Highfather grasped the blade; it was light, almost weightless. It slid easily out of the case. As he lifted it, its blade seemed to drink in the light from the lamp, amplify it, refine it, send it cascading along the polished, golden surface. The room seemed to get warmer, brighter. An odd combination of awe and sadness crossed Bick's face. He nodded, slightly.

"What magnificent creatures," he muttered.

Mutt narrowed his eyes as Highfather raised the blade to examine it, and then the deputy's eyes widened in surprise and confusion. He snapped a glance at Bick and then shook his head.

"She's a fine blade," Bick said. "She will see you through this, Sheriff."

"Not that I'm not obliged, but why aren't you carrying it?"

"Because I can't go with you," Bick said.

"Never took you for a coward," Highfather said. "What is it, then?"

"Like I said, we all have roles to play in this. I . . . I'm . . . not allowed. There are rules. . . . It's complicated. I can't, I wish I could, but I can't. It has to be up to you . . . four."

Highfather stood, sword in hand, and stared at Bick.

"Someday, I will get the whole story out of you, Malachi."

"I'm sure you will."

"Let's go," Highfather said to the others. "We're burning starlight."

"Wait," Jim said. "What about Mutt? He ain't got no fancy sword to protect him!"

The deputy smiled and slapped him on the back. "Don't worry, kid, I think I got something better. I just recollected something my old man told me not too long ago."

Bick rose as they pushed open the doors to the street. He opened his mouth, tried to think of words to say, to express his insides. He failed. He nodded to them. Highfather nodded back, and then they were gone into the night.

"You can come out now," Bick said, pouring whiskey into the empty sixth glass. "Please join me for a drink."

A shadow detached itself from its brethren on the second floor of the Paradise Falls. The figure moved down the stairs to the bar's main floor. The stairs did not creak. A woman, dressed in black, wearing pants and boots best suited to a man, approached Bick. Her graying brown hair was held in a tight bun; her mouth and nose were hidden behind a blood-spattered neckerchief. She had a heavy canvas bag with the strap slung over her shoulder and across her chest.

She stood, her gold-brown eyes boring into the saloon owner. She took the glass from his hand and pulled down the neckerchief-mask.

"Mrs. Stapleton," Bick said. "I never had the chance to offer you condolences for Arthur's death. I am sorry for you and your daughter. He was a good and faithful employee for many years."

"I came here to torture you," Maude said. She paused to toss back the shot of whiskey, then placed the empty glass on the red-felt table with a hollow click. "Find out what I could about Arthur's death and how it's tied to what's happening to the town now, how you are connected to this new misery, and then I planned to kill you, Mr. Bick, because of what this madness that you have set in motion has done to my family."

"What has happened?" Bick said. "Where is your child?"

"She is one of those . . . things now," Maude said.

"I'm sorry," Bick said.

"I heard what you said while the others were here," Maude said. "Is there a way, any way, to bring her back?"

"Honestly, I don't know," Bick said. "The sheriff had your husband's body examined, and he was apparently poisoned by the same black substance. It appears to share certain qualities with venom and blood. At least that was what I was able to ascertain before this night fell and my sources grew quiet."

"Blood and poison . . . ," Maude said, nodding. "I may have something that can help with that."

"Yes," Bick said. "You just might. You are a Daughter of Lilith, aren't you?"

She paused, frowned and poured herself a second drink, then thought better of it and set it down. "Yes, I am. How do you know about that?"

"My . . . family has had a long awareness, and sometimes an association, with those who carry Lilith's Load. I assure you, the world is in danger tonight and your talents and insights can turn the tide."

"All I want is to find my daughter," Maude said. "And I am going to do that and try to heal her of this madness you have brought down on us."

"I believe the course of action you are thinking about is sound," Bick said. "It may save her. It may save us all."

"What are you talking about?" she said. "I haven't even decided— Never mind."

"Do you still intend to kill me?" Bick asked. He wasn't afraid. Maude was troubled by how hard it was to read his body language, his facial cues. They were all there but subtle, so faint as to almost be nonexistent. It was like trying to predict a moving dead man. Perhaps he was.

"No," she said. "There's been enough death tonight, and more to come, I'm afraid. But how much of that death is on your hands, Mr. Bick?"

"A fair portion, madame," he said, reaching for her abandoned drink and cradling the shot glass in his palm, regarding it. "A fair portion."

He drained the glass. When he looked up, Maude Stapleton was gone. Bick rose from his chair; a scar of a smile crossed his face. *Good*. There was another tiny spark of hope out in the darkness now.

The scar faded. His eyes grew wide and dark as it settled over him. She was right. A lot of good people were dead, because of his actions, his pride. It felt like acid hissing in him, burning.

Bick sat down; he stood up again. He picked up the whiskey bottle and began to put it to his lips; then he hurled it in rage. It exploded against the wall and he collapsed again into his chair. He rubbed his eyes and felt the heat of the tears well up behind them. He looked at the empty case that had held his blade, his badge of office, and his battered and torn body was wracked by sobs.

Left powerless in two worlds, helpless to act, forbidden to act. He did something he had often mocked mortals for, in his darkest hours. He began to pray.

The Ace of Wands

Outside the Paradise Falls, Mutt pulled Jim aside. "Don't turn your back on that old Chinese bastard. He's an odd one. Never smelled right to me."

"I'll be fine; don't start fretting like an old lady!"

"Shut your mouth, boy! You be careful, or I will personally kick your ass."

"Yessir."

Highfather and Harry returned from scouting the street for any signs of the Stained.

"Coast is clear, fellas. Jim, you run all the way there, you hear me? Don't stop for nothing."

"Yessir, Sheriff," Jim said.

"Okay, go!" Highfather said.

They headed off in opposite directions; Highfather, Mutt and Harry cut behind Main toward the stand of trees called Lover's Grove and the town well. Past that was a goat path, which would bring them up Argent Mountain to the old ruins near the entrance to the mine.

Jim sprinted down Main in the direction of Prosperity Street. From there, it was a quick left, then a right onto Bick Street and the narrow maze of Johnny Town. The rifle felt heavy in his hands and he wondered if they were okay, back home. He imagined Ma, holding Lottie, singing one of the Psalms, softly, as the stars burned away, one by one.

He pushed the image away; it filled him with a panic, like a horse in a burning barn. It served no good. He wasn't there, he was here, and here he could do something about it; he could save them, save home, even if he could never see it again.

He turned the corner and paused to catch his breath. Three hatchets festooned with emerald ribbons seemed to materialize in the wooden wall beside him. Jim froze. A Chinaman, dressed in black, stepped from the darkness, lowering his throwing arm.

"What are you doing here, boy?" the man asked with a calm menace. Two more Green Ribbon hatchet men appeared where Jim had sworn there was nothing but air and shadow.

"Ch'eng Huang," Jim said as calmly as he could. "Tell him I'm here for the answers he promised me."

The tong soldiers brought him to the Celestial Palace, the bar he had tried to get into a few nights ago. The tattooed man, Kada, who had chased him that night stood guard as he had then, but now Kada had a rifle in his hands and an ammo belt slung over his shoulder. The smaller man, the one who spoke such good English, smiled as he saw Jim and his escorts approach.

"Welcome back, little white eyes. The venerable one awaits you. The guns will stay out here, of course."

"You try to take my pa's eye and you and I will—"

"I assure you, my orders are only to disarm you, nothing more."

Jim heard a piano playing inside. He handed the rifle and then the pistol out of his pocket to the small man.

"Enter," the small man said.

Though it didn't look it on the outside, the Celestial Palace was as fancy as the Paradise Falls on the inside. It looked like a real palace from one of those one thousand Arabian Nights stories he had read in the dime novels. There were silk curtains and dragon statues of jade, vases and urns delicately painted with cherry blossoms and wide columns of blue and gold.

The place smelled funny, sweet, cloying but harsh, choking. Underneath it was a rotted, futile death smell, kind of like what he had caught off of Mrs. Pratt when she had tried to kill Harry at the social. It made Jim feel like someone was slowly smothering him with a silk pillow soaked in perfume and ether.

The tables were low to the ground and there were large cushions instead

of chairs. Large hookahs with individual pipes running off of them squatted at the centers of the tables, like spiders made of glass and brass.

The Palace also had the same odd quality Jim had experienced in the al-
leyways of Johnny Town—it seemed to be larger, more complex, than the
space it occupied would permit.

"Wait please," the hatchet man said, and then hurried off quietly.

The piano player was in the corner, partially hidden by a column and a
paper screen. Jim walked over to him while he played. He was thin, muscular man with long red-brown hair, like a woman or an Indian. He looked up
from the keys his hands moved across, to Jim. He smiled.

"Evening," the man said. "Awful young to be out on a night like this.
Your parents know you're here, son?"

Jim turned, so the man could see the star pinned to his coat.

The piano player smiled and nodded. "Mighty young to be a deputy,
aren't you?"

"Place is pretty slow tonight," Jim said, looking around. The bar was
empty except for a handful of Green Ribbon soldiers, who stood at the bar,
loading guns and sharpening wicked-looking swords.

"Yep, end of the world tends to do that to business," the player said.
"Handle's Ringo. Nice to meet you. . . ."

"Jim, I'm Jim."

Ringo continued to play with one hand while shaking Jim's with the
other, then went back to playing with both hands, with no break in the music.

"Nice to meet you, Deputy Jim. Aren't your folks worried about you being out here with everything that's happening tonight? I mean, the moon
and stars disappearing, people turning into monsters—figure you'd want
your son at home."

"Can't go home," Jim said softly. "Can't never go home again."

"Never is a damn long time," Ringo said. "Why can't you?"

Jim took a chair from the wall and sat down next to Ringo and his piano.
The thoughts of Ma, of Lottie, of Pa all swelled up in him again. He was so
tired—he hadn't realized it until just now. He felt the tension of the last year
suddenly smash into him like a train. The piano whispered to him softly,
like the rain, or his mother's voice. He sighed and slid back into the chair.

"I'm fifteen and I killed a mess of people tonight. I tried to not think of them as people, as creatures, monsters, but I recognized a few of them as folks who tipped their hats or said hello to me a few days ago. I killed folks back home too. I've had more blood on my hands in the last year than a lot of men who were in the war, than Pa. . . ."

He felt like crying, felt the empty sky over him, vacant of hope, of the sun or moon, of God in His Heaven. He felt completely and totally alone in the vast cold.

"I've been trying since I got here. Trying to live up to the fine men I've made the acquaintance of, live up to what they expect of me. But I'm no hero. I'm scared, Mr. Ringo. I'm scared and tired of running and lying. I miss my home; I miss my bed. I miss my family, and now, at the end of things, I want to be with them more than anything in this world. I've wanted to tell someone since I got here, but everyone I've met has been so damned noble, so good, I just couldn't see that light die in their eyes when they knew what I really am. Even the man who saved me, who brought me here. He can't know all of it. But you can. You don't know me and I don't know you and there's a damn good chance that we're all going to die pretty soon anyway, so please, listen."

And Jim told Ringo all of it, even the part that made him weep at night and claw at his face and pray to die, pray to take it back, to change it and make it right. To the strains of "Listen to the Mockingbird," Jim Negrey gave his confession.

The wagon ride back to the Negrey homestead from his father's unmarked grave outside of Albright seemed like a waking dream. Jim's mind wrestled with what he had done, what he had seen. The rage was nestled cold and hard in his chest and he knew, even as part of him was horrified by how he had cut the Professor down in cold blood, that he was going to kill Charlie just the same. He felt all the possibilities of his life, all the dreams, all the fantasies; they all narrowed into a single, desolate road that led to damnation and tragedy. His life had ended the moment he had pulled that trigger back in the bar. Now it was time to finish it, to follow that road to its inevitable end.

The homestead was lit up when he arrived. The lights were on inside and a lantern hung on the front porch, glowing. Dawn was not too far off and the sky was blued steel. He brought the horses to a stop in front of the house, pulled the brake and reached for the rifle. The front door crashed open and Charlie Upton strode out onto the porch, a pistol in his hand. Ma ran after him. Her face was swollen from bruises and tears. Jim climbed down from the wagon, leveling the gun at Upton.

"Drop the gun, you sumbitch," Jim growled, "or I'll kill you where you stand. Pa told me what you done."

Charlie cocked the pistol and aimed it at Jim. "You're just as bug-shit crazy as old Billy was," he said. "You're going dance on the end of a rope, you little bastard. I done sent Rick to fetch the sheriff. They'll be here soon. So you go on and lay that gun down and maybe I'll make this all go away for you, on account of your mama."

"Jim, Charlie, please stop this!" Ma screamed, clawing at Charlie's shoulder and then moving between the two of them.

"Ma. No!" Jim shouted as he tried to take a bead on Charlie. He stepped cautiously sideways to try to get a clear shot.

"Get out of the way, you stupid bitch!" Upton barked. He grabbed Ma by the hair, hard. She was jerked backward by the brutal force of it and collapsed in the dirt beside Upton.

Jim's eyes were blood. All the numb unreality of the night evaporated in white, perfect rage. Upton saw it and had only a heartbeat to react. He squeezed off two quick shot from the Colt even as Jim fired the rifle, cocked it and fired again. An angry wake of heat fluttered past Jim's ear with a whine like a mosquito, before the thunder of his own gun filled his ears with cotton.

Upton charged him, bellowing in rage, the pistol vomiting fire and smoke again. Something tugged at Jim's shirt and he felt heat, like brushing against a stove, at his side. Cock and fire, cock and fire. His nostrils flared at the smell of hot brass as the cartridges flipped from the rifle. He closed the distance toward Upton, his scream of anger crashing into Charlie's own. Their hate was a force, like wildfire, annihilating everything in its way. Less than ten feet separated them and their guns roared again.

Then, as suddenly as it had begun, it was finished. The man-made storm rumbled, echoed across the mountains and was silent. Charlie Upton slumped to the ground, two scarlet blooms expanding across his shirtfront. He coughed up a spray of blood, made a dry rattling sound and died.

Jim, panting, staggered over to him, cocked the rifle again and aimed at Upton's vacant face. All Jim could think of was that before he fell down he was going to make sure there was no pretty funeral for Charlie Upton, no open casket. He would die anonymous and unseen, just like Billy Negrey had.

"Oh sweet Lord in Heaven, Lottie!" Ma screamed.

Jim blinked and looked up. Ma was running onto the porch. Lottie was standing in front of the front door. Her nightshirt looked like it had been dipped in blood. The little girl collapsed into her mother's arms. Lottie coughed and blood dripped out of her mouth.

"Ma, what happened?" Lottie said. "I can't feel nothin'."

Jim dropped the rifle and sprang up the stairs. Ma was holding Lottie's tiny form in her arms, and Jim lifted her head and pushed her blond curls out of her face. She looked at him and smiled a weak, bloody smile.

"Jim, I don't feel good."

"Lottie, Ma, I . . . I didn't mean to . . ." The words were nothing, less than nothing. They fell and broke into a million useless pieces. Ma looked at him in a way he had never seen before. It made him wish with all his heart and soul that he was the one bleeding in her arms, or dead in the dirt.

Ma lifted Lottie quickly and carried her to the wagon. "Hang on, baby. We're going to see Dr. Fleer in town. I need you stay awake for me." She placed her in the back of the wagon and wrapped her in a tarp to keep her warm. Jim stood beside Ma; his arms hung at his sides. As if coming out of a trance, he suddenly removed his coat and put it under Lottie's head.

"Lottie," Jim muttered. "Is that better? Lottie? Lottie! Don't fall asleep, now!"

The little girl's eyes fluttered open. She smiled at Jim again.

"Jim, Pa says he loves us."

Ma was climbing up into the wagon.

"He's taken it all away from me, Jim," she said. "He took Billy; he's taken you. I won't let him take her too. I won't."

She turned to regard her son.

"You have to run now, Jim. Don't ever stop. If they catch you, they will hang you, you hear me?"

"Ma . . ."

"Go on, now." Her voice was hard, almost cracking from the pain. "Take

Promise. Take the money in the box on the mantle and remember to take a good coat. Don't use your real name. Go, Jim. Don't ever come back."

She snapped the reins and the horses pulled the wagon toward the road. Lottie looked at him one more time with her weak, unfocused eyes.

"I love you, Jim," she said.

The wagon rattled down the little road toward Albright. His side was throbbing with pain and wet with blood. The moon was gone; the sun was sleeping. A cold wind caressed his face. He felt no tears. He wanted to cry, knew he should, but nothing came.

He gathered his few belongings, saddled up Promise and headed out just before dawn. He rode away from the sun and its accusing gaze, toward the dwindling darkness, to the west.

The song had ended. Ringo sat still and allowed Jim to finish. Jim looked down, wiped his nose and his eyes on his sleeve. The boy choked back his sob with a wet, sad laugh.

"I haven't cried in so long, I don't even remember no more. Didn't cry when I knew I'd never see my ma and sister ever again. Didn't cry when I shot Lottie, probably killed her. But now, now I'm bawling like a baby to some stranger in a den of Chinamen. I am crazy."

"Nope," Ringo said. "You'd be crazy if all that didn't finally catch up to you."

The piano player drained half his mug of beer and lit another cigarette before he continued. "You got to cling on to some hope, Jim. You don't know if your sister died? Right?"

"The only people they mention on my wanted poster are the Professor and Charlie Upton. I've asked around as cagey as I can, but no one I've ever met can give me a straight answer. I mailed Ma some money a few times, when I had it, but there's no way she can write me back. I don't even know if she would want to."

"Hope," Ringo said softly. "Hope, faith, pigheaded stubbornness, whatever you want to call it, there are times in your life when it's all that keeps you upright, all that keeps you from tasting a bullet, or crawling into a bottle. It ain't rational, and it ain't much, but it's what people got, Jim. You have to hope that we are going to find a way out of this mess, hope that you will make it home someday and that your little sister will come running out to greet you. All those folk who crossed the desert, all those who didn't make it, they got this far, maybe farther, because they had hope that a little farther out west, they'd find whatever it was that would give them their happy ever after. That hope kept them going when nothing else would, or could. You know that; you've been out there."

"You don't seem the type to be preaching," Jim said, rubbing his face dry.

Ringo chuckled. "Places like this, like most of the dives and dens I've called home since I was younger than you, they are full of people who have used up pretty much everything they have, especially hope. You know why most of these places have someone like me, a piano player, a band, a singer? Because music is like hope. Between the strings in this box"—he ran his fingers along the keys of the piano and began to play once again—"and the strings in the heart, there is nothing but air and magic. Songs can lead men laughing into battle, lay strong men low, make you fall in love, let you visit with the dead. Ain't nothing real to it—just words and rhythm—but it's got power, all the same."

A Green Ribbon hatchet man approached Jim and Ringo. He addressed the boy in broken English.

"Venerable one ready to see you now."

Jim nodded, stood. Ringo put his cigarette in his mouth and offered his hand to Jim. Jim shook it.

"Real pleasure to meet you, Jim," Ringo said around the cigarette.

"Hope?" Jim said.

"Hell, you come up with something better, you let me know."

Jim followed the tong member to the far side of the room, up a narrow flight of stairs and through a curtain of wooden beads. There was a small alcove off the top of the stairs. In it, a Chinese dragon of gold and jade expelled a rich stream of incense smoke that slowly trailed down the narrow corridor. The second floor of the Celestial Palace had numerous rooms that could be rented for privacy. Tonight no shadows moved behind their paper walls and screens. Jim was led to an ornate golden door with an intricate carving of two Chinese dragons contending for a central pearl the size of a man's fist. Chinese symbols hovered above and below the dragons. The hatchet man made a contrite bow before the door. The door swung open, seemingly on its own.

"Please come in, my young friend," a melodic voice said. "Leave us, Wei."

The hatchet man bowed and departed. Jim entered the room. It was dark. The only light came from a brazier of glowing red coals. Tapestries, faded maps and yellowed charts of the moon and stars covered the walls. The shelves in the room were packed full of strange bottles and vials filled with viscous liquids of every imaginable color as wells as copper coils and tubes, small oil burners, ancient tomes and scrolls.

In the center of it all Ch'eng Huang sat, still as stone, unknowable as fate. To Jim, he appeared to be exactly the same as when last the boy had seen him—snow-white beard, immaculate emerald silk robes. The dark eyes regarded Jim and a razor-thin smile crossed the old man's face.

"Welcome, Jim Negrey. Please, sit. I took the liberty of having my servants prepare some tea and cakes. I know it has been a difficult night; please relax. You are safe here."

Jim knelt and took a seat on the large cushion across the short table from Ch'eng. The old man carefully filled a small cup on the table before Jim with hot tea from a beautifully painted porcelain pot. Jim nodded. The boy took a small sip and then cradled the warmth of the cup in his hands.

"Obliged, sir. Mr. Bick sent me. He says none of us is going to be safe much longer, way things are going."

Ch'eng leaned back and stroked his white beard. "Bick, eh? Well, he and I have had many discussions concerning . . . philosophy over the years. We come at it from somewhat different backgrounds, you see. What made Malachi think I could be of service in ending this cycle of events?"

Jim regarded his tea. He could make out the leaves setting in the bottom of the cup. He took a deep breath and looked up at the tong lord.

"The eye, sir. He thinks the eye has some kind of power that can help us keep the world from ending. He said it was under your domain, or somesuch. He asked me to bring it to you to help me understand it."

"And I had already extended such an invitation to you previously, yes?" Ch'eng said.

"How did you do that, exactly? I mean, I heard your voice, clear as day in my head, but you were busy talking to the sheriff."

"A disciplined mind can accomplish much, Master Negrey. May I see it, please, the eye?"

Again, Jim looked down for a moment, then returned Ch'eng's infinite gaze.

"Here's the thing, sir. This eye has caused me all sorts of trouble and I think it caused my pa some problems too. I'm afraid of it and I kind of hate it, but it is all I got left of my pa, of my family. So I know you got scary fellas with guns and hatchets downstairs and I know you got some kind of spooky mind-reading wisdom about you, but I intend to keep my pa's eye, no matter what you say or do, 'less you intend to kill me for it. I just wanted to say my piece."

He took the eye out of his pocket, placed it on the low table and unwrapped it from the handkerchief.

Ch'eng Huang let out a hiss of air. His placid eyes widened slightly. "Pangu," he said softly. "Pangu's eye. Master Negrey, may I please?" He reached out with slender hands that looked like they were carved from yellowed ivory.

Jim nodded curtly. Ch'eng lifted the jade eye and carefully examined it, holding it delicately between his thumb and forefinger. The old man nodded as he squinted at the tiny characters that circled the pupil.

"Yes, yes. There have been many forgeries over the centuries. The monks were very careful to hide their tracks and very clever to bring the real eye here to the West. I'm amazed they actually did it, but there is no mistaking it; this is the genuine eye."

"So it belonged to this Pangu fella, before those Chinamen gave it to Pa?" Jim said, leaning forward. "Was Pangu a Chinese too?"

"In a manner of speaking," Ch'eng said. "He was a god."

"Pardon?" Jim said.

"Pangu is the first self-aware being in all creation, the being that created the world," Ch'eng explained. "Before man there was formless chaos—darkness and eternal death. Out of the Void was created an egg."

"An egg?" Jim said.

"After eighteen thousand years, Pangu emerged from the egg and was the first being to contemplate the Void and idealize the concept of its opposite—creation, life. He balanced the forces of darkness with light, the yin with the yang, and created the Earth and the stars. When Pangu finally rested, his breath became the wind, his blood the rivers, his body the rocks and mountains, his voice the voice of the storm. His right eye became the sun. . . ."

Ch'eng presented the jade eye back to Jim. "And his left eye, this eye, became the moon."

Jim shook his head. "So what about all the stuff Ma taught me, about God in Heaven and seven day to make the world and Adam and Eve and Jesus and the Devil? Is that all just made up? Is God a Chinaman?"

"Yes. And no. Tell me, Jim, what do all gods have in common?"

"Um, they're gods?" Jim said. "They don't got to wait in line at the general store? Mr. Huang, I don't know anything about all this, sir."

"People, Jim," Ch'eng said. "Gods all need people. People thought them up; people gave them their names, duties, domains. People raise them to the heights of praise and power or relegate them to the darkness of neglect and antiquity. Gods are nothing without people, and depending on what people you ask you will get many different answers to questions about Heaven and Hell, how the universe was made and how it will end. Ask a Chinese, an Indian, a Mormon, a Christian and a Jew. Each one will give you a different answer and they are all correct; they all exist and have power, within their proper domains, with their chosen people, and, if they are strong enough, even beyond."

"So if all these gods and spirits and haints are real and can do something, then why don't they?" Jim asked. His face was getting red. "All the terrible things that go on in this world, all the suffering and wrongness, why don't they do something about it? Why did my God let my pa get murdered? Why did He let my sister catch a bullet, when, when she hadn't ever done nothing to nobody? It don't make no damned sense!"

He started to rise, but Ch'eng stopped him with a gentle gesture of his hand. Jim sat down.

"The sheriff, he gave you that star, yes?"

"Yeah."

"He sent you to me alone, yes?"

"You know he did, what are you driving at?"

"Are you not too young to have such responsibilities?"

"Mister," Jim said, "I had to shoot a mess of people dead tonight. I've had to decide to take my last drink of water or give it to my poor horse when we were dying in the desert, like all those other poor souls out there before us had. I've had to make a lot of hard choices in my life and I ain't no child, no more."

"No," Ch'eng Huang said. The ghost of a smile had returned. "You most certainly are not. None of you are, Jim. This is a world made for mortals. It has rules, restrictions upon the divine and spiritual. Creation is a beautiful tapestry, a gift and a guide from the ineffable to the mortal, but in the end, it is man's world and men alone must decide their fate and the world's. They decide it through their behavior, their choices, their deeds and their discipline. The gods, the spirits, can only advise, provide counsel and offer indirect aide. The soul of man is what gives the gods their power—the drive, the will, it is the most powerful and terrible thing in the entire universe."

"Faith can move mountains . . . ," Jim muttered the words Ma had said so many times as he stared into his father's eye. "So this thing in the mountain, it's going to tear the world up if it gets loose, right?"

"It is know to us as Chilong—the demon dragon at the heart of all mountains. It was bound long ago when Pangu's bones and body were first laid to rest to form the Earth. It was chained by the August Personage of Jade and his divine court, by chains of celestial fire. If it breaks free, it will rend all of creation. Only the primal chaos and eternal night shall remain."

"Bick thought the eye might be able to help keep this dragon chained up," Jim said. "How does it work? What does it do?"

Ch'eng shook his head in amazement. "Oh—ho! You don't ask for any small thing, do you, boy? The eye was stolen from Chang'e, the Goddess of the Moon, by Sun Wukong, the Monkey King, and given back to man. The eye has power over the dominion of the moon, the twilight worlds, the dream kingdoms—it can be a bridge between worlds and powers. The eye allows one to traffic with the souls of the dead, to speak to them, to entreat them to do your bidding. So much more than that! It is one of the fundamental underpinnings of all creation. It is one of the most powerful artifacts to exist within the middle kingdom. A skilled sorcerer, a master in the disciplines, could use the eye to do almost anything, anything! That is why it was hidden by the monks who gave it to your father, to keep it from the evil and the power-hungry.

"Your father must have been a remarkable man to have been selected by the monks to secure such a treasure. That he was able to endure the burden of the eye's power and not go mad, or die, is a true testament to his honor. You should be very proud of him, Jim."

Jim swallowed. He thought about all the years Pa wrestled with the pain and the dizziness, mostly in silence. "I already was.

"So," he said, "you can show me how to use it, right?"

"Are you a trained sorcerer, master of the esoteric disciplines?" Ch'eng asked.

"No, sir."

"Then, no."

"But I've made the dang thing work for me before!"

"Yes, you have some aptitude; I can see that. That is nothing compared to what the eye is capable of doing."

"Then you use it to lock this dragon thing up and then give it back to me!"

"I can't, Jim. It is not allowed."

"What the hell does that mean? We need your help, or everyone is going to die!"

"I can offer you advice, try to help you figure it out for yourself, but I cannot take an active role in this."

"You said it was up to us to save the world; you said we could."

"Not us, Jim, *you*. You have the power to save the world, you and your friends. My authority ends at the edge of Johnny Town, at the borders of the communities my people have carved out in this new land."

Jim looked at the old man and shook his head. He looked back down at the eye in his palm.

"All this power, all this wisdom, and I don't even know what to do with it."

"Don't sell yourself short. Human beings are remarkable," Ch'eng Huang said. "You possess limitless ambition, near-infinite determination. The same drive that sends you out into this dangerous wilderness in search of new lives, new opportunities, can be harnessed, chained if you will, to accomplish anything."

Jim snorted. "Well, all them pretty words and will ain't helping us right now with . . ." He blinked and looked at the old man again. "What? What did you just say?"

Ch'eng Huang stared at him placidly, silently, for a moment, then replied, "You heard me."

Jim jumped to his feet. "I got to go! Now! I ain't got much time!"

"I understand," Ch'eng said, rising smoothly, almost as if he floated to his feet.

"Thanks for the tea! Thank you for everything!"

"May you meet your destiny with calm understanding and dignity, Master Negrey," Ch'eng said as the golden door drifted open silently behind Jim. "Good-bye."

Jim ran down the hall of the Celestial Palace, past Ringo and the tong warriors and into the endless night.

It didn't take long to reach Clay's livery at a full-tilt run. Jim didn't encounter any of the Stained along the way, but he passed a few bodies, still in the street. The infected townsfolk seemed to have raided Golgotha, abducted as many as they could to swell their ranks and now returned to Argent Mountain to call forth the thing that would end the world.

He threw open the barn doors and found the horses nervous, shuffling and occasionally whinnying wildly. He went to Promise and stroked her nose.

"Hey, girl. I hope you got a good rest, 'cause we've got one more ride to make, and it's a humdinger!"

The boy and his horse exploded out of the barn like a comet. Promise's hooves struck the ground quickly, lightly. They made it to the end of Duffer in no time flat and Jim turned them onto the Old Stone Road. Sparks danced as the little horse flew across the old cobblestones. The horse slowed slightly as the road faded into cold sand, ash and dirt. Jim urged her on gently with a squeeze of his legs.

"I know, girl, I know where we're going too, but we have to. Just one more time. Don't be afraid; I'll be right there with you."

Promise snorted and began to gallop even faster than before. Jim rubbed her neck and hunched forward in the saddle as they rode into the dark oblivion of the 40-Mile.

The Knight of Cups

Auggie led Gillian by the hand through the chaos. People who minutes ago were dancing, gossiping and laughing were now a mob, rushing away from the hissing swarm of their infected brethren. Fear swirled around them like toxic gas. He clutched a broken table leg in his free hand, the only weapon he could find in the middle of the screaming, shouting and shooting.

"Auggie!" Gillian shouted behind him. He spun to see Kenneth Burel, one his regular customers, tugging on Gillian's arms and screaming for her to come with him. Burel wasn't infected by the malady of the weeping blackness, but he was in the throes of another dangerous affliction—panic. Auggie turned, pulling Gillian out of Burel's grasp and behind him. He brandished his makeshift club at Burel and the man bolted back into the current of frightened, running humanity.

"This way," Auggie said. He led Gillian between two row houses that were neighbors of Dale McKinnon's homestead. Pratt Road was to their west, as was the Baptist church. Auggie figured they could get their wits about them inside the church for a moment and then figure out how to get Gillian out of this madhouse of a town. He knew he needed to get back to the store, to protect it from looters and to make sure Gerta was safe as well. The thought of one of these strange creatures ransacking their home and hurting her made the knot in his gut tighten.

"I am sorry I could not get you to the wagons in time," he said as he and Gillian walked hand in hand again, Auggie leading.

"It's all right," she said. "I wouldn't have gone anyway."

Auggie stopped and turned. "It is too dangerous here, Gillian! We have to get you out of here."

"This is my home too, Augustus," she said. "I have a responsibility to my boarders and my friends. Besides, we both have to stay to make sure your store is safe."

He shook his head. "You are very strong. Aren't you afraid?"

"Of course I am; only a fool wouldn't be! Aren't you?"

"Ja." He smiled and nodded. "Terrified. Come on; let's get to the sanctuary and off the street."

When they turned back toward Pratt Road, they saw the church was burning. A hulking figure stood between the end of the alleyway and the flames.

"Figured I'd find you eventually, bitch," the shape said as it lumbered toward Auggie and Gillian. "Ain't that big a town and I knew you'd be at your little party tonight, Gilly-girl."

The creature that had been Otis Haglund, the butcher, Stained with the infection and wearing a necklace of severed human hands over its leather apron, advanced toward them, its eyes tunnels of night.

"Run!" Auggie bellowed to Gillian as he charged Otis, raising the table leg to strike. Auggie was a big man; he was used to having about half a foot and at least a hundred pounds on most of the men in Golgotha. Otis was one of the few exceptions. The butcher caught his club as it descended to strike and drove a crushing right into Auggie's gut. The shopkeeper gasped and stumbled backward. Gillian screamed and charged Haglund.

"Gillian, no!" Auggie wheezed.

Otis backhanded her. Her glasses exploded as they flew off her face and she smashed against the wall of the row house and slid down into the dirt. Auggie roared and drove his whole mass into Haglund, tackling him at the waist. The butcher staggered backward but stayed on its feet. It grabbed Auggie by the throat and slammed him against the other wall of the alley, holding him there.

"I'm gonna have a good time with old Gill, there, Shultz," Haglund said, its face moving closer to Auggie's. Something black and wet vibrated in its mouth. "But first I'm going to bring you over to God and then we can take turns with her; won't that be fun? Open wide, fatso."

Haglund suddenly stiffened, convulsed and released its grip on Auggie's throat. A row of slender metal spikes poked through its chest and thick black ooze spread out from them, soaking its apron. Over the butcher's shoulder, Auggie saw Clay jam the pitchfork deeper into Otis's back. Haglund groaned and its eyes fluttered shut for an instant; then they snapped open again, wide and black. The impaled butcher began to turn toward Clay. Auggie knelt, grabbed the fallen table leg and struck Otis's head with all his might. There was a hollow crunch. Haglund collapsed and finally lay still.

"Thank you, Clay," Auggie said, gasping. Clay nodded, dropped the pitchfork and pushed his wild halo of hair out of his eyes.

"It's lucky you came by," Auggie said.

"My wagon is around the corner. I ran home to fetch it when the commotion started. I saw you struggling with Otis as I passed."

Gillan was up and hugging Auggie. "Thank you, Clayton," she said.

"I didn't do it for you," he said as he turned Otis over and examined the black goo still leaking out of its chest. "I did it for Auggie."

Clay lifted the apron. "This is fascinating. Impaling his heart and lungs didn't kill him or, to be more specific, didn't kill the thing inside of him. Look here."

He opened Otis's mouth wide. Something was still squirming inside. The thing shivered, slowed and then was still.

"Trauma to the head seems to be the most efficient way to dispatch it," he continued.

"Clay . . . ," Auggie said.

". . . His blood seems to have been converted into the same fluid that was used to poison Arthur Stapleton," Clay continued. "I would hazard that eventually the toxicity of the substance accounts for Stapleton's internal organs liquefying and—"

"Clay," Auggie repeated. "We have to go now, before more of them come. We have to get Gillian out of here."

"I told you, I'm not leaving without you," Gillian said.

Clay stood. He recovered the pitchfork. "I agree. We all need to leave town as soon as possible. The rate at which this has spread is remarkable. I doubt there are too many uninfected people still alive in Golgotha. This is going to get much worse before it gets better."

"We need to go to the store before we head out of town," Auggie said. Clay nodded.

"Why?" Gillian said. "Augustus, if we aren't going to stay and protect it, why risk going all the way across town?"

Clay's eyes burned into Auggie. Auggie sighed. "Gillian, there are . . . things. Precious things . . . They belonged to Gerta. I can't just leave them to those creatures."

Gillian took his hand. "Then let's go get them," she said.

Clay drove the wagon down Pratt Road and crossed over onto Dry Well Road. Over the buildings they could see the glow of fires. The streets were silent, save for an occasional scream that cut the cold night like a knife. They passed Gillian's boardinghouse. It was dark and quiet.

Clay pulled the horses over at the old stone well at the end of the road. The town legend claimed two lovers had met their end in the depths of the well and that their ghosts stood sentinel over it. If the legend was true, and most townsfolk swore it was, the spectral couple thought better than to be out tonight.

"We'll cut through here," Clay said softly. "The store's back door is just one street over."

They moved through the brush quietly. Auggie scanned both ways. The alley appeared vacant. He slid the key out of his trouser pocket.

"Now, go!" he hissed. They crossed the open space quickly, three shades fluttering loose from the darkness for an instant, then swallowed up by the gloom of the building's shadow.

Auggie clutched the door handle with one hand and fitted the key into the lock with the other. Clay stood ready with an unlit lantern and match while Gillian scanned the street for any signs of activity. The door clicked open. They hurried inside and closed the door behind them.

Clay struck the match and lit the lantern. He placed it on top of a wooden crate, one of many in the cluttered storeroom. The open door leading to the stairs to the overhead apartment was yawning darkness.

"Gillian," Auggie said, taking her hand, "why don't you get us some provisions from the storefront for the trip? Fill some canteens and grab whatever food you can. Stay away from the windows and keep down, *ja*?"

She nodded and squeezed his hand. She opened the door a crack and slid inside, shutting it behind her.

"Nice way to distract the 'other woman,'" Clay said with a rasp that passed for a chuckle from him.

"Be quiet," Auggie said, ascending the stairs. "Come on."

The light from the lantern below was a feeble comfort. The apartment was dark and the window blinds were drawn. Auggie moved as quietly as he could, quickly lifting a framed photograph off the end table—the only photo ever taken of Gerta. He used his free hand to grab the old family Bible they had brought with them on the crossing from Germany. It had been in Gerta's family for six generations and it contained the only record of their son's birth and death.

Clay watched Auggie collect the artifacts of his life. "You need to tell them, both of them," he said to Auggie's back.

"After we get out of here, after they are both safe. Then, I'll do it," Auggie said. "I'm sorry for what I said to you at the dance."

They entered the bedroom. Auggie pulled a large carpetbag from under the bed. He snapped it open and dropped the photo and Bible into it.

"Don't be," Clay said. "She seems like a decent enough female. No Gerta, mind you, but acceptable. Come on; let's get Gertie's case. I brought her repair kit; it's in the wagon already."

There was a crash below them, a scream; it was Gillian. Auggie dashed toward the stairs. He heard glass shattering, angry voices. He reached the storeroom in time to see Gillian struggling in the doorway with Doc Tumblety, Stained and snarling.

"Come here, you little whore!" Tumblety bellowed. "You'll change your tune soon enough, bitch! Let me get my mouth on you!"

Gillian scratched at the doctor's face. Clearly she was frightened, but she also looked angry.

"Get your filthy drunkard hands off of me, damn you!"

The creature that had been Tumbelty winced and reached for its torn face, releasing Gillian.

She spun, bumped into Auggie and fell into his arms. "They were outside the store, all over Main Street," she said, gasping. "They saw me; I'm sorry!"

Auggie hurled a punch at Tumblety as the infected doctor lunged again at Gillian. The doctor flew backward into the store. Auggie saw other figures in his store, Gerta's store, climbing through the shattered front windows, knocking over shelves, breaking things. He felt the tears welling up in him, the anger and the sadness. He remembered holding Gerta here, on this patch of desert before all of this had existed. The shadows crept closer. Tumblety was scrambling to its feet, laughing. There was more crashing, more breaking.

Gillian's voice was close to him. "Augustus, we have to go upstairs, now. Come on, darling. Please, we have to go."

Blood crawled down the side of her face. He touched her hair; it was wet with blood. Her eyes rolled back into her sockets and she went limp in his arms.

"Gillian!" he screamed. He lifted her in his massive arms and slammed the door to the stairwell. He secured it with an iron bolt and hurried up the stairs, even as the pounding began on the barred door.

"Clay! Trouble! Gillian is hurt!"

Auggie laid her on the bed. Clay had already pulled down Gerta's case. It rested on the small chest by the water basin.

"How are we going to get out of here?" Clay asked.

"Is she all right?" Auggie asked, pushing Gillian's bloody hair out of her face. "Is she going to be all right?"

Clay examined her head briefly. "Looks like a nasty scalp wound. She probably has a mild concussion, or she passed out from blood loss. She should be fine, if we get out of here with our skins intact."

There was more pounding and another crash; then both men began to smell smoke.

"Damnation!" Clay said. "They set the place on fire, trying to smoke us out."

"We have to get them out of here, Clay! How about the window?"

Clay pushed back the blinds. "The alley is still clear and I see smoke pouring out of the building. It's too far to drop either of them. I'll climb out and go get the wagon. You can lower them down to me."

"Go," Auggie said.

Clay tried to force the window open, but couldn't. Finally he smashed it, wincing in pain as a shard of the glass sliced his hand. He climbed through the jagged opening, out onto the narrow awning. Smoke was starting to fill the apartment. The pounding and shouting had stopped, replaced with the snap and crack of approaching flames. Auggie figured the Stained, as he found himself thinking of them, had withdrawn to either let him, Clay and Gillian burn or wait for them to run outside.

Auggie heard a faint moan. It was from Gerta's case. He opened it. Part of Gerta's skin—the part that had covered her jaw and chin—had come loose and was floating at the top of her tank. Her teeth and jawbone were partly exposed and a thin trail of bubbles slipped from her barely moving lips. Auggie wound the key several times and saw her eyes flutter open.

"I'm going to get you out of here, Gerta; don't be afraid," he said.

She smiled at him.

"I . . . was . . . dreaming," she said.

"What were you dreaming about?" he asked, stifling a cough. Smoke was clawing at the back of his throat. On the bed, Gillian stirred, coughing too. He heard the groan of wood giving way below him. He looked out the window—no Clay yet.

"Please tell me, Gerta."

"Do you remember when we rode up Rose Hill and had a picnic for your birthday? That was a beautiful day. I always see that day whenever I think of what Heaven will be like. I fell in love with you again that day, Augustus. I fall in love with you again every time I see you, did you know that?"

"Ja, Gerta. I know." He was crying.

The head pursed her lips. Part of them drifted away in the fluid from the effort. "Don't be sad, darling. Everyone dies. It is fair. We have had a wonderful time together. We shared pain and joy, anger and comfort. We took two lives and made them into so, so much more."

There was a whoosh as a jet of flame erupted in the living room. The Swiss clock's frozen face was burning. The whole building breathed and shuddered. The floor was hot now and the smoke was everywhere, becoming thicker.

"No! You can't die; I won't let you die. I'll save you! I can't do this alone, Gerta. I can't bear this alone!"

The fluid in the tank was beginning to bubble as it started to boil.

"I can't stay, Augustus. Please understand, my love. I pray to be free of this pain, of this cage. You can save me, beloved—you can let me go; you can set me free."

The flames were licking between the planks of the floor in the bedroom.

The whole world now was unbearable heat and smoke. The floor creaked under its own weight.

"Gerta, I need to tell you something. I love Gillian, very much. I'm sorry, I never wanted to hurt you, but you deserved the truth. I love her, and I want a life with her."

Gert smiled. *"She is a very good woman. I couldn't ask for a better person to look after you. I just want you to be happy, Augustus. As happy as you made me."*

The clockwork beneath the tank began to grind to a stop. The lights in the tank dimmed, but the head remained animate.

"I want that for you too, love. I've been selfish for too long," Auggie said, running his hands along the glass of her jar. It was hot to the touch. "This was never about love; it was about fear, my fear. I'm sorry, Gerta."

"Auggie!" It was Clay's voice shouting above the death knell of the building. "Out here! Get a move on; it's all coming down!"

Gert's eyes were closing. She was still smiling. *"I'll wake from this dream to finally find myself in Heaven. Sing to me again, Augustus. I was dreaming of singing. It was beautiful."*

The floor was cracking and collapsing by the bed. Auggie ran to Gillian and lifted her up. She groaned and coughed painfully. He tossed the carpetbag out the window.

"I . . . love you . . . Augustus," Gerta said, her voice beginning to distort. *"Thank . . . you."*

Auggie pulled Gillian over his shoulder and struggled through the broken window. He looked over his shoulder back at Gerta, wreathed in flames.

"Rest now, beloved," he said.

The floor of the apartment crashed down and part of the wall gave way as well. Auggie fell toward the bed of the wagon below. He managed to turn his body to protect Gillian from the impact with the wooden bed. He groaned in pain as he hit, then turned to cover her from the rain of debris that followed him down.

"Where's Gertie?" Clay shouted from the buckboard.

"She chose," Auggie said. "She finally got to choose for herself, Clay."

Clay opened his mouth to speak, but no words came. He looked at Auggie blankly, then to the rapidly collapsing inferno that had been Shultz's General Store. He climbed down from the wagon.

"Get Mrs. Proctor out of here, Auggie," he said. "Be careful and good luck to you. You've been a good friend. Better than I deserve."

Clay walked toward the burning building. Ash and glowing embers drifted around him, like fireflies. He stopped and looked back at Auggie.

"I love her. I've always loved her."

He walked into the fire, vanishing into the smoke.

Auggie struggled onto the buckboard and took the reins. He watched as his and Gerta's life here in Golgotha turned to hot ash. He waited for Clay, but he knew he'd never come out. After a moment, Auggie looked back at Gillian, breathing softly in the bed of the wagon. He tugged on the reins and felt the wagon lurch forward. He headed south, out of Golgotha.

Death

There were no guards at the entrance to the mine. Highfather, Pratt and Mutt approached cautiously anyway, blades and guns drawn.

"Where is everyone?" Harry asked.

"In there," Mutt said. "Doing what we came to stop, I'd reckon."

"Grab some lanterns," Highfather said as he watched another star flare and fall from the firmament. "We don't have long."

They descended the main tunnel, Highfather and Pratt to the sides, lantern in one hand and sword in the other, Mutt in the middle, taking the advance, his shotgun sweeping across the dark gulf that stretched before them. They paused often to make sure there were no oil-faced sentries waiting for them behind the wooden timbers that framed and supported the massive sloping corridor.

It took them fifteen minutes to reach the first annex. There were two smaller shafts extending off from the main tunnel in either direction. Crude chalk markings on the wall provided directions to the different shaft designations. Highfather examined them for a moment and then nodded to the left.

"This is the way to the new vein. Bick said that was where the chamber was. What's our time?"

"My watch is broken," Harry said. "I don't know."

"About noon," Mutt said. "Give or take. I'm pretty good 'bout stuff like that."

"All right, keep moving," Highfather said. They continued down the left corridor. It was narrower, and they had to go single file. Highfather took the lead.

"Any ideas how we're going to stop whatever it is we're supposed to be stopping, Jonathan?" Mutt asked.

"I'm working on it," he said.

The tunnel branched off again. Two of the shafts were sealed with wooden boards and warnings in red paint. The third looked new but poorly braced. The earth tricked down between the shelves of rock and timber; particles of dust floated in the beams of the lanterns.

"My ears just popped," Harry said. "We must be deep. I hope there aren't any gas leaks down here."

"It's getting hotter too," Highfather said. "I think we're close."

Mutt suddenly cocked his head. He raised a hand and everyone grew silent and still. He sniffed the air and turned back to the tunnel behind them.

"Talk to me," Highfather said.

"Company coming," Mutt said. "One. Moving fast and damn quiet. It ain't one of them, though. Smells like—"

The figure appeared at the edge of the lantern light. Slight, dressed in a heavy black miner's coat, gloves, pants and boots. White skin, but with long hair, pulled back into a ponytail, Indian-fashion, and half the stranger's face was hidden by a dirty bandana.

Jon and Harry leveled their blades, but Mutt sniffed again, shook his head in bewilderment and lowered his scattergun.

"Bick sent me," the stranger said. The voice was a low growl, male. "I'm here to rescue one of the infected. I'll help you as much as I can."

"And we're just supposed to trust you?" Harry said.

"Malachi Bick as a character reference isn't exactly the best means of introduction," Highfather said. "And I don't know you from town, stranger. Mayor's got a point."

Mutt knew this was Maude Stapleton. He recognized her scent and this was her, but somehow she had changed not only her voice but also her body language, her posture. Everything she presented now was a deception that this stranger was a man, and a damned good deception too.

"I'm here to save a child, a young girl," Maude said in her new male voice. "Every second you delay deciding if you want my help is another second people are dying."

She looked to Mutt, only for a second, her brown eyes softened just a little.

"Please," she said. "Let me help."

"It's okay, Jon," Mutt said. "I know this fella. He's solid. We can trust him."

Highfather looked at his deputy, frowning.

Mutt nodded. "I'll vouch for him," Mutt said. "He's my . . . friend."

Highfather lowered his blade and nodded for Harry to do the same. Sheriff extended a hand to the stranger and the two shook. Jon noted the stranger's grip was strong but odd in some way.

"Good enough for me," the sheriff said. "Can use all the help we can get."

"Thank you," Maude said.

"Let's go," Highfather said. "Mutt, you fall back. You and your friend here guard the rear."

"Okay, Jon," Mutt said.

"And sometime you gonna have to tell me when you got so damned social all of a sudden," Highfather said.

They traveled in silence for several more minutes. The shaft opened eventually into a rough-hewn chamber. Wooden crates lined the cave wall to the left, dozens of them. To the right was a jagged cleft of an opening, recently blasted and with only the most basic of support in place.

"Dynamite," Highfather said, carefully lifting the lid off one of the straw-filled crates.

"Never heard of it," Harry said. "Some kind of explosive?"

"Fairly new," Highfather said. "It's like blasting gelatin, but more stable, and more powerful. Still pretty dicey to mess with, though, but it could be the answer to our problem."

"We set this stuff off and seal the chamber they are using to bring this thing up from," Mutt said. "Can we do that and get out of here in one piece?"

"Wait a minute," Harry said. "We're not blowing anyone up! Those are our friends and family in there; we can't just write them off as gone. We can save them, Jon; I know we can!"

"We're running out of damn options here, Harry," Mutt said. "I'm powerful sorry about Holly, but we've got to stop them, and if that means people got to die, then that's just the truth of it."

"I agree with the mayor," Maude said. "I may have the means to save them. This may require a more subtle solution, Deputy."

"Fellas . . . ," Highfather said as he placed the lid back on the crate.

"Right. What do you care?" Harry said to Mutt. "It's not like you actually give a damn about anyone in this town, do you? You can count the people who even give you the time of day on one dirty hand, can't you?"

Mutt looked to Maude, then looked down.

"Enough!" Highfather said. "We're not giving up on those people in there, until we have no other choice. And if that happens, we'll be ready to blow Ambrose's god all the way back to Hell.

"Now it will take me a bit to wire this stuff with some blasting caps and a good, long fuse. You three go in there and try to stop the ritual and save our people. I'll join you when everything is ready. Agreed?"

"How you know all this about dynamite, Jon?" Pratt asked.

The sheriff kept working on the wooden spool of fuse he had found behind a crate. "I've had to blow things up from time to time in this job," he said.

"That two-legged horse, Phillips, is mine," Mutt said

"You be careful," Highfather said. "He whupped both of us pretty good at the mansion. Didn't look too tuckered out from the experience either."

"I got a little surprise for him this time," Mutt said with a grin.

"Watch out for Ambrose too—he's not a scrapper," Highfather said, "but he's the heart of this and he's a believer. That makes him dangerous."

"Very astute," Maude said. "If he becomes a problem, I can take care of him."

"He will be a problem," Highfather said. "Count on it."

"I'll deal with Holly," Pratt said.

"Don't get yourself killed doing it, Harry," Highfather said. The mayor was silent.

"I'll get the girl and as many of the townsfolk out as I can," Maude said, fiddling with something in her canvas bag. "You may not see me, but I assure you, I'll be around if you need me. I won't let any of you down."

"Sounds kinda like a plan," Highfather said. "Let's go earn our pay."

"See you in a spell, Jonathan," Mutt said.

Mutt took the point, lantern and shotgun in hand. Harry followed. They had to turn sideways to squeeze through the narrow, uneven passage. Ahead of them was the sound of chanting, of many throats straining under the cadence of painful words.

"You ready?" Mutt whispered.

The mayor nodded; so did Maude.

"Good luck," Pratt said.

"You, too, Harry," Mutt said. Then to Maude, "You be careful in there, y'hear me?" She smiled beneath the bandana and her eyes smiled too. She nodded.

They entered the massive chamber, its floor made of polished silver and etched with bizarre symbols, its ceiling lost somewhere to the roots of the world. Burning sconces encircled the chamber, giving everything a dim, shaky, dreamlike light. A few dozen of the Stained townsfolk stood around the well at the center of the silver floor. As they continued to sing their blasphemies, one by one they eagerly stepped off into the void of the well, falling from sight. Constance was in the group awaiting a turn to plunge into the darkness.

"No!" Maude said, her voice slipping for a second back to her own.

"The townsfolk, the squatters?" Harry said. "Where are the rest of them?"

"Gone," Mutt said. "Already gone."

"Ah, gentlemen!" Ambrose's voice boomed across the chamber. "So glad you could join us. I'm afraid you're a little too late to stop it, but you are just in time for a splendid view of the end."

Promise's hooves thundered across the cold, still desert. Her breath trailed behind her, like a spectral banner. Jim was crouched low in the saddle. The eye was in his hand, burning with cold, emerald fire. He let it guide him forward. He tugged on the reins, left, then right.

Ahead was a sloping ridge rising out of the desert. He urged Promise toward it, up it. They reached the apex and Jim brought Promise to a halt. From here he could see across the vast expanse of the 40-Mile. Jim remembered the bleached bones, the discarded personal artifacts, the residue of so many lives and dreams crushed by the wastelands that guarded the promise of the West.

He recalled how it had felt when he had finally dropped in his tracks while leading Promise across the desert. His last thought was, *I came all this way, I went through so much, just to die out here—alone, forgotten.*

The jade eye was growing colder in his palm, colder than the desert night. Jim looked at it. It was glowing green like it had that night with Pa in the graveyard, like it had with Arthur Stapleton. He looked up into the vast dark sky. Only a few stars remained sheltered overhead.

I know Mr. Huang said you got to believe in something to make it real, Jim said silently to the empty sky. *And I rightly don't know enough about any of you, or this eye of yours, to even figure out what to believe in, but I sure could use your help right now. My friends are back there in that town and they are fighting and dying to save all of this—to save you in whatever Chinaman's paradise you all are in, to save Heaven, to save Golgotha. To save Ma and Lottie. So I'm asking for help. I don't know if I believe in you-all, or not, but I believe in my friends. Please, show me the way to do what I set out to do out here. Please, let it be the right thing; please let it work.*

Something moved across the sky. It swirled like sediment in muddy water, pushing aside the darkness. A thin sliver of silver moon appeared in the sky over the 40-Mile. It was just a sliver, but it was more than he dared hope for. He held the eye above his head and let the moonlight caress it.

"I know you-all are tired!" Jim said, shouting out across the desert. "I know how bone weary you-all are. I know what it feels like to fight for the next step, to push on, when everything in you screams to lie down. I can imagine how frustrating it is to not make it, to feel like you failed, like you made a promise you couldn't keep."

There was movement on the plain below him, vague, at the edge of moon shadow and sight.

"You have a chance, now, tonight, to make it not have been in vain. To push yourselves one more step, take one last ride. None of you are quitters. If you were, you would never have made it this far. I'm asking you to be ornery, as stubborn as a mule, one last time. Don't let it end like it did—in failing, in being forgotten."

The moon's light struggled against the vast darkness. It faltered for a moment, then held. Jim looked down at the desert plain; green light shimmered off the desert floor like reflections of sunlight off of water. His eyes widened at what he saw. Promise snorted and shuddered wildly.

"Easy, girl," Jim said, stroking her neck.

He shouted down to the plain, "Okay, we've got one more trip ahead of us—the most important one you've ever gone on! What do you say?"

A wind ripped across the desert, moaning, then howling, rising in pitch. Jim's hair whipped in the wind. He clutched the eye, green light spilling out between his fingers, and nodded.

"Then let's ride," he said.

Mutt edged to the left of the chamber's entrance, Harry to the right. Maude vanished into the shuddering shadows of the chamber.

"Where are all the townsfolk? The squatters? The people you infected with your sickness, Ambrose?" Harry asked. "Where is Holly?"

"Oh, them," Ambrose said. His voice was close to the central pit; Harry couldn't see him and Mutt couldn't get his scent. "Some of the faithful remain in the town, doing God's work, but most of them went down the well, to feed our Lord. He is hungry after his unjust imprisonment and needed sustenance to free Himself from His bonds."

"Oh, merciful Savior," Harry uttered.

"An odd epithet coming from you, Mayor Pratt," Ambrose said.

Harry was edging closer to the center, staying in the shadows between the blazing sconces. He could see another of the Stained, old Edna Hull, step into the void, smiling, and fall silently from sight. There were only a handful of the Stained left now. "You, who have spat upon your faith your entire life, who have experienced firsthand the unjustness of the divine tyrant. Yes, I know your secret. Holly and I have spoken at length. Isn't that right, dear?"

Harry stopped. It seemed ridiculous to be paralyzed by fear of discovery now, at the end of everything—the height of ego and pride. But he was genuinely terrified that his secret was no longer safe. He closed his eyes, wincing in pain. Holly's voice snapped him out of it.

"Yes, beloved." Holly's voice dripped with passion, and with venom. "Hello again, Harry. So you finally found enough courage to come down here. Pity it's too late to be of any value. I see you are still hiding in the shadows, though, like you've hid your whole life. You're a coward, Harry, and I always despised you for that."

"Come unto her, Harry!" Ambrose called. Harry could see them both now. A few of the Stained remained near the pit. Ambrose and Holly stood with them. "Come unto her and take the communion of the Greate Olde Wurm. You will know peace, you will know yourself and you will know freedom, for the first time in your wretched existence. Freedom without guilt."

"I've had that," Harry said, stepping into the light, sword in hand. "It took a long time, but I finally found that, in the arms of the person who loved me, and who I was supposed to love."

Ambrose smiled. "How sweet! And what do you think your God would say to that, Harry? Do you think He would embrace you and call you son? Or would He cast you out and disown you for embracing the nature He gave you?"

"That's between Him and me, I suppose," Pratt said. He turned to Holly. "I am sorry, Holly. You're right; I have been a coward. I'm sorry I ruined your life. I should have set you free a long time ago. I do love you; I always have. And I'm sorry I let you down."

"Let me kill him, now," Holly hissed in Ambrose's ear. "You promised!"

"But it would be so much sweeter to give him communion, Dark Mother," the old priest whispered. "To let him revel in the glory of the Wurm, as He tears His way out of this sham of a world and ascends to Heaven to drink the blood of the divine pretender. Perhaps he and I could fornicate as the world falls apart. How does that sound to you, Harry?"

"We're going to stop you," Harry said, stepping forward. "I don't care if I die doing it. You're not going to destroy my home."

Ambrose and Holly laughed.

"Ah, there's my knight!" Holly said. "Once again, too little too late, Harry. It's done."

"Those of the faithful drawn to the ritual were especially succulent," Ambrose said. "Their souls carried the greatest light, doused in the beautiful darkness of the One True God. They were a veritable feast for Him, and they have awoken Him, made Him strong, and now He will be free!"

Harry looked to Holly, frantic. "Holly, your soul is still in there—he just said as much. You can fight this, Holly; you don't want to do this. Think of your mother, your brother, your little niece. Please, Holly, fight!"

"Perhaps another, for good measure," Holly said. "Come here, dear Reverend."

The Reverend Prine, eyes wet and black, staggered forward, a look of sublime happiness upon his black-stained face.

"For the glory of the Wurm," he mumbled as he stepped toward the pit. "For His glory . . ."

"I am the Black Madonna, Harry," Holly said, smiling, darkness dribbling down her chin. "The soul of the woman you know is gone, fed to a slumbering god while her last terrified thoughts were of you—how much she loved you, how much it hurt her that you didn't come for her. Holly didn't hear your sweet words, Harry. She never will. Die knowing that."

The reverend stood at the edge. He looked to Ambrose, who nodded. Prine smiled and stepped out.

"Enough of this guff!" Mutt shouted as he launched himself from the shadows, knife in hand. "You damn white people talk too much!" He hurtled toward the pit, toward the reverend to knock him away from the well even as Prine took a step into oblivion. Mutt would have made it too.

Phillips, moving like a locomotive, was suddenly there, smashing into the deputy in mid-flight, knocking them both into the darkness. Prine, smiling, weeping black tears of joy, stepped off into oblivion. He fell, and was gone.

"No!" Harry shouted, stepping forward.

Holly's strong, Stained hand was on his shoulder. "One more failure as your epitaph, Harry," she said. "Fitting."

The chamber began to shudder violently. Debris tumbled down from the dark vault above. More of the Stained eagerly walked into the pit, many hand in hand, singing the inane alien hymns they had been chanting earlier. The rumbling grew in ferocity.

"Hallelujah!" Ambrose shouted. "Praise be to the One True God! *Nyarl'ohtha, hub-ia, ia-vultgmm!* The end is here!"

A dark figure stood between the remaining six Stained and the well. The figure had not been there an instant before. Maude, hands loose, legs slightly bent, ready.

"Who," Ambrose said, "the fuck are you?"

The voice came from inside herself, outside herself. It was her voice, a woman's voice, all women's voices gathered as one. Maude felt strong, stronger than she had ever felt before. All the years of doubt, all the fear and uncertainty, fell away.

"I am the Mother's blade, the Mother's wrath," she said. "You have poisoned her, raped her and her children. Left her to die. Now you will suffer. You will fail."

"Take her!" Ambrose shouted to the Stained as he backed away from Maude. "Carry her into the pit with you!"

They fell upon her, hissing like serpents. Maude went after Constance first for two reasons: Maude didn't want her daughter getting any closer to that well, and if she had retained any of her training, she was the most dangerous opponent of the six.

The girl lurched forward, like the others, her muscles seeming to be under the dominance of the alien force inside her. She moved with none of the grace or balance Maude had taught her. Good.

Maude lunged low, tumbled and drove two stiff fingers into a nest of nerves in the small of Constance's back. The girl shuddered, fell and remained still. Maude completed the tumble on the other side of the cluster of the Stained, crouched. As the infected floundered to keep up with the sudden movement of their prey and reorient themselves, Maude went to work.

She launched herself again, driving a knee and forearm into the chest of one of her attackers. The infected staggered backward, and Maude came along. The blows would have floored a normal man, but did little to the Stained, and Maude knew that by now. However, she rode the momentum to use her target as a ram to break the circle they were trying to form around her and as a shield. As she and the Stained fell, Maude's hands flashed out and struck two of the infected, one on either side of her. Her fingers, light as a firefly, hard as lightning, landed in the exact spots on each man's side to paralyze them for a time.

As her shield struck the silver floor, Maude, crouched on the man's chest, stood. She ground her heel into the infected man's collarbone at the exact spot she had practiced since she was Constance's age. The Stained raised its arms toward Maude's legs and then the arms dropped, and the man was still like a wind-up tin toy that had run down.

In less than three seconds, she had dropped four of her six attackers. The room shook again with thunder from deep in the earth. Debris and dust rained down around her. Her bandana had slipped to around her neck and her face was bare. Her breath was coming in ragged razor-blade gulps. Her whole body ached as if she had been beaten from head to toe. She felt alive, powerful, and it was all worth it when she saw the look of fear slide across Ambrose's smug face for just a second.

"Avast, ye right bastard." Anne's words coming out of Maude's mouth. Anne's evil grin that could turn a cutthroat's blood to ice stitched across Maude's face. Everything became clear, sharp focused, like the point of a knife. "You're next."

"Kill her!" Ambrose bellowed. "Kill the bitch!"

The last two Stained shuffled toward her. Maude prepared to greet them with open arms and a pirate queen's smile.

Phillips scrambled to his feet a second ahead of Mutt. The deacon drove a powerful hammer of a fist into the deputy's jaw, knocking Mutt to the silver floor again, in a spray of blood. The floor under Mutt was trembling.

"Too late, half-breed," Phillips said. "That's the death of this half-assed world, of everything."

Mutt sprang at Phillips and tackled the giant. Straddling him, Mutt landed blow after blow into his face—left, right, left, right. Phillips freed his arms and slapped Mutt off him, like a dog shaking off a flea. Both men struggled to their feet again and circled each other. The chamber shook. There was a cracking sound and more debris rained down.

Mutt scanned the floor for his knife as he wiped the blood from his mouth. Phillips, unbloodied, lunged forward and snapped a punch at Mutt's head. The deputy ducked it, barely, and drove two quick body blows into Phillips's side. It was like punching granite. The deacon grabbed at Mutt— *He's faster than a man his size should be,* Mutt thought; he needed to watch that. Mutt darted away, his hands aching from his ineffectual blows.

Phillips managed to grab Mutt's hair. He yanked, hard. The Indian's neck snapped backward and he crashed to the floor with a grisly snapping sound, and lay still in a cloud of settling dust.

Harry jerked away from Holly's steel grip. The sleeve of his jacket tore as he pulled free. He discarded the ripped coat as he circled her, keeping the point of the Sword of Laban between them.

"What are you going to do, Harry? Run me through with your angelic pego?" Holly chuckled. "Not exactly the way to save your poor wife that you just apologized to, now is it?"

She moved toward him, her dead, wet eyes searching his face for weakness, for hesitation. There was none.

Harry advanced, a classic lunge—his legs scissored, together then apart, as he closed the gap, blade unwavering, rear arm raised. Holly sidestepped, grabbing at his arm. He pivoted, spinning like a dancer—feet close together, knees slightly bent—and in that instant he saw his opening. He took it. Holly's arm erupted in golden flame as Laban's blade pierced her above the elbow. The sound that fell from her open mouth could never be made by the apparatus of a human throat. The whole room seemed to spasm in her pain as she frantically beat out the golden, sparkling flames. Now her hands were on fire as well, and the unearthly conflagration was spreading over her. The black ichor from her eyes, nose and mouth began to smoke and burn away.

"Damn you!" she screamed, lunging at him. "I'll sheathe that damn sword in your arse!" Holly charged him, like a rabid dog, head low, those strong, clawlike hands outstretched, desiring to choke the life from him. Harry stood his ground; his face was a mask of stone, feet planted in an *en garde* T, the angel's blade before his face as if to salute her. She was on top of him, burning hands seeking his throat. Harry turned his arm at the wrist and elbow smoothly and with blinding speed. The blade flashed out. Holly's snarling charge drove it into her chest. Her eyes widened, still bleeding smoke. She blinked and tried to say something. The angelic fire swirled about her whole body.

Holly's hands flashed out, wrapping tightly about Harry's throat. Harry felt the terrible heat, then numbing cold. His throat ached and his vision dimmed. Bitter smoke clawed at his nostrils, into his nose and eyes, but there was no air. The blade rested in her heart, up to the hilt. Husband and wife stood, separated by the gulf of a single breath, a single heartbeat.

The blackness in her eyes boiled away, replaced by devouring golden fire. Her grip loosened and he greedily gasped and gulped in air, but there was little of it. The smoke poured from her tear ducts, her nostrils. It smelled of stale pipe tobacco and sweat—it was the smell of his father's death.

The Black Madonna opened her mouth again, fighting to hiss out a final epitaph perhaps, or maybe it was Holly frantically trying to hang words off of the tatters of her soul that were rolling out, up, away from this burning, dying home. But there were no words; all that rolled across Harry's face was black smoke, smoke that smelled of damp earth and wet skin. Smoke that wept, whispering for a time when the world was young and everything was promise and potential—nothing was final; nothing was impossible. It was the smell of their first kiss, and it showed him exactly how much he had truly taken from her in this life.

The smoke swirled up out of her, old pain and memories given black wings. It dispersed into the guttering darkness of the collapsing vault.

"I love you, Holly," he tried to croak, but, like her, his voice was gone. She slumped against him, and was still.

Maude's muscles were on fire. It felt like her insides were made of broken glass. She had torn ligaments and ripped cartilage she had forgotten she even had, and now the balm of the thrill of combat was departing her and all that remained was the damage done to an out-of-shape body. She lay near the edge of the well and cradled Constance's limp form amidst the unmoving bodies of the infected Maude had incapacitated.

She wiped the black ooze off her daughter's face with a handkerchief, but as quickly as Constance's features would appear from beneath the oily morass more of the substance would leak out of her eyes, nose and mouth and pool up. Constance moaned and a bubble of the Wurm's black, oily milk popped over the girl's mouth, like a tar pit bubbling.

Maude pulled Constance tight and rocked her.

"Shhhhhh, baby girl. It will be all right," she said over the sounds of the world ending, of life and death struggling for supremacy. Of everything falling down. "Momma's got you. It will be all right."

It didn't feel like a lie. It didn't feel like a foolish, futile thing to say to a dying animal thrashing. Maude believed it; she actually believed it. With no evidence to support it and plenty to the contrary, she knew it was going to be all right. She held her child tight and knew the faith most holy men dream of possessing.

With a free hand, she pulled the chain from out of her pack. The ancient flask, green with age, still wrapped in a web of silver filaments, dangled at the ends of the flat linked iron chain. It was the same flask Maude drank from so many years ago.

She remembered Anne once sitting by a fire on the beach, looking out into the infinite.

"Why me?" Maude had asked. "I'm no one special. Why do I get this gift you are giving me?"

"I was . . . a wicked person," Anne had finally said. "I spent my life killing, lying, cheating and stealing. I was selfish, small. I asked the woman who gave me this gift the same question . . . 'Why me?' She told me what I'm about to tell you. . . . She said to me, 'Go find out why.'"

Maude wiped Constance's face clean again and lifted her daughter's head. She uncorked the jeweled stopper from the flask. There was a hiss, and a faint trail of smoke wafted out of the mouth of the flask. Maude tilted the container to her daughter's dark lips.

"Please, *please* ... Constance, honey, please come back to me. Please."

Lilith's blood dripped into the girl's open mouth, a thick drop at a time, swelling to ripeness, then falling to gravity's demand. Maude remembered the coppery fire of it, burning down her own throat, filling her with alien memories and a sense of connectedness to everyone, everything. Constance began to convulse, thrashing as if she were being beaten or burned. Maude quickly corked the vial and slipped the chain about her neck. She wrapped her arms around her daughter and held on tight.

The chamber shook, the stone walls and ceiling cracked and rocks and dust rained down around them. Maude closed her eyes. The embrace of her child became her universe.

Constance coughed and then began to gag and choke. Maude leaned her forward as the child flailed wildly as if she was going to be sick. Maude patted her gently on the back as her daughter began to retch onto the silver floor.

A pool of oily black vomit splashed on the vault floor. Gallons of it seemed to gush from Constance's mouth, and then, after what seemed an eternity, the child gurgled and then ejected a fat, black multi-segmented wormlike thing. The creature was about six inches long and it thrashed about like an eel out of water for a moment, then convulsed and lay still, smoking faintly.

Maude wiped the black ooze from her daughter's face again. This time it did not well up again from her nostrils and eyes. Constance blinked and tried to talk; only a croaking sound came out.

"Save your strength, darling," Maude said, hugging the girl. "It's over. Mother is going to take you home now."

Maude stood and tried to get Constance to her feet; the girl tried valiantly but simply couldn't rise. Maude made an assessment in a split second. It felt good and terrible all at once to know she had the capacity to make decisions of this magnitude in an instant. If she could get her daughter moving, she had strength enough to carry one of the immobile townsfolk out on her back. But now she knew she would be saving only her daughter today.

Across the chamber in the shaking, wavering firelight Maude saw Mutt being brutally beaten by the deacon, Phillips.

"Rest," Maude said. "We're going, but I need to take care of something first."

The girl shook her head and pointed to the well.

"Muh . . . Mother," she croaked, "it's coming for all of us; it's coming for home too. . . ."

"Well, then . . . ," Maude said, kissing her daughter on the forehead and clutching the flask to her breast. "Mother is just going to have to kill it, dear. I'll be right back."

Mutt became vaguely aware, in a distant corner of oblivion, that there were flashes of exquisite pain, like watching lightning dance off the coast of the ocean. He didn't want to examine it any closer, but some stupid, stubborn part of him insisted that he had to go back, that it was damn important that he go back. So he did, pulling the heavy covers of stupor off of him and letting the cold and the pain jar everything back into focus.

He was on the floor of the chamber, on his back. There were sounds of crashing—massive rocks shifting and tumbling. The taste of dust on his wet, numb, shredded lips. There was weight on him—Phillips, one knee resting on Mutt's chest, while the deacon held his blood-soaked shirtfront and drove blow after blow after blow into his face. He could vaguely see through one eye, through a film of red haze. He had an idea, more an instinct. Something his father had said . . . It swam in and out of his collapsing mind. The punching stopped. There was a voice.

"Let him go," Highfather said to Phillips, hefting the cavalry sword. "You so keen to kick an ass, come try kicking mine."

The weight came off Mutt's chest as Phillips stood and faced the sheriff.

"With pleasure," the deacon said. "I've been trying to figure out why everyone in this town is so scared of you, Sheriff. I'm going to enjoy this."

Suddenly Ambrose was behind Highfather, locking the younger man's arms into a fierce hold, above the sheriff's head. The sword clattered to the silver floor.

"Hello, Sheriff Highfather. I was hoping you'd be with us for the end," the preacher said. His breath reeked of decay. "Phillips, please give me Sheriff Highfather's heart, if you will."

"No!" Mutt bellowed. He was staggering to rise, his face a swollen mask, matted with his bloody hair. "Ain't gonna do nothing to him, you big stupid sumbitch. We ain't done yet! I ain't done with your cowardly, crazy ass! Come on!"

Phillips turned back to Mutt, smiling. The deputy was on his hands and knees crawling around, groping across the debris-strewn floor of the vault. Blood spattered in thick, quick droplets from his smashed face. The deacon strode toward Mutt as the chamber shook again and more debris crashed down.

"You too damn dumb to know when to just lay there and wait to die, half-breed?" he said, closing on the crawling man. "Want a little more pain before the end?"

Highfather drove his head back into Ambrose's nose and was greeted with a satisfying crunch. The old preacher grunted and loosened his grip. Jon slipped loose, spun and drove a powerful right hook into the old man's jaw. Ambrose gave him a black, bloody grin and launched himself at Highfather.

"It's fitting it ends with us locked in battle," Ambrose said, laughing. "Order battling until the last, even as chaos unravels it all at the very seams of creation."

Phillips stood over Mutt's crawling form, shook his head and drove a powerful kick into the Indian's guts. The force of it lifted Mutt off the ground. He dropped back to his hands and knees, gasped and hacked up a huge glob of blood.

A voice in the red haze of pain. Sweet, soft and kind just for him.

"Mutt, I know you can hear me. It's Maude. Do you want me to take him?"

The deputy shook his head slightly. Blood dripped off the long strands of hair. "No," he croaked. "Mine . . ."

"Stubborn man." Maude's voice murmured in his ear, like cool water gurgling over rocks, easing the pain, making it bearable for a little longer. "I'll be your eyes, then. He's to the left of you . . . more . . . more . . . turn a little more left— Watch out!"

Another savage kick. Mutt's insides were broken glass and fire. Vertigo. He had no idea where he was . . . where *Phillips* was. Mutt wanted to retch. He was having trouble breathing. When he did, each ragged breath was etched with a razor blade of pain.

"He's going to kill you, and then I will have to kill him," Maude's ephemeral voice echoed in his ears. "You are being a damn fool!"

"M . . . mine," was all he muttered. He didn't hear her moving through the pain, through the crashing of the chamber's demise, through the sounds of Highfather and Ambrose's battle and the world-shattering bellow of a thing never born of woman, awakening. Mutt knew she was, though, by the change in her voice and then the soft thud of a kick and then the tingling sound of metal on metal skittering across the silver floor. Closer to him close. Sliding.

"Your right hand, now!" she whispered.

Mutt's hands shook as they flailed out across the floor.

"Lose something?" Phillips asked, smiling.

"Um-hm," Mutt said. "I just found it."

The deputy sprang to a crouch, his big fighting knife in his hand. He shook his face, spraying blood all over the wide blade, and without missing a beat slashed out at Phillips's stomach. The giant didn't bother to try to dodge the blade. Suddenly the smirk left his face. He winced and staggered backward, clutching his abdomen. When he raised his hands, they were covered in his own black blood. More of it stained his ripped shirt.

"Well, now ain't that a fascinatin' development," the deputy said. He whispered to the darkness, knowing she was there, "Thanks."

"Kick his ass," the darkness whispered back.

Mutt stood, wiping the blood from his face and rubbing it into the knife's blade. His face was still a mess, but it seemed to not look as bad as it had a few minutes ago. He managed a smile, even.

"How?" Phillips asked, a look of long-forgotten fear creeping into his visage.

"Remembered something a wise old coyote told me once," Mutt said. "Well, not that wise. See, you and me, we're more alike than you know. Both got power in our blood. Me, I've jist been a little more afraid to use mine. But you, you done gone and got me pissed off. So I reckon I'm gonna use it. Thanks."

He moved toward the larger man, the stiffness and pain leaving Mutt's form with each step, the bloody blade twirling in his hand.

Phillips backed away, hands out, ready to grab at the deputy. "It doesn't matter if you kill me," the deacon said. "The Greate Olde Wurm is free now. This world and all others will perish. Death shall reign supreme."

"Then why you backin' up?" Mutt said. "You want death? Come and get it."

Phillips charged Mutt. He was still preternaturally fast and his fear and anger drove him now to even greater velocities. Mutt sidestepped the giant with a hop, a duck and a lightning flourish of the knife. Phillips staggered in pain and now his chest and arm bled. Mutt tossed the knife to the other hand and spit more blood onto the blade. He twirled it, the blade facing downward now, and bounded in for another strike, this time connecting with Phillips's lower back. The deacon grunted in frustration and pain.

Highfather and Ambrose's fistfight had carried them near the well. The sheriff discovered that while Ambrose appeared to be far his senior, the blood of the Wurm, perhaps in concert with his madness, gave him a degree of resilience and strength that was unnaturally difficult to overcome. Highfather had landed dozens of blows to the preacher that would have killed a younger man, had broken Ambrose's nose and most likely his jaw, but he barely seemed to notice.

"Getting tired?" Ambrose said. "The blood of my God sustains me, Sheriff. What do you have to keep you going? Faith, hope, will? They all falter; they all fail you at the end of things, Jonathan—you know that better than most, don't you?"

Highfather drove another hard right into the preacher's jaw. Ambrose's head snapped to the side for an instant. The old man slapped him across the face. Blood sprayed from Jon's mouth and he flew backward from the sheer force of the blow. He landed on his ass at the edge of the well. Ambrose laughed. A huge shelf of rock crashed down behind him. Several of the sconces jumped from the impact, then smashed to the floor, spilling glowing coals and scattering fire and shadow.

"I wish I had found you first, Jonathan—what a deacon you could have made! The war was so good at turning nice young men like you and Phillips into husks, looking for any way to ease your pain, or inflict it on another. The frontier is full of you—walking wounded, casualties of the war that were never counted."

Highfather pulled his pistol, cocked it and took aim at Ambrose's head. He groaned as he climbed to his feet.

"If you had any silver bullets left, you would have used them," the preacher said.

The gun blasted fire and thunder in Highfather's hand. The vault shuddered and groaned as the mountain buckled under the strain of an angry god. The bullet blew a hole through Ambroses's forehead, above his left eyebrow. It blew out the back of his head, igniting a patch of his scalp and white hair as it passed. The preacher staggered backward, driven by the force of the blast.

"It's a special bullet," Highfather said. "I've carried it every day since the war. Saving it for a special occasion. Figure the end of the world is good enough, don't you?"

Ambrose's right eye twitched. He made a gurgling scream and charged at Highfather, even as his hair continued to burn and his brains slid out the back of his skull, splattering on the silver floor. He crashed into the sheriff and grappled with him as they edged toward the pit. Ambrose's strength was that of a thing kept animate by forces that did not acknowledge reason, did not answer to nature.

Highfather pistol-whipped him with the barrel of the Colt to no effect. As they struggled, Jon felt his boot heels slip against the raised edge of the well. The gun was lost, dropping to the floor. The room dipped and swelled. More debris crashed down around them.

A horrible sound—the essence of skeletal hunger and bone-scraping pain amplified through a billion red-swollen screaming colic baby throats, vibrating like a trapped moth's beating wings. The sound came from the heart of the void, from the depths of the well. It was an anthem of rage and pain. It was at Highfather's back, waiting for him after the fall.

Ambrose pushed him backward, another inch, two. The old man no longer felt pain; he no longer spoke. He was beyond such human frailties. His hands tore at Jon's face; his forearm pushed the sheriff back, back.

Was it today? Was this it? Was this why he lived and so many others, so many better men and women than him, had died? So he could stop this madman? This would do—it was as good a way to go as any, better than most, if only it would end the madness and the death.

Please, Lord, if You're there, let me be the last one to die today. . . .

He grabbed hold of Ambrose, tightly, and began to pull them backward toward the well.

"Jon! Catch!" It was Harry, running, dodging, through the stone rain, throwing something to him. He pulled an arm free and reached out. The cavalry saber dropped into his hand, landing like a hunting bird returning to its master. He slashed down at Ambrose's shoulder. The blade tore the arm cleanly off at the joint in a jet of white fire. The burning arm bounced and fell into the darkness of the well.

Highfather grabbed Ambrose by the collar of his shirt, bent him at the waist and drove the sword deep into his belly. More opalescent fire erupted along the blade protruding from the preacher's back. Jon sidestepped as he pulled the blade clear and shoved Ambrose over the edge of the well.

The priest fell, burning, tumbling into blackness, the flame guttering, fanning wildly before vanishing, swallowed up by the ravenous dark.

Highfather stood on the edge of the well, panting. The cavern was beginning to collapse. Whole sections of the ceiling were tumbling down, exploding as they shattered against the silver floor. The fire and the smoke from the smashed sconces gave the place the look and feel of Hell's waiting room. The thing in the well roared again. It sounded like it was coming closer.

Harry was beside him, grabbing him by the shoulder.

"It's all coming down! We've got to go! Where's Mutt?"

Highfather realized that Harry had Holly's smoldering body slung over his shoulder. His eyes looked dead. "Damn, I'm sorry, Harry," he said.

"Jon! Where the hell is Mutt? We have got to get out of here!"

There was a blur of movement on the far side of the chamber.

"There!" Highfather said.

Mutt was knife-dancing. Moving around, under, over, encircling Phillips, the crimson-splattered blade flashing, sparking, as it struck stray pieces of falling rock. The deacon stumbled, but continued, like some damaged machine, to drive blow after blow into the deputy. More missed than landed, but each one that did drove Mutt to the ground with a terrible crash, a spray of dust and blood, but Mutt tumbled, rolled and sprang up anew, knife flashing, with a yip and a snarl.

Once, when Highfather had been a boy, he had sat very still beside his brother and his father and watched a brown bear take on a pack of wolves. The wolves had worn the bear down, a death of a hundred bites.

As Highfather watched his deputy now slash and whirl around the deacon, it brought the memory back to him.

"Damn," Harry muttered. "Look at him go."

Phillips was bleeding everywhere. His face radiated the pain and humiliation that had rapidly become his world. He swung wildly at Mutt and missed this time. He was rewarded with another ugly slash under his armpit.

Mutt's face was intent, his eyes dark and focused, scanning each move, each response—predator's eyes. He wasn't quite grinning as he cut the man again and again, but there was a cruel slit of a smile on Mutt's smashed and swollen face.

Phillips groaned and began to sprint toward the well.

"Into Your hands I commit my spirit!" he bellowed as he dived toward the well. Mutt dashed after him, sprang and landed in a crouch. He slashed at the larger man's legs in a wide, powerful arc of the knife, severing his hamstrings. Phillips gasped in pain and surprise as his legs failed him. He slid to a stop a few feet from the well, the sheriff and the mayor.

"Nope," Mutt said. "You don't get to die all fancy. You don't get to go be with your sick preacher and your slimy god, all special-like."

He pulled the deacon's hair, yanking his head up. He spit fresh blood on the blade and put it to Phillips's neck.

"You get to die just like all those folks you killed—scared and confused and full to the brim with regrets and unfinished business. Just regular folk."

"It doesn't matter," Phillips hissed. "It's free and—"

Mutt opened his throat from ear to ear with the knife. The stuff that gushed out was black and thick as it splashed out onto the silver floor.

"You don't get to have the last word either," Mutt said. "Ain't that a pisser?"

He dropped the dead man facefirst on the ground, in a pool of his god's black ichor, and looked up at Highfather and Pratt, panting.

"You done playing?" Highfather said over the groan and crash of the rock buckling.

"Reckon so," Mutt said. His eyes rolled up into his head and he collapsed on top of Phillips's corpse.

"Damn it!" Highfather said. He ran to Mutt and hefted him up, throwing him over his shoulder. "C'mon, run!"

And they did, as great stone boulders tore loose from the ceiling, tumbled and exploded like bombs across the chamber.

Highfather looked back and saw the stranger with the bandana mask kneeling by the edge of the well, a young girl, maybe Constance Stapleton, slung over the stranger's shoulder. He waved for the stranger to come. The stranger nodded and returned to whatever task he was about at the well's edge.

"Come on, Harry, we got to get a move on! Don't stop; go, go!"

"We didn't stop them, did we?" Pratt asked as they dodged tumbling debris, headed for the scar of an entrance.

"I don't think so," Highfather said. He looked back to see if the masked stranger was following. The stranger was nowhere to be seen.

"Then why keep running?"

"Harry, shut up and run!"

And they did.

Golgotha was dying. The Earth was dying. The sky was dying. Only a few stars remained glittering in the dark heaven. The ground trembled, as if it were afraid. Many of the buildings on Main Street had collapsed; others burned. The few people in town who were still human cowered. Most of them prayed.

There was a sound—like thunder, like the roar of a cannon repeated in staccato time, magnified a thousandfold. It shook the ground as mightily as the tremors did. Those with eyes that still saw more than darkness turned to the east, to the desert, where the sound rolled in from. There was an eerie green glow, like the northern lights, billowing across the desolate peaks and dunes. The glow grew brighter, closer, and the sound rose with it.

Jim Negrey rode as fast and as hard as he ever had. Promise's head was low and her eyes fixed with certainty and intent as they crashed through the brush, darted between the buildings at the edge of town and galloped onto Main, headed north, toward the pass, toward Argent Mountain.

Jim knew what was behind him, but he dared not look back for fear it was all a dream. That he would awake back in Albright, or in a cinder-block cell beside the gallows. Or, worst of all, that there was nothing behind him, that he was mad, like his father, and he had failed, one last time, and this was the end.

No.

He pulled the reins tight to the right and Promise turned tight and fast onto the narrow mountain road. They began to ascend Argent even as the mountain began to shake and crumble.

"Go, go, go!" Jim shouted over the sound of the world ending. He stood in his saddle, willing Promise to even greater speed.

No more time.

The Mother had no more time. The thing that had been locked in her womb since before the stars burned in the sky was free and it was killing her as it clawed its way toward the sky, toward Heaven. It had always been there, darkening her heart, poisoning her blood and dreaming its obscene dreams of a universe of nothing but endless death.

Maude crouched at the edge of the well. Constance was unconscious and slung over her shoulder. She held the ancient flask, uncorked its jeweled stopper again. She suddenly noticed that many of the symbols carved crudely onto the flask matched symbols that spiraled about the well's mouth. The realization made her feel an odd sense of calm. This was the right thing to do; maybe this was why the blood had survived, why the line of women who carried Lilith's Load had come into existence, had crossed the millennia.

She leaned over the well. It was coming. Rushing up out of the vertigo of darkness, free after time out of time. Maude could feel it, a roaring blast furnace in her mind, destroying reason, annihilating thought. Hungry. Enraged. It was everything she had ever feared, everything she had ever allowed to devour her, her every failure, her every mistake. The darkness had a face and it was her own.

She held the flask over the well; her hands were steady, her mind certain.

Your heart is sick, she said silently to the shuddering cavern, to the broken sky and, truth be known, to herself. *Poisoned. I know that feeling, very well. This thing has wrapped itself around the core of you, black and rotten and eating away at your peace, at yourself, at your soul. It has made you weak and it has stolen your resolve, your true self. It has taken away the clear light that is at the core of you; it has stolen you from you and filled you with fear and instability.*

She turned her wrist and the blood began to pour freely from the ancient vial, draining down into the darkness.

It was not here of your doing but put here, dumped here through the cowardice and weakness and fear of another, your creator, He Who you should trust first amongst all others He Who betrayed you to His own selfish goals.

More of the old blood flowed from the flask. More than could possibly be held by it. Maude could feel the heat radiating off the streaming blood of the first woman, the first rebel, the first human being to say no to the indomitable intent of the inevitable, the ineffable. The first human being with a sense of themselves and their place in the universe, alone.

The first Free Will.

And now is the time to cast it off, to heal it and kill it and take away all its power over you. The time to know yourself again, to know your core and embrace it and repair it. To be the Mother, to be the Woman, your own creator, your own author! I return this gift of power, of strength. I add it to your own endless reserve. You are the source of all strength, all weakness. All. Heal: cast the poison out. Fight. Fight!

The last of the bloodstream trickled out of the flask as Maude completed her healing prayer, her declaration of will. It felt as if her own blood, Anne's blood, the vital essence of all those who had come before, had been spilled down into this wound in the world. She pulled the empty flask back from the abyss.

It's up to you now, she thought, rising from the side of the well with her daughter on her back. *Only you can heal yourself, Blessed Mother. You have to want to live, to be whole, to thrive, not merely survive, poisoned and wounded. This world, this existence, this breath is a gift, not a curse.*

Maude stepped between the curtains of deadly debris and made her way toward the opening to the mine.

Breathe, Mother, live.

And Maude was gone, fighting her own way back, her daughter's way back, to the shattering sky.

Outside the chamber, Highfather felt the last ember of hope he had to salvage this grow cold and die. He was still carrying Mutt, and Harry carried

Holly's body. It hadn't been easy going through the narrow corridor, back to the mine shaft. He paused when he had cleared it. "What?" Harry said.

Part of the tunnel had collapsed on top of the explosives Highfather had rigged to bring down the whole level and well chamber. The long fuse he had run up the ramp to the higher levels was buried under a ton of rock.

"I can't blow it from the upper level," Highfather said. "There's no more fuse to run. I used it all."

"What difference does it make?" Harry said. "You heard Bick—you honestly think collapsing that room will make a bit of difference?"

Highfather shook his head. "It's all we've got left. If Malachi or Jim or whoever is going to find some kind of solution, this might buy them a little more time.

"Here," he said. He pulled Mutt off his shoulder and carefully laid him over Harry's.

The mayor groaned a little under the weight of two bodies, but did not falter. "What the hell are you doing, Jonathan?" he said.

"I'm going to light what little fuse I've got left down here and make a run for the top."

"You can't outrun an explosion or a collapsing mine," Harry said. "That's crazy. You'll die."

"I don't do that, remember?" Highfather said, handing him the last lantern they had.

"Now's not the time for that nonsense!" Harry shouted.

The corridor shook and the horrible wet growl rumbled from the well chamber again. More debris dropped.

"Go on, Harry. Trust me, I'll be right behind you. I'll give you five minutes' head start. 'Less if it sounds like that thing is coming up sooner. Now go!"

The mayor nodded. "Five minutes," he said, and then started to run up the ramp to the higher levels as fast as his load would allow.

In a moment he was gone and Highfather was alone in the hot, stale darkness listening to the mountain spasm and heave. He fumbled around and found the other lantern, crushed by the rocks. He wrapped his kerchief around the end of the saber and dipped it in the leaking remnants of the lantern's oil. Struck a match, and began to count.

Harry's lungs burned, his legs and back ached, but he did not stop. He followed the bouncing circle of lantern light as it led him up the ramps, down the corridors. Support timbers crashed down around him and behind him he heard the crash of the rock ceiling and he feared he would never see Jon Highfather again.

Mutt groaned on his back but lay still. Holly was painfully still. This was not how Harry would have chosen to spend the last minutes on Earth, but there was a strange sense of peace in him here. It was something he hadn't felt most of his life, only in his times with Ringo. Harry felt like he was in balance, like this was not a bad note to end on. He just wished they could have won.

Ahead was the entrance and while it was still darkness, it was discernable as open air. He trudged forward a few more steps and then he felt the charges go far below him. The mountain shook and the mine heaved and began to collapse.

"Good work, Jon," he mumbled to no one. "Very good."

Highfather gave Pratt seven minutes. Then he turned to light the remaining fuse. It would give him about three minutes before the blast. He knew Harry was right and his prospects were not good. But if this bought the world, bought his family and his town, five more minutes, then it was worth it. He lit the fuse and began to run up what remained of the ramp.

A boot stomped out the lit, sputtering fuse, silencing it.

It was Phillips, or what still occupied his corpse. Fat black worms, like convulsing tentacles, pushed through the gash that ran along his throat. His expression was unchanged from the moment of his death. The deacon stumbled, dumbly, arms outstretched, toward Highfather, who stood on the ramp.

Highfather drew his pistol, took careful aim and fired. The bullet struck the dynamite. The narrow passage was filled with unbearable light and sound. The blast ripped what was left of Phillips's body apart. It was the last thing Jon Highfather saw before the blast overtook him as well.

Outside the Argent Mine, Harry Pratt sat on a wooden bench, exhausted. His dead wife and Deputy Mutt both lay at his feet. The mine was collapsing, dust was rolling out through the yawning entrance and rock and debris began to tumble out as well. A single star remained above. It began to flare, to wobble in the firmament. Harry looked down at the blade in his hands, at Holly, and thought briefly about Sarah, about Ringo, and hoped they were somewhere pleasant in their last moments. He wished they were together.

The cacophony of hooves shook him back to awareness. Jim appeared at the gates to the mining camp, his horse in a full gallop, flecks of foam at the edges of her nose and mouth. The boy was followed by a growing nimbus of green light.

Jim pulled Promise to a stop beside the mine entrance. More rock and debris continued to fall; more dust plumed from the hole. The glowing procession following him rumbled into the camp, toward the mine.

"Here!" Jim yelled. "Down here, hurry!"

Harry could hardly comprehend what he was seeing. A glowing green spectral procession of covered wagons full of families; prospectors on shimmering horses; Indians riding bareback; Mormons; Chinamen; Buffalo Soldiers; explorers; settlers; immigrants; pioneers.

They all roared down into the collapsing mine, as if the constraints of space meant nothing to them. They traveled past in a wave of sound and fury—laughter, cussing, weeping, music, oaths, hymns, prayers. They carried the desert's wrath with them, carried the hope of a new horizon just past the next rise, carried dreams spun of nothing more than promise and determination—dreams stronger than steel, stronger than the 40-Mile, than any desert. Stronger than death.

Then they were gone, buried under the earth beneath tons of rock. All that remained of their passing was a swirling desert wind and the fading echo of thunder. The mine entrance was sealed in debris. The ground no longer shook. Everything grew very quiet.

Jim climbed off Promise and patted her neck.

"Good girl, very good girl. I didn't know you could run that fast. You've been holding out on me."

Harry rushed over to the boy.

"Jim, what did you do?"

"Found something strong enough to hold it down there a while longer," the boy said. "Least I expect so. Those folks don't do nothing half-measure."

"Where's Jonathan?" Mutt said. The deputy was on his feet and looking better than he had in the chamber, but he was still a mess, still barely standing.

Harry looked down, and then to the mine entrance. "He . . . stayed to set off the dynamite. I'm sorry, Mutt."

The deputy staggered to the entrance, he began to pull out rocks and toss them aside.

"Mutt . . . ," Harry said.

"Help me," Mutt said, continuing to dig.

Jim ran over and began to work loose the debris he could manage.

"Mutt, he was my friend too, but there is no way—"

"Damn it, Harry, it's Jon Highfather! Please!"

Pratt joined them and began to help the deputy move some of the larger rocks. The sky was lightening, but none of them had noticed.

After about twenty minutes, they heard a faint groan from about thirty feet back. They kept working, even harder now, making a narrow path through the debris. They found him in a small open space created by two support timbers falling on top of some larger pieces of debris. He was blackened, burned, scraped and cut badly. Mutt and Harry pulled him free and carried him out into the orange and indigo sky.

Highfather's eyes were swollen shut. His lips moved, barely, and Mutt knelt to hear what he was trying to say. The sheriff muttered for a moment, tried to laugh and then, exhausted by the effort, slid back into unconsciousness.

"What did he say?" Jim asked.

"He said it's not his time yet," Mutt said, shaking his head and laughing.

From the east came the dawn, long denied, and even more beautiful for the waiting. It followed the laughter down the mountain, into the streets of Golgotha and across the world.

Judgment

The almanacs and the newspapers called it a solar eclipse. The sun and the moon were back where they were supposed to be, and from wherever they had tumbled to the stars had managed to make it back to their rightful places in the crown of the night sky. That was good enough for most folks.

In Golgotha, it was decided an epidemic of the Black Vomit had run through the town making folks so sick they could scarcely recall much of the last few days. At least that was the official, and loudly announced, explanation from Doc Tumblety, as soon as the good doctor himself had recovered from the malady.

Those who had been infected and managed to avoid getting killed during the madness made a full recovery complete with a terrible recollection of illness, vague nightmares of suffocating and the horrific experience of vomiting up dead wormlike things and viscous black fluid for days.

Other events could not be so easily put aside. The damage to the town, to the Argent Mine and the old Reid mansion, all was explained as caused by either locals mad with illness from the plague or earthquakes caused in some unexplainable way by the odd machinations of the eclipse—it really depended on who told you the tale as to what the explanation was. Most folk in Golgotha had learned long ago to quickly grab hold of any explanation in the daylight that might make it easier to sleep in the dark.

One fact of the dreadful mess that couldn't be explained away or ignored was that eighty-six people had died during the "epidemic," by most people's accounting. Others vanished and were never seen or heard from again.

Clay Turlough kept pretty much to himself in the days following the fires and the plague, but he sent word that his main barn could be used as a morgue for the dead, until proper burials could be arranged.

Clay had moved his workshop to a smaller building and his horses to the old stables that he had used before raising the main barn. He watched, through the curtains covering the small window on the door, as families and friends wandered in and out of the barn. Most were weeping, holding each other, consoling one another. He felt a coldness slip through him; it slowly became anger, then resolve. What a waste death was.

Gillian Proctor suddenly came into view, carrying a basket. She stopped to speak with, to console, several of the mourners, hugging them, patting their hands, sharing a moment of despair with them, wiping tears from her eyes as she did. Also giving strength and hope to them. It had not occurred to Clay until now that Mrs. Proctor was physically perfect. Her proportions, her measurements and symmetry, were flawless. She was lovely, to be sure, if in no other way than mathematically.

She approached his workshop door and he withdrew from the curtain quickly. She rapped on the glass gently.

"Clay? Mr. Turlough?"

Clay growled and covered his work with a stained cloth. He strode to the door. The damnable woman would peck all day like a bird until he relented. He threw it open.

"Yes, Mrs. Proctor, I am in the middle of some very delicate experiments right now and—"

Gillian presented him with the basket. Clay's nose caught the scent of ham and fresh-baked bread.

"I know; I'm sorry, Clay," she said. "We were just worried you weren't eating."

"We," Clay said.

"Auggie, me. He's afraid you're angry at him, still."

Clay shook his head. "No, not angry. I just feel it is inappropriate for me to be on display given my current . . . condition."

"Oh," she said.

He had to give her credit; she hadn't automatically lowered her eyes like everyone else who had seen him. He still wore dressings on the side of his face and on his forearms and chest where the burns were the worst. It was not for the benefit of others' sensibilities but a matter of survival. He was working on a compound to help protect him from infections until the burns would scar over. Clay had never been a good-looking man and the burns were simply the final affirmation of his total disdain for the vanity of the flesh. They were the price he paid, and it was a cheap price.

"May I come in?" she asked.

"I, I think not," he responded. He took the basket with one hand and began to close the door with the other. "Thank you for the victuals, Gillian."

She pressed her hand against the door, stopping him cold. He had never experienced a display of such gentility married to such strength. Her eyes never left his.

"I never had the opportunity to thank you for saving my life."

"Don't have to. Thank Auggie."

"I understand," she said. "But I wanted you to know you have people who care about you, Clay. Auggie cares about you so very much, and so do I. You're our family."

She released the door and he closed it. She stood for another moment, hoping there would be more, but that was not Clay Turlough's way.

She walked back to the wagon where Auggie waited.

"Well?" he said, taking her hand and helping her up onto the buckboard. "Is he all right?"

"He took the food," Gillian said as Auggie climbed on the wagon beside her. "That's a start."

"Speaking of starts," he said. "I want to show you the property up on Rose Hill I'm looking at buying. It'd be a good place for a house."

"Shouldn't we take care of fixing up the store first?" she said.

Auggie laughed, it was a beautiful sound to Gillian, any time she heard it.

"*Ja*, we probably should, but no work today! Today I want to show you where our home is going to be, where I'd like it to be."

She smiled at him and took his thick, rough hand in hers.

"I'd like that very much," she said.

He shook the reins and the wagon jumped forward, down the road, toward Rose Hill.

From his window Clay watched them depart. Behind him on the work-table was the blackened and warped jar holding Gert's head. The head was mostly mummified by the heat of the fire. The brass cogs and wires below the jar were a melted, twisted mass. Hoses, tubing and wires ran from a box-like device into the tank and attached to Gert's head, which nodded lazily, immersed in a new, bubbling nutrient solution. The eyes were squeezed closed in a shriveled mask, like the skin was too tight. Her hair tumbled, drifted in the currents.

"I know you were sad this way, Gertie," Clay said, "powerful sad, but I ain't never had much of anything in this life that mattered to me . . .'cept you. I love you. I need you. And I'm gonna make this all better for you. Just like it was before you got sick, even."

He turned away from the window. On the wall behind the worktable there was a drawing, an anatomical sketch of a woman's body. The drawing had no head. Clay had done his best to make the drawing perfect. Mathe-matically perfect.

"I swear," he said.

Malachi Bick drove another nail into the new wall, replacing some of the damage done to the Paradise Falls. He wore shirttails and suspenders as he worked.

"Making good progress, Malachi," Highfather said as he entered. The sheriff's arm was still in a sling, and his face was still covered with cuts and bruises. "Should be open by the end of the month."

"That's my intention," Bick said.

"You're going have to go pretty far ways to find another mirror for be-hind the bar."

"There's a place in Virginia City that makes them," Bick said. "Surpris-ingly, they get a lot of business in replacing barroom mirrors."

Highfather nodded. "I came to pay my respects, for Caleb."

"I see; thank you, Sheriff." Bick steadied another nail and began to drive it in.

"I lost the saber!" Highfather shouted above the hammering.

Bick stopped and turned.

"In the mine. After the explosion. I lost it. I'm sorry."

Malachi nodded, put the hammer on the bar. "It's all right. It served its purpose, and I doubt I'd ever be able to use it anymore, anyway."

"What was its purpose, really, Malachi? What is yours?"

"Whatever I was, I'm not anymore. Not really. And for the first time in a long while, I'm good with that," Bick said. "As for what I am, I am a businessman. I see opportunities and seek to profit from them."

"The mine," Highfather said, shaking his head.

Bick smiled. "And I am a civic leader. Those poor souls up in the squatter town deserve a fair shake, don't you agree, Sheriff?"

Highfather laughed. "I thought all of this might have changed you, but I guess not."

"It did, Jonathan," Bick said. "It did. But you must understand I doubt I'll ever be able to give you the full story of what I do or why."

"Then I'll keep poking around on my own," Highfather said, "till I get the answers."

He walked toward the doors, and then stopped, smiling.

"I'll be keeping on eye on you, Bick."

"I feel safer already, Sheriff," Bick replied, returning the smile.

The saloon doors thumped open, then closed, swinging for a moment. They stopped suddenly and the noises from the street faded to silence. Bick picked a bottle of rotgut off the bar and poured two shot glasses.

"Care for a drink?" he said.

"Always," Lucifer replied, stepping from the cool shadows by the faro tables. "Congratulations are in order. Your pawns succeeded in sealing the bottomless pit and restraining the Darkling. Most impressive." He picked up the shot glass. "Why reopen the mine, though?"

Bick raised his glass.

"It would draw more men like Deerfield and Moore if left unattended," Bick said. "Open, under my auspices, I can direct them away from the chamber and the pit. And I get to make a fortune in the process. Oh, and by the way, not pawns," he added. "Part of a design."

"Oh please," Lucifer said, eyes rolling. "After all of this, you honestly think the Almighty had a hand in how this shook out. He was pissing Himself, just like the rest of us."

"Why give the greatest power in all creation to a bunch of monkeys?"

Bick said. "A power greater, stronger, than the will of God itself? Why give them free will? Why give them a world they can damn or save, all on their own?"

"A test?" Lucifer said. "You think all of this was just another one of His little experiments? I think you give the Architect far too much credit."

"To the human soul," Bick said, raising the shot glass.

Lucifer tapped it with his own. "Keeping us all in business for a long, long time," the Devil said.

They tossed back the shots.

"You water down your whiskey," Lucifer said incredulously.

"The good stuff is for paying customers," Bick replied.

"Offer still stands, Biqa," Lucifer said. "A job, a home. The company of your kin."

"I have those," Bick said. "Just took me a spell to realize it. Besides, despite your opinion, I think the Almighty is a hell of showman and I can't wait to see what He's got in store for them next."

"You're not going to hear from the home office, you know that?" Lucifer said. Bick nodded. "You are alone here, Biqa. This place has tainted you, in their eyes. There will be no order to return, no reward for being a good soldier. You never get to go home."

"I know," Bick said, picking up the hammer. "But this will do."

He looked up. Lucifer was gone. Bick gathered the nails and got back to work.

Mutt, hat in hand, knocked on the door. Maude Stapleton opened it, dressed in black. The purple smudges of bruises covered her face. She was still beautiful, Mutt thought.

"See you made it out in one piece," he said. "Good."

The deputy's face was a road map of pain and suffering. Swollen, broken, split and jagged. He somehow managed a smile through the wreckage.

"Your face!"

"Not as bad as it looks," he said. "You should see the other fella."

"I did. I was very proud of you down there, Mutt. Even if you were a stubborn fool."

"Thank you for saving me," he said. "You really did, you know?"

"Thank you for trusting me," she said. "When I had trouble even trusting myself."

They stood silent for a moment, but more passed between them than words were capable of holding.

"Have you been to Dr. Tumblety?" she finally said.

"Nah, I heal pretty quick, and he's a jackass."

They both laughed. They both winced from the pain the laughter brought.

"I just wanted to check on you," he said. "Make sure you and your girl were okay."

"Yes," she said. "She's sleeping a lot. There are nightmares, but she remembers less every day. She is mending, getting stronger, in fact. Thank you. I'll tell her you asked after her. I appreciate your concern."

They stood there, no words again, and that was all right. The afternoon wind was blowing up clouds of dust in the bright sunlight.

"I gotta go," Mutt said. "Just wanted to, you know."

She nodded. "Yes."

He started to walk away.

"Why aren't you asking me?" she said. "You must have a lot of questions."

"Not really," he said. "I know what I need to know. I know what counts. The rest is just conversation."

He began walking again.

"Mutt," she said. He turned back. "Arthur's funeral is tomorrow. Most of our associates are really Arthur's associates. I was hoping you could attend, as my friend. I don't have too many. I never have."

Mutt nodded. "Me too. I'd be honored."

"Thank you."

He stood in the street, watching as she closed the door. He put his hat back on and then walked away.

Many families held vigils with the bodies resting in Clay's barn. With so many dead, it was taking a while to bury them all properly.

Tonight, Harry was alone with Holly on the black watch. The huge barn was silent except for the sounds of the wind coming off the desert, rustling through the high sacaton grass. The moon was swollen and bright—almost like day—and the stars chased each other like cats, racing across the desert sky.

Ringo and Sarah had both offered to sit the night with him, but Harry had declined. This was his duty alone. The least he could do for her after all he had stolen from her—the chance for a family, for a man who could love her as she had deserved to be loved. For failing to save her, for killing her. For every lie, every bitter, hurtful word. For not being able to say good-bye to her, just the thing that wore her body those last days. For not being able to tell her it wasn't all fake, it wasn't all untrue. There had been love, but she would never know that now. Her soul was gone, devoured.

He wanted to cry, but there was nothing left. He hadn't been home to the mansion, to their home—her home—since the night she died. He knew who he was, why he was, and he accepted it. But the price she paid had been too high for his security, his fear and denial. Harry sat looking at her shroud-covered body, wishing it could be him there.

A few more tears arrived from the dregs of his soul. He lowered his head, shook.

"Mr. Mayor, sir?"

Harry looked up; he wiped his wet eyes and sniffed. It was Jim Negrey.

"Yes, Jim, what can I do for you?"

Jim's hands were stuffed deep in his pockets, his head down.

"Sir, the last time I saw my pa alive, he was drunk and angry and in pain. I wished that wasn't the last living memory of him I had, but it is. The last time I saw my ma and sister, they were scared and hurt and it was all on account of me."

He looked up at Harry.

"Regrets will eat a man up. My pa told me that. Said you should always try to make your peace when you can, 'cause no man knows what the Lord has in store for us tomorrow."

"I'm burying her tomorrow," Harry said. His voice was small.

"Yessir," Jim said. "That's why I'm here." He pulled a rawhide cord with a small leather bag from around his neck. He placed it in Harry's hand. "I'd give anything to hug my pa again," he said. "To kiss my ma and tell her how sorry I was, to see my little sister smile and know she's all right."

Jim walked out the huge, open barn doors.

"Good night, sir," he said.

Harry opened the bag; the jade eye dropped into his palm. He lifted it to his own eyes to examine it and the brilliant moonlight fell upon the orb. Glittering motes of emerald drifted in slow orbits around the eye. The barn began to fill with cool green light.

"Hello, Harry," the woman's voice said from the shadows on the other side of the body. She stepped forward and Harry's eyes widened. He began to smile and to cry.

"Hello, Holly."

The sun was huge and red, crawling down behind the jagged peaks that were the sentinels of the desert, casting long twisted shadows on the floor of the wasteland.

Jim sat in the saddle. Promise waited calmly, nibbling on a patch of grass. Golgotha was behind him. There was a thud of hooves and Mutt, astride Muha, pulled up next to him.

"Thought I might find you out here," Mutt said. "You figuring on leaving?"

"Well, things have kind of quieted down, now, and . . ." Jim let the words die. He didn't know what else to say. "Yeah, I reckon."

"Virginia City or back to . . . where the hell was it?"

"Kansas," Jim said, smiling.

"Right, Kansas," Mutt said. "Here." He tossed him the leather necklace and pouch. "Mayor said, 'Thank you.'"

"Mayor," Jim said. "You called him Mayor, not Harry, not Pratt, or sumbitch. Mayor."

"Yeah, well, don't mean nothing," Mutt said. "He's still a Fancy Dan."

They sat quietly and let the time pass. A covered wagon ambled over the dunes and climbed onto the road toward Golgotha. Dark bird silhouettes sailed into the ruby eye of the sun.

"It's pretty here," Jim said. "It'll kill you, if you're not careful, but it's the prettiest place I ever did see."

"I talked to Jon," Mutt said. "Says you can keep that star you're wearing, if you want—you earned it. He wants you to stay on, be a deputy."

"Mutt, that's gonna get complicated. I've got a price on my head. I done wrong, back home."

"Well, you did right here, and that counts more in my book, Jon's too. We'll stand by you, come what may."

"Where is the sheriff?"

"Old cemetery, said he had some business to attend to before sundown—make sure all the commotion didn't stir anything up. Old, bad business."

Jim shook his head. "It's a miracle anyone stays around here."

"Maybe," Mutt said. "But more folks came back after this mess than kept going. It's a good town, with good people. Worth protecting. Good place for a man to pay off a debt, if'n he had one."

Jim smiled. "Really?"

"Yup," Mutt said. "Credit would pile up quick, I'd reckon."

"I already gave my notice at Mrs. Proctor's," Jim said.

"Yeah, I told her to never mind that."

They both laughed. "Pretty sure of yourself," Jim said.

"I know a sure thing when I see one," Mutt said.

Jim stuck out his hand. Mutt shook it.

"Let's git home," Jim said.

"Nice to have one," Mutt said, "ain't it?"

They turned the horses and began to gallop back to the road and into town. The sinking sun was at their backs, painting the sky, smearing it, in oranges, reds and purples. Behind it was the cool, whispering promise of night, of stars and moon, silver and shadow.

"Be dark soon," Mutt said. "Time to earn our pay."

Golgotha, mother to the lost, destination of all the hardest roads, opened her arms to them, and to the coming night.

Acknowledgments

Thank you to my mother, Mabel T. Belcher, for a lifetime of encouragement, guidance, friendship and love. You always believed in me, supported me and taught me to never give up. I love you, Mom.

To my wonderful children: Jonathan, Emily and Stephanie. You are the light of my existence and each of you has made me so happy and so much more than I would have ever been without you. Thank you for the love you show me every day. I love you all to the moon and back.

To Leslie Barger: My editor, my fan, my muse. Your love is my cool water in the desert. You are my moon and stars. Thank you for your dedication to my writing and for your belief in my ability, even when I had none. I love you.

To Phil Rowe: Smartest man I know, full of wisdom, kindness, patience and affection. Thank you for all your help in editing and sage counsel. Thank you for Robert Parker and John D. McDonald and William Goldman and a million, million other treasures. Most of all, thank you for your friendship and brotherhood—the greatest treasures of all.

Thank you, Pam and Allen Trigger, for your gracious generosity; you have truly been my patrons and truest friends in dark days. I hope this thank-you in some small way shows you how much I truly appreciate all you have done for me and my family.

Thank you to Vicki and Tony Ayers and David and Susan Lystlund for love and support over all the years. Thank you for being my family; my brothers and sisters.

Thank you to Bob Flack: brother and wisest man I know. Your friendship has kept me sane and alive. Thank you.

Thank you to Meg Hibbert and Dan Smith for having faith in me as a writer and for giving me my shot. I owe you both so much.

Thank you to my uncle, John Weddle, for being a father to me every time I needed one.

Thank you to Stacy Hill and Greg Cox of Tor Books for taking a chance on me, and my writing, and for patience, unwavering support and guidance.